Daughter of
Providence

DAUGHTER OF PROVIDENCE

A NOVEL

JULIE DREW

THE OVERLOOK PRESS
NEW YORK, NY

This edition first published in the United States in 2011 by
The Overlook Press, Peter Mayer Publishers, Inc.

141 Wooster Street
New York, NY 10012
www.overlookpress.com

For bulk and special sales, please contact sales@overlookny.com

Library of Congress Cataloging-in-Publication Data

Drew, Julie.
  Daughter of providence : a novel / Julie Drew.
  p. cm.
  1. Family secrets—Fiction. 2. Domestic fiction. I. Title.
  PS3604.R486D38 2011   813'.6—dc22   2011017406

Book design and typeformatting by Bernard Schleifer
Manufactured in the United States of America

ISBN 978-1-59020-462-7

10 9 8 7 6 5 4 3 2 1

In memory of my sister, Cathy.

*What we would have been to each other
in our grown-up lives is still my favorite fiction.*

It was not death, for I stood up,
And all the dead lie down.

—*Emily Dickinson #355*

PROLOGUE

In the stifling train car a dozen dark men, covered with the day's sweat, sit reading month-old foreign newspapers. Old women who once conquered oceans talk of marriages and births, the names familiar and fading, and think of their parents' graves, which they will never see.

Winter's gray palette is spent at last, and the western edge of Narragansett Bay turns the train's windows blue. The eyes of the passengers slide toward the salt-streaked glass, straining to make out the objects outside—the boats and the buildings, the dunes and the sea grass—until the sun's glare forces them back to the train's murky interior.

A dark-haired young girl sits on a crowded bench seat, wedged between two heavy adult bodies clothed in layers of cheap wool. The stench of perspiration is overpowering. Tobacco smoke thickens the air near the ceiling, obscuring the faces of those who are standing. The girl is jostled as those on either side sway against her with the moving train. Her attention wanders restlessly around the interior of the car. She is searching, perhaps, for just enough room to breathe.

She is small for her age, making her seem younger than she is. Two old women in the back of the car ask each other, Who could have let her travel alone, so young? But Maria Cristina sits quietly. Only her eyes move as she surveys the passengers. A sinewy young man, hands blackened by engine grease, gnaws on a hangnail. A pregnant woman crosses and uncrosses her bloated ankles while she knits something small and pale. Two thick-waisted men argue in a language Maria Cristina does not recognize.

An old woman dressed in a high-necked black dress from the old country—though which particular old country is unclear—stares back at Maria Cristina without blinking. The woman's forehead is heavy and smooth under her thinning white hair, but the lower half of her face is compressed, the mouth collapsing in on itself beneath the wrinkled, spotted skin. The woman and the girl hold that stare for a full, long minute, the challenge implicit. The old woman, used to silent wars with nothing at stake, retracts her thin lips, revealing blackened gums and a single, rotting tooth. A thread of spit, dark with tobacco juice, dribbles from the corner of her mouth, but her eyes never leave the girl.

A movement at the old woman's feet breaks Maria Cristina's concentration. Already unnerved by the suddenly gaping mouth, she is startled further by the motion and looks down at a small wire cage nearly bursting with two live chickens. They are an indistinguishable mass of filthy white and red-gold feathers save their hard, bright eyes. The birds blink rapidly, clucking, their feet scratching at the floor for food that isn't there. Maria Cristina feels a spasm of fear in her gut.

The old woman, thinking nothing more menacing than What a pretty little thing, *chuckles softly as the train rumbles toward Warwick, where I wait.*

This is how I think of Maria Cristina, on the train and speeding toward us that day in late June. I know that train and its passengers, having ridden it myself for years. I wonder, sometimes, if some sense of foreboding came to her, surrounded by strangers in that crowded car. I wonder if she was afraid.

Still, I find comfort in the thought of her on the train, before we met. Whatever she did or did not do during that short journey from Providence to Warwick, it remains a moment suspended between the sad events that left her orphaned and the greater tragedy that lay ahead. A moment of possibility, even in its uglier incarnations, as I may write her life—and death—as many times as I like. As many times as I can. It is easier to think of her as a character I have invented, a shadow without flesh or blood, rather than as someone real whom I came to love, and then lost—the choice of a coward, perhaps. A choice I have made more than once.

We were good Christian people. And yet we have blood on our hands. I have asked God a thousand times how both these things can be true. It is only recently that I have begun to wonder if the question itself is flawed, to wonder if the problem is not, after all, an inability to know what is true but rather a colossal misunderstanding of what truth itself is. And, more important, what it is not.

It has been almost two years since I put her in the ground, but the events that led to Maria Cristina's death still haunt my dreams and waking thoughts. The loss of those I loved, the betrayals. Everything I left behind.

I want you to understand who I really was. What I saw, what I felt, and—God help me—what I did. I do not ask for your forgiveness. Perhaps understanding is enough.

CHAPTER ONE

Although it began in solitude and menial chores, everything changed that day, June 28, 1934. Dawn burst through the window and hurled itself at the copper teakettle, sparking off of it like flint, but the sun quickly rose over the house, turning its attention elsewhere, and by mid-afternoon the light had begun to weaken. All I could think was *She's coming today*. I did not yet know that Maria Cristina's arrival would be, for some of us, overshadowed by that of another: a young man who was at that moment being gently caressed by the receding tide in Kingston Cove.

These were our last moments of innocence; had I but known, I might have savored the simplicity of the morning. But I turned mindlessly from the sink to the hardwood cabinets and back until the last plate from breakfast had been dried and put away, then took off the apron Mrs. Hatcher made for me. I frowned, my mouth pursed unattractively, as Father was fond of pointing out. I could feel the crease between my eyebrows deepening, but I didn't care. I tossed the apron over the back of a chair and climbed the kitchen stairs to take one more look at Maria Cristina's room.

I stood in the doorway and bit my lip, frowning. Will she like it? I wondered. I had agonized over this—such a small detail, really, which room to put her in. We certainly had plenty to choose from, but I felt compelled to get it right. I finally settled on the room next to mine. It wasn't the biggest, but the ceilings were high, and there was a small fireplace with a mantel in one corner with white oak panels above. It had a large window, and I knew that on a clear day Maria Cristina would be able to see the sun sparkling on the whitecaps in the cove at Ezra's boatyard, just as I could from my window. I hadn't done much to prepare the room for her, but had managed, with Mrs. Hatcher's help, to sew new curtains that matched the yellow squares in the quilt I had used as a child, and which I had placed on the bed. The wallpaper was old and a little faded, but the small bouquets of yellow and blue flowers on a white background seemed hopeful.

I walked to the bed and smoothed the covers again, though they didn't need it. There didn't seem to be anything else I could do, so I went back downstairs, my solitary footsteps echoing off the woodwork, resounding through the empty house, muffled only slightly by the white sheets covering the furniture we never used. The house was absurdly large for us, but Father had insisted we stay. He had told me years ago that if we carried on as if nothing at all had happened we might avoid pity and gossip. I was no more eager for the town's scrutiny than he, but I thought we called attention to ourselves by rattling around in that old mansion year after year.

I glanced in the beveled mirror hanging in the hall and tucked a long strand of dark, curling hair behind my ear in an attempt to smooth its wild appearance. My father was an important man in Providence, as was his father before him. I had learned early that we *were* Rhode Island. As the daughter of Samuel Dodge, I had a responsibility to uphold—a responsibility I did not always meet, despite being almost twenty-four years old. But I wanted Maria Cristina to think well of me.

Shaking off my distraction, I looked at the clock on the table beside the telephone. I could hear it ticking, but the hands did not appear to have moved at all. There was still an hour, maybe more, before I had to leave. The waiting was torture. I made a sudden decision and left the house, closing the front door behind me and pausing just long enough to run my hand over its surface, which teemed with thousands of intertwining carved figures. The writhing sea serpents, surfacing whales, floundering ships, glowering thunder clouds, leaping mermaids, towering waves, jagged lightning, capsized boats, grasping, giant squid, hurtling harpoons, and drowning men were all in motion, their lives and their stories tumbling into and through one another. Like the work of Hieronymus Bosch, it was beautiful but primitive and repellant and violent, a nightmarish vision of every seafaring legend and ocean life form I had ever heard of.

I turned from the door and hurried toward our still-shiny black Ford parked in the crushed-shell driveway. The car was clean and reliable, but whereas before the Crash its luxury would have announced our social and economic standing, five years later it merely served to remind everyone of better days. I reached for the car door, my handbag clutched in my other hand, just as Mr. Hatcher ambled into view on the sidewalk in front of the house.

"Going to get her, are you, Annie?" he called. I could hear in his voice the phlegm from a lifetime of smoking. "Esther says today is the day!"

"I am, Mr. Hatcher, and it is. Father and I are going together in a little while. I'm heading down to Ezra's right now, though, while I wait."

Mr. Hatcher nodded a half dozen times, carefully considering this information. He turned to go, clearing his throat loudly, then stopped, remembering something. "You tell your dad I'm grateful he put in a good word for me with Mr. Dekker. Me and Mrs. Hatcher, we both appreciate his help."

"I certainly will," I said quickly. "I know he was happy to do it. How are you liking the work at Dekker's?" I was far too anxious for a leisurely chat, but I didn't want to be rude.

"I like it just fine. Bookkeeping suits me. I'm too old for mill work anyway, so it's all worked out the way I'm sure the good Lord intended," he concluded, waving and continuing on, passing the house without another word.

I climbed into the car, tossing my handbag and the lawyer's letter onto the seat, then pushed the starter and drove—too fast, I'm sure—the two blocks to the courthouse. I glanced at the old building as I paused in the intersection. Milford was a small town, and all public business was conducted at the courthouse, including town council meetings, over which my father, as president, presided. On the opposite corner sat the Milford Congregational Church, where Reverend Brown stood trimming the hedges in his shirtsleeves. I waved as I turned right and drove down the mill road, turning once more onto the narrow sand-and-shell path that led to Ezra's.

Ezra's road was scarcely wide enough for a car, and the low-hanging tree branches and underbrush scraped its sides as I drove, the tires slipping a little, making the car slide as if it were moving across ice. The sun had long since risen past the tree line into a cloudless summer sky.

Ezra Johnson's place wasn't recognizable at first glance as either someone's home or a working boatyard. He had cleared much of the land himself, a bit at a time, leaving narrow stands of trees at what he thought each time would be the far edge of the new section he had cleared. Grass grew more or less regularly down toward the water, giving way to sea grass, and then sand about twenty feet above the high tide mark. Thirty yards or so from the northern edge of the property, between the house and the retreating forest, was a crumbling, smoke-blackened stone foundation. Ezra's father had told him the Indians burned out the family, but that they had come back and built another house, and had lived there for many years. Ezra didn't know any of the details, but I had liked the story as a child, imagining myself a daughter of that family, bravely fighting the Indians, surviving the flames as they engulfed our home, maybe saving a baby brother as I leapt from the highest window to safety.

I pulled the car close to the workshop, wondering too late if I would have time to do any work. Anything was better than wandering around the house, I thought, waiting and worrying. But before I could even turn the engine off, I saw two boys running toward Ezra's house from the water's edge. Although they were still twenty yards away, I did not see them as children playing. There was a tension in their bodies, a determination, and the second boy, who lagged a little behind, glanced over his shoulder as he sped toward Ezra's house.

They were running from something—something or someone.

I opened the car door and climbed out, calling to them. "Hi! Boys! What's wrong?"

They turned toward me, startled, but did not slow down as they veered from their course and raced up the inclined yard toward me, their relief apparent. I recognized one of them.

"Finbar Sullivan, what are you doing down here?" I asked as they stopped in front of me, breathing hard and exuding excitement—and something else that made my scalp crawl.

"We're lookin' for Ezra," he panted, and the other boy nodded. "We were clammin'," he said, his explanation rushed, words tumbling over each other as he pointed beyond where the beach curved out of sight, back up toward the mill. "We've been out since dawn, and we found somethin'—somethin' bad. We need to tell somebody, an' Ezra's was closest."

The other boy had not stopped nodding, and when I looked at him more closely I could see that his eyes were wide and unblinking, his hands trembling.

"What did you find?" I asked.

They looked at each other, conferring in silence. Fin looked back at me, as though they'd reached a decision. "It's bad. And scary. And you're a girl. We should tell Ezra."

"Okay, let's go get him," I said, assuming that I'd hear the details sooner if I let them tell Ezra.

We walked quickly up to the house, and I climbed the steps to Ezra's door. I knocked. I glanced back at the boys, who'd waited below in the yard, but nothing happened. I knocked again, harder.

"Ezra! It's Anne. Are you home?" I yelled at the door. When we heard nothing, I walked back down to where they stood, waiting.

"I'm all you've got, boys. Whatever it is, I can take it." They hesitated, but before they could refuse me, I decided they weren't in charge, after all. "Come on, let's go see what you found," I said, turning and walking toward the water.

After a moment they ran to catch up with me, and we walked swiftly, Fin leading the way in single file along the shoreline from Ezra's up toward the mill. The hard-packed sand began to turn mucky, pulling at my shoes as we approached the edges of the marsh that separated Ezra's property from the mill.

"It's . . . it's right over here," stammered the other boy, whose name I had not asked.

Something in his voice made me stop and turn around. His face was pale, and tears stood in the corners of his eyes.

"You don't have to go the rest of the way," I said gently. "Just point out where I should go."

"I'll take you," said Fin. "It's just right there, up ahead."

I turned and followed him, the tall grass clutching at my skirt. I looked down as we walked, noting the mud and silt splattered on my ankles. My shoes were completely ruined. I would have to change them before I picked up Father.

I pulled up short to avoid running into Fin, who had stopped in front of me. I looked over the top of his head at the body of a man lying facedown in the marsh not three feet from where we stood.

"Oh, no . . ." I whispered.

"Yeah," said Fin. I put my hand on his shoulder, and we stood there, taking it all in. The course black hair, matted with mud and seaweed, the face turned away from us toward the horizon. The sodden clothes, stiff with drying salt water. I couldn't look away.

Get a hold of yourself, I thought. I tightened my grip on Fin's shoulder and turned him around to face me. He was pale and shaking, but he looked me steadily in the eye.

"Fin, here's what we're going to do. You and—What's your

name?" I asked, turning back to the other boy who stood a few yards behind us.

"Paul," he said.

I turned back to Fin. "You and Paul are going to go straight to the sheriff and tell him there's been an accident, looks like one of the local fishermen has drowned. Tell him you found me at Ezra's and showed the— showed it to me, too. But that I couldn't wait, I had to go to the train station. Tell him I'll talk to him later. Can you do that?"

Fin nodded without taking his eyes off mine.

"It's okay," I said. "You boys were very brave, and you did the right thing. Let the sheriff take care of it now."

They turned and raced back the way we'd come, and I knew they wouldn't stop until they'd reached Sheriff Tucker's door. I realized suddenly that I was alone. My heart pounding, I turned back to the body, took a few steps closer, and knelt down beside it.

I knew better than to touch him—even had I wanted to, which I certainly didn't—but I found myself leaning over him to get a glimpse of his face. I couldn't help it. I'd never seen a dead person before, and I had to learn if he was someone I'd known.

Leaning over him, I could see his ear and half of his face in profile. The other side of his head appeared to be partly buried in the sand— fresh, wet sand. He'd been in water earlier and must have been here long enough for the high tide to go back out, I reasoned. Maybe he'd died at sea and washed up on shore. His skin was dark—darker than mine—but it had a pale, bluish tinge to it, and while I couldn't quite put my finger on why, something about that skin made me know he was dead, even without listening to his chest for a heartbeat or some small trace of breath. I knew if I touched him he would feel cold, like meat taken from the icebox, still chilled but in danger of spoiling if left out too long.

I did not know him. He might be one of the local fishermen, someone I'd seen around town—he looked vaguely familiar—but I did not know him. I stood up, ashamed of my relief. I reminded myself that others did know this man, and there would be shock and loss and pain. This day would always be a tragedy for some family.

And just that quickly I remembered: Maria Cristina. *She's coming today.* I turned and made my way as quickly as I could back to Ezra's, back to my car. I drove home and went upstairs to bathe my hands and face and feet, and to change into fresh shoes and stockings. I drove into town, a little anxious when I saw the clock in the square. As soon as Father was finished, we would drive to meet Maria Cristina at the train station in Warwick, a good fifteen miles away.

My hands shook on the steering wheel. I tightened my grip against their tremor, eased the car up to the curb in front of the courthouse, and pulled on the parking break. I took a deep breath and willed myself to calm down. *Everything will be fine,* I thought, repeating it over and over again. *You've just looked at a dead man, and Maria Cristina is coming today, but everything will be fine.* I forced myself to look around, to note the familiarity of the town I knew so well. A few people were sitting on the steps of the courthouse, enjoying the warmth of the afternoon sun. People walked along the sidewalk, drove their cars along the street. The building right in front of me loomed large and comforting. I had looked at the courthouse nearly every day of my life, watching it change and grow along with me, like the town. It had been the centerpiece of Milford since the town was settled in the late 1600s, though it had been altered numerous times, not always wisely. Broad steps had been added leading up to the courthouse's front doors and, later, columns along the front of the building. I felt a great deal of affection for its quirky appearance.

I grabbed my handbag and ran up the steps and through the doors into the cavernous room where the council meeting was just breaking up. In marked contrast to the raw oak beams and exposed pins at their joints, an ornate crystal chandelier—six feet deep and nine feet across—illuminated every corner, as well as the portrait of an illustrious Dodge ancestor, the same one whose likeness graced the rotunda of the Rhode Island State House in Providence. These adornments were supposed to lend a certain formality to the proceedings, but I thought they highlighted the dirty, workday clothes worn by most of those present.

The members of the council were gathering up papers, some still sitting, others standing and conferring with one another. The reporter for the *Warwick Post* who covered local politics was finishing his notes for tomorrow's column. A dozen or so townspeople were clustered in small groups, talking or moving toward the door.

And there, up at the front of the room, of course, was Father: a tall, angular man in an immaculate suit and spats, with a youthful color to his face despite the thick, startlingly white hair. He stood with the other elected officials, as serious and solemn as the room, then took the pocket watch out of his old-fashioned waistcoat, checked the time, and snapped it closed again with a brisk, commanding motion. Though in a hurry, he took care to keep his papers in order, making the stack neat before laying it in his soft leather briefcase in such a way that no corner would be bent, no page creased.

He strode past the council table, moving quickly through the room toward the double doors someone had thrown open at the meeting's end, and brushed so close to a short, compact man covered in masonry dust that the man stepped quickly back in order to avoid being run down. The mason, who had no doubt forfeited an afternoon's pay for the chance to converse with the president of the town council, opened his mouth to speak, but my father, unaware, had already passed, leaving the man standing with mouth open and hat in hand.

The mason's face flushed with shame, and I felt my own answering flush. I knew that the only reason my father would have forgotten his obligations to anyone in Milford was my presence here and the task that awaited us.

Father saw me waiting at the back of the room, and when he reached me he leaned in and kissed me on the cheek. We left the courthouse together, walking abreast through the double doors and down the steps to where I'd parked the car.

"How was your meeting?" I asked with some effort. We never spoke about anything of importance unless we were alone.

"Fine, fine. Nothing much to speak of. We approved the

expanded business zone up to Cedar and Fourth streets, and Alma Smith has again petitioned for car horns to be restricted on her street"—a note of exasperation crept into his voice—"because the noise upsets her dog."

I smiled weakly, but Father frowned as we reached the car.

"Why didn't you come around and park on the other side?" he asked. "It would have saved time since we have to drive north." He thought I lacked a certain attention to detail—the kind of attention, he said, that makes for efficient living. Nothing wasted—not a thought, not a precious second.

"I'm sorry, you're right," I said automatically as I went around and climbed in the passenger's side. Father settled into the driver's seat and shut the door.

He put the car in gear and, after looking behind him and waiting for an old farmer's truck to pass, crossed the street to merge with the light traffic heading north on Main.

"Father, something happened this morning," I began. He must have heard something in my voice because he glanced at me immediately in concern.

"What is it, dear? What's happened to upset you?" he asked.

"I drove down to Ezra's before I came here and met with two boys from town—Fin Sullivan and another boy—who were looking for Ezra or any adult, I guess, because they'd found— they found a dead body. In the marsh."

"Oh, my God," he said softly, shocked.

"I know," I agreed. "Ezra wasn't home, so they took me to it, and—"

"You saw it?" Father interjected, clearly displeased.

"It's okay," I assured him. "It wasn't pleasant, but I'm all right. It was a man, a young man from what I could tell. No one I know— at least I don't think so. I didn't turn him over."

"Turn him over—I should think not! You didn't touch the body, did you?" Father asked quickly.

"No, of course not," I said. We both sat quietly then as he drove, lost in our own thoughts. We didn't see many accidental deaths in Milford, but when it did happen it was almost always one of the workingmen. Finally I shook my head to clear it, determined to push the morning's events from my mind. "Have you had any luck identifying investors for the mill?"

"Nothing definite, but I have a lunch meeting in Narragansett next Tuesday with some men from the Pier who may be interested. I should have a better idea of what I can expect after that."

"That sounds promising," I said. After another brief pause, I found myself thinking about the body in the cove again. "I wonder who the dead man was."

"There's no point in speculating," said Father, ever practical. "Dr. Statham will be wearing his coroner's hat this afternoon, I suppose, but until he's identified the body I doubt we'll hear anything." Father seemed reluctant to talk about it and changed the subject back to the meeting he'd just left.

How like him to want to spare me, I thought.

I stared out the window while he talked. The forest along the roadside was lit by dappled sunlight that succeeded only intermittently in pushing its way through the dense, dark foliage, giving the passing scenery the jerky, high-contrast look of the silent films I had loved as a young girl. I stared at the flickering light and shade, the dark vertical tree trunks flying past like frames in a projector.

Nervously twisting the handle of my handbag between my fingers, I realized we would arrive at the train station in just a few minutes. I wondered if Maria Cristina would look like me. Or maybe like Inêz. Not that I would know—I didn't even know if *I* looked like Inêz, or if her absence had somehow erased all resemblance. It had been many years since I had recalled her face with any certainty.

I felt Father's glance and realized he had expected a response to his last comment, which I had not heard. I examined his profile while he drove, noted the set of his jaw. "I'm sorry, Father. You know I'm interested. It's just . . . I'm a little distracted today."

"Of course you are, dear. As am I," he said, clearing his throat. "This will be a big change for us, Anne, but opening up our home to the girl is the only decent thing to do. I've had a long conversation with Reverend Brown, and he agrees completely."

"Father," I said impulsively, "her name is Maria Cristina." I wanted to stop, but I couldn't. "I don't want her to feel like this is charity. I want her to feel welcome. After all, this is going to be her home, and we are—I am—her family."

He pulled up to the train station and parked the car. I felt a familiar pang of remorse. Why was I always so quick to speak? I hated, more than anything, to cause my father pain, perhaps especially because he had borne this pain so well for so many years. He had never spoken ill of Inêz, and out of respect for him, I never spoke of her at all—or of anything that was connected to her—but those days were clearly gone.

I looked at Father, sitting in the car beside me, and I wanted nothing more than to touch him tenderly, in love and in sympathy. But I could not. Even had I known how to do such a thing, he would have recoiled in embarrassment.

"I know this can't be easy for you . . ." I managed to get out, but my voice faded away to nothing. His ability to be here at all, to speak calmly of Maria Cristina's arrival, was a brutal reminder to me of his goodness, and the terrible thing Inêz had done to him.

He did not look at me as he turned off the car. He took out his pocket watch and checked the time.

"We'd better get inside," he said, his voice a little tight. "Her train's arrived." He reached over and patted my hand without looking at me, and I said nothing. It was the best we could do.

He closed the door after himself, but I hesitated, alone in the car, prolonging that last moment before Maria Cristina irrevocably became a part of our lives. I picked up my handbag and the letter I'd received a month ago from the lawyer in Providence. The letter that had so abruptly announced the existence of Maria Cristina—a sister, after a lifetime as an only child!

That letter had exploded in our midst like a bomb, leaving small cuts in unexpected places. Inêz—wife, mother, deserter, whore—had had another man's child, and here we were, my father and I, at the train station to meet her. I got out of the car and followed Father into the building.

The station at Warwick was small, and not much frequented by either trains or travelers. We walked into the simple waiting room, with Father just a little ahead, past the benches and the handwritten schedule of arrivals and departures posted on the wall. We approached the ticket window where Pat Tully worked, free to spend the better part of each quiet day reading poetry.

"Hello, Mr. Tully, how are you today?" I asked.

There was no answer, though I could see the top of his head below the windowsill, which meant he was either asleep or reading. Mr. Tully was just a little younger than Father, a sweet, wounded man with thin red hair. He lived alone. Father said he had been a drinker in his youth but didn't touch it anymore.

"Mr. Tully?" I said, a little louder this time.

"Patrick Tully, you have customers," said Father.

"Oh! Sure, of course. Sorry, folks. Walt Whitman has me that distracted today," he said. "Ahh, t'day's yer big day, isn't it, Annie-girl?" Mr. Tully asked, looking me in the eye.

Whatever pleasure I might have felt at Mr. Tully's affectionate familiarity, and his interpretation of this occasion as a happy one, was lost as soon as I glanced at my father's stony face. I had accepted long ago that everyone in town seemed to know our business only moments after we ourselves did, but Father hated it. He loathed gossip even more than he did the assumption of familiarity by mere acquaintances.

"Mr. Tully, has the 4:10 come in?" I asked quickly.

"It's just stopped full. The passengers'll be disembarking in a moment or two. Would ya want t' go out t' the platform?" he asked, his thick brogue more pronounced than usual as he spoke loudly over the train whistle just outside.

I looked at my father, trying unsuccessfully to read his expression.

"I'll go," I said. "Father, why don't you wait in here where it's cool and quiet? I'll bring her right in."

He gave a quick nod, and relief flooded through me, so intense that for a moment I feared my legs would not carry me.

I turned toward the door that led to the station's only platform and strode forward. I tried not to run, feeling both Father's and Mr. Tully's eyes on my back as the door loomed close and then suddenly I was through it. I felt the breeze on my face, hot with steam from the train, blowing my hair across my eyes.

And there she was, standing right in front of me, giving me no chance to breathe, to arrange my face into the calm welcome I had planned. I had imagined this moment every day for weeks, lain awake at night wondering what she would be like, but I found myself completely unprepared and all I could think was *I'm not ready.*

She was a little thing, fair-skinned with long, straight dark hair and hazel eyes just like mine, but without my ill-tempered furrow between her black brows. She didn't move, or speak, or blink. She just looked at me, a little defiant, and thrust out her pointed elfin chin, sending me reeling because I knew that chin, its narrow stubbornness, and in that instant of recognition my breath was gone, sucked from my body in a grief I had never allowed myself to feel.

My sister's small body seemed to shimmer, and I impatiently pushed the hair back from my face only to realize that it wasn't my hair but tears that were blurring my vision. I laughed as I swiped the water from my eyes and bent down a little to see her up close.

"Hello, Maria Cristina," I said. "Welcome home."

The other passengers from the 4:10 walked around us to get to the door, talking and laughing, but Maria Cristina remained stoically silent in front of me. She very nearly ran from me, she later confided, as I stood in front of her on the platform at Warwick station.

"You must be tired, and this must be so strange for you," I began again. "Why don't we go inside? My father is there, and we can all go home and get you settled."

She weighed my words with a deliberation surprising in such a young girl. Then she nodded. Just once, and with finality. I almost smiled but refrained, noting her rigid self-control and assuming from it that she did not want to be found amusing.

She carried one small suitcase, a once-expensive valise that was old but still fine, its caramel-colored leather supple and rich. I took the bag from her to carry. The gold initials underneath the braided handle were I.C.D.: Inêz Caldeira Dodge. My mother's bag! Jealousy pressed hotly behind my eyes, and in an instant I felt monstrous, swollen, and ugly. Barely formed resentments flashed in quick succession through my head. *I have nothing of my mother's!* We walked silently toward the door to the station and I struggled for control. *There isn't time,* I thought. *Father's just inside, and you've said nothing yet. Talk to her!*

I stopped, and she stopped beside me. I looked at her, but she looked straight ahead, her back like a ramrod. She seemed young and tragic, left alone in a world of strangers, not yet thirteen according to the lawyer's letter, and I reminded myself that I had long ago recovered from my loss, while her wounds were fresh. I put my hand gently on her thin shoulder, feeling the bones beneath her faded cotton dress, willing her to turn my way.

"Maria Cristina, I can't imagine how hard this must be. I don't pretend to know. But I'm glad you've come, and I hope you'll like it here." I heard the quiver in my voice and swallowed hard to control it. "I hope you'll like me."

She looked at me then, her eyes a shade greener, and smiled tentatively. There was a small gap between her front teeth, and I knew I would love her.

"*Perdóe-me—*" she began in Portuguese.

"What?" I interrupted, startled by the language and by her unexpectedly deep, resonant voice.

"Excuse me," she said again, this time in English. "Excuse me, I also hope I will like you."

We looked at each other for just a moment, then soldiered on toward the door, side by side, and the tight, twisted knot inside me began to ease. When we entered the station it took me a moment to find my father among the dozen or so people milling about. His eyes were already on us, though, and I knew he'd seen us the moment we came through the door. He was not looking at me but at Maria Cristina, and I saw more in his face than I cared to. He recognized Inêz in her just as I had, and though he succeeded in masking it before we reached him, I saw the pain—and something else.

Revulsion.

It was I, then, and not Maria Cristina after all, who felt a sudden spasm of pain in my gut—fear—as Patrick Tully, who could not know what a cruel blow he dealt my father, exclaimed in honest appraisal of my sister, "What a pretty little thing!"

Chapter Two

We left the train station in an awkward silence. Father did not look directly at Maria Cristina after that first glance. He nodded and said a polite, formal hello when I introduced them and then made a fuss over carrying her bag so he could look at it and not her. We climbed into the car with Maria Cristina in the backseat. She was quiet and pensive, and I kept looking over my shoulder at her, wondering what she was thinking, then worrying that I was looking at her too much.

Unexpectedly, Father began to speak.

"The Dodge family has been an important force in the state since the 1700s," he began as he drove south through Warwick, pointing out a colonial armory, now in imminent danger of collapse, built and stocked by a patriot who also had the good sense to be born a Dodge.

At first his comments appeared innocent, even helpful, as if he were merely pointing out sites of local interest he thought Maria Cristina might like to see. But it soon became apparent that this was a lecture focused entirely on our family history. My brief irritation was replaced with pity that his discomfort was such that his usual charm was all but absent.

"Moses Brown, of Providence, and the Englishman Samuel Slater introduced the cotton-spinning frame at the Pawtucket Falls mill in 1790," he intoned. "My great-grandfather, John Henry Dodge, was their good friend and business partner. The Dodge fortunes were made in the Blackstone Valley, in the textile mills that boomed here."

I glanced back at Maria Cristina, but she was dutifully noting the monuments to the Dodge pedigree that Father was pointing out to her. There was absolutely nothing in all of South County with the name Caldeira on it. In fact, as Father cheerfully explained, most of the Portuguese immigrants lived in a poor area in west Warwick. On the other hand, the county was lousy, as they say, with Dodges. Our name was everywhere, from the huge family mausoleum in the Milford cemetery, to the statue of J. H. Dodge under the clock in the town square, to the name inscribed in granite over the Milford public library, which had been donated by my grandfather in memory of his late mother.

"Sheer grit and the entrepreneurial spirit, that's what's lacking today," Father said, as if to himself. I said nothing. I felt quite certain that any presumption of grit from either Maria Cristina or me would have met with his strenuous disapproval.

Maria Cristina remained silent in the backseat, as did I, my hands held tightly in my lap, staring straight ahead at the road.

"By the time my father had finished school," Father went on, "my grandfather owned and operated one of the largest textile mills in the valley, employing more than three hundred workers. Eventually, my father and his brother persuaded him to build a mill in South County, which was entirely undeveloped then. Nothing here but a few farmers. Within two years the mill was successful and growing, the first water-powered mill in this part of the state, and to this day the largest. My grandfather deeded the mill to my father, and it eventually came to me. Someday it will be Anne's," he said proudly. He was speaking directly to Maria Cristina for her edification, so she would know exactly where things stood in regard to who was the daughter of the house and who was the guest.

My irritation returned.

"We hope to reopen the mill by the first of the year, and then you'll see Milford restored to its former prosperity," he assured her.

I knew that he was thinking of an era and lifestyle long gone, the mansions in Newport whose owners had been friends of his father's, the politicians and industrialists who had come to our house when I was a young girl. I knew that he wanted to add, *And when the mill is restored, the Dodge family will be restored as well,* but could not. It was one thing to brag about one's ancestors in the guise of local history, quite another to insinuate oneself into that history, revealing personal ambition.

I glanced back at Maria Cristina as we drove down Main, past the courthouse. She pressed the side of her face up close to the glass, craning her neck to see the top of Reverend Brown's pride and joy, the recently painted bell tower atop the Congregational Church. Its needle-sharp spire, newly, startlingly white, captured and reflected the brilliance of the late-afternoon sun.

Then we were home, and Maria Cristina and I were immediately and unexpectedly left alone when Father surprised me by announcing, as he pulled in to our drive, that he would leave us to get settled. He had several more hours of work in town to finish, he said.

"How long will you be?" I asked. "What time should I have dinner?"

"No need to wait for me," he said, his voice a shade too jovial. "I'll be busy well into the evening and can get a bite later." My face must have reflected my surprise and disappointment because his softened immediately. "Give me a little time, dear. I'm doing my best." He spoke quietly and Maria Cristina gave no indication that she heard his plea.

"Of course, Father. Just let me know what you need. We'll be fine."

Father put the car in reverse, grinding the gears so badly that I winced, and left us on the front steps with Maria Cristina's leather valise. As he drove away, I suddenly had a vision of our future: me, standing between my father and my sister in false cheerfulness, attempting to draw them into the same world, each of them forever a ghost to the other, invisible, untouchable.

God help me, I thought.

Maria Cristina was staring at the front door. "Excuse me, this is very beautiful. Did my *avô* make this?"

Confused, I could only ask, "Your what?"

"My *avô*. My grandfather." She looked at me pointedly. "Your grandfather."

"No," I said, frowning. "My friend Ezra made it." The door had been a gift. Ezra had hand-carved it and presented it to me when I had framed my first hull at the age of eighteen. Father did not approve—of the old man or the door, or of my building boats for that matter—but he loved me and let me go my own way for the most part.

She looked at me for a long moment and said nothing.

"Why don't we go inside." I hesitated when she did not move, then reached around her to open the door. "Please," I said, gesturing for her to precede me into the house. I suspected she might be a little intimidated.

Modeled after John Brown's home in Providence, the Dodge family's massive, square mansion sat resolutely on its well-kept corner, its outlandish, carved front door only fifteen feet or so from the street, surrounded by a low wrought-iron fence. The gracefully curved gambrel roof and widow's walks with turned spindle railings added a decorative, slightly feminine touch to the heavy brick house that gave an impression of squatness, despite its three stories. It was impressive, I knew, and I wondered what her grandfather's house had been like.

She walked inside, out of the sunshine and into the darkness of the formal entryway that extended toward the back of the house in a long hallway. The front staircase curved elegantly upward on the right, just beyond the double doors that led to Father's library. Doors on the left led to the dining room and, beyond the kitchen, to the servants' dining room and butler's pantry. A small telephone table sat against the wall beside a delicate, upholstered chair. Above them hung an old portrait in oil—the colonial ancestor—framed in ornate gold leaf.

I waited while Maria Cristina took it all in. Some days I hated that hallway, with its dutifully polished cherry paneling, its Founding Father casually displayed. Each time I found myself in its dark confines, I felt the undertow of desire pulling me toward the front door, the perennial, unspoken desire of women to walk out of the house and simply leave, carrying nothing and speaking to no one.

"Are you hungry?" I asked, breaking the silence.

"No, thank you," she replied.

"Why don't we put your bag in your room? You can get settled in, and I can show you the house if you want."

"Excuse me, that would be fine." She was excruciatingly polite.

I couldn't think of a thing to say, so I turned and climbed the stairs, and she followed a few steps behind.

I stood aside at the door to the bedroom I'd chosen for her, my hands clasped tightly behind my back. "This is your room—unless of course you don't like it. We have others, so you could choose another one that suits you better. If this one doesn't suit you, I mean." I had never felt more awkward.

She stood in the doorway, the valise in her hand, taking a long, deliberate look at the room. The afternoon sun shone on the faded yellow quilt, and a breeze blew in the open window, moving a strand of her long hair and carrying the salty scent of the cove into the room. I heard the far-off *scree* of gulls.

"Excuse me," she said, turning her head and smiling at me—the first real smile I'd seen. "This room suits me."

My shoulders relaxed and I wiped my sweaty palms on the sides of my skirt. "I'm glad you like it. If you think of anything that will make you more comfortable, just let me know."

I sat on the edge of the bed while she put her few meager possessions in the drawers of her bureau. I felt the discomfort of awareness—awareness of my own good fortune and her lack of the same—when I saw how little she owned. Besides the plain cotton dress, old-fashioned straw boater, and scuffed brown shoes she wore, she owned two dresses, three blouses, a pair of long pants, underwear, and a comb and brush. The only item worth having at all was the brilliantly colored woven scarf she had worn on the train, wrapped loosely around her shoulders, its fringed end hanging down her back and half hidden by her hair. It looked soft and well-cared for, and though clearly not new, the deep blues and greens and purples, like deep ocean water shot through with sunlight, were gorgeous. Still, it was a poor tally, even for a thirteen-year-old.

I was suddenly reminded of a woman I had met on the train a couple of years ago. For four years I rode the commuter train to Providence to attend Rhode Island College. At the end of the day I would get back on board with the people who worked in the mills, or the garages, or the big houses that could still employ servants. I breathed their sweat, and my clothes picked up the dirt from their bodies when I brushed up against them in the crowded car. Once I sat next to a woman who called me "miss" and told me she had three daughters at home and that she supported them by cutting wool from the bolts in a factory up in the valley. Her husband had died, she told me without self-pity. She interrupted her story to cough, violently, from deep in her chest. When she took the handkerchief away from her face I saw that it was covered with the wool fibers she inhaled each day, wet with mucus and thick, dark blood.

I wondered if that woman was still alive, and what kinds of things her daughters might carry in a valise if she was not. I turned away from the thought.

Once her clothes were neatly folded and put away—taking up only two of the eight drawers—Maria Cristina reached into her bag one last time before closing it for good. I knew in the instant before her hand emerged from its depths that she held a photograph. She looked around the room for just the right spot, settling at last on the mantel of the fireplace, just as I would have, and moved with certain steps to place it there, right in the middle. I tried not to appear too interested, but my heart was pounding as I strained to see through her, around her from my perch on the bed.

She turned to me, and the picture was in plain view just beyond her shoulder.

"Excuse me, does it look nice here?"

My eyes darted to the photograph, and I stood up and took a step nearer.

An old man, surprisingly slight, stood next to an old woman. Both had gray hair, though hers was still mostly black. His face was weathered, but hers was startlingly beautiful, despite her age, with high cheekbones and a smooth forehead, her eyes pale and set wide. Between them and just in front sat a much younger woman, small like the old couple. She shared the wide, light eyes of the woman and her dark hair held no hint of gray, but her expression was more like the man's. They looked stubborn, both of them, but particularly the young woman, whose pointed chin was echoed in the face of Maria Cristina, who stood looking at me expectantly.

Startled, I realized I'd walked right up to the mantel to see their eyes, catch the nuances of personality, maybe hear the echo of their voices. It was the first time since she left us—when I was six years old—that I had seen a picture of my mother. Seen my grandparents. They weren't quite strangers, but I did not know them.

I turned to Maria Cristina beside me. "It looks just right here."

We explored the rest of the house and even shared a laugh when Maria Cristina said she was sure she would get lost. She was incredulous when I told her that only Father and I lived here, but as we went from room to room and she saw the closed draperies and covered furniture, her skepticism disappeared. I felt sharply the hollow quality of the house as we made our tour. It had been different when Inêz was there, of course—the feeling of fullness was something I remembered. The house had been alive then and people had filled the rooms—until that morning in January when Father had announced that she was gone. Her note dangled from the very edges of his fingertips as he stood in my bedroom doorway, telling me that my mother no longer loved us. I watched that paper, so precariously held, the blank white back of it telling me nothing. I thought, *Be careful, Father, you'll drop it*. But he never did.

When we finished looking over the house, Maria Cristina and I went downstairs to the kitchen, where we ate the chicken salad Mrs. Hatcher had brought over that morning.

"Do you like the salad?" I asked, unsure what she was used to eating.

"It is very good," she said.

I smiled. "Mrs. Hatcher made it—she's an excellent cook. In fact, she's asked us over for breakfast in the morning." Maria Cristina looked a little alarmed, so I hastened to reassure her. "You'll love Mrs. Hatcher. She's very kind. She practically raised me."

I stopped short, realizing what I'd said. Mrs. Hatcher had practically raised me because my own mother—Maria Cristina's mother—had abandoned me. It was probably unavoidable, but I had not intended we should discuss anything difficult on her first night.

But Maria Cristina was unperturbed. "Excuse me, she sounds very nice."

I exhaled and realized I'd been holding my breath. "Yes, she is."

"My *avó*—my grandmother—was the good cook. And she took care of me when *Mamãe* died. Like your Mrs. Hatcher."

I squirmed a little in my chair, not sure how to reply. I had no memories of my grandparents Ben and Lucia Caldeira. It was nice for Maria Cristina that they apparently had loved *one* of their granddaughters, I thought. The only contact I'd had with them was when, at fifteen, I'd received a letter from my grandfather informing me in three terse sentences that Inêz had died of Spanish influenza. I had given the letter to Father, my hand shaking as I imagined what this news might mean to him. He had read it, his face gaunt, and thrown it away without a word. It had merely confirmed the central truth of our lives: my mother was dead and gone.

Maria Cristina yawned then, and I felt relieved. I knew how to respond to that.

"You must be tired," I said briskly, standing up from the table. "I'll show you where the towels are so you can bathe and get some sleep."

She yawned again and followed me up the stairs.

Later that night, in my own room, I lay awake staring at the ceiling. I had known, of course, that when she arrived I would be faced with a living reminder of my mother and grandparents. But it was going to be harder than I thought.

I turned over and plumped my pillow into a more inviting shape. I tried to think of other things—the boat, what I would be working on the next time I went down to Ezra's, but that brought back images of the dead man in the marsh. I didn't want to think of him, either. It was no use, so I gave in: I thought about my mother, or at least I tried to. The effort left me frustrated, as always. My memories of Inêz and her family had become increasingly vague and unsatisfying until eventually I could no longer recall the expressions they wore, what they said or how they spoke. I had nothing left but odd, jagged fragments of them, like scraps of pages torn out of a book: Food in front of me, brown and spicy-hot. A woman with tall hair who held me on her lap.

I still dream of them sometimes, just as night is ending, and in those dreams Inêz is always singing. And then I wake, struggling to capture the thin wisps of memory that waft away like smoke from a snuffed-out candle, left with nothing but the faint sound of birds rising at dawn.

As we walked through the gap in the hedge to the Hatchers' the next morning, I thought about how I might enlist Mrs. Hatcher's help in easing my sister into Milford. I knew that people would stare at Maria Cristina, for a while at least, and I dreaded it for her. No one would deliberately make her uncomfortable, but she had appeared suddenly out of a history that the town had been witness to: my parents' unexpected marriage and my mother's disappearance when I was a child.

I anticipated the worst, and figured Mrs. Hatcher would be a good person to start with. She'd be kind, and she'd do what she could to both satisfy the town's curiosity herself and keep the worst of the gawkers in line. The Hatchers had been our neighbors my entire life, and after Inêz left Mrs. Hatcher had decided it was up to her to teach me how to cook and sew and clean—none of which I was very good at or particularly interested in. But she had taken me in, given my life a structure those first few years that had kept me from feeling too lost or lonely. I knew she'd do the same for my sister.

Maria Cristina was quiet, hanging a little behind me as we walked up to the back door of their modest home. When we arrived, Mrs. Hatcher stole a quick, curious glance at her as she hustled us into the kitchen.

"Mrs. Hatcher, this is Maria Cristina," I said.

"Well, it's a pleasure, I'm sure," said Mrs. Hatcher warmly. She was looking intently at my sister, and I could see Maria Cristina begin to withdraw from that look.

"Mrs. Hatcher, I'm so glad you invited us. You are the perfect person to become Maria Cristina's first friend. To help ease her into the neighborhood, you know. It can be hard to be the new person." I weighted my words with significance I hoped Maria Cristina would not understand. Mrs. Hatcher turned from her examination of my sister's face and nodded.

"I understand, and you're right. Don't give it another thought."

She seated us at her scrubbed table and set before us a hot pan of just-baked cinnamon rolls and a bottle of cold milk. She brought out plates and glasses and served Maria Cristina first, telling her to dig right in.

"I've got a luncheon tomorrow, and I'll be sure that folks know there's nothing much of interest about any of it. Just a child coming home. When I explain it, they'll fall all over themselves to see who can be the kindest."

"Thank you," I said simply.

"Go ahead, dear. Try one," Mrs. Hatcher urged Maria Cristina, who sat looking at the plate. With no other choice before her, Maria Cristina picked up the gooey roll with thumb and third finger, the remaining fingers held carefully out of the way, and took her first bite with more than a little suspicion. The expression on her face changed from wariness to delight, and she polished off the sticky pastry in no time as Mrs. Hatcher busied herself about the kitchen and continued a steady stream of chatter with little interruption from us.

"I've had a letter from Katie this week, and the baby is finally over that nasty cough she's had since spring. Lord love her, she's a sickly little thing, but seems to be getting stronger lately. Jimmy hasn't written," she said, with a ghost of hurt or disapproval in her voice. "But then nobody expects boys to stay in touch with their mothers like girls do."

Although I was glad to hear that Katie and her baby were well— Katie had been my closest friend growing up, and I still missed her— I had no idea how to respond to Mrs. Hatcher's comment about her son and took a huge bite of cinnamon roll so I wouldn't have to: I was chewing vigorously and could only nod when she glanced my way. She turned back to the already spotless stove she was scrubbing, and I marveled anew at the physical force she exerted in her household chores, a force surprising in such a small, slim woman.

"Well, Mr. Hatcher's finally up. I hear him thundering about upstairs. I swear that man stomps across the floor on purpose," she said, rolling her eyes skyward.

I didn't hear anything, but I was used to her caustic comments about Mr. Hatcher. I drained the last of the milk in my glass and sat back, satisfied.

"Since he's been out of work he's become a regular layabout, that man."

"Isn't Mr. Hatcher working for Mr. Dekker at the store now?" I asked, drawn into the conversation despite my better judgment. Maria Cristina sat across the small table from me, eating and listening.

"Well, yes. But even with keeping the books at three stores it's not a full day most days, and he just seems to be here all the time.

Not like when he was at the mill. Then he was gone from early to late, which suits me better."

Maria Cristina looked at me, but I ignored her.

I heard footsteps on the stairs, and Mr. Hatcher entered the kitchen.

"Good morning, Annie," he said, then looked at Maria Cristina expectantly. "And who have we here?"

"Mr. Hatcher, this is my sister Maria Cristina Caldeira. She's come to live with us."

"Very nice to meet you, my dear," he said, loudly clearing the phlegm from his throat before turning to me. "And how is your paramour, young Mr. Dekker?" Mr. Hatcher had always teased me in the manner of an uncle.

I blushed, giving him just what he wanted.

"That boy they fished out of the cove yesterday was a Portuguese—his folks came down from Warwick last night to identify him," he suddenly announced. "I saw Dick Statham this morning on my walk. He said the family is devastated."

I looked quickly at Mrs. Hatcher, who immediately began to flap her dish towel in her husband's direction—to shush him, I supposed—while glancing pointedly at Maria Cristina, who sat quietly, taking it all in.

"Would coffee be too much to hope for?" Mr. Hatcher asked, dutifully abandoning the subject.

"Yes, it would. The pot's empty—we've had guests" she said by way of an explanation, though neither Maria Cristina nor I had been offered coffee, and we certainly hadn't drunk any. I said nothing, avoiding Maria Cristina's attempt to make eye contact. Perhaps I should have prepared her better for the Hatchers.

"That's fine, Esther. Don't give it another thought. It probably would have given me an acid stomach, anyway. I'll stop at the lunch counter for a cup of Gracie's coffee, which is better. Don't you worry about me. I'll just get my hat and be off. Have you packed me a lunch?" he said, turning back to look at her as he passed through the kitchen door into the living room.

"Yes," she chirped sweetly. "I'm just finishing it now"—indicating with a wave of her neatly manicured hand the sandwich and slice of pie in waxed paper sitting on the counter.

With a nod and a smile, he left to fetch his hat.

Mrs. Hatcher turned back to the counter and made sure the pie was secure in its wrapping before carefully putting it into a battered workman's lunch pail. Then she reached for the sandwich she had just made—chicken breast with tomato, it looked like—and before I realized what she was doing, she lifted the top piece of bread off, reached over the sink, picked up a bar of soap, and rubbed it carefully, thoroughly, across the inside of the bread. I heard Maria Cristina gasp, and thought Mrs. Hatcher must have heard her, too, but she didn't turn around. She put the sandwich back together, wrapped it up, and was just putting it in his lunch pail when Mr. Hatcher reappeared.

"Thank you, dear," he said, taking it from her. "I may be late tonight."

"That's fine. Don't hurry home on my account. Enjoy your lunch," she said, smiling and handing him the pail.

Mr. Hatcher whistled an off-key rendition of "Night and Day" as he walked out the door, and the discordant sound faded as he made his way down the street. His wife turned back to wiping down the counter, and I stared at her back and wondered as I always did what drove her to do such things. Granted, they were small, relatively harmless little revenges, but I could not see for the life of me how Mr. Hatcher had wronged her beyond insulting her coffee.

I steeled myself for Maria Cristina's confusion over the Hatchers' inexplicable behavior. I had so far been able to ignore her, assuming she would blurt out an inappropriate question, but I figured I might as well get it over with, and at least Mr. Hatcher was safely out of the house now. I looked right at her, prepared for the worst. Her eyes were squeezed down to mere slits, her lips pressed tightly together. She was laughing! She might well be confused, but she wasn't horrified at all. She thought it funny.

Feeling like I, too, was thirteen years old and in danger of laughing in church, I turned away quickly to find Mrs. Hatcher looking at both of us.

"You girls will be married some day, too, and you've a lot to learn," she said. "I've been trying to teach Annie how to cook for years, Maria Cristina, but she doesn't seem to have a knack for it. Maybe you'd like to learn a few things?"

"Yes, please," said Maria Cristina, surprising me. "I like very much to cook. Excuse me, maybe you will teach me your special dishes." The laughter was in her voice, and this time I knew that Mrs. Hatcher had heard it.

They looked at each other for a brief span of seconds. Then Mrs. Hatcher smiled and nodded.

"Good," she said. "We'll start with sandwiches."

CHAPTER THREE

Maria Cristina wasn't at all what I'd expected, I thought, walking along behind her as she chased Will's dog, Ruth, down the sandy road that led to Kingston Cove. Will had come by after dinner to meet my sister, and we'd decided to take her for a walk down to the water and show her the mill. I was eager to get to Ezra's place. Maria Cristina was having a wonderful time playing with Ruth and seemed almost carefree. She was reticent, polite—foreign, I had to admit. I saw moments, of course, of her personality, but she was still recovering from the loss of her grandfather—the loss of all of them—and only gradually becoming more comfortable with me.

Ahead of us, Maria Cristina was speaking Portuguese to the dog.

"*Salta! Salta!*" she ordered. I wasn't sure what that meant, but the dog responded by jumping for the stick Maria Cristina was holding over her head.

Will had gotten the black spaniel a few months earlier, trying to persuade me after the fact that she was our dog. I'd kept my distance, liking her just fine but wary.

"You know I named her Ruth with you in mind," he said sud-

denly. "It seemed fitting. Ruth, the good woman, cleaving to her husband." I could hear the laughter in his voice. And the sincerity. "What
is it she says? Oh, yeah. 'Wither thou goest—'"

"I wouldn't go around claiming I was a biblical scholar if I were
you," I countered, watching him brush the pale hair out of his eyes,
as he did a thousand times a day. "Ruth says that to her mother-in-
law, not her husband."

"You're most beautiful when you're clever," he said. "And your
eyes look greener when you're mean. You're like some warrior god-
dess who slays every man who falls in love with her."

"I am not!" I said, uncomfortable and indignant. I hated compli-
ments. I knew quite well, whatever he said, that I was too tall and too
dark—and certainly too blunt in manner—to ever really be pretty. I
could only conclude that either his judgment or his honesty was lacking.

Ruth had run to him with her stick, and he bent down and
picked her up. "You're wrong," he said, smiling and holding out the
squirming puppy for me to take. I ignored him, refusing to hold her.
I didn't want to love her and be that much closer to the gravitational
pull of his intentions.

"You're the loveliest thing in the world," he said, unwilling to let
it go. "Your one flaw is your poor opinion of yourself."

He missed the irony that I trusted my own opinion—in this, at
least—over his.

"Annie," he said, in a tone that made me clench like a fist. "Stop
being so difficult. Marry me—you know you will eventually."

I said nothing but kept walking. I did love him. We'd grown up
together, our fathers the two most powerful men in Milford, maybe
in all of South County. Will's father owned half a dozen dry goods
stores here and in the surrounding towns, and he had recently been
elected mayor of Milford. Ours was old money and an older name,
but the Dekkers, having arrived in America from the Netherlands only
thirty years ago, had made a small fortune in business and smart
investments. Mr. Dekker had survived the Crash better than most,
and his business appeared to be thriving again.

Will's mother, Elsa, had mothered me, but only to the degree I would let her. She was a quiet woman, a full ten inches shorter than I had grown to be, with a huge, solid wall of bosom that defied any attempt to imagine actual breasts. She had a great capacity for love, and was clearly disappointed to have had only one child. She had smothered me with bear hugs whenever she saw me, made a fuss every time I skinned my knee. I adored her. It was her dearest wish that Will and I marry, and she had never hesitated to tell me so.

It was what Will wanted. It was what his parents wanted. It was what my father wanted.

I wanted— I didn't know what I wanted, but I was filled with desire, the desire to do and see and live. When we were children, I was the one with the crazy plan, the wild, make-believe game filled with danger, feats of physical strength, and treasure in the end. I wanted to be a pilot and a jungle explorer, the first woman to climb Mount Everest, a Nobel Prize winner for some extraordinary service to humanity. Mine were the ego-driven dreams of childhood, while Will's dreams had seemed small and stagnant to me even then. It made me sad that it was I who made his modest dreams unattainable, but the thought of marrying him—of marrying at all—left me cold.

"Hello?" he said softly by my side. "Are you actually considering saying yes? Finally?" His tone made it clear that he didn't hold out much hope, but my silence had encouraged him.

"Will, you know I care for you," I began.

"I know, I know," he said glumly, throwing the stick for Ruth again. We walked in silence for a few minutes, and then he seemed to brighten a bit. "There's no rush," he said. "I've got to get my practice off the ground. There's plenty of time."

Will spent most of each weekday in his little office next to the courthouse. He had graduated from law school in Boston, passed the bar two years ago, and set up a small practice in a downtown office— which sounded a lot more impressive than it was. His office consisted of one unpainted room on the second floor of a small, two-story building that housed an insurance company, a tailor who moonlighted as a sail maker, and a dentist. The room featured a battered desk and two chairs, a barrister's bookcase filled with his law books (a gift from his parents when he'd passed the bar), and a bare bulb hanging from the ceiling. The building's tenants shared a common telephone that sat on a little table in the hallway just inside the front door of the building. It rarely rang.

My sympathy for him disappeared. I had refused him many times, but he always bounced back. Perhaps I needed to say no a little more forcefully, so that he heard it as "no" rather than "not yet."

"Did you see her?" Maria Cristina called, turning to us with an eager, open smile. The dog had gone tearing down the sandy track after a rabbit.

What a change had come over her! We had been together nearly every moment since she'd arrived, and already she seemed taller, more substantial, as if she were growing right before my eyes. I felt I was beginning to know her, though she was often an enigma, speaking foreign words, asking to be excused every time she opened her mouth, picking suspiciously at everyday foods that seemed exotic to her. Her moods swung wildly, reminding me of myself at sixteen or so. She was not yet thirteen, but she was approaching adolescence already, sometimes seeming like a child, at other times more like a young woman.

"Yes, we saw her," I said. "Ruth loves having you here to play with her. Will's an old man already, so he's no use." I butted him with my shoulder as we strolled along, letting him know I wasn't angry.

"Now that's just mean," said Will quietly, making me laugh. "One of us has to be a grown-up, and since you seem incapable, it falls to me to be the serious one."

"Excuse me, Ana, did I tell you yet that we had a *cão*, a dog?" Maria Cristina asked, walking back toward us.

I loved the deep tones of her voice, the round, full vowels of her English. The way she called me Ana.

"My *avô* took him in the *barco*."

I felt my stomach tighten, but only a little this time. Already I was getting used to her frequent, easy references to her grandfather, her *avô*. She spoke of her grandmother and Inêz less frequently, and rarely acknowledged that they were related to me. She clearly felt a proprietary right to them, though we had both lost them at an early age.

"Tristâo—he was our dog. He barked too much, so *avó* called him Noisy. Tristâo could swim. Excuse me, can Ruth swim?"

Will assured her that she could, and they chatted about dogs as we walked.

"I see it!" Maria Cristina yelled suddenly, running ahead of us. "Excuse me, I see the mill!"

The road curved gently ahead, away to the left, leading down to my family's mill, which sat about a hundred yards away on land that had been built up at the mouth of the Misquamisett River, where it widened dramatically as it approached Kingston Cove. The mill sat at the water's edge, reinforced by a sea wall constructed of enormous rocks culled from the surrounding countryside, larger versions of the same rocks the pioneers had gathered to create the labyrinthine walls that crisscrossed New England. The mound of rocks and boulders pushed up tightly against the exterior walls of the mill, and then fell away into the brackish water, almost as if they had spilled out of the mill itself, tumbling like an avalanche down the slope, until the last few came to rest in the bay.

Local children sometimes swam and canoed in the cove on hot summer days. In a serious storm, though, with a lee shore, the wind could blow a small craft onto the rocks and break it into kindling. This made the shoreline just beyond the mill a good place to scavenge seasoned timber. The tidal patterns washed all sorts of things up to the mill, and farther down the cove by Ezra's dock, as well. A dead body was unusual, to be sure, but we were used to the Atlantic depositing oddities on our shores. Over the years Ezra and I had plucked countless buoys, still attached to ropes and rigging, out of the surf. We'd salvaged decking and spars, even an unbroken mast once, a sail wrapped around it, the air pockets beneath making it billow out and undulate in the water like a jellyfish. I had dismissed most of this bounty as a total loss, but Ezra insisted there was always something worth saving.

Ruth barked, and I looked up. The dark, soot-stained brick walls of the mill loomed in the approaching dusk, soaring to sixty feet in some sections, unadorned but for the dozens of small windows whose broken shards of glass reflected the last of the sun's rays. Some in Milford said the deserted mill was frightening, menacing even—children tried to scare one another with tales of ghosts flitting about the property. A dead boy discovered in the marsh next to the mill would add fuel to that fire, but my father always dismissed such comments impatiently. He said that dime-store crime novels were eroding the good sense God gave people and remarked on how odd it was that they appeared to enjoy being afraid of their own shadows.

Even though I didn't share the children's macabre views, I felt it was neither stupid nor irrational to feel uneasy at the sight of the mill. The buildings comprised a massive, hulking structure, an unsealed crypt containing the skeletons of abandoned machinery, with weeds grown up over the walkways and parking areas. For me the mill exuded the faint, sad scent of failure and decay.

To our right the road forked and became much narrower, obscured by the heavy foliage and densely packed, twisting trunks of scrub oaks and knotty pines. Will and I stopped at the fork, and he called to Maria Cristina.

"Let's go to Ezra's, Maria Cristina! It's not really safe to go all the way down to the mill. It's been empty for a long time, and there's a lot of broken glass around. Ruth might get hurt." He whistled for the dog, and she spun abruptly and raced back toward us.

"Okay," Maria Cristina said. She reluctantly turned around, her eyes lingering on the mill down the road, and followed Ruth back to where we stood in the road.

"It'll be fun," I told her. "You'll like Ezra, and I want to show you something special that no one but he and Will have seen."

Maria Cristina was immediately interested. She could tell that the excitement in my voice was no ploy. I couldn't wait to see my boat, to run my hands over her.

We turned right onto the narrow track that led to Ezra's, plowing through the sand, which tended to drift in spots. So few cars came down this way that the road never got tamped down, the sea shells never crushed to create a harder, more stable surface. We leaned into it, heads down and arms swinging for momentum, and trudged along in silence. Only Ruth, who raced ahead and back and among us, seemed unaffected when, fifteen minutes later and a little winded, we left the trees and entered a large clearing that extended to the edge of Kingston Cove.

CHAPTER FOUR

Over the years Ezra had made additions to the house left to him by his father, additions that suited his functional needs. No one, not even Ezra, would have claimed that they met anyone's aesthetic needs. I wasn't sure how long he'd lived there—at least fifty years. The original structure was a one-room house, heavily framed in oak, with an end chimney made entirely of stone. The exterior walls were shingled in weathered gray cedar that had seen better days. The cedar had a dank brownish hue that was redolent of mold and wood rot from too many years of the unrelenting assault of humidity and salt. At some point Ezra had added a kitchen ell with a fine mullioned window, salvaged years ago from a shipwreck, and a steeply pitched roof, much like the larger, older roof adjacent. The newer shingles on the kitchen had weathered to the soft, opaque color of early morning fog. I smiled to myself as my gaze fell on the tiny shed two dozen steps from the low door behind the kitchen—1934, and Ezra Johnson still had an out-house. There was no living room. Ezra maintained that he had no need of such a room, since he could typically be found in the rocking chair on his front porch or on the wreck of an upholstered sofa he kept in the workshop, by the woodburning stove he kept stoked there in winter. I suspected that he slept on that sofa, rather than in his bed, half the time.

The workshop, the largest building in the clearing, sat closest to the water. It was covered in a hodgepodge of found materials—sheets of corrugated tin, timbers from an old barn that had come down in a storm on a neighbor's property, even some bricks that I knew had been filched from the mill. A low stone wall, hundreds of years old, ran along the southern edge of the property. A dark, tangled forest of ash, oak, paper birch, and towering pines like Corinthian columns crowded right up to the wall along with rhododendrons and wild roses, wildflowers and curling ferns.

Between the workshop and the dock that ran about thirty yards out into the bay were two sets of carpenter's horses, their supports inverted to form cradles, and on each we had erected a boat, Ezra and I. The two small vessels were in various stages of construction. Mine, the one furthest from completion, sat upside down. She was framed, though, her bottom planked.

I tore my eyes away from it as Ezra stepped out onto the porch of his house.

Ezra's effect on people was more than the sum of his physical appearance. He was a big man—not fat, but dense and heavily mus-cled, with a barrel chest and massive arms from a lifetime spent in physical labor. He was a study in grays and browns, not unlike the shingles of his house, and, he would have joked, he had more than a touch of the same rot from too many years living with the sea. His skin was deeply tanned; his tangled long hair was iron gray, like his eyes beneath the bushy ridge of his brows. He rarely smiled through his thick, matted beard, and when he did it wasn't pretty. He looked, I suppose, too physically powerful, too roughly hewn, too lacking in hygiene and social graces for most people to feel comfortable in his presence.

He had been a whaler in his youth, but a blow to his knee from a block and tackle that had ripped loose in a storm had left him with a permanent limp and a life ashore. He seemed content with what he did.

He designed and built boats.

Technically, there were dozens of boatbuilders in this part of the state, but none was as skilled as Ezra (at least not that I'd ever heard). Most in South County had been forced to turn to other work during the Depression, but Ezra had hung on, claiming that his needs were so few that as long as he could fish and grow a few vegetables behind the house he'd be just fine.

There were a few boatbuilders whose businesses had survived the Crash, one or two who built bigger craft, schooners and yachts for rich men who summered in Newport or Narragansett. Those builders had impressive boatyards, and dozens of carpenters on the payroll, and I'm sure they were good enough at what they did.

But Ezra's knowledge of design and craft was built upon his love of every minute he had ever spent upon the water, every board he'd sanded and caulked. He knew small boats from every angle, and he brought to life one vessel at a time with painstaking care. Each one was a thing of beauty. He made outboard runabouts, cruisers and two-man trawlers for people he knew—fishermen, most struggling to survive—and occasionally a sailboat, like the centerboard sloop he'd made for Mr. Dekker six or seven years ago, commissioned as a surprise for Mrs. Dekker, who had dearly loved to sail with her father when she was a girl in Holland.

We approached the house together—Will, Maria Cristina, Ruth, and I—with Ezra standing above us on the porch. He didn't talk much, wasn't even particularly friendly, but I found his silences comfortable, and the quiet allowed me to focus on my boat when I was there.

"Evening, Ezra," said Will.

"Dekker," said Ezra with a curt nod as he limped down the decaying wooden steps that led from the porch to the yard, turning his hip awkwardly at each step in order to swing his bad leg over and down because his knee didn't bend anymore.

"Ezra," I said, "this is my sister, Maria Cristina Caldeira. Maria Cristina, this is my good friend Ezra Johnson." I spoke slowly and clearly, hoping to ward off any reaction of shock or fear she might feel at the sight of him.

They looked at each other for a moment. Then to my surprise Ezra smiled, and Maria Cristina smiled right back. He came slowly down the remaining steps and held out a ham-sized hand to her. Without hesitation she put her small, pale right hand into his calloused, dirty one, and they shook.

"*Bom dia*, Maria Cristina," said Ezra.

I was shocked to hear him speaking Portuguese. Ezra Johnson had lived in South County his entire life, and I had known him all of mine. His father had been a Congregationalist minister. Ezra was as white as my father—our people had all been colonial pioneers in Rhode Island. But I quickly reminded myself that Ezra had gone to sea as a whaler when he was a boy—against his father's wishes—and had lived a sailor's life among immigrants, many of whom were Portuguese.

No less shocking was the gentleness and enthusiasm with which he pursued a conversation with Maria Cristina. She was obviously delighted to hear the language of her grandparents again. She answered him briefly in Portuguese, then with a glance at me switched to English in mid-sentence.

". . . and the house is very large. I have a yellow-flower room, right next to Ana's room. We both can see your water—your bay—from our windows."

I must have looked dumbfounded by their exchange because Ezra turned to me and said, not unkindly, "Close your mouth, Annie. You look like a codfish."

Will ducked his head quickly so I wouldn't see the smile on his face, but Maria Cristina giggled.

"Want to see the workshop?" Ezra asked Maria Cristina.

"Excuse me, yes, please," she replied.

It was one of the ways she was subtly but unmistakably differ-

ent. The casual—my father would say disrespectful—way most children spoke to adults was obviously foreign to Maria Cristina, who
had been raised to display a reverence for age.

With his stiff, lopsided gait, Ezra led us to the workshop. The exterior of the building, though it appeared somewhat stitched-together,
was in better shape than the house. Ruth barked once, happily, as our
little group crossed the yard, and Maria Cristina fairly vibrated with
anticipation. Ezra's limp began to seem like a dance step to me, and
we were suddenly a party.

Ezra lifted the simple, heavy oak beam from its cradle, a latch
system that kept the twin doors shut even in the fiercest wind, and
opened the doors wide—to create a dramatic effect for Maria
Cristina, I suspected. The building sat on level ground so he could
move heavy lumber and unfinished boat hulls in and out as necessary,
but it meant that the workshop flooded a couple of times a year.
(Thankfully, we'd had a fairly dry summer so far.) It was one of the
many ways he paid for his lameness, since navigating steps with a
heavy load was out of the question for him. He stood aside for the rest
of us to enter, and we marched in, single file behind Maria Cristina.

I closed my eyes when I crossed the threshold, breathing deeply
the slightly smoky flavor of the sawdust that permeated the room. I
opened my eyes to find Will looking at me with love and understanding. He raised one brow comically and performed a little soft shoe in
the thin layer of dust on the floor.

Ezra had taken Maria Cristina to the back of the one-room
building and was showing her his drawing table, a smooth, unfinished
hardwood surface mounted along the length of the back wall, higher
at the back and sloped down toward his chair, which was on castors.
Above the desk the entire wall was pane after pane of window glass,
and I knew that for most of the day the room was quite brightly lit,
though there was little daylight left now. Taped to the surface of the
desk were various blueprints and drawings. A tiny eight-foot punt, a
flat-bottomed skiff, the Sullivan outboard—and something new, I
noted, trying to see over Maria Cristina's head. The sleek lines, shal-

low waterline, and centerboard keel in the rough drawing suggested a racer. The half-breadth view, showing the shape of the deck and water lines; the side views that depicted the height of the deck, the depth of the rabbet and the keel bottom—I could read them all knowledgeably now, at a glance, after working with Ezra for the past five or six years.

"Excuse me, what is this one?" asked Maria Cristina, pointing to one of Ezra's drawings.

"That's outside," said Ezra with customary brevity.

"And this one?" she asked, pointing to another.

"Ask Annie," he grunted.

I pretended not to hear the pride in his voice.

"Excuse me," said Maria Cristina, turning to me. "You have drawn this, Ana?"

"She drew it, and she's building it. It's the boat that's sitting upside down outside," Will answered for me.

"My avô made boats, too," Maria Cristina said. "But bigger than these, I think."

"Yep. I built whalers with him," said Ezra.

"You knew my grandfather?" I asked, incredulous. "Why didn't you ever tell me?"

Ezra shrugged. "Never came up."

He continued to walk Maria Cristina around the shop, pointing out the tools, explaining what we did here. An eight-foot-square workbench with shelves underneath occupied the center of the room. Rollers, wood planes, and a carpenter's bevel hung on hooks on the wall, and sandpapers and cork, clamps and caulking cotton sat on nearby shelves. The steam box sat out of the way in a far corner. Cans of putty and caulk, varnish and turpentine lined the upper shelves. Lumber lay stacked against the left-hand side of the building, between the door and Ezra's desk, and the lower shelves held half a dozen chisels, sharpened and ready for use, boxes of rigging cleats and jars of fasteners, galvanized nails and screws—brass screws, because Ezra said the threads were much sharper and clear-cut. The rope I had used for practicing knots when I was not much older than Maria Cristina hung on the wall where it always had.

I watched silently as Ezra gave her the tour. I suddenly felt an outsider in the place I loved the most, the place that was mine. I had known my mother's father had built boats—I had wondered on more than one occasion if he would have been proud of me—but it had never occurred to me that he and Ezra might have known each other. I thought my grandfather had lived up the coast from here, up near Barrington.

"I don't understand—you knew my grandfather? Did you know my grandmother, too? My mother and my uncle, Estevão?" My voice was too loud, I knew. Will put his hand on my arm, but I shook him off.

Maria Cristina froze, and Ezra turned from her and looked at me, scowling.

"Of course I did. It's a small town, an' I been here for sixty some-odd years." He sounded impatient, and it hurt me.

"Well, I . . . I think you might have told me, that's all. It seems odd that you've never mentioned them to me." *Especially,* I thought, *when it's practically the first thing you mention to her.* I knew it was petulant, that I sounded younger than Maria Cristina, but I felt somehow betrayed. "It's like you've been lying to me all these years!"

He hesitated for such a brief moment that I thought I might have imagined it. Then he turned away from me, saying with uncustomary gentleness, "Lies there may have been, but they wasn't mine."

Will stood just to my left, watching me and saying nothing. Maria Cristina was looking at me, too, uncertainty marring the confidence she had shown earlier.

I struggled to be the adult when what I wanted to do was turn my back on all of them and run home.

"I'm just surprised, Maria Cristina," I explained stiffly, unable to keep the hurt from creeping into my voice. "This hasn't been easy for me. Your grandfather was my grandfather, too," I reminded her, a challenge in my voice that I had not intended. "And I didn't get to know him."

I tasted the resentment in my mouth and felt the urge to spit it out on the sawdust-covered floor.

Maria Cristina's eyes began to tear up, and Will stepped forward.

"Let's go outside and look at those boats," he said, sweeping us all out of the workshop, as if a simple turn around the yard would make it all go away.

I took a deep breath of the cool evening air as we walked across the yard to the cradles that held my boat. I felt oddly thin and light, as if in the dusk I might be nearly invisible.

"Maria Cristina, come feel the side of this hull," Will called as she lagged a little behind. "The sanding makes the wood feel like it's covered in silk."

As Maria Cristina went to Will's side, Ezra came and stood next to me, saying nothing. The tide was rising. We looked out at the waves gently rolling in over the sand, listened to the sucking sound they made going out.

A mosquito whined loudly in my ear as Ezra cleared his throat beside me.

"Your grandfather was the most gifted boatbuilder I've ever known. I was lucky to work with him when I was a boy." His voice was gravelly, uneven; like a tire rolling over rocks, it slipped and rose and fell unexpectedly. "Lucia, your grandmother, was just a girl when they married—fifteen or sixteen, I think. Ben was older, and rough. He was nothing but a sailor at that time. But he loved her." The simple statement was meant to sum up their lives.

I listened to him with a painful constriction in my throat.

"Did you know Estevão and Inêz, too?" I asked.

"I was already at sea when the boy was born, but I was back in a few years with my knee," he said, with a rare, impatient gesture toward his twisted leg. "By then Estevão was three, maybe four, and Lucia was pregnant with Inêz. I played with Estevão. I made him a rocking horse. I was Inêz's godfather. So yes, I knew them. I was part of the family. I never talked about 'em because you don't. I figured you'd rather not."

I couldn't think of a reply. It was the longest speech I'd ever heard from Ezra, but even so, all too brief. I hungered for stories of them, after a lifetime of willful ignorance, and the ache was made worse by Ezra's point that this was a pain I had caused myself. My father and I had always dictated the terms upon which any and all knowledge of them might be revealed or discussed.

What was wrong with me, I wondered, that I had never asked about these people—my own family?

I needed time to take it in, and this was not the moment.

"Ezra," I said suddenly, "did you know that Portuguese boy who washed up in the cove?"

"Sheriff Tucker says it's Matt Da Silva, Cezar's boy. I knew the father—knew of him's more like—some years ago. They're up in Warwick.

"Sorry I wasn't here an' you had to go with them boys." He waved a hand, moving a mosquito out of his vicinity, still not looking at me. "Sheriff told me you went up into the marsh grass 'tween here and the mill to see the body."

"It's okay," I assured him. "It wasn't that bad. I didn't have to get that close. The truth is, I was curious. I wonder what happened to him?"

Clearly uncomfortable, Ezra shifted his weight restlessly. His knee must be bothering him, I thought. Before he could answer, we were interrupted by Maria Cristina calling me over to the hull she was examining. The hull of my boat.

"Ana," she said with some caution, probably wondering if I was still upset. "Your boat looks the same as your drawing. It's fat, *redondo*—I mean round."

I moved toward her, relieved to abandon the conversation with Ezra—for now, at least. "You're right, it is fat," I said. "I worked up the design from the boat Ezra's building but modified it to suit me. See here," I said, pointing, "how it's wider just aft of the center, and also shorter than Sullivan's boat over there?"

She looked over at the other boat and back to mine, nodding.

"And here, the way the hull is rounded for stability?" I asked. "She's fourteen feet long with a beam of five feet, and will sit a little lower in the water, which gives her that fat look. She'll be fitted with a 'kicker'—a small motor," I explained, "only six or eight horsepower. That's because my boat is just for fun—picnics or camping. Ezra's is meant for long runs to the fishing grounds in open water, but I'll use mine to motor around in the coves. I'm going to explore the nooks and crannies of the bay from Warwick and Barrington down to Portsmouth, Jamestown, and Newport."

Will and Ezra stood shoulder to shoulder with their arms unconsciously crossed over their chests in identical fashion, smiling with unapologetic delight, as though I were their child, performing for company. I ignored them and concentrated on Maria Cristina.

"It's getting rather dark, but can you see the forward deck, here? And the raised sheer?" I asked. "I've made space to stow blankets and cooking gear under the deck, and I'll put a small anchor and rope locker here, through the forward hatch."

She nodded her head, her eyes traversing the elevated hull that reached just up to her shoulders. "Excuse me, I very much want to drive this boat when it is finished."

I was becoming increasingly delighted by her unusual phrasing, and more so by her enthusiasm for my boat. "Well, certainly you can take a ride in it, but maybe we'll do it together. And I'll drive."

Maria Cristina didn't offer her usual polite response but continued to examine the boat for a moment before walking toward the dock with Will and Ruth. She didn't argue, but she gave no sign of acquiescence. Her mouth was set in a hard line, and while I was happy to see that she had spirit, it made me a little uneasy. She might prove to be a handful over the next few years. I hoped I would be up to it.

Ezra had walked down to the boat he was currently finishing, the one on the cradles next to mine. He was building it for Stevie Sullivan, Fin's older brother, who had just turned eighteen. Their father caught sea bass, flounder, and cod and sold them to the restaurants in Newport, and on the Pier when he could compete with the bigger outfits. He had one small boat and his family had barely been surviving for a number of years now, but the economy was beginning to strengthen, my father said, and things would be looking up soon for the local fishermen as the resort and restaurant business picked up again. Stevie had just graduated from high school and would go out on the water with his father to help support the family. He could have been fishing with Mr. Sullivan years ago, but his parents had insisted he finish school, which was more than either of them had been able to do. Stevie was grateful, but he couldn't wait to join his father, and he would love the boat Ezra was making for him. He had taken to hanging around at Ezra's, eager for his boat—at least as often as Ezra would let him.

Ezra was inspecting the coat of varnish he had applied earlier, when the sun was high and hot, which kept the consistency of the varnish like that of thin oil for easy, even application and caused the fresh coat to dry hard in less than an hour. His brow was furrowed in a deep, angry-looking scowl. I knew this meant he was very pleased with the results of the day's work, and I came closer to stand beside him.

"How long before she's ready?" I asked.

"Another week," said Ezra. "They pick her up Friday next."

"She's a beauty. Stevie will love her," I said with absolute certainty.

"She needs another coat or two. If we stay dry, I'll be polishing brass by Saturday. Maria Cristina can help," he said gruffly, then shrugged. "If she wants to."

"I'm sure she will—I used to love it when you let me. I'll ask her," I said.

We left Ezra's soon after, walking back to the house while darkness fell heavily around us. The wind picked up, shoving us forward as we traveled inland, then dying down as we moved farther away from the cove and under cover of the trees. Maria Cristina appeared tired, saying little and swatting at mosquitoes. I felt Will glance at me from time to time.

"I'm fine," I told him quietly, without turning.

"Are you sure?" he asked, touching my hand without attempting to hold it. "Do you want to talk?"

"No," I said, then adding, belatedly, "Thanks."

We walked the rest of the way without speaking, and Will went home, declining my less-than-sincere offer to stay for lemonade. The Ford was in the driveway, which meant that father was home.

I was suddenly bone-tired. Maria Cristina went upstairs to wash up before bed, and I went to the kitchen for a glass of water. I was looking forward to sleep.

I crossed the threshold of the hallway into the kitchen and saw my father standing in the dark, both hands on the sink and his head bowed and sunk down below his shoulders. He was always so upright that this unexpected moment of visible weariness caught us both off guard.

"Anne!" he said, straightening up and turning to me as I entered the room. "You startled me. Where have you been?"

"Will came by, and we took Maria Cristina down to the cove after supper. Not all the way to the mill, of course. We stopped by Ezra's for a few minutes."

He scowled. "What were you doing down there?"

"I wanted to show her the boat."

Father said nothing for a moment. "It might be better if you stayed away—for now at least. Farley Tucker is investigating that boy's death, and his men will need access to Ezra—to his place—without any interference."

"Interference? How would my working on my boat interfere?" I asked.

He seemed reluctant to answer. "I just don't want you involved. Any more than you already are, I mean. Dr. Statham will convene a coroner's inquiry the day after tomorrow. He's got to give that poor boy's family permission to bury the body. And determine the cause of death. He asked me to tell you that he wants you there. Officially."

I couldn't imagine what I could add to the statement I'd already given to the sheriff. "But what— Why does he want me?"

"The body was found at Ezra's. You're there a lot. And the Sullivan boy, too. He wants all three of you— Don't look like that, dear," he said gently. "It's his job. He needs to ask you all some questions, see if maybe you know some small detail that might help him figure out what happened. The boy's parents deserve to know."

I nodded. "Of course. I should have expected an official inquiry."

"How is your— How is Maria Cristina adjusting?" he asked unexpectedly.

"She seems fine," I said, trying to keep up. "She becomes more comfortable every day. I think she's sad, and she misses her grandfather, but it is clearly getting easier for her."

"Good. I'm not surprised with you helping her," he said. "You'll make a wonderful mother, you know."

I was surprised, and more than a little pleased with his unexpected praise. But I had to know. "Father, why didn't you ever tell me that Ezra knew Inêz and her family?"

I couldn't read his expression. He was looking right at me, but he was focused inward, examining his feelings, searching his memory for the truth before he answered me. A traitorous little voice in my head suggested that maybe he was trying to decide how much of the truth, if any, he was willing to tell me.

"Many people in Milford knew your mother and her family," he said finally. "Why would I enumerate them?"

"That's not really what I mean," I said. "Of course people knew her. She shopped at Dekker's. She went to church. But Ezra said he was a friend of— of her father's, a good friend, that he made a rocking horse for her brother. He *really* knew them. He was Inêz's godfather. Why didn't you tell me?"

Father stood, his back up against the sink.

"I'm sorry you feel I've been remiss, Anne. If Ezra Johnson was a friend of Benigno Caldeira and his family, perhaps he is the one who should have spoken of it to you."

My grandfather's name fell quickly from his mouth, as if he were eager to be rid of the unpleasant sounds. His tone was just injured enough to make me hesitate, but not so much that I could be sure it was deliberate and therefore resent it.

"According to the sheriff, Caldeira's not the only thing he's being closemouthed about. Now if you'll excuse me, I'm going to bed. I'm very tired tonight."

He turned to leave but paused at the foot of the stairs and said, with his back still to me, "I've invited Will for dinner tomorrow night. Seven thirty. I assume we'll be four." He paused, then added, "I'm sorry I've been so busy these past few days. I'll try to be home for dinner more often."

He had won, so he offered me the consolation prize of his presence at a family dinner that would include Maria Cristina. He thought the discussion was over, and he had every reason to. This was our pattern: he set the tone, decided what we could and would talk about, and I allowed it, swallowing whatever inconvenient things I might have to say. But suddenly I found I didn't want to allow it. Perhaps I had been manipulated and shoved off balance once too often that day.

He began to walk up the stairs.

"Father," I said, my voice ringing out in the kitchen, "I'm not finished yet. It's only natural that I would be curious about my mother, and about the rest of my family. If you can't talk about it, I understand. I've always understood." My voice began to quiver, but I cleared my throat and continued, stronger. "But I am not betraying you by asking questions about them."

He paused on the second step in the darkened stairwell and turned toward me, his head in shadows so I couldn't see his face above me. I knew he was hurt, maybe even angry. There was no sound for a moment, and then I heard a floorboard creak overhead and the unmistakable sound of Maria Cristina's bedroom door softly closing.

"I see," he said. He spoke quietly, his voice perfectly controlled. "I have tried to shield you from the pain of your mother's infamous actions. I have done so out of love, and because I believe that is my responsibility to you. You may choose to despise me for it, but I have felt it my duty to protect you."

"Father," I said, my hand instinctively reaching out to him but falling back to my side in the shadows, having found nothing. "I know you want to protect me, but –"

"I can't do this, Anne. Not tonight. I'm sorry," he said, his dignity intact, as he turned and slowly ascended into the dark.

I stood there until I heard his bedroom door close. I was so tired that my body felt alien to me, and I watched in a detached sort of way as my hand moved slowly to turn off the lights, as though it wasn't I who controlled its movement. I was exhausted, shaken by the effort of attempting to take a stand with my father, by the arrival of my sister, and by the notion that the old man I'd known and loved my entire life was capable of a subterfuge I never would have believed possible. He knew things about Inêz, about my grandparents—and, if my father's ugly hints were to be believed, he knew something about the dead boy in Kingston Cove.

CHAPTER FIVE

The next morning dawned clear and dry without a trace of fog. I woke early, eager to get to work from my first moment of consciousness. I washed up quickly, donning old dungarees that I knew would set Mrs. Hatcher's tongue clucking in gentle disapproval if she saw me walking out of the house in them. More scandalous still, I took great pleasure in putting on an old work shirt of Will's as well. He'd left it at the house last spring when he was here and had spotted a second-floor window casement that needed to be repaired. He'd decided on the spot to fix it so Father wouldn't have to. The day had become brutally hot, and Will had taken his shirt off under the blazing sun, inadvertently leaving it draped over the boxwood hedge below the window, where he'd flung it. I'd given him an old, clean shirt of my father's to wear home when he was finished.

He had asked for his shirt once or twice shortly after discovering it was missing, and each time I replied vaguely that I would return it soon. Eventually, of course, he saw me wearing it, and had thoroughly enjoyed calling me a thief and a liar ever since. The worn cotton pleased me, and he knew I had no intention of giving it back.

I went downstairs to find my father already gone. He had indeed been busy recently, I thought with a pang, focused as he was on reopening the mill. He worked tirelessly to improve not only our circumstances but also those of Milford as a whole, and I hesitated to make things more difficult for him. Even so, I was determined to ask Ezra more about my family. Father would surely come to understand that my loyalty to him was not diminished by my desire to know more about the Caldeiras. As I made coffee I heard Maria Cristina and smiled. For a small girl, she sounded like an extremely large horse coming down the stairs—exactly what Father used to say about me.

I loved any similarity I could find between Maria Cristina and me. It made me feel like we were true sisters, girls who had grown up in the same house together and developed the same habits and characteristics. This was what made Milford's big clans, such as the Sullivans, identifiable as families—the things they all shared. The Sullivan brothers and sisters had the same quick temper and their mother's sandy hair—traits that identified them to one another and to outsiders, that made them real and gave them substance.

Now Maria Cristina made me more real every time I saw some new way we resembled each other. And when I walked through the house now, dusting or putting away clean towels, I heard the sound of her voice calling to me from some other room instead of the hollow echo of my own footsteps.

"Good morning," I said as Maria Cristina entered the brightly lit room.

"Mmm." Her eyes were only half open, her hair a dark tangled mess around her shoulders.

"How about some toast and jam and a glass of milk?"

"Okay." She moved her hair off her face with the back of her hand. I smiled, wondering if she was picking up Will's habit.

"You are awake very early," she said, put out by the hour.

"I thought I might work at Ezra's. Would you like to spend some time with Mrs. Hatcher today, if she's willing?" I asked.

"Excuse me, I very much want to go with you."

"Well, you can if you want to, but it won't be much fun for you today. I thought maybe you and Mrs. Hatcher could make some cookies or a cake for dessert tonight. Will's coming for dinner, and he'll love it if you make the dessert," I said, shamelessly bribing her. Of course she had already developed a crush on Will. He was undeniably handsome—blond hair bleached almost white by the sun, clear blue eyes like the shallows after a good, cleansing storm has passed.

"Okay," she said, with as much enthusiasm as I could hope for this early in the morning.

I toasted bread while she poured her milk in silence. It was a nice kind of quiet, companionable and without anxiety, and it occurred to me how rarely I felt such ease in the presence of another.

"Excuse me, can we dress tonight?" Maria Cristina asked suddenly.

I paused a moment, frowning, before I grasped her meaning. "You mean dress up, like a fancy dinner?"

She nodded, chewing her toast.

"Sure, why not?" It was easy enough to indulge her, and this would be the first time she had sat down to dinner with my father since she arrived.

"And I'll make a beautiful dessert. Something special for Will," she said.

Sitting at the kitchen table, I planned my workday in my mind as I sipped my coffee and Maria Cristina ate her breakfast. I would have to finish up in time to get home, get cleaned up, and have dinner ready by seven o'clock. It would be close. I was glad I was getting an early start.

When Maria Cristina had eaten I hustled her upstairs to get cleaned up and dressed. Then we walked next door to Mrs. Hatcher's.

As we came through the hedge our way to the house was blocked by walls of white sheets hanging on clothes lines. We could hear Mrs. Hatcher humming somewhere within this freshly laundered maze.

"Mrs. Hatcher," I called, ducking behind the nearest sheet and finding myself hemmed in from behind and in front, my vision reduced to the few feet of dewy ground on which I stood.

I called again, and heard her laughing response to my right. I lifted a damp sheet and Maria Cristina and I came up in the narrow row from which Mrs. Hatcher was hanging her clean linens to dry in the morning air.

She was dressed in a neatly pressed, crisp cotton dress and apron. I would have fallen over in shock to ever find her barefooted, or wearing trousers.

"Girls! Come in to the kitchen—I've just finished up here," she said, leading us out and into the open air again.

"What can I do for you this morning?" she asked, clearly happy to see us, though she raised an eyebrow at my old work clothes.

"Well," I said, "I've got a day of work ahead of me at Ezra's, and I wondered if Maria Cristina might spend the day with you. She'd be a little bored at the workshop today, and what with the Sheriff's investigation, it's probably not the best place for her right now anyway. I thought perhaps you two could bake something for dessert tonight, if you aren't too busy. She'll have more fun with you than sitting at home alone, and since school doesn't start until September she hasn't had a chance to make any friends yet."

"And, excuse me, Will is coming for dinner and I will make something he likes," Maria Cristina said.

"I think that's a fine idea!" Mrs. Hatcher told her. "I make a very good cake, you know. We'll go to the grocer first. I understand that Mrs. Jablonski has fresh strawberries coming in today, and you caught me on a day when I have plenty of sugar on hand. I'm supposed to bake something for the DAR Fourth of July picnic anyway, so we can do both."

"Okay." Maria Cristina smiled at Mrs. Hatcher, and I knew I could leave her without a qualm.

"Anne, would you like a cup of coffee before you go?" she asked.

"Sure, a quick one, thank you," I said.

I sat down at the table and sipped my coffee while Maria Cristina ate a fresh doughnut dusted with sugar.

"Let me just clear up this sewing so we'll have room to work later," said Mrs. Hatcher, swiftly removing the pins from the hem she had just sewn in Mr. Hatcher's suit coat. "Well, maybe we'll leave just this one," she murmured, burying a straight pin deep in the back of her husband's coat. Then she gathered up scissors, thread, and coat and hurried out of the room to put them away.

When Mrs. Hatcher came back I left for Ezra's after assuring them both that I'd be back by four. I hurried down the street and turned onto the old mill road for the walk to Ezra's.

The sounds of a summer morning in downtown Milford—cars, voices, radio music heard through an open window—vanished just a few steps down the mill road. The thick tangle of woods on either side of the road, plus the sand of the road itself, served as a sound barrier that effectively separated Milford proper from the outskirts of this side of town, and from Kingston Cove. The last fingers of morning mist clung to the ground and the tree trunks on either side of me, hiding from the sun that would burn them away.

I was wide-awake, eager, bristling with energy. I marched down the hard-packed sand road, making lists in my mind of the things I would accomplish today. Birds chattered and flitted among the trees on both sides, and I occasionally caught a glimpse of a blue jay or a pair of catbirds as they chased each other in and out of the branches. The sun shone brightly in my face, having risen just high enough to peek above the trees in front of me as I drew closer to the cove.

Shafts of light cut diagonally through the trees, looking solid enough to touch. The chiaroscuro of sun and shadow gave the wood a surreal aspect; it seemed impossible that the pale, verdant leaves trembling in the clear morning light were the same as those that lay in gloomy shadow mere inches away, struggling in darkness.

I shivered. The air was still chilly, despite the warmth of the rising sun, and I was glad of the sweater I'd decided to wear.

When I reached the turnoff to Ezra's place I paused and looked at the mill down the road. It stared blankly back. I hoped that my father would find his investors and the mill would rise like the phoenix he envisioned. The residents of Milford certainly needed it, but I wondered anxiously what effect Roosevelt's presidency would have on my father's dream. Not so many years ago, when the mill was running at capacity and Father had not yet developed the near-constant look of worry he now wore, there had been no question of a labor union. But things had changed.

I read the papers religiously, looking for articles and editorials about the New England textile mills—about Roosevelt's plans for a minimum wage, and the fate of mills that had moved down South or closed their doors forever. I had been weaned on such dinner-table conversations when the mill was flourishing and the house was often filled with businessmen and politicians. I was always present at the dinner table, and many of the meetings as well, but not because anyone thought it prudent to educate me on such topics—my father and everyone else assumed that when I eventually inherited the mill it would rest in my husband's capable, masculine hands.

No, I was there as my father's hostess, standing in for his absent wife whom nobody ever mentioned.

I had listened to hundreds of discussions involving labor, capital, and politics, and I read widely enough now to know that all the mills, including ours, were going to be deeply affected by Roosevelt's New Deal—affected in ways that Father was certain would hurt us.

My father was a nativist and a businessman, positions he had inherited from his father along with the mill, the house, and an extensive stock portfolio—though he was too fine a man to say to our neighbors and friends who happened to be Italian, or Irish, or Lithuanian that he did not think they should have too much political or economic power, despite their growing numbers, especially if they were Catholic and answered to some foreign Pope rather than to the government of the United States and the free market.

I remembered a morning, years ago, as Father and I sat at the breakfast table drinking coffee and reading the *Providence Journal*, when I had expressed the opinion that the property requirement for voting seemed wrong.

"That's because you don't understand it, dear," he had said kindly, but I bristled. I was seventeen or so at the time, and believed myself wiser than I was.

"Maybe I don't understand all the details," I said, "but it seems to me that this requirement means that poor people get no say at all."

His mouth tightened and his color deepened across his cheeks and the bridge of his nose.

"I support a property requirement, as do many reasonable men in Providence and elsewhere, and as the Founding Fathers did. I support that requirement because it is we, the property owners, who have invested our lifeblood here, and we have far more to lose than those who have not. With immigration out of control, and the cities filling up with laborers from who-knows-where, we've got to protect our interests. They already outnumber us in the cities."

He said this as though it were so self-evident that he was slightly embarrassed for me.

"But Father," I had said, "how can you support such a thing and still claim to support democracy?"

It was the first time in my memory he ever yelled at me. He had been furious, outraged, shouting phrases at me like "no daughter of mine" and "you have no idea what you're talking about."

I followed the narrow, sandy track off to the right, and my thoughts followed suit, leaving the mill behind. I kept a brisk pace trudging through the soft sand and soon emerged from the trees into the clearing where I found Ezra already at work, sealing the lid on a can of varnish. As early as it was, he had already applied a coat to the Sullivan boat, taking full advantage of the promise of a hot, dry day.

"Good morning!" I called, advancing into the clearing.

Ezra looked up and nodded.

"We've good weather for working today," I commented. "With any luck I'll finish the transom."

Ezra frowned. "Don't hurry it, girl. You'll make costly mistakes."

"So you've told me a thousand times." I pulled my sweater off, already too warm now that I was out from under the trees, and headed toward the workshop.

The sun had not yet risen sufficiently to fully light the room, and I squinted in the dimness, mentally ticking off the tools I would need. I had already framed my boat, including stem and keel, and planked her from the bottom-up. The transom, cut from a single wide board, marked from a pattern and cut to shape, lay on the floor, propped up against the workbench where I had left it the last day I was here—a week ago, I thought, shaking my head. I'd never finish her at this rate.

I would attach the transom to the center cleat, then caulk the seam and begin planking her sides. If all went well, I might even glue the transom frame to the planking today.

I bent and lifted the transom—feeling grateful that I was strong and relatively tall—then carried it to the door and leaned it up against the wall. I went to the shelves and chose my fasteners, three-and-a-quarter-inch brass screws—number twelves—and the hand drill and corresponding bit. I laid everything on the workbench, then went back to the wall, picked up my clamps, and added them to the pile of tools and hardware I had gathered there. I grabbed work gloves and the old leather tool belt that Ezra had said I could consider mine whenever I was here. I put the screws in one of the belt pockets and hung a hammer, screwdriver, and drill in the loops on either side. Then I dropped a stubby carpenter's pencil, measuring tape, and chalk line into a second, larger pocket, and tucked the gloves into the waistband of my dungarees. I was ready.

The familiar weight of the belt filled me with purpose, and I picked up the transom, remembering to lift with my legs, and walked out into the brilliant sunshine.

Ezra sat on a rickety, handmade chair he kept down by the dock. He liked to sit outside and smoke a pipe while a coat of paint or varnish dried in the sun. He claimed something in the foul-smelling smoke made the finish last longer.

Ezra looked up from beneath his shaggy brows and peered at me through a haze of smoke as I approached. I picked my way slowly across the yard, then carefully propped the transom up against the legs of the horse that supported the stern of my boat. Ezra got up with some creaking from his old joints, walked the few steps over to the transom, and slowly, painfully leaned down, holding the stem of his pipe between his teeth in order to free both hands, which he ran gently over the surface of the piece.

"Well?" I asked, a little anxious despite myself.

"She'll do," he said. He could do that—could tell if a surface was level or a joint square just by eyeballing it or running his hands over it. For the first few years I'd worked with him, when I'd heard him make such pronouncements with absolutely no confirmation from an instrument, I'd secretly gone back to check.

I no longer checked.

"Of course she will," I said, with a bravado that was slightly marred by the note of relief even I could hear in my voice.

A snort was his only reply as he lowered himself back into the chair to enjoy his pipe and the sun on his back.

"Hi, Annie! Hi, Ezra!" came a shout from the road as Stevie Sullivan drove his dad's open flivver into the clearing. The old jalopy coughed and shivered as it came to a lurching stop midway between the workshop and the dock. Stevie pulled the brake up and climbed out.

He stood, hands in his pockets, somehow managing to look both bashful and nosy as he craned his neck to see what I was doing with my boat, blushing all the while.

"Morning, Stevie," I said. "How is everything at your house?"

"Oh, fine, fine. Ma's on a tear about the little ones digging up her garden, so I thought I'd come down here. You know, see how she's coming." He gulped as Ezra sent a scowl his way. "Thought I might be able to help."

"Your dad's not paying me to have you build her," was Ezra's only reply.

"Oh, yeah, okay. That's true, I guess," he stammered. "I guess I'll go an' see my girl."

"Oh, have you got a girl?" I asked, forgetting for a moment that he was nearly a man and thinking only, *How sweet.*

"Well, I hope to," he said, his eyes on the sand he was digging with the toe of his shoe, looking like the little boy I'd always thought him.

"Good for you," I said, as if I were his grandmother.

Ezra and I were only minimally polite as he waved good-bye, and barely waited until he was back in the car before we were back at work.

"That boy's here more'n I'd like," Ezra grumbled. He was in a worse mood than usual, I thought. "I told him to stay away, but he don't learn."

"Well, you're just so loveable—who can resist you?" I asked cheerily.

After lifting the transom to the frame, I spent the next hour or so positioning it carefully and then clamping it in place. I did not ask for Ezra's help, and he didn't offer. I had been determined from the very beginning to build her entirely by myself, and I wasn't about to revert to being an apprentice at this late date.

By the time I got the transom up and stable enough to free my hands, I was sweating in the hot, late-morning sun, and Ezra, who had long ago finished his bowl, was tamping down another. He seemed to be in no hurry to continue the work on his own boat, content as he was to watch me struggle with mine.

"Are you enjoying this?" I asked, pausing a moment to get my breath.

I felt a bead of sweat run down my face from temple to chin and impatiently brushed the irritating drop away with the back of my gloved hand. Strands of hair that had escaped from my ponytail clung damply to my cheeks and neck. I was annoyed, by both Ezra and the heat.

"Go get some water," he said, clearly amused. "Cool off, or you'll take it out on the boat."

I went to the rusty old spigot by the workshop door and pumped the handle vigorously, taking it out on Ezra's medieval plumbing instead. A stream of fresh, icy water shot out, and I cupped my hand under it. Splashing the back of my neck and face first, I finally took a long, cool drink. When I straightened back up, I saw Sheriff Tucker's long, black car emerge from the trees into the clearing. He parked midway between the house and the dock, and as soon as he turned off the engine, all four doors opened. The sheriff and four other men climbed out of the car and walked somberly toward Ezra, who hadn't moved from his chair. I realized I'd left the spigot open and quickly pushed the handle down. I was standing in a little puddle, my shoes muddy. I'll never finish her at this rate, I thought.

Wiping my hands on my dungarees, I walked quickly toward the men, who were already talking. The sheriff stood closest to Ezra, like the point in the V-formation of an aerial attack, with the others— his deputy, Mac Donovan, and three men I did not know—fanning out behind him. They all wore heavy waders.

"True enough, Ezra, I have been down here asking you questions already," Sheriff Tucker was saying. "That don't mean you've been answerin' 'em, though." Farley Tucker was well liked in South County, and though his manner of speaking was slow, it was a mistake to assume that his thoughts were moving at the same pace. My father had a tremendous amount of respect for the man, and Father couldn't abide fools.

"All I can do is tell you what I can, Farley," said Ezra from his chair. "It can't be helped if what I can tell you isn't much."

Sheriff Tucker stood over Ezra, looking down at him for a moment and saying nothing. I thought he looked unhappy, but whether it was with Ezra or the job he was compelled to do, I did not know. He looked at me suddenly.

"Your dad tell you you're needed at the inquest tomorrow?" he asked.

"Yes, yes, he did." I was shocked by how nervous I sounded. How guilty.

He nodded once, then turned to his men. "All right, boys, let's go. Smitty, Mac, you two follow the shoreline. Stay abreast, one of you shin-deep, th' other knee-deep. Sweep the silt with your feet, all the way to the rocks at the mill. You boys"—he turned to the other two men—"you'll come with me. We'll cover the marsh and the high grass between here and the mill." They left and began walking along the shore, two of them in the water, the other three up on the shore.

I returned to the transom of my boat, saying nothing to Ezra. I knew he wasn't looking for conversation. Within minutes the sheriff and his men had rounded the point, following the curve of the shore-line out of sight.

After a time, my mind returned to the questions it could not escape and I spoke. "How did you first meet my grandfather?" I asked.

I felt Ezra's sharp, swift glance but didn't look up. I kept my eyes on my caulk line, kept working. When he spoke, there was no indication in his voice that he was either surprised or reluctant to pursue the topic. I suspected that after last night he was expecting this, and he seemed relieved that I did not ask about the sheriff's at-titude toward him.

"I went to work in the shipyard 'cause I didn't want to be a preacher," said Ezra. "I wanted to build boats. Ben Caldeira's father was a whaler, brought his family from the Azores to Massachusetts when Ben was a boy. The old man started repairing boats when he got older, and Ben quit school at eleven to help him. Even as a boy, it was clear he had a gift. Time he was thirty, Ben was chief carpenter at the Barrington shipyard. I was just a kid then, happy to do the scut work as long as I could hang around. We became friends."

I was pleased by this unexpected wealth of information. I pressed my advantage, knowing that Ezra could decide at any moment that he was through talking for the day.

"How did he meet Lucia? When did they get married?" I asked. I wanted to get everything I could, as quickly as I could.

"They met at St. Mary's in Barrington. She went to Mass every morning, her an' her mother. She caught Ben's eye. She caught ever'body's eye."

He glanced at me then, caught my surprised look.

"Well, she did," he said, surprisingly defensive. "I went with him sometimes. Nobody could take their eyes off her." I could only imagine how his father, who had been the Congregationalist minister in Milford, had reacted to Ezra attending Mass.

"Did she like him, too, right away?" I asked.

"She never showed it if she did. She kept her head covered an' her eyes on her rosary. She was little more'n a child, but Ben spoke to her parents right away. They was poor, an' Ben wasn't, at least not by their reckoning. An' the Portuguese hereabouts thought him a good man, which was good enough for Lucia's parents. They was married that same year."

I had stopped even pretending to work while he talked.

"And they were happy?"

He shrugged. "Happy as anybody. Though they had their share of troubles," he said more darkly, and I knew he meant Inêz.

"What was Estevão like?" I asked after a moment, postponing any discussion of Inêz for as long as possible. I wasn't sure why, but where Inêz was concerned my eagerness was tempered by the old reluctance. Surely, I thought, no new information could be worse than what I already knew.

"Estevão was a sweet child but an angry man," was his surprising answer. There was a pause, while I waited for more, but Ezra said nothing.

"Angry in what way?" I prodded.

"He was proud. Proud of his family, proud of being Portuguese. But they was immigrants, and Catholics, and things was done and said, and it hurt him. It was hard to put your finger on it. Folks weren't so welcoming, I s'pose, or even polite, an' he felt it more'n most. After he was grow'd he might've stayed among his own people. That's what a lot of 'em did, including his parents. But he went the other way. He got angry, and he got loud. He wanted things—things he thought was his right, same as anybody. A lot of folks disagreed."

"What kinds of things did he want?" I asked.

"Some things you could name, and some you couldn't," Ezra said, shrugging. "They had a nice house, and Lucia didn't have to take in washing or clean rich folks' houses. They didn't lack for nothin', Estevão or Inêz. But he wanted . . . respect, I guess. An open space in front of him. It wasn't about money, he told me once. It was about being a man."

"What did he want to do?" I asked, confused.

"Well, for one he wanted to go to college," said Ezra, pausing in the pacing he'd been doing for the last few minutes, too restless—or maybe too agitated by the conversation—to just sit and smoke any longer. "Maybe you should ask Samuel."

"What did Father have to do with it?"

"That's for him to tell you," he said, and abruptly walked away from me, toward the workshop.

Ezra stayed inside for a while, and I finished caulking the seam between the transom and the center cleat. I knew, of course, that Ezra and my father disliked each other, had always sensed that their animosity was in some way about my mother since she was the one thing that neither of them ever discussed, but what Ezra was telling me now suggested that I might actually be getting to the reason for it. I was both excited and afraid. I had begun to ask questions, and the questions seemed to have a life of their own, gathering speed and carrying us all forward. I finished up my caulk line, then went and sat under the little copse of pines nearby to eat the cheese sandwich I had brought with me from home. I chewed slowly, as if I might bite into something unexpected.

From my lunch spot under the trees I watched Ezra emerge from the workshop and make his awkward way down to the boats. I remained, enjoying the shade while he applied another coat of varnish after thinning it slightly with turpentine. He worked quickly, efficiently, and I wondered if, were I to put a brush in his hand in the dead of night, he could varnish a hull in his sleep, wake in the morning, and find not a single bubble in the finish. It wouldn't have surprised me at all.

Balling up the wrapping from my sandwich, I returned to the boats and threw it into the rusted oil barrel Ezra used for trash when he was working down by the dock. He had put together a comfortable little camp there over the years. Some days he sat down by the water from sunup to sundown. He had his chair, his current project up on horses, a trash barrel, an old stump to prop his feet up (or for me to sit on), even an old oil lantern and some matches, hidden in its brass base, in case he stayed out past dusk working.

"How's it coming?" I asked.

"Fine," he grunted, not looking up.

"How many more coats you figure?"

"Maybe two," he said.

I nodded, even though he wasn't looking at me.

"I've just got the fasteners left," I said. "Then I'm finished with the transom for now. I think she's coming along."

Ezra didn't reply, so I set about measuring, marking, and drilling starter holes for the screws in my pocket. I worked carefully, knowing that if I rushed I would make a mistake. Then I screwed the transom and frame together, and finally removed the clamps I had so carefully placed, reconsidered, and repositioned no fewer than three times. I had once had to recut a transom I was helping Ezra with, which had proved far more time-consuming than if I had done it right the first time.

We worked in silence as the sun beat down on our heads and the tide went out, the watermark of each successive wave slipping lower on the dock's pilings as the afternoon wore away. When Sheriff Tucker and his men returned, something about their determined, faster pace—as compared to the slow, meandering way in which they'd set out—told me they'd found something. I steeled myself, glancing over at Ezra, who appeared unconcerned.

Sheriff Tucker approached with something wrapped in his jacket. He stopped a few feet from Ezra's chair. "You missin' any tools, Ezra?" he asked.

"Don't believe I am, Farley."

"This look familiar?" asked the sheriff, unwrapping the bundle and holding out the object inside for us to see.

"Looks like a chisel. I'm pretty familiar with those," said Ezra. He had barely looked at it.

What are you doing? I thought, though I gave nothing away. Of course he knew the chisel—I had recognized it at once. It was one of a set, the big one, its flat, sharp blade easily eight inches long, the distinctive handle made of maple, flat and broad at the end for the mallet. Now it was dirtied with muck, a strand of seaweed, and just a trace of rust—or blood—on the blade halfway up to the hilt.

The sheriff carefully wrapped the chisel back up and signaled to his men that they were through. Before they'd taken three steps toward the car, Farley Tucker turned back toward us. "I'll see you tomorrow at the inquest, Ezra. And you, too, Miss Dodge. You folks think about how you might be able to help me out here. Help that boy's family learn what happened to him, and why. You do the right thing. You hear?"

Without waiting for a reply, the men climbed back into their car and left. I stood looking after them, and when I turned to Ezra he was looking at me, waiting. Suddenly I heard the tentative cry of a young owl from the trees beyond the stone wall. The sun was approaching the tree tops at the western property line.

"Ezra, what time is it?" I asked in a panic.

He glanced at the sun. "Five, five thirty."

"Oh, no!" I wailed. "I'm late for dinner!"

"Go," he ordered. "I'll clean up."

I tore off my tool belt, dropped it in his lap, and ran.

The sandy track opened up and pulled at my feet. My legs felt heavy and slow, like in those dreams where you're running and not getting anywhere. Finally I reached the mill road, red-faced and breathing hard, and I cursed out loud because no one was there to hear me and it felt good. I turned left toward town, my feet now flying down the hard-packed road. Within minutes my lungs were burning and I felt a stitch begin in my side, but I kept going, refusing to slow down until I reached Mrs. Hatcher's back door.

CHAPTER SIX

I knocked, then leaned against the door jam, shaking and weak as I forced air into my lungs, my heart pounding, rattling the bars of its cage.

"Excuse me, you are very late," said Maria Cristina as she swung the door open.

"I'm sorry," I managed to get out. "I lost track . . . Are you ready to go?"

"She's more than ready," laughed Mrs. Hatcher, coming up behind Maria Cristina and carrying a vision of a cake on a raised platter. "Eight hours is a bit long for a baking lesson, even for me!"

"I'm really, really sorry," I said, meaning it. "You were so kind to take her . . ."

"Don't be silly," she said briskly. "I've loved every minute of it and can't wait to do it again. Only next time, Maria Cristina's going to teach *me* how to cook something. Something Portuguese, right, Maria?"

I smiled, both at the affectionate shortening of her name and at the idea of any sister of mine developing culinary skills, but I could see that Mrs. Hatcher was not joking.

I looked at Maria Cristina with surprise, and she smiled back at me.

"Excuse me, *Avó* let me help her, and when she got sick I cooked a lot," she explained.

"Well, aren't you the accomplished young woman," I said, hoping after I said it that they'd heard admiration in my voice, not envy. "We should?" I asked, then turned to Mrs. Hatcher, embarrassed to ask another favor of her but seeing no way around it. "Mrs. Hatcher, I've been called to the inquest tomorrow. I'll probably only be gone for a few hours in the morning . . ."

"Of course, dear. Bring her over when you have to leave."

I took the cake from Mrs. Hatcher, who called after us that there was no hurry to return her cake stand, and we picked our way carefully through the gap in the hedge. Maria Cristina opened the back door, and I deposited the cake on the kitchen table with a sigh of relief. It was magnificent, easily six inches high and perfectly round, decorated with plump red strawberries rolled in powdered sugar and thick, creamy white icing swirled into flowers and leaves.

"This is gorgeous," I said. "Did you make it yourself?"

"Yes," she said. "No," she amended her answer. "Mrs. Hatcher helped. I was not skilled in the icing. I practiced the flowers first on some little cakes—cupcakes—we made. We cooked many for her picnic, and some for Mr. Hatcher, but mine were not pretty. So she made the flowers on the big cake."

"Well, it looks almost too good to eat. Not that that would stop Will," I said, and we both had a laugh at his expense.

"Did anything, uh, unusual go into Mr. Hatcher's cupcakes?"

"Excuse me, but I don't know. Maybe. We went to the market first. Mrs. Hatcher bought strawberries and a fish for their dinner. When she stirred the cupcakes in the bowl, I believe she poured juice from the fish into her bowl. But her back was to my face, so perhaps not."

"Did she say anything?" I asked, amused.

"No. But later, when we painted the icing on my cake, I said, 'Excuse me, but with the flowers and leaves can we make some little icing fish as well?'" said Maria Cristina, starting to giggle. "She looked angry, but it was pretend anger, and she said, 'Don't be fresh, Maria.' Is she trying to kill Mr. Hatcher?"

"No," I laughed. "No more than he is really trying to hurt her with his insults about her cooking. It's just what they do."

After a quick bath, while Maria Cristina was washing and dressing, I took the pot roast out of the icebox. I bought all our meat from Mr. Jablonski, who ran a butcher counter at the back of their grocer's store. The boy who worked there, Giovanni, would deliver in the afternoon if I telephoned my order in the morning. We had worked out a deal, Giovanni and I: I gave him a twenty-five-cent tip if he came right into the house through the back door and put the meat in the icebox, and if he didn't tell anybody. My father would not have been pleased, and neither would Mr. and Mrs. Jablonski. But I never locked the doors anyway—no one in Milford did, to my knowledge—and doing it this way meant I didn't have to wait around in the house when I could be outside doing something more to my liking.

Working quickly, I dredged the roast in flour, then lightly seasoned it with salt and pepper and thyme. I browned it all around in an oiled Dutch oven on the stove, then added carrots, potatoes, and water, and put the lid on. I shoved the cast-iron pot into the oven, turned the gas on and lit the pilot light, and then ran upstairs to dress.

I knocked on Maria Cristina's door and opened it in response to her call to come in. I hadn't been in there since I'd brought her bags up that first day. I wanted her to feel that the room was hers in every way, that she had private space that would not be entered by anyone, even me, without an express invitation. I glanced around the room, knowing that she couldn't have added much to it, given that she'd carried only a single suitcase off the train. She had, however, managed to make it her own. She had moved the bed closer to the window that faced the cove, no small feat in itself as the bed was made of solid bird's-eye maple. She had cut some of the flowering wisteria that grew along the back of the house and put it in water in an old blue bottle I'd picked up years ago on the beach at Ezra's and given to her when she'd said she liked it. The flowers sat on her bedside table right next to the window, and the fading gold light of a spectacular sunset shone gently on the white blossoms and through the cobalt glass.

Maria Cristina was sitting at a low dressing table on a small upholstered stool. The table was an old piece that had been in one of the spare bedrooms, and I thought she might like it. It was a little ornate for me, and certainly too low. When I was a child I had loved it, but in adolescence I had begun to grow alarmingly tall, and by the time I was fifteen I could no longer sit at the table because my knees wouldn't fit under it. It was perfect for Maria Cristina, I thought happily, watching her finish her toilette—a word that came unexpectedly to my mind and that I associated with my father's mother, a sour old woman who had taken a brief interest in me after Inêz left.

I was taken to visit her once a month, driven in a big black car by Albert, a man with an odd-looking hat, but it didn't last long. She had found me wanting in some fundamental way, in my "disgusting and unacceptable toilette," she had said once in exasperation, and which I took to mean that I didn't wash my hands enough. I felt only relief when she decided that her own toilette included washing her hands of me.

She had insisted when I visited on what she called "proper comportment," which meant hats and gloves and sharp pins pulling my hair back tight. It meant uncomfortable shoes and sitting quietly, and it most certainly meant no running down her long marble hallway in my stocking feet and sliding into the maid, who shrieked and carried on in the most ridiculous way the one time I had done it.

Grandmother Dodge had been a formidable woman. She was as tall as Father—age had never caused her to stoop—but with iron-gray hair instead of white.

On my forced visits, which included a stay overnight, she had instructed me in bathing. I remember vividly the stiff brush her maid had used to scrub my skin as I sat shivering in the old porcelain tub, trying not to cry, while she looked on with her arms folded across her chest.

"You're so dirty," she muttered once, pausing with the brush she had taken into her own hand in frustration. "How do you get so dirty?"

I recall my confusion as I looked at the skin on my arms and hands and feet, the only parts of me that might have been exposed to any sort of dirt. They were the same color as the skin on my stomach, my thighs—all the parts that remained covered by my clothes.

"It's okay, Grandmother," I'd said, relieved to know that I had not failed her. "Look—I'm not really dirty. I'm just the *color* of dirt."

She'd stopped then and looked at me, really looked at me, as I held out my arms for her to see. She was sitting on a low stool beside the tub, and we were, for the first and last time, eye-to-eye.

"Yes," she said slowly, apparently struck by my view of the unfortunate reality of my coloring. "I suppose you are. And I suppose it's never going to come off."

I remember the delight I felt as she said this. I had taken her at the time to mean she would stop scrubbing me so hard.

Not long afterward, Albert stopped coming for me.

I focused again on Maria Cristina, who was facing the mirror and smiling at me in the glass. When I put this room together for her I had included the silver comb, hairbrush, and handheld mirror that always sat on the dressing table. Maria Cristina was slowly combing her long hair, watching herself in the mirror, humming something haunting and sad. The light from the window was faint, a mere memory of illumination. I realized that I was holding my breath, watching Maria Cristina in the dim light. She put the comb down and gathered her dark hair at the crown, pulling it up and turning it with a practiced twist of her wrist into a knot high on the top of her head, and then she looked right at me in the mirror. I reached blindly behind me, my hand groping for support as I stared at her reflection. My hand found the edge of the bed, and I sank onto the neatly folded quilt at its foot.

No specific memory presented itself, but I knew as surely as I breathed that on many evenings I had stood as a child, just so, watching my mother at this very table, putting her hair up as she dressed for dinner. Maria Cristina was still smiling at me in the mirror, as though nothing had happened—and for her, of course, nothing had. She dropped her hands, and her hair fell back down around her shoulders.

"We must put our hair up," she said imperiously. "It is difficult to do alone. When I was little *Mamãe* used to do it for me, just like hers, and after she died *Avó* would try when her hands didn't hurt too bad."

I nodded, swallowing hard and staring at her. Her likeness to Inêz, with the wide-set eyes, the face narrowing to the pointed chin, was so much more striking with her long hair up off of her face. I breathed deeply, willing myself to calm down, to smile back at her. She was looking at me for approval.

She had dressed in the only nice thing she owned, a cream-colored satin dress with a wide sash and a voluminous little-girl skirt made of net. It looked a little small for her—I had not noticed before, but she was beginning to develop. She looked like a woman, not a child.

"Excuse me, do I look pretty? This was my *crisma* dress. I wore it for the Mass when I finished my catechism. *Avó* remade it. It had the long sleeves, but she had to cut them more short when I became tall. She made a new skirt," she said, indicating the layers of net.

"It's beautiful," I said, "and so are you." I hesitated, then decided to just say it, unsure whether I did so for me or for her. "You look like our mother. I hardly remember her, but when you held your hair up, you looked just like she did when I was a child."

"Really?" she asked, clearly pleased. "*Avô* said that I looked like her, too." And then, intensely excited, "You must get dressed, and then we will put your hair up, too!"

And suddenly that was exactly what I wanted to do. I wanted to play dress-up with my sister.

"Come on!" I cried, and we tore out the door and into my bedroom. I threw open the old mahogany wardrobe I rarely used because it held the formal clothes I had so few occasions to wear, and that I viewed primarily as uncomfortable. I quickly rifled through the few garments hanging there and then I saw it—the red one. Father had insisted I buy a new, expensive evening dress two years before, when I graduated from college. I had protested weakly, then given in happily when I saw the red silk. After commencement, Will had taken me to a ball at the Pier. We danced and drank bootleg gin, and afterward we had . . . I blushed, remembering his mouth, his hands, the red silk pushed up around my waist. He had asked me to marry him the next day. Alarmed by his proposal rather than our intimacy, I had not so much as kissed him since that night.

My fingers caressed the thin, watery silk, and I smiled. I loved this dress. It was long and slippery, brilliant ruby-red in the light, a deeper bloodred in its shadowy folds. I pulled off my robe, kicked off my scuffed slippers. Maria Cristina laughed and did a little jig where she stood as I pulled the dress over my head and twisted at the waist to fasten it. I pushed the fabric down over my hips and felt its cool whisper as the hem grazed the tops of my feet.

"Well?" I asked Maria Cristina, turning to her.

Her eyes were huge, her hands clasped over her chest. "*Estás linda*," she breathed.

I turned to the mirror set in the door of the wardrobe to see for myself. I had forgotten I could look like this. Green eyes, a long straight nose, thick dark brows. My mouth was too wide, of course, but tonight my plain, strong features seemed to complement my height. The bodice of the dress was cut on a bias, the neckline draping softly and falling from the edges of my bare shoulders. The hollows under my collarbones lay in shadow, and my skin took on the warmth of the red fabric. A good deal of my back was left bare by the dress, which followed the curves of my waist and hips, clinging like the fragrance of soap on skin. I caught Maria Cristina's eyes in the mirror and giggled.

"Now your hair!" Maria Cristina said.

I rummaged around in the boxes on my bureau, pushed aside

an early sketch of my boat, threw a dirty shirt on the floor, and finally found what I was looking for: hairpins. I gathered them up, handed them to Maria Cristina, and sat on the edge of the bed. She worked quickly, humming that same melody I knew instinctively she had learned from Inêz, or maybe her *avó*. Our *avó*, I thought, trying it on. As Maria Cristina worked, gathering my hair and brushing it upward into her other hand, I felt the unusual sensation of its weight at the top of my head, rather than pulling back and down from the ponytail I fashioned each day for convenience. Her breath on my neck gave me chills, the delicate skin there unused to even that light touch.

"Now me," said Maria Cristina. She handed me the rest of the pins, sat on the bed next to me, and turned around. I began, clumsily at first, to pull her hair into my hands. Then, with increasing confidence, I lifted it up the way I'd seen her do a few minutes before, twisting my wrist, and coiled it around in a knot on top of her head, securing it with the pins.

"Okay," I said. We stood up and looked at each other. She was very serious, surveying me from head to toe.

"Do you have jewels?" she asked. "For the throat, the wrists?"

"Yes!" I shouted, and we both laughed as I ran to the bureau and started turning boxes over, spilling their contents everywhere.

"Here!" I yelled, victorious. "I have this, a jet necklace and matching bracelets. You should wear them," I insisted, pressing them into her hands.

"Oh, I love them!" she exclaimed, turning so I could clasp the necklace around her slim throat. She put the bracelets on, then turned to me, a question in her eyes.

"Perfect. Now shoes, and we're ready for company. Hurry!" I shouted, hearing voices downstairs and wondering how long they'd been here.

Maria Cristina ran to her room and I turned back to the wardrobe. Way in the back I found my one pair of heels, black. I should have satin sandals, dyed to match this dress, I thought with uncharacteristic vanity. My black Louis heels would have to do, though, and I bent down to buckle them, wondering as I did so what time I had actually put the beef in the oven. I had forgotten to check, but surely it hadn't been more than an hour.

I finished just as Maria Cristina came back in the room.

"One thing more," she said as I straightened up. "Sit on the bed again."

I did as she asked, and she pulled out from behind her back some of the wisteria blooms from the bottle-vase in her room. She worked carefully, a little frown of concentration on her face so close to mine, and then sat back with a self-satisfied grin.

"Ana, go look," she commanded without so much as an "excuse me."

I rose and went to the mirror, and I looked. My thick hair was twisted into a heavy knot at the crown of my head, a few curling strands already escaping and a half-dozen tiny flowers peeking out at one side, soft and white. The red dress seemed to breathe with me, reflecting its depth and warmth and life onto my skin—and my skin, no longer the color of dirt, shone like living oak, like the deep, rich velvet of a young buck's antlers.

I was magnificent.

Maria Cristina came and stood next to me, and we gazed at ourselves and each other in the mirror, standing close so we could see ourselves together in the narrow glass. Our arms were touching, we leaned in a little toward each other, and she clasped my hand in hers. She smiled her impish, gap-toothed smile at me in the mirror, and when I smiled back, we both looked like our *mamãe*.

CHAPTER SEVEN

When I was seventeen I became briefly interested in dramatics. Like most of my friends, when our drama teacher, Mr. Thiessen, announced that we would stage *Romeo and Juliet*, I studied hard and auditioned with great determination. When I won the part of Juliet I was elated, despite my knowledge that the director had to cast someone tall enough that the audience would be able to see her clearly above the already-constructed balcony wall.

I read the play and learned my lines quickly, but as rehearsals commenced I found myself increasingly uncomfortable as Juliet. *Be patient*, I wanted to counsel Romeo, despite my inability to change the outcome of the story. *Don't trust what you see, what you think you know*, I wanted to warn him. *Things are not what they seem.* As opening night approached, I became agitated. I knew the tragedy that lay ahead, the waste of it all. The die was cast, the lines written, our deaths inevitable, and walking out on that stage and just letting it happen was almost more than I could bear.

But when the curtain rose I spoke my lines with feeling, my phrasing and intonation exactly what Mr. Thiessen had asked of me.

The play's the thing, I suppose, but it strikes me that only the authors of our little dramas ever say such things.

My high school theatrics were short-lived, but I was reminded of my brief time under the lights as Maria Cristina and I, dressed for the domestic stage, went down to join my father, Will, and Reverend Brown, whom Father had included at the last minute. We all—all but Maria Cristina—had long since become comfortable in our well-rehearsed roles. We had been an ensemble cast my entire life.

Here was Will, I thought, the grateful guest, interpreting his presence as a sign that our eventual marriage was, despite my protestations, a fait accompli. And there, center stage, was my father, concealing his fears and his plans behind the incongruity of humility and moral certainty. And over here, for comic relief, perhaps, was the Reverend Brown, a portly, graying man whose ministrations to the faithful were well intentioned, if unimaginative, and whose community leadership consisted of agreeing with everything my father said. Maria Cristina, the ingenue seated at Will's left, served as the catalyst for the evening.

And though she had been in Milford for nearly a week, this is where we all took up the mantle of our respective parts: Maria Cristina and I, having buttoned, buckled, and tugged our costumes into place, raced to the top of the stairs in response to Father's call, asking if anyone was at home. We composed ourselves and walked carefully down the steps, listening to the sound of men in quiet conversation below in the hall. We reached the landing, still hidden from view, where we paused, looked at each other, and smiled before turning and following the stairs the rest of the way down, our hands gliding along the polished banisters, as ladies in evening gowns do, to where the gentlemen awaited the pleasure of our company.

My father, Will, and Reverend Brown stood in the well-lit hall at the bottom of the stairs, talking quietly. The sound of our footsteps caused them all to look up, and the expressions on their faces told us our efforts had not been in vain. Will, seeing the red dress with which he had once had such intimate contact, blushed beneath his tan, and his eyes, suddenly intense, caught and held my own. Reverend Brown looked serious, even a little disapproving, as he took in my ensemble, its artfully draped silk leaving too little to the imagination. My father, on the other hand, was staring at Maria Cristina, and in that moment before he turned to me and greeted us with his impeccable courtesy, I knew that he hated her.

I was shaken, but the show had to go on, naturally.

"Good evening, gentlemen," I said smoothly, tuning my voice to my dress and laying a languid hand on Will's arm, the kind of sophisticated greeting I had seen Garbo pull off so effortlessly on the big screen at the Rialto.

Will took my lead immediately, kissed my hand lightly, and then did the same to Maria Cristina's hand, which she had proffered in exact imitation of me. "You both look lovely this evening," he said.

Maria Cristina murmured a gracious thank you, eyes cast downward at first, before looking up quickly and intently at Will from underneath her thick dark lashes, her lips curved slightly upward. It was a deliberately seductive glance that took me by surprise and made her look far older, and certainly more knowledgeable, than her thirteen years.

Will seemed a little taken aback and dropped her hand.

I asked Father if he would make drinks for any who cared for them before dinner while I finished preparing the meal. Reverend Brown accepted the offer of a whiskey, and they walked into the library where Father kept a decanter, though he rarely drank himself. I watched him through the doorway as he poured each of them a drink. Will declined, saying he would help in the kitchen instead.

I gave Maria Cristina the task of setting the table, pointing her toward the china cabinet in the butler's pantry whose glass doors and felt-lined drawers held the monogrammed Dodge silver, the Waterford crystal, the herringbone china. Meanwhile, I covered my dress with a large white apron and lifted the pot roast out of the oven while Will hovered, awaiting instructions.

Meat fork in hand, I ordered him about like a general with a baton, and he jumped to, an excellent second-in-command. He washed lettuce, sliced tomatoes, and dressed the salad, glancing at me often. I tried to ignore him, placing the beef in the center of a deep platter and arranging the carrots and potatoes around it. The roast looked suspiciously dark. I hoped I had not left it cooking too long.

I picked up the pot, now empty but for the roasted juices an inch deep in the bottom, and placed it on the stove over a high heat. In moments the savory brown liquid was bubbling, and I whisked in a little flour, as Mrs. Hatcher had taught me, stirring constantly until the gravy was thick and simmering. Will put the salad on the table, helped Maria Cristina arrange each place setting, then poured the gravy into a deep handled dish with a matching ladle. As Maria Cristina carried it into the dining room, each measured step carefully executed so as not to spill her precious cargo, I took off my apron and called to Father and Reverend Brown that dinner was served.

I stood aside in the doorway of the butler's pantry to let Maria Cristina, then Will precede me into the dining room, and as Will passed me he paused, leaned in close, and whispered, "I love you in that dress."

His lips were almost touching my ear, and his breath moved a strand of hair that had escaped and curled softly down my back. The silk dress moved with me as I turned, and the fabric sliding across my breasts felt like his hands. I glared at him, frowning, which appeared to delight him.

"Stop that!" I hissed.

"Stop what?" he asked, trailing a finger lightly down my bare arm as he walked past me into the dining room.

"Will, would you carve, and Father, would you pour the wine?" I asked briskly, all business, handing Will the monogrammed sterling-and-ivory carving set that had been in the Dodge family since before the Revolutionary War. Father poured red wine into the bowls of four of the stemmed glasses I had set out, hesitating only briefly before pouring the fifth for Maria Cristina. I wanted her to have the elegant, grown-up party she'd dressed for. I passed the glasses around while

Will carved the roast beef, and we all tried not to notice how much effort he was exerting, despite the razor-sharpness of the knife. Clearly,
the beef was a little well-done. I sighed in resignation as he struggled
manfully on. I was horrible in the kitchen—this was a fact established
long ago. I looked forward to the day when we could once again
afford a cook.

No doubt everyone else did, too.

"May I serve you, miss?" Will asked, looking at Maria Cristina.

She nodded, regal and composed. Her eyes, more obsidian than
hazel-green in the candlelight, shone like the jet beads around her
throat. We passed the other dishes around and served ourselves, talking lightly of the heat and the upcoming storm season. When I took
my first bite of the roast beef, I was thankful for the wine to wash it
down. I wasn't the only one. Father was already on a second glass.

"Mr. Dodge, any progress with the mill?" asked Will.

"I have a meeting with potential investors in a few days in Narragansett, and I'm very optimistic," Father replied.

"Are they interested in a working partnership or simply a capital
investment?" I asked.

Father responded to Will. "I'm hoping for an infusion of capital,
a loan only. I don't want strangers getting their hands on the mill.
They don't know me, and they don't know the men. If they insist on
taking a hand in operations as a condition, however, I'm not sure what
I'll do."

"Well, I hope you can work it out," said Will. "And, of course,
if there's anything I can do . . ."

"Thank you, my boy, I appreciate that. Your interest means a
lot to me," Father said warmly, glancing at me.

I knew I was supposed to say that it meant a lot to me, too, but
I thought I was too old to be reminded of my manners, so I said
nothing.

"Thank you, sir," Will said, "but I was also thinking about the
men. Most of the town has gotten by the last few years, but only just.
They desperately need you to reopen the mill."

"Let's not forget how much Samuel has done already, and continues to do, for the workingmen of Milford," Reverend Brown reminded Will.

"Of course not," Will replied. "We're all grateful for everything he's done."

"Excuse me, what did you do?" Maria Cristina asked my father, who seemed startled to be addressed by her directly.

"He's done a lot," I said, happy to be able to present either of them to the other in a positive light. "The *Providence Journal* published a story this past winter about his efforts in South County."

"Mr. Dodge," said Reverend Brown, "is a pillar in this community. He held on after the Panic, kept the mill's doors open at a loss for more than a year. He paid workers out of his own pocket for months so they could put food on their tables. And," he added with quiet emphasis, "when he finally had to close, he persuaded those who could to hire the unemployed mill workers to paint their homes, build new fences, cut firewood—anything they could, and all before Christmas, so the men and their families would survive the winter."

Father, I noticed, was looking much more relaxed, and I beamed at him, remembering his efforts on behalf of the men and their families.

"That was a very good thing," Maria Cristina said, smiling at him.

"Milford is lucky to have him," Will said. "He works hard for everyone who lives here, which is more than I can say about a lot of politicians and businessmen."

"Well," said Father, "while this is all quite flattering, I could name others—like your own father, Will, and you, Reverend—who are equally committed to Milford and to South County. It's a long, hard road back, but through the efforts of many, we're making progress. I'm very hopeful that the mill will be up and running soon, the last and most important piece in Milford's recovery."

"Hear, hear," said Reverend Brown, raising his glass.

It sounded a little too like a stump speech, but I was pleased, despite my earlier annoyance. Father *had* worked tirelessly, entertaining business associates and longtime family friends here at the house, calling on them in their homes and their offices, persuading them to hire the unemployed mill workers for odd jobs. And it had worked. I had no doubt—nor had the town—that my father's efforts had single-handedly saved more than one Milford family from starvation, or the desperation and decline that the constant fear of it could induce.

I had seen the faces of the truly destitute on the train and in the streets of Providence and surrounding mill towns when I was a student traveling back and forth nearly every day. The shabby, thread-bare coats that could not keep out the bitter coastal winds, the newspapers shoved inside shoes whose soles had long since worn through. The unshaven men who stood on corners, their haunted eyes darting at me, then sliding away in humiliation, their hands working silently at nothing, used to productive activity and moving out of an unconscious need to have something, anything, to do. It was heart-breaking, the utter hopelessness in their blank stares, and by all accounts it was the same almost everywhere.

While Milford had seen hard times, we had escaped the worst of it, through luck and the determination of people like my father.

"Maria Cristina, how are you finding our little town?" asked Reverend Brown.

"I like it very much, thank you. Everyone is kind—Mrs. Hatcher and Mr. Johnson, especially. I have been to Mr. Dekker's store and Mr. Sullivan's fish truck with Mrs. Hatcher to buy cod," she said.

"Ezra Johnson?" Reverend Brown asked, surprised.

"Yes, Ezra Johnson," I interjected firmly. I had battled hard when I was Maria Cristina's age to be allowed to visit Ezra's place—battled against my father and Reverend Brown, neither of whom thought I should be spending time down at the cove.

Father was scowling now, and Reverend Brown seemed disturbed.

"You know, it might be wise to give Ezra Johnson a wide berth just now," suggested Reverend Brown.

"What do you mean?" I asked, though I knew exactly what he meant.

"Well, it looks like he's in trouble with the law. You don't want to be pulled into that, even if only by association."

"Are you suggesting that Ezra is guilty of something?" I asked aggressively.

"I'm not suggesting anything, Anne, except a little prudence on your part," he replied gently.

"I think I know him better than you do, and he's done nothing," I said.

"You don't know that," my father interjected. "I've known him for more than thirty years, and if you think he's not capable of violence you don't know him at all."

There was an uncomfortable silence while I sat, fuming, my eyes on the uneaten food on my plate. They *didn't* know him. Yes, physically he was a powerful man, and he was abrupt, even unfriendly, but only because of the hard, solitary life he'd led. I was beginning to feel alarmed. If everyone felt this way, he'd be railroaded right into jail.

"I like Ezra—" Reverend Brown began.

"Do you?" I interrupted.

"Yes, of course," he assured me, wiping his mouth with his napkin. His white collar appeared a little tight as he swallowed with some difficulty the piece of beef he had been chewing for several minutes.

"Everyone in Milford is a friend or neighbor," he said. "A child of God—a sinner, as we are all sinners, but a sinner who might be saved through God's grace. Including Ezra Johnson."

"Perhaps he should be confessed," Maria Cristina said, with every appearance of trying to help.

"In the Congregational Church we do not confess in the way you mean." His voice was gentle but firm.

"We are Protestants, not Catholics," said Father. "And that includes Ezra Johnson, though you're unlikely to see him in the pew on Sunday morning."

"Well, Ezra's not the only person in town who doesn't go to

services every Sunday," said Will. "And I'm not sure that he should be held to a higher standard because of who his father was." He turned to Maria Cristina. "Ezra's father was the minister at Milford Congregational Church a long time ago, before Reverend Brown came to Milford."

"Ezra has been known to attend Catholic Mass, though, as well as your services," I pointed out, feeling argumentative. "And he's been to the Jewish synagogue in Providence, more than once, in fact. Surely such an interest in God and in worship would suggest that he's very interested in God's grace, wouldn't you say?" I turned, smiling, to Reverend Brown.

"Well, interested in an academic way, perhaps, but interest is not the same thing as faith—or faithfulness."

"But that's such a personal, interior thing. Invisible, really. How can you judge a person's faith on such flimsy evidence?"

"I am not judging him, Anne. Don't be so defensive," he said quietly.

"Well, it sounds like you are to me," I said.

Maria Cristina's head moved back and forth, watching us all in turn. Will was watching only me. He knew how much I loved Ezra, and that displays of piety got under my skin. Reverend Brown was a decent man, but he approached matters of religion strictly by the book, and he and I had crossed verbal swords before. I usually got mad, while he got calm, which, of course, made me madder. Each time, I told myself that even though he appeared calm in my presence he likely went home rattled, alternately cursing me and praying for the salvation of my soul. It made me feel better to think so.

"Anne," said Father with quiet authority.

We exchanged a private look. Father understood my frustration with Reverend Brown, but he insisted that I respect both the man and the office. At the very least, he had told me once, I should not antagonize him, if for no other reason than that it wasn't sporting. I remembered that and smiled at Father.

"Here, Reverend, let me pour you some water," I said, filling his glass. My anger dissipated and I turned to Will. We would talk about something else.

"Stevie Sullivan will be fishing with his father in a week," I said. "His family has been very patient, with all those little ones to feed and only Mr. Sullivan out on the water. They've had as difficult a time as anyone in town this past year. Stevie's been at Ezra's place every day for weeks. He can't wait until it's finished."

"Yes, it's time they got a break," Will agreed. "They're good people, and they sacrificed a lot so Stevie could finish school."

"Excuse me, is that the boat Ezra is making?" asked Maria Cristina.

"Yes, the one up on the cradles next to mine," I told her.

"You're making another boat?" Reverend Brown asked.

"Yes, but it's really my first one," I replied. "I've always helped Ezra with his projects. This one's my own. I designed her, and I'm building her, every inch, by myself." I knew I sounded proud, but I couldn't help it.

"Well, that's very nice," said Reverend Brown, though his tone suggested that he thought it anything but very nice. "I'm surprised that you're still fooling around with carpentry, though. Isn't it time you started preparing yourself for the work of marriage and family? Surely the prospect of little ones of your own appeals to you?" He was smiling, concerned. I knew he was actually thinking of my happiness, making it far worse than if he'd been baiting me.

"Why can't she do both?" asked Will, flicking his hair back from his face.

"That's hardly the point," I said indignantly. How dare they discuss my life in this way, as though I wasn't necessary at all in determining what it should look like?

"Nor is it realistic," said Father, entering the fray. "When Anne marries and has children there simply won't be time to run down to Ezra's every day. She'll have responsibilities—happy responsibilities, to be sure. She knows that."

"And there is the question of propriety," Reverend Brown

added. "It's one thing to indulge children, to give them the freedom of the town while they're young. It's quite another for a married woman, a mother—the daughter of one prominent man, the wife of another—to run around in dungarees, covered in sawdust."

"That's ridiculous!" I said, turning from one man to the next, trapped.

"No, Anne, it's not," said Reverend Brown. "Do you really think it appropriate for the adult daughter of Samuel Dodge to spend her time in a shed with Ezra Johnson, hammering nails and covered in engine grease? Especially now, with the inquiry into that poor boy's death pointing at him? You've been called to the inquest yourself, I understand, as a direct result of your relationship with that man—surely you can see how this embarrasses your father. You are not a child, my dear. It's time to grow up. Time to think about how your actions affect others."

I felt flushed and hot. I pushed my glass of wine away from me, wanting more control, not less.

"First of all, if I ever do become a wife and mother, it will be because I've chosen to, not because I'm expected to," I said, my voice tightly controlled. "I make boats, and with all due respect, Reverend, I will keep making boats, regardless of what you think. As for the rest, even though Matt Da Silva's body was found on Ezra's property, even if his death was no accident—and that has not yet been determined—it doesn't mean that Ezra killed him, or that he knows anything about it!"

I sat breathing heavily, fists clenched under the table, ready to do battle. Maria Cristina sat quietly, taking it all in, her wide, unblinking eyes the only indication of a reaction. Father, however, had fought with me about Ezra—and probably with Reverend Brown, privately—many times before, and he made a halfhearted attempt to end the hostilities, choosing to ignore, for now, the Da Silva issue. No doubt he felt the Reverend had made his point.

"Reverend," he said, "I learned long ago that Anne is one of those people who needs a hobby. It makes her happy, and I choose to indulge her in this, so long as the proper perspective is maintained. So that's all that needs to be said on the subject, at least for tonight, I think. There is no reason we should assume her hobby will interfere with her other responsibilities. In fact, I'm certain it will not, but will run its course in due time and be left behind, as are all childhood preoccupations. And I have no doubt that she will stay out of Farley's way. She has never disappointed me yet," he finished, taking my side in a way that left me utterly abandoned.

"Of course," said Reverend Brown. "I suppose you are still young. There's time yet. How old are you now, Anne, twenty-two?"

"Almost twenty-four," Will offered.

"Really?" said Reverend Brown, one eyebrow raised. "Well, perhaps someone else needs to take a stronger hand in the matter." He looked at Will with such pointed meaning it would have been funny had it not been so infuriating.

"Oh, for Christ's sake!" I blurted out.

Reverend Brown recoiled, and Will laughed out loud.

"Anne!" said Father sharply. He hated it when I cursed, saying it was common and made me sound like a sailor. I was secretly pleased by the latter, which would have dismayed him far more than any expletive I could come up with.

The room felt small, pressing me. The candlelight, which had seemed romantic, now made the room look murky. I longed for fresh air and an absence of walls around me. The weight of everyone's expectations, even while they claimed to be thinking of my happiness, was getting heavier by the day.

"Let's discuss something else, shall we?" urged Will, stepping into the breach.

"I know!" said Maria Cristina excitedly, turning to my father, who was pouring more wine into his glass. "You pointed out, Mr. Dodge, excuse me, when we drove from the train station, the Portuguese town, West Warwick. I would like to go there," she said, turning to me.

"And do what?" I asked, hearing this idea for the first time.

"Excuse me, but we could just walk. Talk to people. Perhaps we will go on a festival day and eat *chouriço.*"

I was immediately tense, but she kept talking, increasingly enthusiastic.

"The Festas de San Antonio is already past, but there are other saints. We can see the puppets and the bonfires, and there is always singing and dancing," she said, her eyes shining.

Before I could respond, my father weighed in.

"There's no reason to go up there," he said, looking at me and not Maria Cristina. "That neighborhood is dangerous. Look what just happened to that boy."

"But Father," I objected, stunned by the illogic of his argument, "even if he was murdered, that boy was a victim, not a criminal himself. And his death occurred here, in *our* town, not in Warwick."

"My point, Anne, is that where they are, you may expect to find trouble. I won't allow you to go there—nobody goes there but the Portuguese."

We all sat quite still. I wondered if Maria Cristina understood what he'd said.

"But I *am* Portuguese," she said quietly. She had understood him perfectly.

"Well, yes, of course, I know that. But now you live here," Father said, glancing at her quickly, then away again.

"But, excuse me, I am Portuguese, wherever I live," she explained.

"I've said no, and that's all there is to it," he said, his words clipped and heavy. "You'll have to trust that I know what's best for you."

I saw her chin tilt up and her expression harden, and I thought, *Don't say anything. Not right now.*

"My *avô* would take me," she said. "He would say it was okay."

"I could take them, sir, if it would ease your mind," offered Will.

"No. I've said they won't go," said Father. His tone brought a stillness to the room. He would brook no argument—that much was clear.

I realized then that, between the whiskey and several glasses of wine, he had drunk far more than he was used to. His last two words had been dragged out too long in their pronunciation—not slurred, exactly, but it was there. He stared moodily down at his plate.

"Why don't we move to the living room," I suggested. "Maria Cristina has made a lovely cake for dessert. Would anyone like coffee?"

But no one moved.

"I will go," said Maria Cristina, so quietly that I barely heard her.

"Maria Cristina—" I began.

"I *will* go," she said more loudly, looking at me. "He cannot tell me what I can do, what I cannot do. Only my *avô* can, and he is gone!" She was upset, and I realized she was still grieving. I turned to my father, hoping he would relent because she was a child who had lost her family.

"Father, perhaps we could—"

He slammed his palm down hard on the table, and I jumped along with the silverware.

"I won't have it in my house again!"

Reverend Brown put his fork down carefully, folded his napkin, and placed it gingerly on the table. Without looking up from his plate, he mumbled something about a parishioner needing him and his regrets about having to make it an early night.

"Annie, have you read Hemingway's *Death in the Afternoon*? If not, I'll lend it to you. You're going to love it," said Will quickly.

His tone was urgent, and I recognized the sound of my own voice in his, our mutual weakness in the face of my father's displeasure. Inexplicably, I despised him for it.

"Perhaps you and Reverend Brown would be more comfortable if you left. We don't want to embarrass you with our family squabble." It was a nasty, unfair thing to say and I knew it.

"Fine," he said, fed up at last and perhaps a little relieved. He rarely displayed temper of any kind, but I was too angry to care. He didn't look my way again as he and Reverend Brown pushed back from the table, stood up, and retreated from the room.

As the sound of the front door gently closing reached us, I turned back to my father, who sat glowering into his wineglass. He picked it up and drained it with one swift motion.

"Father, what did you mean?" I asked, my stomach in a painful knot beneath the red dress. "You won't have what?"

He said nothing, though his face had darkened. He just sat there, glaring at me from the other end of the table.

"You won't have what, Father? You won't have Maria Cristina be Portuguese?"

"Well, that's a rather ridiculous way of putting it, but yes, if you must. I won't have her be Portuguese, not if she's to stay in this house."

"You can't change the fact that she's Portuguese, Father, any more than you can change the fact that I am," I said without thinking.

"You shut your mouth!" he roared, half out of his chair, both hands on the table as he leaned forward.

"I will not," I said, shocked to see him like this. I stood up suddenly, accidentally knocking my chair over behind me. "I did not spring fully formed from the head of Zeus." I flung my napkin down with shaking hands and faced him furiously across the table. "I am a Caldeira as much as I am a Dodge!"

My body was a rope pulled taut from head to toe, and I crossed my arms and pressed them tight across my stomach to still their trembling. Anger flared in me, stronger than ever, like coals raked up to reveal the smoldering heat they harbored deep inside.

"Don't be absurd—you're no more Portuguese than I am," he spat. "I've made sure of that. None of it means anything to you. It's all completely foreign—the language, the music, the religion, the food. It's not about blood. It never has been, never will be. *It's about how you live and whom you live among!* You're a Dodge, and nothing you do can change that now. It's too late!" He shouted his last words, throwing them at me, the triumph in his voice unmistakable.

"It can mean something now if I want it to!" I shouted back. I fought back a sob and the effort left my throat raw.

"No, no, Anne, listen to me!" he said, his tone suddenly soft and wheedling. He'd overplayed his hand, and now he walked carefully around the table, past Maria Cristina, who had crept into the corner of the room and stood with her hand in front of her mouth.

Father felt his way around the table like a blind man, inching toward me, his eyes never leaving my face.

"Anne. Annie. I didn't want you to grow up confused, wondering who you were, corrupted as she was corrupt."

"Stop it!" Maria Cristina suddenly cried from the corner where she stood. "My *mamãe* was good!"

Father continued as if she hadn't spoken, as if she weren't there at all. "Anne, I did it for you. I could give you a history you could be proud of, that people would respect. The kind of future you deserve. What could they give you?" He stood by my side, close enough that I could smell the alcohol and the desperation.

"You've seen them—the poverty, the way they live," he said. "That's not for you—that's not us! What would have been served by letting you grow up thinking you were one of them? By letting people like us see you as an immigrant? They would have painted us all by association. It was unthinkable!"

His voice was at its most persuasive. He might have been arguing passionately in front of a jury, working the city council to sway a vote his way. Stirring the rich and the powerful to acts of charity so his workers wouldn't starve—he had done that. I had seen it. That's the kind of man he was. I wanted to believe he meant well now, that he was just confused, but his open disdain—for Ben and Lucia, as well as Inêz—felt like a slap full across my face, and I felt the pain in my jaw as though he really had hit me. I could not even think how this was making Maria Cristina feel. I could not bring myself to look at her. I didn't understand how he had married our mother at all, feeling like he did. He must have hated her, and she must have known!

I realized that my face was wet, and when I raised my trembling hand to my cheek I felt the tears I had not known I'd cried.

"But it doesn't change anything if I know about them. I just want to know . . . Father, why can't I know?" I cried.

"Of course it changes things—use your head, Anne. What we know always changes things!"

He leaned in, and I could see the bloody veins in the whites of his eyes, like cracked pieces of glass barely holding themselves together. A mere whisper of movement could shatter them into a million pieces.

He grabbed my arm, hard. "Do you think the life you've had, and the one you have ahead of you, would be possible if you were Portuguese? Of course not! That's why I've worked so hard—for you!"

Breathing heavily, he gripped my arm like a vise and then flung me away from him, and I stumbled across my fallen chair to the floor.

"Everything I've done has been for you!" he said, as if he were accusing me.

I gazed up at him, shaking. "Everything you've done," I repeated, as if waking from a deep sleep. "Father, what is it, exactly, that you've done?"

He looked at me blankly, blinking once or twice, letting his words and mine catch up with the moment.

"I've done what I had to, of course," he said. "What any father would do."

And with that he quit the room for the library. I thought he hesitated as he passed me. Just for a moment I believed—I still believe—that he wanted to touch me, or say something to evoke the love we had always felt for one another as the two lone survivors of Inêz's betrayal. But he walked past me, leaving us trembling in his wake.

CHAPTER EIGHT

Milford's only doctor, Dick Statham, was rarely called upon to act in his official capacity as coroner. The occasional violent, unnatural, or sudden death whose cause was, at least initially, unknown was far from a common occurrence in our little village. Even when he had to perform this onerous duty, Dr. Statham usually determined the cause of death to be accidental, like a drowning or machinery-related incident, or natural, after all, like heart failure. In the case of Mateo—Matt—Da Silva, most of the town had already decided that the deceased had met a violent end. This widespread conclusion was exemplified by the shockingly high turnout for the inquest—the room was filled to capacity with dozens of onlookers who had no business there at all, save morbid curiosity, plus the doctor, Sheriff Tucker, Deputy Mac Donovan, the court stenographer, witnesses called upon to testify, and the bereaved family and close friends.

My father sat across the courtroom from me, on the right side of the aisle that separated the gallery into left and right sides. He had been there when I arrived, and I hesitated for a moment before choosing a seat. I had looked at him first, and when I received only an embarrassed little smile, I thought to spare us both and sought a solitary seat as far from him as I could manage, on the left and up front in the second row. The courtroom occupied the back of the building, behind the main meeting room, and had its own entrance off Third Street. It was set up in the customary way: a judge's bench and witness box front and center on a raised platform, and two tables, one for the prosecution and one for the defense, in front of and equidistant from the bench. As these proceedings were merely an inquest, however, Dr. Statham sat at one table with several stacks of papers before him, a sheaf of blank paper and a pen in his hand for note-taking. The other table—as well as the judge's bench and the jury box—remained empty. The gallery, however, was full, and several people stood at the back of the room by the heavy oak door, which remained open to let in any breeze that might relieve the oppressive heat that had already suffused the building.

At nine o'clock sharp, Dr. Statham looked at his watch and rose, straightened his tie, and then walked around the table to stand at the front of the room before the judge's bench. The moment he stood up all whispering and restless movement came to a stop, save a few women who continued to fan themselves with their gloves or a piece of paper—anything that would stir the air.

"Ladies and gentlemen, this is an informal proceeding, in that we are not here to determine fault or mete out punishment. Still, what we do here today is required by law. As coroner—as an officer of the court—it is my job to determine how, when, and where the deceased died. I have examined the body, and Sheriff Tucker has begun an investigation into the circumstances surrounding the death of this young man. At the end of today's proceedings I expect to render a decision on cause of death, and release the body of the deceased to his family for burial."

All eyes turned to the family, sitting in front of me in the first row. I couldn't see their faces, but the older woman bowed her head, her husband's arm around her shoulders, while the other children— there were four of them: a girl of sixteen or seventeen, maybe, and three little ones—sat with their heads turned toward their mother, their profiles stricken, more terrified by her grief than by the loss of one of their own.

The steady, gentle scratch of the court stenographer's pen was the only sound.

"Mr. Da Silva, if you please?" asked Dr. Statham, indicating with his hand that the grieving father should take the witness stand.

Mr. Da Silva stood up slowly and made his way to the front of the room, short and solid in his ill-fitting suit. He opened the gate and sat in the chair, closing himself into its box. *Like his son will soon be,* I thought, then quickly pushed the thought from my mind.

"Mr. Da Silva, I know this is a terribly difficult time for you," began Dr. Statham, "but we need to ascertain, for the record, the identity of the deceased." He paused, and Mr. Da Silva nodded, his eyes never leaving the doctor's face.

"Mr. Da Silva, you came to my office eight days ago for the purpose of identifying a body found in Kingston Cove, is that right?"

Mr. Da Silva nodded, but when Dr. Statham did not continue, he realized that he had to say it out loud. "Yes," he said, his voice a mere whisper. He cleared his throat and tried again. "Yes."

"And were you able to positively identify the body?"

"Yes."

"Mr. Da Silva, please tell us the name of the deceased." His voice was exceedingly gentle.

"It was my boy, Mateo," the man said, still looking at the doctor. "Mateo Da Silva."

His wife sobbed into her handkerchief, only once, but her shoulders shook silently for some time.

"We are all very sorry for you and your family, sir, and sorry to put you through this. I only have a few more questions at this time."

Mr. Da Silva nodded. He did not look at his wife, or at anyone besides the doctor. I realized that he couldn't. If he did he would break down. The doctor's gentle, authoritative voice kept him focused on the thing at hand, rather than the context and its larger meaning.

"Mr. Da Silva, when was the last time you saw your son alive?"

Mr. Da Silva licked his dry lips. "I saw him nine days ago—on the Wednesday, we come in from the boat, me and Mateo. His mamãe has dinner for us, we eat, and Mateo left. He's a man now. He goes out sometimes."

"Thank you, Mr. Da Silva. I have only one more question. What time was it when your son Mateo left the house last Wednesday evening?"

"I don't know, doc. Maybe seven, maybe eight. It's not quite dark yet, I know. I seen him clear in the road from our window, arguing with his sister Susana." Here he paused and lifted a shaking hand to point to his eldest daughter, the young girl who sat on one side of her three remaining siblings, their mother on the other. "They always fighting. Both are"—he struggled for the right word, then found it—"Both are hot—hot-headed."

"So you last saw your son Mateo alive on the evening of Wednesday, June twenty-seventh, 1934, sometime between seven and eight o'clock, before the sun had set, standing in the road in front of your house arguing with his sister Susana. Is that right?"

"Yes, that's right," said Mr. Da Silva. "And we don't see him no more. He ain't come home again and never will now." His voice broke on the last word, and now Susana Da Silva was crying, too. I heard more than one sniffle in the room behind me, and my own throat felt constricted.

"Thank you, sir. You may step down."

Mr. Da Silva rejoined his wife, his shoulders held painfully rigid. Dr. Statham looked at his notes and called Farley Tucker to the stand.

"Sheriff, please describe your discovery of Mateo Da Silva's body on June twenty-eighth."

Sheriff Tucker looked flushed and a little embarrassed. He was much better in quiet conversation with one or two people than he was speaking before a large audience, and he was well aware of his lack of polish. He nervously smoothed his hair, on which he had lavished pomade for his courtroom appearance.

"Well, doc, as you know we was notified that a body had been found by some local boys a week an' a half ago, June twenty-eighth it was. The boys run straight to Ezra Johnson's place, it being closest to where they was, an' found Miss Anne Dodge there. She went with 'em to see the body, then sent the boys to fetch me. They come to my house, and then I went to Mac Donovan's and picked him up in the patrol car. We headed out the old mill road, parked, and started walking in toward the marsh, where the boys had said they'd found the body. And there it was, just like they said."

He paused for a moment, his eyes going to Mrs. Da Silva, who was crying softly again. "Sorry, ma'am."

"Please continue, sheriff," said Dr. Statham, gently but firmly.

"Right. Well, we come up on the body, facedown in the high grass, where it seemed the high tide'd left him. The area'd been trampled pretty good—the grass was flat an' broken down. I felt for a pulse, but he was dead all right. We seen no sign of injury—until we turned him over, that is. I'd assumed he'd drowned, but he had an ugly wound, left side of his neck." He indicated with his hand a place on his own body, just below the jawline. "The wound looked deep and long, like some kinda blade." He cast a furtive look at Mrs. Da Silva. "I am sorry, ma'am. He fell on somethin' sharp but good, or somethin' sharp come at him real hard."

"Thank you, sheriff," said Dr. Statham quickly, and a little sternly. "That determination is made by the coroner. Please present only the facts as you observed them. Now, please tell us how the investigation has progressed since the discovery of the deceased's body and its delivery to the coroner for examination."

"Sure, doc, sorry. I've been out to Ezra Johnson's place a couple a times—once to interview him, tryin' to as-cer-tain if he seen or heard anything, and once with a couple of fellas to look around the property for the murder wea— I mean, for the thing that cut that boy."

"Was Mr. Johnson able to tell you anything on that first visit? Had he seen or heard anything?"

The deputy snorted, clearly not thinking much of Ezra as a potential witness. "No, to hear him tell it he don't know nothin' about nothin', even if it's happenin' right under his nose."

"Thank you, sheriff. Now, yesterday you returned to Mr. Johnson's property with additional men."

"Yeah, some fellas from Warwick. I've used 'em before when we needed extra manpower. You'll remember last year when Hal Peterson's little girl wandered off—the whole town and then some turned out to look for her. It was one of these boys from Warwick found her up in that boathouse, scared and hungry."

"Yes, that's right. Can you tell us, please, what transpired yesterday at Mr. Johnson's property?"

"Well, we went down there to search the area. Ezra and Miss Dodge was workin' on some skiffs down at the dock. I sent two fellas through the shallows, all the way up to the rocks at the mill. Then me and the rest of 'em went through the marsh up at the high tide mark. Sweepin' the area."

"And did you find anything?"

"You bet we did—a big carpenter's chisel, musta weighed seven, eight pounds. Looked like it had blood on it, too. I wrapped it up and we took it back—dusted it but no clear prints was on it. And then I gave it to you."

"Yes, you did. I was able to determine that the substance on the cleat was, in fact, blood. Further, the wound in the deceased's neck matched the depth and breadth of the chisel blade."

So it was murder, after all. There were excited murmurs throughout the courtroom, and though I knew I shouldn't, I turned slowly and looked at Ezra. He was looking straight ahead, despite the whispers and furtive glances from his neighbors. I thought he looked a little pale.

"I'm going to call a short recess," Dr. Statham said, frowning at the noise. "We'll reconvene in fifteen minutes and adjourn, I hope, before noon." He picked up his papers and, without another look at the room, walked through the door in the back wall that led to the judge's private chambers.

People were talking excitedly, most of them standing, as I made my way toward the open door at the back of the room. I wanted to get outside.

I passed Stevie Sullivan, standing awkwardly by the door but making no attempt to leave the building. He wore a stiff white shirt and dark navy tie, both of which he had outgrown years ago. He looked horribly uncomfortable and touchingly young. I smiled reassuringly at him as I passed.

"Don't worry, Stevie. Dr. Statham asked me to come, too. It's just because we've been at Ezra's so often these past few weeks—he's hoping we might have seen something that will help clear this up. It doesn't mean you've done anything wrong." He tried to smile and then looked away.

Outside I found Ezra sitting on a bench behind a tall hedge, out of sight of the crowd that stood on the steps of the courthouse. He was rubbing his knee, his leg stretched out straight before him.

"Hi, Ezra," I said as I approached. "May I join you?"

"Free country," he said darkly.

Undeterred, I sat down beside him. "So I guess the Da Silva boy was killed. With that chisel."

Ezra shrugged, saying nothing.

I frowned, puzzled by his odd behavior. He was always gruff and certainly wasn't much for conversation, but I knew how kind-hearted he was. Matt Da Silva's death was a tragedy for that family—surely Ezra knew that, felt it. I couldn't understand why he seemed angry.

"Ezra, what's wrong?" I asked. "This isn't like you—is it because people might think you had something to do with it?"

"People'll think what they will. I got no say-so over that."

"That's true. But it's at least possible that the chisel came from your workshop. The handle is maple, just like yours, like the whole set—you bought them a few years ago in Mystic. It'll be easy to figure out if one's missing, and you've never locked the workshop door. Just tell Dr. Statham that. If someone took one of your tools and used it to kill that boy, it doesn't mean it's your fault."

He looked at me then, finally, and his face was thunderous. He spoke through clenched teeth, to keep from shouting at me. "I know all that, girl. I don't need you to mother me. And I'll thank you to keep your mouth shut about my workshop."

He stood up slowly and limped back toward the courthouse. I stayed a few minutes longer, letting the heat from the sun beat down upon my bare head, staring at nothing, my hat in my lap.

It took a good twenty minutes for everyone to reassemble in the courtroom, to find their seats and settle in. The moment the last person was seated, the judge's chamber door opened and Dr. Statham walked briskly into the room carrying a small, open box and a stack of papers. After putting these items on the table, he turned to the gallery.

"Ezra Johnson, please take the witness stand."

Ezra made his laborious way to the witness stand, but though he had trouble with the steps leading up to the box, Dr. Statham knew him well enough not to offer his arm. We all waited until he was seated, his clean shirt suggesting a respect for the proceedings that his glowering expression belied.

"Mr. Johnson, please tell us where you reside."

"You know where I live, doc."

"Yes, Ezra, I do. Please state for the record where you live."

"I got a house on five acres on Kingston Cove, from the mouth of the Misquamisett River, just south of the mill, down to the road that runs northwest through South County. It was my father's land, and now it's mine. That's where I live."

"And the marsh on the edge of the salt pond, the marsh that lies between the mill and your house, that's part of your property?"

"Yep."

"Sheriff Tucker has testified that the body of Mateo Da Silva and the chisel with the blood on it were found in the tall grass between the marsh and the beach. On your land. Do you agree that it was?"

Ezra paused for a moment, considering. Finally—reluctantly—he nodded his head yes. "That's what Farley says. I wasn't with him, but I got no reason to doubt it's true."

"Thank you." Dr. Statham walked to the table and picked up the box, and then came back to Ezra. "Have you seen this chisel before?" he asked, taking it out of the box and holding it up for everyone to see.

Ezra hesitated. He did not look at the chisel but rather at Dr. Statham. "Don't know, doc. It's a chisel, and I seen a lot of 'em. I use 'em in my work. But this chisel? I can't say for sure if I've seen this chisel before."

"Mr. Johnson, I'm trying to establish the time and place of death," said Dr. Statham wearily. "I need folks who were anywhere around the vicinity to speak up about what they know. Were you at home, sir, on Wednesday evening last week?"

Ezra never took his eyes off of Dr. Statham but set his lips in a firm line that I knew all too well.

A moment passed, then two. Finally, Dr. Statham turned and walked back to his table, putting the chisel back in the box. He faced the gallery, not looking at Ezra. "I'd like to remind everyone of the serious nature of these proceedings, and to make it perfectly clear that while this is not a court of law, and no one is under oath, it is from these proceedings that the court will determine whether to pursue a criminal investigation and, ultimately, whether to charge someone with a crime."

Ezra merely glared at the back of his head.

"Thank you, Mr. Johnson, that will be all. For now," said Dr. Statham without turning around. "Miss Dodge, will you take the stand?" he asked, looking up at me.

I passed Ezra as he made his way back to the gallery, and then I, too, sat in the witness box, behind the little gate. It was an odd feeling, sitting on the raised platform, the focus of everyone's attention. I felt their eyes on me, and I clenched my hands in my lap.

"Miss Dodge, how often do you go to Ezra Johnson's place, and for how long do you stay?"

My voice shook a little when I answered. "It depends. My other obligations permitting, I try to work on my boat—which is at Mr.

Johnson's place—several days a week. And when I go, I try to stay for the whole day, though that's not always possible."

"Do you ever see anyone else there?"

"Sometimes. Lately, Stevie Sullivan. Ezra is finishing up a boat for him, and he's been waiting anxiously for it. He's been helping a little with the finish work."

"Anybody else?"

"Not often. Sometimes a fisherman will come by and make arrangements for some repair work. Sometimes the delivery boy from the Jablonskis' grocery. I've seen some of the kids from town playing in the cove up by the mill wander down the shoreline to Ezra's. Once he sees them, they don't stay long."

Dr. Statham smiled, and I heard a chuckle from the gallery. "No, I don't suppose they do." He walked back to the table, thinking, turned on his heel, and walked back toward me. "Miss Dodge, have you heard or seen anything at Mr. Johnson's place, or anywhere on the mill property, that might shed some light on the death of Mateo Da Silva?"

"No, I have not," I said, my voice strong, the relief apparent. "I was shocked to hear of it. I had absolutely no idea that anything had happened."

"Thank you, Miss Dodge. One more thing," he said, pausing and looking sharply at me. *Please don't ask me if I recognize the chisel,* I thought. I did not know if I could lie—or, worse, if I could tell the truth and make a liar out of Ezra.

"Were you at Ezra Johnson's place, or on the mill property, on Wednesday last week?"

"No, I was not," I said firmly, looking him right in the eye.

"Thank you, that will be all for now." And I was done.

He called Stevie Sullivan next, but it was over almost before it began. Poor Stevie was pale at first and then flushed a deep bloodred, his face and neck peppered with angry-looking blotches. He sat in the witness stand biting his nails, his eyes continuously roving the gallery, stopping on nothing and no one.

Dr. Statham asked him only one question. "Stevie, did you work on your boat at Ezra Johnson's the Wednesday in question?"

Looking like he was slowly deflating, Stevie dropped his hand from his mouth, relaxed his hunched shoulders, and brought his eyes to meet Dr. Statham's. "No, sir. I didn't work on my boat at all that week." He paused, sensing that this somehow made him look a shirker. "Don't get me wrong, I wanted to," he said. "But Ezra, he got fed up with me, told me to beat it."

"Thank you, that will be all."

Stevie hesitated, not daring to believe that was all there was to it. He'd been worried for nothing. He stood up and crossed the front of the courtroom, stealing a glance at the bereaved family—at Mr. Da Silva, silent and staring straight ahead; Mrs. Da Silva and Susana, teary-eyed; the little ones, not really comprehending.

And then it was over. Dr. Statham released the body to the Da Silvas for burial and pronounced the cause of death to be a stab wound to the neck that had severed the carotid artery. He asked the principle players—the family and the day's witnesses—to make themselves available to Sheriff Tucker, who would be continuing the investigation for the South County prosecutor's office. It seemed we had a murderer in Milford.

After a hurried meal at the town lunch counter, where Gracie Baldwin served good coffee and acceptable sandwiches, I hurried home to Maria Cristina. Gracie, who was a couple of years older than I, had talked incessantly, wanting to know everything that had happened at the inquest. She hadn't been able to close up shop to attend and had sorely missed the opportunity to hear firsthand the details of what she clearly considered to be one of the most exciting events in recent Milford history. I was vague and reluctant, refusing to gossip, and eventually she gave up in disgust.

No sooner had I opened the front door of our house than Maria Cristina ran straight to me from Mrs. Hatcher's house, bored and looking for something to do.

"Ana, we can go to Ezra's today and swim" was her first suggestion.

"I don't really want to swim today, Maria Cristina. I have a lot on my mind."

"Then, excuse me, we can go and pick up shells. Your mind has less on it this way, right?"

I had to laugh. She was so sweet, so funny.

"Okay, we can pick up shells. And we can swim, too, if you want."

So we set out for Ezra's, and I was grateful for the excuse to go, to talk to him about what had happened in the courtroom.

When we arrived Ezra was nowhere to be seen. He wasn't down by the dock, and when we knocked on his door there was no answer, no hint of movement inside the house. He was moving so slowly these days, I wasn't surprised to find he hadn't made it back from town yet.

"Maria Cristina," I said, the idea occurring to me only then, "why don't you walk down to the water and see what you can find? The tide's out, so there should be some nice shells and lots of those little gray stones you like." She was looking at me, the question already on her lips, but I forestalled her. "I'll just run up to the workshop and get a bucket to hold everything in."

"Okay," she said happily, moving down toward the water.

My faith in Ezra had seemed, only yesterday, absolute, but here I was, full of doubt and suspicion, intending to snoop around. And it was only possible for me to do so because he trusted me completely—on his property, with his things, in his life. My sense of disloyalty, and the accompanying guilt and self-loathing, sat like a stone in my chest.

I entered the building and quietly shut the door behind me—itself an unusual thing to do, particularly in nice weather. I felt like a sneak, and with good reason. I went immediately to the long plank shelves where Ezra kept his set of chisels, still new by his standards, handles facing out and arranged in order of descending size. Looking nervously over my shoulder, I searched the shelves, shuffling my feet sideways as I moved along the wall, checking each shelf and box, although I knew exactly where he kept everything. He hadn't changed a thing in this room in all the years I'd known him. I covered the entire wall twice until finally I had to accept what was obvious.

The chisels were gone, every one of them—and in a boatbuilder's shop, their absence was glaring. Everything else on the shelf had been shifted over to fill in the two-foot long space they had occupied. And only this single shelf held no trace of the thin film of sawdust that covered every single surface in the building.

"What're y'lookin' for?" Ezra's voice right behind me scared me senseless, and I jumped, crying out a little. My heart was pounding, my hands shaking as I turned to face him.

"I— I was just looking for a— a bucket. Maria Cristina is picking up shells and rocks and I told her I'd find one." I tried to make myself look at him, meet and hold his gaze to show him I had nothing to hide, but my eyes kept sliding away.

He looked at me hard for a moment, and when he spoke, I knew he was as disappointed in me as he had ever been. "Yer lyin'. Since when do we do that?"

I flushed, ashamed, and hung my head for a moment. When I looked up I had tears in my eyes. "I'm sorry, Ezra. You're right. But— well, that's just it. I think you're lying to *me*."

Now it was his turn to look away.

"I can see that the chisels are gone," I said. "You should have at least put your old ones in their spot, cleaned the dust everywhere, not just where you were trying to cover up what you'd done. And in the courtroom today . . . lying is one thing, but not saying anything at all—you just looked guilty! Are you trying to get arrested?"

Oddly enough, he looked relieved. He seemed confident again, sure of his ground. "I'm sorry, girl. But I won't talk about it." He turned to go then, as though that was the end of it, but I couldn't let it go.

"Ezra, wait," I said, taking a quick step forward and grabbing his sleeve. Surprised—and more than a little annoyed—he turned back to face me.

"What d' you want from me?" he asked.

"I want you to tell me what you know about that boy's death. I know you didn't kill him—you couldn't do such a thing—but I think you know something about it."

He hesitated. He really did. But whatever he was struggling with, whatever he knew, was bigger than his relationship with me. I saw this, I felt it, and it was as though I were riding one of those towering wooden roller coasters. I could almost hear the clacking of the wheels as we climbed higher and higher, the time to turn back long past. Any minute now we would plummet to the ground.

"Can't," he finally said, turning away and walking out into the sunshine. "It's better if you don't know," he muttered as I stood in the doorway, watching his broad back move away from me toward the water, where Maria Cristina combed the breakers for little things she could call her own.

CHAPTER NINE

In the days immediately following the inquest, my father and I were cautious and inclined to avoid each other. I didn't want to discuss the murder investigation, and neither of us wanted to talk about what had happened at our disastrous dinner party. Maria Cristina and I saw little of him for the next couple of weeks. When I encountered him at all we dealt with each other minimally, and with great formality. We had mastered long ago the kind of civility that allowed us to avoid the truth when we deemed it necessary.

Unexpectedly, my little declaration of independence from Father at dinner that night helped me begin to overcome the walls I had inadvertently built between my sister and me from the moment I learned of her existence. Until I spoke aloud that I was half Portuguese, I had scarcely realized it myself. In hiding from that essential truth, I had spent those first precious weeks reluctant to ask her questions about our family, jealous that she had had them in her life and I had not.

Maria Cristina and I spent the days exploring the sandy trails that led down to the water and the roads, paved and unpaved, that meandered around the marshes and salt ponds and led west, away from Milford into dense wooded acres, where we climbed ancient stone walls and forded narrow streams. We trekked across farmland, some of it fertile with crops, some lying fallow, as free as either of us had ever been.

We spent a lot of time at Ezra's, mostly doing nothing—though Ezra himself kept busy. He cleaned the workshop thoroughly, saying only that it was long overdue. His old set of chisels mysteriously reappeared on the shelf (although one was missing), and in no time I felt as though they had always been there. The sheriff did not seem to be interested in either Ezra or me, and I was happy to accept this unexpected reprieve. These were the dog days of summer, hot and sultry, the sun baking every ounce of energy out of our bodies. Ezra tolerated our presence as long as Maria Cristina and I expected nothing from him, including conversation most days. Sometimes we swam in the cove, or fished off his dock. We dug for clams in the marshy area between his yard and the mill, and ate our catch raw, standing in knee-deep water, braced against the gentle push and tug of the lapping tide as it rolled in and out, frothy and spitting. We sat under the trees and ate our picnic lunches, lying in the shade and talking, staying some days until the sun had set and the mosquitoes were eating us alive.

Maria Cristina was often more mature than I expected, but she was also exceedingly childlike. Our grandparents had been old-fashioned, and she had been isolated, babied, and protected by Lucia and Ben after Inêz died. They had rarely let her out of their sight, it seemed, though she had attended Catholic school with a small group of girls in their all-Portuguese parish. She'd had almost no interaction with anyone outside her immediate family until now.

To this day one small joy, one comforting bit of knowledge, pushes up through my guilt like a single, fragile blossom: that she was with me long enough to run down to Dekker's by herself, without a second thought, or over to Mrs. Hatcher's to see what was cooking. She went to Ezra's alone on occasion, or came back home by herself when I was working and she got bored. She became friends with Stevie Sullivan's little sister, Deirdre, and they were often at our house, whispering their secrets and walking arm in arm. She was happy.

While we explored Milford like Wampanoag braves scouting the lay of the land, Farley Tucker was quietly interviewing the young Portuguese men in the area, the boys who fished, worked on cars and pumped gas, or labored in the mills and factories. His interrogation style included a friendly smoke and a discussion of the weather or fishing. He asked them who they knew, what they'd heard, and what they thought. He made his quiet way through west Warwick, talking to every boy who'd ever known Matt Da Silva, until he eventually found his way back to the dead boy's family. Sheriff Tucker was methodical and closemouthed, taking it all in and saying nothing of his suspicions. The town began to lose interest when nothing more seemed to happen after the inquest, and I was no better. When Ezra was not immediately arrested and charged, I let the incident fall from my mind like a scab that has healed. I didn't see it peel away—I only realized later that it was gone.

I was busy with my sister. Maria Cristina was teaching me the Portuguese names of things, and I tried to mimic the unfamiliar sounds, embarrassed at first but with growing confidence. She was a good teacher. She never once laughed at my faulty pronunciation, never lost patience with me. We made it a game, and she encouraged me, lavishing praise upon me when I was able to commit words to memory and pull them out later in the appropriate context.

During our language lessons the years between us evaporated, as though we had been born on the same day, at the same moment. I felt sometimes that if we could just talk long and hard enough, tell each other every thing we had ever thought or felt, that she would be me and I would be her and I could never possibly feel lonely again.

She taught me a children's song in Portuguese, and I taught her some in English. We were a strange sight, no doubt, to any who might have spied us, clamoring over field and stream, swimming in the cove at Ezra's, splashing, laughing, and calling to one another in two languages, singing songs usually heard from six-year-olds.

I asked her about our grandparents, and she told me stories

that brought them to life for me. Ben, strong and certain, a force to be reckoned with—not unlike Father, perhaps, but less formal, more demonstrative. He had played the guitar, and Maria Cristina said she remembered Inêz and Lucia dancing in the kitchen while he played. Lucia, with her sweet disposition, had been crippled by arthritis in her last years and had drawn increasingly on her faith to sustain her as she died in excruciating pain. Lucia's death, Maria Cristina said, had killed her *avô*. He never fully recovered, following his wife to the grave in less than two years. These were the things we talked about—we could spare nothing for the murdered Portuguese boy. Discovering my own family—even if they were dead—was all I cared about, not worrying about who had destroyed someone else's.

On Thursday, July twenty-sixth, surely the hottest day on record, Maria Cristina and I decided to walk down to Ezra's and swim. Later, when the temperature dropped a bit with the sun, I planned to begin planking the sides of my boat. I wouldn't need to rush home today, as Father had left a note in the kitchen that morning telling me that the men he had met in Narragansett the week before were driving down to see the mill before making any decisions about investing in it. He would be busy all day.

The heat was already unbearable when Maria Cristina and I got up and left the house. We packed some sandwiches and our swimsuits and began a leisurely stroll down to Ezra's. We trudged down the sandy path that forked off the mill road, the cicadas throwing up a steady hum all around us, and Maria Cristina swinging her lunch pail in a way that did not bode well for her sandwich.

"Excuse me, Ana, why does Mr. Dodge hate the Portuguese?"

I cringed inwardly. "He doesn't, not really. It's complicated. Father was hurt very badly by Inêz—by our *mamãe*—when she left him so many years ago." I felt my face flush as I called her that, saying *mamãe* out loud for the first time, but Maria Cristina didn't seem to notice. "Because our *mamãe* was Portuguese, he wants nothing that is Portuguese in his life. It reminds him of her, of his pain." I felt a twinge of discomfort telling her something I wasn't sure I believed myself. "Do you understand?"

She didn't answer immediately, and I glanced sideways at her as we ploughed slowly and steadily toward Ezra's.

"No, excuse me, I do not understand. If a dog bites me, I should not hate all dogs. I should not kick another dog when I meet him. How is this right?"

I struggled to come up with an answer. I had felt this criticism of Father myself over the years, but had never spoken to him about it. What would be gained, I reasoned, by arguing with him about an attitude he could deny or, worse yet, claim he had a right to feel in light of what he had suffered?

"Ana, excuse me," Maria Cristina was saying. "Please explain what you said—*Mamãe* left Mr. Dodge?"

Of all the things Maria Cristina might need explained, I had not thought that the fact of Inêz's desertion of her husband and daughter would be one of them. Still, I had no way of knowing what Inêz or, more likely, what Ben and Lucia, had told her.

"She didn't want to be married to him anymore, and one day she just left us. I woke up one morning when I was six years old and she was gone. I never saw her again," I said.

"She would never leave you," Maria Cristina said quietly and with absolute conviction.

The tone of her voice, with its gentle certainty, told me I was wrong, but I'd lived with this truth for more than fifteen years, and her certainty about what she could not know—had not been forced to know, like I had—upset me. "Well, she *did* leave me. That is indisputable."

"But I don't think so," said Maria Cristina. "She was a good mother, and I know—I *know*—she could not have left you, no more than she could have left me."

"She left us both, eventually," I said, my own pain making me cruel. "Inêz was having a love affair with someone. She left a note for my father, admitting it. She said she was in love with someone else, a

Portuguese man. That her marriage to Father had been a mistake. So one day she left. They left, together."

"I do not believe that," Maria Cristina said with finality. I envied her delusions, but I had lost the capacity long ago to ignore the hard realities of my childhood, because it was upon them that I had built my adulthood. What would I have—who would I be—without them?

"Well, I'm sorry," I said, "but it's true. And if you think about it, if you put the pieces together, you'll see it."

I hesitated, though I suspected that at some level she already knew what I felt must be said between us. "She had you, Maria Cristina. You are the proof of what she did to us."

We continued walking, saying nothing, and the trees receded up ahead as we approached Ezra's yard. We emerged into the blistering heat. The trees that had shaded us on the narrow, sandy road ended abruptly, and the stark, brutal light beat down upon us both.

Ezra's kitchen chimney was smoking, and I figured he was baking soda bread for the week, which he sometimes did in the morning.

"Want to swim?" I asked Maria Cristina.

"Okay," was all I got, but I knew her now, knew she liked to consider things, turn them over before she spoke. In that way she was far wiser, and more mature, than I perhaps have ever been.

So we swam, and the cold salt water washed away our pensive moods until we were laughing, diving for shells, riding the waves into shore, our bodies held arrow-straight, heads down, arms rigidly out in front, and toes pointed behind. Ezra had taught me how years ago, and I had taught Maria Cristina. In a day she learned how to gauge where the wave would break and launch herself at just the right moment. She understood instinctively that her success depended far more upon her giving in and letting go than it did on mastery.

It had taken me much longer, despite the advice Ezra had shouted from the shore. I thought that with practice, with athletic skill and the force of my will, I would best the sea. Through that long, hot summer I had struggled against the waves. Every day I tried to ride them in, and every day I failed. Ezra had gotten so frustrated he stopped coaching me and merely worked on a boat up by the dock, glancing up every now and then to make sure I hadn't drowned.

Then, after school one day in early September, shivering in the weak sunlight and icy water, I stood chest-deep, looking at the blue-black wall of water racing toward me. The summer was over, and I still couldn't do it. I would never get it, I knew. Exhausted, dispirited, and intending only to come in out of the frigid Atlantic waters and warm up by Ezra's fire, I turned toward shore. I took a deep breath, put my face in the water, lifted my feet, and simply gave myself to the ocean, allowing the waves to do with me what they would. It had been the most exhilarating moment I'd ever experienced.

Together, Maria Cristina and I rode the waves, springing back up each time, our stomachs scraped from the shells and rocks, eyes stinging from the salt, and racing back out for another run. We finally tired and went up to eat our lunch by the cluster of pine trees closest to the workshop, our hair stiff with brine and dripping onto our shoulders, the breeze raising goose bumps on our arms and legs and obliterating, if only for a few moments, the intense heat of the day. We had just unwrapped our sandwiches when Ezra came out of the house and began his slow, awkward walk toward his chair by the carpenter's horses at the water's edge.

"Hi, Ezra!" I called, in case he had not seen us earlier from his window.

I preferred not to surprise him, having learned my lesson years earlier when he had thrown open the door of the workshop where I was working, a loaded shotgun in his hand, having seen from his house that the door was slightly ajar.

He answered, the sound more a grunt than a discernable word, and proceeded to ignore us.

Maria Cristina and I stayed put, damp and cool from the breeze and shade.

"I did not meet my *pai*," Maria Cristina said suddenly.

"Never?" I asked, surprised.

"No. *Mamãe* told me he was a Portuguese man who died before I was born. She did not like to talk about him."

I marveled now that she could remember things Inêz had said to her since Inêz had died when Maria Cristina was only four. I had never challenged her memories of her mother, but in my own mind I had concluded that either she was inventing details or she was remembering conversations with Ben or Lucia.

"I asked *Avó* about my father," Maria Cristina continued, as though she had read my thoughts, "but she did not like to talk about him, either. She seemed very sad when she thought about him, and she told me to leave the past in silence."

"She probably just wanted you to be happy, didn't want you to focus on something you couldn't have," I said. "*Mamãe* was Catholic, even though she broke with the church to marry my father." I was struck by this new layer of longing and loss that we shared.

"Maybe," said Maria Cristina.

Suddenly there was a shout from Ezra, who was down by the water where my boat lay, unattended by me, in its cradles.

"You gonna finish her or quit?" he yelled.

"Of course I'm going to finish her. I'm planking today!" I shouted back.

He didn't respond, merely looked at me across the yard before turning and limping toward the workshop. I felt a pang of guilt as I forced myself to acknowledge how lazy I'd become. It didn't matter how hot it was—I should be finished with her by now. The Sullivans had picked up their boat weeks ago, and when Stevie claimed her for his own I had seen his pride, the fierce joy of physical freedom and mobility, and the independence having his own boat would mean.

Stevie had shaken Ezra's hand, swallowed hard as he thanked his father and boarded the boat bobbing at the end of the dock. After he checked her over, Stevie took the rebuilt motor his father handed him and mounted it on the transom. He poured the premixed gas and oil into the gas tank and closed the choke. Then he started her up, and gravity pulled the fuel into the carburetor. A faint cloud of blue smoke rose from the engine as it roared to life, the blast of sound startling a group of gulls from their afternoon walk on the sand. They rose into the air, circling and screeching their displeasure, the tips of their wings lavender in the sun.

I asked Maria Cristina if she would be able to amuse herself for a couple of hours while I worked on the boat. Having spent most of her life with ailing grandparents and thus, I reasoned, amusing herself, she seemed content to wander back down to the water and search for shells while I worked. I was grateful that she understood I did not want her help, or anyone else's for that matter, and turned all of my attention to the boat.

I put my light cotton blouse and trousers on over my mostly-dry swimsuit and walked briskly toward the workshop. I would need to haul my lumber outside first. The boat's frame, including the keel and stem, was white cedar. The hardness and close grain of the cedar would hold the fasteners well, and since I would use this wood only in narrow widths, its tendency to twist or warp was not a serious defect. I figured the lightness of the cedar planks would offset the weight of the teak I planned to use for the deck and seating. She would be fast enough, and built to last.

I was feeling pretty good as I moved my planking and tools outside.

I began with the wider boards near the bottom of the boat, then continued planking her sides with increasingly narrow widths. Hot weather shrinks even the driest lumber, loosening putty and caulking, but by keeping the planks narrow I hoped to minimize this. I used four- and six-inch boat clamps for bending planks at the bow, with a couple of ten-inchers for longer reaches and a cast-steel jambing dog for edge setting. I didn't know how far I would get before I ran out of daylight, but I was optimistic that I'd soon be rolling the boat over in her cradles to build the half-deck and seats.

I worked steadily in the heat, looking up occasionally to check on Maria Cristina, who shuttled back and forth between the shallows and the shade trees. Ezra came and went, sometimes working in the shop, sometimes going back up to the house for a time. He came down to the water once or twice and looked at my work. He didn't speak, which I knew could mean that I was doing exactly what I should be doing, and doing it well, or that I was destroying my boat through incompetence and he figured I needed to learn that hard lesson without any interference from him. I looked critically at my work, but didn't want to start second-guessing myself. She was a beauty, I thought, running my hand over her planks. I had already taken off any lumps or bad spots in the strake's edge with a rabbet plane, so the planking was fair and identical—Ezra had taught me to always make planks in pairs with a band saw. I had tacked two together and sawed them out at the same time, one for port and one for starboard, except for shutters. The wood grain was so nice, it was almost a shame to paint her.

I went back to work, fastening the planks that were clamped to the frame. I drove the chiseled point of each nail so it cut the grain of the frame, which meant they would hold much better, and they were less apt to split the frame if I had to pull them back through later for repairs. I hummed while I worked.

The sun had nearly slid down to the tops of the trees just beyond Ezra's stone wall. Sunset was not far off. I had just straightened up to call to Maria Cristina to help me bring the remaining lumber and hardware back to the workshop when I heard the sound of an approaching car, an unusual sound at Ezra's.

I stood, stretching, the breeze on my sweat-soaked shirt cool and welcome, the relief in my back making me aware for the first time how long I had been hunched over, and how cramped and sore I was. I stared at the woods that separated us from town, at the gap in the trees where the road emerged and where, suddenly, two long black roadsters appeared, one right after the other, driving slowly, their tires slipping and spinning a bit in the deep sand. They pulled up on the grass near the workshop, and the men inside opened the doors and began to spill out.

One of the men in the first car was my father, I noted, feeling strangely unnerved by his presence here. Six other men, most in suits and fedoras, climbed out of the cars and assembled in Ezra's yard.

Ezra came out of the house and stood on the porch, and Maria Cristina looked up from where she stood, ankle-deep in white foam and the receding tide, down near the dock. The men were closest to me, and spotting me, my father led them over to where I stood by my boat.

"Oliver," he said, "I'd like you to meet my daughter. Anne, this is Mr. Fielding, who's come up from the Pier to take a look at our mill."

A man stepped forward from the group; he was younger than my father, the only one in the group without a jacket or a hat. He had loosened his tie beneath his unbuttoned collar, and his shirtsleeves were rolled up to the elbow. He offered his hand, and I shook it firmly.

"How do you do, Mr. Fielding?"

"Call me Oliver, please," he said, easy in a self-possessed sort of way. *You can always tell who's got money,* I thought.

"What brings you gentlemen down here?" I asked, wondering if smoothing down my hair, which had dried from the salt water into an exaggerated form of its natural, mad state, would only make matters worse by calling attention to it.

"I've given Mr. Fielding and his associates a tour of the mill, and as we were heading back to town, Mr. Cohen asked what was down the turnoff. I explained that it was a private home, but Mr. Fielding asked if we might see it," Father explained.

He sounded perfectly agreeable, but I knew him too well not to detect the note of resentment in his voice. He did not want to be here at all and, compounding his frustration, here was his only daughter, filthy and sweating, in men's trousers and working like a day laborer.

I tried to make up for it in some small measure by making myself as charming as possible.

"Well, I'm sure I speak for Mr. Johnson when I say we're delighted to have you here," I said, smiling broadly. "Although there's not much going on here but boatbuilding."

Maybe I wasn't really trying to be charming after all, I thought, as I had just highlighted what was surely rankling my father. But I was hurt that he should be embarrassed by me.

Maria Cristina had crept up quietly and stood behind me, to my left. I turned toward her.

"This is my sister, Maria Cristina," I said.

"Miss Dodge," said one of the men, nodding at Maria Cristina. I felt my stomach turn, and out of the corner of my eye I saw Father's face blanch.

"Excuse me, my name is Caldeira," she replied. "Maria Cristina Caldeira, Ana's sister. I am happy to make your acquaintance." She spoke formally, her English accented more noticeably than usual. I wondered if it was deliberate, but dismissed the thought almost immediately.

"Ah, sorry. Miss Caldeira. Pleasure," said the man, his confusion unmistakable.

"Why don't we go say hello to Mr. Johnson," my father interjected hastily, leading the group up toward the house where Ezra stood waiting on the porch.

Maria Cristina and I, left standing out of earshot of the men in suits, watched them from the water's edge.

"Why are they here?" she whispered.

"I don't know," I said. "They were at the mill with my father, and I guess they're just exploring the area."

It appeared as though introductions were taking place and Ezra was being his usual gruff self. One of the men was asking questions, about the boats, maybe, or about Ezra himself—I couldn't tell from where I stood. Ezra was at least listening, if not answering. He hadn't thrown them off the property yet or shown them the business end of his shotgun, which was something.

After only a minute or so, Oliver Fielding broke away from the group and walked back to where Maria Cristina and I stood by the water. He was only an inch or two taller than I, with warm brown eyes and hair that was just starting to gray at the temples. He smiled easily at us as he approached, his eyes on mine.

"I apologize for interrupting your work," he said, indicating the boat.

"That's all right," I assured him. "I was out of daylight anyway."

"Your father mentioned you, said you'd recently graduated from Rhode Island College, but he didn't tell us that you worked with Mr. Johnson." He seemed interested, and I could detect no hint of criticism in his question.

"Ezra is a family friend. I've been coming down here since I was a little girl, learning how to build boats. It seems to be in the nature of a calling for me," I said, daring him to find me unfeminine, a freak of nature, an embarrassment to my father.

"Is she yours?" he asked, turning to the boat without responding to my challenge.

"Yes," I said, reluctant but unable to resist talking about my favorite subject. "I designed her myself."

"Really?" He looked at me now with some intensity, and certainly with greater interest, and I found myself blushing.

I showed him the boat, explaining my plans for her. She was a pleasure craft, I told him, but built as tough as any working boat. I had modified her for stability and comfort, since she was to be mine and I was not a terribly experienced sailor. He asked a few questions, wanting to know how many she'd hold, how her design made her more stable in choppy seas. I was surprised by his interest, and flattered.

I did not immediately perceive that my father and the other men had approached, realizing it only when I saw Maria Cristina's expression change. I turned and saw them standing just behind us.

"I beg your pardon, I didn't know you were there," I apologized, stepping back to include them in our small group.

"We've really got to be going if you gentlemen want to make it back to Narragansett for dinner," said Father.

They all murmured good-byes and thanks and made their way back to the cars, but Oliver Fielding turned and walked back to where Maria Cristina and I stood watching them leave.

"Miss Dodge—" he began, but I interrupted him.

"Anne," I insisted.

He smiled. "Anne it is. Listen, Anne, I'd like to talk to you again, when we both have more time, about your boat design. Among other things," he added.

He was smiling, and I felt far from offended.

It was all so completely unexpected, these men at Ezra's, this man in particular, standing in front of me, talking about my boat, and looking at me like, well, like *that*. Like he was really seeing me. I could only nod and shake his hand as he offered it in parting.

"May I telephone you?" he asked. "Perhaps we could have dinner."

I felt, rather than saw, Maria Cristina standing next to me, completely agog. I had a sudden urge to laugh.

"Perhaps," I said, too startled to think it through right then.

He smiled, turned, and walked briskly back to the car where the others waited. He did not look back. In a moment they were gone, and we stood watching the car disappear into the dusk and trees.

At home later that night I sat waiting up for Father in the library after Maria Cristina had gone to bed. He and I had spoken little since that awful dinner, but I wanted to know how his meeting had gone, and if Mr. Fielding, Mr. Cohen, and the others were going to invest in the mill. I found myself going back over my conversation with Oliver Fielding, and then over it again.

I was just nodding off in my chair when I heard Father drive up and saw the glare from the car's headlamps sweep across the living room. The front door opened and closed again softly, and then Father was in the doorway, drawn to the sitting room where a lamp was still on.

"Anne," he said, surprised to see me. "Is everything all right?"

"Yes, Father, everything's fine. I just wanted to see you. I wanted to ask if your meeting went well. I know it's late, but we haven't talked for a while. I miss our talks."

He smiled then, in his familiar way. I felt a rush of tenderness for him, and my eyes were suddenly filled with tears. I brushed them away quickly as he walked into the room, hoping he hadn't seen.

He sank heavily onto the Queen Anne sofa opposite, loosening his tie. I smiled, remembering that I used to call it the "Queen Me" sofa. It had been our little joke, Father's and mine.

"You look tired," I said.

"I am," he admitted. "Very tired indeed."

"How have your meetings gone? I assume that these men are interested in investing since they drove up to inspect the mill."

"Yes, they are," he said, "though they have made no commitment as yet. They're still only cautiously optimistic. Although they certainly didn't get rich by being cautious. I'm counting on them to remember that."

"What did they think of the mill?" I asked.

He sat for a moment, frowning before he spoke. "I don't really know," he finally said. "They appear to take their cues from Fielding, and he plays his cards close to the vest. He asked a lot of questions. A lot of good questions. He knows what he's doing," he admitted with grudging admiration.

"He seemed like a nice person," I said, keeping my voice casual.

"Yes, I suppose so," Father said.

"He, um, asked if I'd like to have dinner with him," I volunteered. I figured it was better to determine right away if Father thought this a bad idea since I would certainly erase Oliver Fielding from my thoughts if it in any way compromised Father's hopes for the mill.

"Really?" he said, alert again. He thought for a few moments, staring right at me but not seeing me as he considered all the angles.

"I wonder what he thinks you can tell him about the mill that I either can't or won't," he mused. "What did you tell him?"

"I told him he could call me, but we've not made a date. I wanted to ask you first," I said. "He's a business associate of yours, not a boy from college."

"Good, good." He nodded in firm approval. "If you'd like to go, I think it's a fine idea. You're a good spokesman for the family, for me, and there's nothing you can say about the mill or about our operations that I can see would do any harm at all."

"Thanks," I said, though I wasn't really sure I'd been complimented. "Father, what's happening with the Da Silva murder?"

He frowned, clearly bothered. "I wish I knew. Farley isn't telling me much. At this point he's still gathering information, trying to determine what might have been happening in the boy's life that could have led to this. He's trying to find a conflict, I suppose, that would point him toward a motive."

"Is Ezra still a suspect?"

"I honestly don't know, dear. I can't help but think of that boy's family. They lost their son in a horrible fashion, and they haven't the vaguest notion of why—or at whose hand—this has come to pass. I can't imagine the horror."

I looked at him, surprised by the depth of his compassion for the Da Silvas.

"I've been trying to steal some time away from the mill and council business, meeting with church leaders in Warwick. They simply must encourage the locals to speak freely with the sheriff. They're usually so reticent when it comes to law enforcement, but this is too important."

We sat quietly, each occupied by our own thoughts, our own imaginations.

"Father," I began, changing the subject. "About what happened at dinner a few weeks ago—"

"I know, I know," he said, talking over me. "We all had too much to drink. Some unpleasant things were said. Unfortunate things. I think it's best if we forget all about it."

He got up then and crossed the short distance between us to where I sat curled up in my chair. He leaned down and kissed me on the forehead, like he had when I was a little girl. It was a rare gesture of affection. Then he straightened up and walked toward the door.

Just before he left the room, he turned back to me, his expression more relaxed than I'd seen it in a long time.

"I think everything's going to be all right, Anne," he said. "Maria Cristina is here, and the sky has not fallen. And I think Fielding, if not the others, will sign on, and we'll reopen the mill. You and Will— Well, I know you won't disappoint me. I have a very, very good feeling." And he was gone.

I listened to his footsteps above, the old floorboards creaking for a few minutes until they, too, became as silent as the rest of the house. I reached up and turned off the floor lamp beside my chair, holding myself completely still. I was a deer trembling in the forest, hardly daring to breathe for fear of giving myself away.

I want so little, a voice inside me suddenly cried. *Why is this so hard?*

The answer came, and I didn't like it. *It's hard because you make it hard.*

Maybe I should just marry Will and put the boats and the dungarees away once and for all.

No, not yet, I thought. *There's still a chance, if I can just hold on long enough.*

I shook my head in an attempt to dislodge such gloomy thoughts and stared out the window, seeing nothing but my own faint reflection in the glass. *There are people out there who are happy,* I told myself, but as the night deepened, I felt only the vast emptiness of the world, not the weighty comfort of all it contained.

CHAPTER TEN

I did not have to wait and wonder if Oliver Fielding would call. The following afternoon the telephone rang shrilly and Maria Cristina darted into the hall and was speaking into the receiver before I had even reached the kitchen doorway.

"Yes, this is Maria Cristina Caldeira. Yes. Excuse me, I am very well, thank you. How are you, Mr. Fielding?"

Was he calling for me or my father? I wondered.

"Yes, excuse me, she's here. We are cooking." Maria Cristina smiled, listening, then said, "I am, but only because she does not try."

I could hear his laughter over the line from several feet away, and I frowned at Maria Cristina. She merely shrugged her shoulders, unimpressed by my disapproval. She was thoroughly, annoyingly, my little sister in that moment.

"Okay, I will. Good-bye," she said, then handed the phone to me. "This is Mr. Fielding."

"No kidding," I said. Cradling the phone between my ear and shoulder so I could wipe my floury hands on the towel I had carried out of the kitchen with me, I spoke into the receiver: "Hello?"

"Hello, Anne." His voice sounded thin and far away, and I wondered where he was calling from. "I hope I haven't called at an inconvenient time?"

"No, not at all. Maria Cristina and I were just making some dinner. Although you might think we were making a mess more than anything else, by the look of us."

"Yes, she told me you were cooking. I asked her who was the better cook, and she confided in me that it's not you," he said with mock severity.

"She is certainly right about that." I felt giddy and oddly strengthened by my impulse, both at Ezra's and now, to proudly announce my womanly failings to this man. To dare him to imagine, as I did in my most outrageous moments, that they were not faults at all. "I am not especially gifted in the kitchen."

"Well, if it doesn't interest you, leave it to those who like it and do it well," he said. I was thrilled by such sacrilege.

Maria Cristina stood mere inches from me, leaning in as she tried to hear what Oliver was saying on his end. I covered the phone with my hand and whispered to her to give me a moment's privacy. When she hesitated, that stubborn chin tipping up toward me, I sniffed the air in sudden alarm. "Do you smell something burning?" I asked. She turned and raced back into the kitchen, and I put the phone back to my ear. "I'm sorry, Mr. Fielding, you were saying?"

"Please, Anne, I thought we had agreed that it's Oliver."

"Of course. Oliver."

"I was saying that I hoped you might be free Friday night for dinner. I have business in Providence early in the day but should be back in Narragansett by six o'clock. I could send a car for you and we could meet at the Pier, if that suits you."

It suited me very well indeed. I hadn't been there since my college graduation. I was eager to see it again.

The Pier operated as though there were no Depression, with restaurants, shops, lovely women and powerful men—and dancing. Famous dance bands were de rigueur, and dinner was a real dress-up affair, catering to the wealthy summer people visiting from New York, Providence, and Boston. And, of course, now that Prohibition had been repealed, nightclubs and taprooms were springing up everywhere. People were starting to go out again at night, and I was excited by the prospect of joining them.

"I would love to," I said, "but there's no need to send a car. I can drive myself."

"I'm sure your father would not appreciate me taking such poor care of you," said Oliver, "sending you out on the road at night to drive home alone."

"Mr. Fielding—Oliver—I am hardly a fragile flower. Besides, it's what I prefer."

"Then that's what we'll do," he agreed readily. "Shall we meet at Henri's, at the maître d' stand, seven thirty? Dinner and dancing?"

"Yes," I said. "It sounds perfect."

"It certainly does. And I wasn't joking, you know. I do want to talk about your boat."

We hung up, but by then Maria Cristina had finished preparing our dinner by herself. She had made some sort of stew of lamb and potatoes. It was delicious, but when I asked her to tell me how she'd cooked the ingredients we'd bought together, washed and chopped together, she refused.

"Excuse me, you have secret telephone conversations, I have secret cooking."

I laughed at her, teased her, but she would not forgive me for the rest of the day.

The next morning, despite the fact that I was itching to go down to Ezra's and work, Maria Cristina and I went shopping. The previous night's dinner had depleted what staples we had left, and we needed soap and a few other items, so we planned to stop at Dekker's and then go on to Jablonski's. I also wanted to buy some flounder or cod and maybe two dozen quahogs from the Sullivans, but they sold their catch out of their truck later in the day, after they came in from the fishing grounds. It was difficult to predict what time they would open their doors for business, as it were, since the length of each workday depended on both the weather and the size of the day's catch. That meant two trips to town, effectively killing any hope I had of digging in at Ezra's for a good stretch of work.

We set out for Dekker's first, and when we entered the store, the bell attached to the screen door jangled, announcing our arrival. The whole place smelled sharply of the briny pickle barrel that sat up front by the window that looked out on Main Street. I smiled, remembering how I used to stick my arm in that barrel, all the way up to the elbow, feeling around for the biggest, fattest pickle.

Mr. and Mrs. Dekker looked up to greet us and, to my surprise, so did Will, whom I had not seen recently, except from a distance in town. "Hello, beautiful," he said, clearly delighted to see us. Apparently we had moved past any remaining awkwardness between us after that horrible dinner some weeks earlier.

"Will, please," I said, embarrassed by the endearment, especially in front of others.

"Believe me, Anne, you will someday wish for the days when you were greeted by a handsome young man in such a way!" laughed his mother, Elsa Dekker, from behind the counter where she sat at their behemoth of a cash register. "Your small waist will one day be gone."

"There's a cheery thought," I said, laughing.

"Now, just a moment!" protested Mr. Dekker, shaking a finger at his wife. "Wasn't I just remarking this morning on my great good fortune in having a wife as beautiful as you?" Will's father, a slightly shorter version of Will, had the same clear blue eyes but thinner blonde hair that seemed to be fading rather than turning gray.

Mrs. Dekker waved him away with her hand as he approached, both arms out, as though to embrace her right there in the middle of the store. "What nonsense! I'm as fat as an old cow," she said, frowning.

"Lies! You're a stunner, woman," said Mr. Dekker with such enthusiasm that her face shone.

I turned away in embarrassment. "What do you hear about the sheriff's investigation?" I asked, eager to change the subject.

"Oh, it's all too sad, isn't it?" asked Mrs. Dekker.

"It is sad," agreed her husband. "I'm afraid momentum has already been lost. Farley's a good man, but the Portuguese are reluctant to talk, and folks here in Milford won't see any of it as having much to do with them."

"My father said he's been trying to help, trying to get people to cooperate with Sheriff Tucker," I said.

"He has. I went with him this morning down to the docks, before the trawlers went out. Your dad's a good man—he told them how important this investigation is, and that the law is on their side."

I felt torn, wanting to see justice done but hoping that it wouldn't include destroying anyone I knew and cared about.

We all stood awkwardly, lost in our own thoughts about the case and the ways in which it served to highlight the chasm that existed between west Warwick and Milford.

"What brings you two by this morning?" asked Will, bringing us back.

"Food!" said Maria Cristina, which made him laugh.

"We've run out of just about everything," I said, "so we're shopping this morning. We're going to Jablonski's next, and Sullivan's truck later. Why are you here?"

"Dad's got a delivery this morning, and I came in to help unload the boxes. He's getting too old to do the heavy lifting," he said, teasing his father.

"Such a smart mouth he has!" said Mr. Dekker. "Isn't he awful?"

"Yes, a terrible son. The worst," I said, playing the game they always played.

"Say, Annie, let's go clamming this weekend. Saturday afternoon, at low tide," suggested Will.

"Oh, Saturday I can't, Will," I said quickly.

"Why not?" asked Will, tossing his head to get the hair out of his eyes. "Are you working at Ezra's? I could meet you there if you like when you're finished for the day."

"Ana is not working—she is dancing on Saturday," said Maria Cristina, lifting the lid off of a large glass jar that sat in a prominent place on the counter and carefully removing a peppermint stick for herself as Elsa looked on approvingly. Their affection for each other—and Elsa's indulgence—was already firmly established.

"Dancing? With who?" Will asked, looking at me.

"No one," I said, and promptly blushed. I sounded, and now looked, as though I was hiding something. "I mean, no one you know. A business associate of Father's. One of his investors, he hopes. And it's dinner—a meeting, really. Father thinks I'm a good representative for the family," I quickly added, wondering if I was lying by implying that this dinner was really about the mill. I actually didn't know for sure, but either way I was furious with Maria Cristina. I didn't want to discuss this, not with Will, and especially not in front of his parents. But it was out of my hands now. Maria Cristina did this sort of thing on purpose, I thought, so sweet and innocent on the surface, but underneath so very aware of what would stir things up and make people uncomfortable. Make *me* uncomfortable.

"What's his name?" asked Mr. Dekker.

"Oliver Fielding," I said.

"I know Mr. Fielding," he said. "He owns a small resort and half a dozen summer houses in Narragansett that are doing very well. I believe he also has an interest in a woolens factory up in Cranston. Or is it in Johnston?" he mused, more to himself than to us. "He has a reputation for being very smart—and very tough."

"What do you mean?" I asked, curious.

"Labor problems," said Mr. Dekker. "The unions have come in to organize his people."

"That's happening everywhere, though, isn't it?" I asked, hoping I didn't sound as though I were defending Oliver. Or as though he needed defending.

"Yes, but Fielding's taken an unusually hard line. People say he blacklists and fires workers for even attending a speech—he uses spies and keeps records on his employees."

"I don't like this. Who would spy on the men who work for him?" asked Mrs. Dekker. She was indignant already, and I rushed in to calm her down.

"Maybe it's not like that," I said. "Maybe he is simply monitoring his business. Surely he is right to be concerned if agitators are coming in to his place of business and stirring up the men."

"Well, there's been some violence, too," Mr. Dekker said. "A couple of incidents—one where a man was shot, though he recovered. The other time a man was beaten to death with a baseball bat. There was a hearing, of course, but Fielding wasn't anywhere near the factory when it happened, so he was in the clear."

"Sounds like a swell fellow," said Will, his back to me as he bent to pick up a case of flour and move it to the store room.

"Well, this is just gossip, of course," said his father. "He certainly knows what he's doing in terms of business. He's very rich."

Will said nothing as he walked down the center aisle of the store toward the back, the wooden crate held in both arms, his muscles accepting the burden but straining under its weight. He passed the shelves stocked with sacks of flour and sugar and cornmeal, the old wooden casks filled with nails, coils of rope, hammers and hatchets, wrenches and various pipes and fittings, and disappeared into the storeroom without so much as a glance my way.

"Well, Maria Cristina, let's get what we need," I said quickly. "Then we'll walk over to Jablonski's and be home before lunch."

We hastily made our purchases and left before Will reemerged from the storeroom. After we left, Maria Cristina and I each toting one of the new brown paper shopping bags the Dekker stores now carried, we walked the short distance to Jablonski's, which sat half a block down and two streets over, nestled between the luncheonette and a boarded-up, empty storefront that used to sell women's ready-made apparel before the Panic had put it, like so many stores, out of business.

I was still angry, but now that we were out of the store I felt better, less nervous. Perhaps it was better to have it out in the open that I'd made a date with Oliver Fielding. I had no obligation to Will, after all. Hadn't I made it perfectly clear that we were not engaged? I could see whomever I wanted to, I thought, as we approached the Jablonski's store.

Jablonski's competed with Dekker's on only a few items since the Dekkers carried very few perishable goods. Jablonski's sold fresh fruits and vegetables, baked goods, and dairy products, all from the surrounding farms outside of Milford. We bought milk and eggs, early corn and blueberries, some bacon and a fresh chicken at the tiny counter in the back where Mr. Jablonski ran the store's small butcher service. I arranged for Giovanni to deliver the meat, plus ice, later in the day, and we made our way home, leaning a little into our heavy packages as we followed the sidewalks back to our house.

It was hot, humid, and hazy. Looking out over the bay I could see darker clouds, but in town the sky was a brilliant milky white, the cloud cover high and dense, without even a hint of a breeze. The thick, sultry air stifled any impulse we might have had to talk. We walked home in silence, sweating.

Around four o'clock we set out again with the burlap bag I used to carry fish home. Mr. Sullivan parked most days just a few dozen yards from the Dekker's store and sold his catch if he had anything that the local restaurants hadn't taken. I liked to buy from him whenever I could. The Sullivans were some of my favorite people.

Maria Cristina and I were walking toward Dekker's, enjoying the breeze we were delighted to find had sprung up. Rain was clearly moving in, indicated by the dark-gray clouds now heading inland fast. I tilted my head up and breathed deeply, tasting the impending rain that would bring cooler air in behind it. One of the best things about New England summers is that no matter how hot it gets, cool air is never far away.

We passed the Hatchers' and the old Bertolucci place, turned the corner onto Main, and saw Sullivan's truck in its designated spot.

Rather than a customer or two at the truck's tailgate examining Mr. Sullivan's catch, however, some two dozen men were gathered there—a few women and children, too—and a man I didn't recognize was standing up in the truck bed speaking to them.

We approached cautiously and hung back behind the crowd, close enough to see and hear without actually joining the group.

"Do you know what's happening in Massachusetts, in the wool and worsted mills, in the carpet factories? In Massachusetts they can't make our men work more than forty-eight hours a week. It's in their contract. Here they can work you fifty-four hours a week!"

"Friend, there ain't a man in this town wouldn't jump at the chance to work fifty-four hours a month—let alone a week!" said an amused voice from the crowd. Several of the men in the audience chuckled at this.

The speaker was a good-looking man, with neat brown hair and strong hands that he used to punctuate his sentences. He looked like any young mill worker might, before too many years at the looms had stooped his shoulders and crippled his hands and back, but he was far more articulate.

"I hear you—the most important thing right now is to have work, to get that mill reopened. But I think you know what you'll find," the man continued. "You'll have to work faster, increasing your chances for injury on the job, because your production quotas will be up. Their efficiency experts have decided you can speed up and stretch out. In Pawtucket they've got fifteen-year-olds running thirty wide-looms from before sunup to after sundown!"

There were some murmurs now from the crowd, and men turned to each other, denying that this could be true—or saying instead that, indeed, they had heard these rumors. The speaker's voice gained confidence, fed by this new restlessness.

"Two years ago, in Fall River, it was the same. The men were working fifty, sixty hours a week, and some of the women and children were, too. Kids running more looms than a grown, experienced man can properly handle. Pay so low families were barely surviving.

Then we came in, told them what we could do for them, what we had done for others, and they voted us in. And it hasn't hurt the factories—far from it! Fall River is recovering faster than anywhere in Rhode Island, and I've got the numbers to prove it."

He paused, his hands resting easily in his pockets, and looked at them with an open, confident smile from his perch on the truck bed.

"How so?" asked Mr. Sullivan, up front in the crowd. He sounded impatient, either to hear the man's answer or to have this event over so he could sell his fish before the ice melted and they rotted in the sun. I saw Stevie standing shoulder-to-shoulder with his dad, his arms crossed self-consciously over his chest in identical fashion. He looked very young, his attention focused on the crowd rather than on the speaker, as though we were all watching him.

"I'll tell you what we did. We put the strength of our national organization behind them. We got other unions to come out and support their cause. We told them we could offer food and even money to tide over their families in the event of a strike. And we went to the bargaining table on their behalf," he said, reciting his list slowly and with emphasis so none within hearing would miss a single detail.

"How'd it turn out?" asked another man whose face I could not see.

"It turned out good. Real good," said the man, turning his head and scanning the crowd as he nodded in agreement with his own statement. He was trying to make eye contact with as many of the men as possible, a formidable task as more and more people approached the group out of curiosity, and stayed because what he was saying compelled them to remain. The air was heavy, and the wind had picked up, moving the clouds fast. A woman standing near us and holding her young daughter's hand had to quickly reach up and clamp her hat onto her head to keep it from blowing away. I heard a low rumble of thunder off to the south. It was an angry, threatening sound.

"It turned out so good that now they've got an eight-hour workday in Fall River. They've got a twenty-loom maximum—eighteen if the operator's a woman or a child under the age of seventeen. They've got a minimum wage that is the highest in the industry, and auditing rights if the mill claims they've got to let workers go. If the audit confirms the need, workers have the right to vote to share jobs so that everybody eats and nobody starves."

"Sounds good," said a voice from the middle of the crowd, "but it don't add up. Back in twenty-two in the big mill strike, the men was out of work for eight, nine months. Some of the mills didn't last and shut down for good, or moved south. The strike destroyed jobs, didn't make 'em better."

"True enough, friend," agreed the man in the truck bed, "but it's a new day. We're better organized, better funded. Workers are speaking with one voice now, and the owners will have to meet the needs of those who actually do the work, even down South. If they can't divide us, they can't conquer us."

"The *Pawtucket Times* says that's communism," said another voice from the crowd, but whoever had spoken was immediately drowned out by others. Everyone seemed to be talking at once.

The babble of excited voices got louder as everyone competed to be heard, in dozens of separate conversations or by the speaker up front. The crowd had easily doubled in size, and I could hear individuals calling out to their friends and neighbors in the crowd. I heard it in their voices—the excitement, the hope, the camaraderie. I saw Pat Tully up front, and several mill workers I knew. That young girl from the inquest, the dead boy's sister—Susana Da Silva—stood to the right of the crowd, her lovely oval face reflecting both her grief and the excitement of the moment, the combination startlingly beautiful. Mr. Meyer and his wife had joined the group and stood only a few feet away from Maria Cristina and I. Everyone seemed to be vibrating with energy.

I felt it myself. The thrill was contagious, and so was the anxiety. The tightly packed and shifting bodies, the cacophony of voices and the speaker's words ringing through the air, the darting glances and the grim expressions all suggested that reason and control were fragile things.

"And it's all put down in a legally binding contract," the union organizer concluded, his deep voice pitched to be heard above the now-noisy crowd. "You have rights, my friends. They don't own you anymore!" he suddenly shouted, and my stomach clenched hard as though steeling itself for a punch. After a startled moment the men exploded with approval, clapping, whistling, shouting, fists pumping the air. Maria Cristina moved a little closer to me and took my hand.

"You have the power, as a collective, to demand a decent living and to secure your own jobs!" he shouted. "They don't own you—no sir, not anymore!"

The crowd went wild as the first fat raindrops plopped around us, and Maria Cristina and I instinctively stepped back, as though the rain was coming from the man speaking to the crowd. When he jumped down off the truck to mingle with his audience, dozens of men and women, people I'd known all my life, crowded around to shake his hand, to tell him stories about how hard it had been here, some with tears in their eyes. They slapped him on the back and shook his hand, this man who had characterized Samuel Dodge as their enemy. I found that I was shaking and holding Maria Cristina's hand too tightly.

From our position on the fringe I saw three or four men whom I had not noticed before, strangers who now moved in and out of the crowd with pencils and small white cards as they encouraged every man and woman present to authorize the American Textile Workers Union to bargain with the Dodge mill on their behalf.

The rain was beginning in earnest. Suddenly a flash of lightning rent the sky, illuminating the crowd milling about in the rain. Almost immediately we felt the answering crack of thunder that shook the very sidewalk on which we stood. The heavens opened, and rain poured down upon us. Maria Cristina and I turned and ran for shelter. I was badly shaken and forgot all about the fish we had come to buy. I had been moved by the man's speech and caught up in the crowd's reaction—I knew these people, after all, and their welfare was important to me. But the realization that it was my father they were organizing against came crashing in, and as I ran home, torn in my loyalties in a way I had never experienced, I wondered for the first time if Father and I had anything to fear from the people we lived among.

It had always seemed clear to me that the interests of the mill as a functioning, moneymaking enterprise were the interests both of my family and of the men and women who worked for us. I knew the arguments, of course, that this was not the case, but I had never experienced the passionate speech-making of an agitator, or peered into the faces of neighbors I knew and cared deeply for, familiar faces suddenly naked at the prospect of real hope that they might be relieved from the brutal uncertainty of their lives. I knew them as a strong, even stoic lot, and I felt strange—embarrassed, really—to have seen them naked in this way.

My father and I were not their enemies—the idea that Father thought he "owned" his workers, as the man had suggested, was absurd—and yet, it was undeniable that we had grown rich from the mill. My father was not torn about such things. It was his absolute conviction that our good fortune was not an accident, and he slept very well. So I had tried, all these years, to focus on his certainty rather than the fact that we had not lost either our home or much of our wealth in the Crash and ensuing panic, as so many others had.

I staggered up the steps to our grand home, soaked through and shaking. I felt the difference, the gap between those people at Sullivan's truck and myself. I shook with it as I struggled with the wet doorknob, my Portuguese sister by my side, the voices of my Irish Catholic and Italian and Russian neighbors ringing in my ears, pouring out their troubles, their fear and their anger to a stranger.

When Saturday evening finally arrived I was running late and found myself racing to get ready. I had given some thought to what I should wear and had decided that a suit, rather than an evening gown, would be the better choice, especially since my long red dress was out of the question for a first date, and it was the only evening gown I owned that wasn't hopelessly outdated. My graduation from college served me still, however, and I chose the smart white suit I had worn under my robes at the commencement ceremony. It was perfectly appropriate for the occasion, and would serve as a suggestion that I considered our dinner to be more business meeting than romantic tryst. Will's reaction to the news that I had a date with Oliver had decided me on that point. Neither I nor my father needed the townspeople gossiping about my social life, especially if it might hurt our chances for reopening the mill.

Maria Cristina begged to help me get ready, though she bounced on the bed and chattered about Deirdre Sullivan and her four brothers more than anything else. Apparently Stevie was on the outs with his mother for fishing all day, coming home, and then leaving for the better part of each night.

"Deirdre says Stevie's immortal soul is in jeo–, jeop–," Maria Cristina stammered.

"Jeopardy?" I asked, amused.

"Yes, that's it. Oh, I like this hat very much!" she said, distracted by my efforts.

In addition to my only pair of real silk stockings, the black Louis heels, and my white linen suit, I wore a small hat I had borrowed from Mrs. Hatcher for the occasion. It was a ridiculous little confection of a hat—just a tiny, rounded white cap, really—that sported a curved ebony feather and a small veil of black net that covered my eyes and came just to the tip of my nose, throwing my mouth into high relief. I felt silly when I'd agreed to try it on next door, but when I looked in the mirror I knew I would wear it. It was enormously flattering, making me look and feel a sophistication that simply was not a part of my life. The jet necklace and a pair of soft black kid gloves completed my outfit. Maria Cristina forced my wayward hair into a sleek knot at the back of my head and pinned the hat on top at a slight angle. She pronounced me "just right," but when I examined myself in the mirror, I added red lipstick.

I drove myself to Narragansett, preferring the independence of knowing that I could come and go as I pleased without having to depend on an employee of Oliver's—or Oliver himself—to drive me home. I wasn't sure how long I'd want to stay. I felt somewhat conspicuous in my clothes, not because they were outlandish in any way but because I was unused to wearing them. My everyday clothes, my dungarees and heavy work shirts stained with paint and varnish and dried caulk—*those* were unusual, I reminded myself, not this lovely suit.

I spent the thirty-minute drive to the Pier thinking about the union organizer I had seen and heard a few days before, trying to settle in my mind how I felt. In the abstract, I could not help but side with the workingmen, especially in these increasingly volatile days when strikes were apt to turn violent, with hired thugs brought in to intimidate and beat workers into submission. It happened, I knew, despite the loud proclamations by most politicians, industrialists, and newspaper editors to the contrary. The larger constitutional questions behind these ongoing battles, questions about freedom of speech and the right to assembly, became complicated and difficult to hold onto in the face of a battered economy and businesses struggling to survive.

And yet, we were mill owners, Father and I. I had been witness to my father's concern for his neighbors and employees my entire life—it was not a lie. Where did we fit into this nameless, faceless scheme of labor versus capital, I wondered. What was our responsibility, and what was our due? We certainly benefited enormously from the mill, but my father's family had turned privilege at birth into wealth and power and jobs and community responsibility, where other men with equal privilege might have been content to live comfortably, producing nothing, or even to squander their wealth in reckless speculation.

They had not gotten off scot-free, my family, not when cheap labor drew their competitors to the southern states, and not when the stock market had crashed. In 1930, after a decade of steadily declining profits, the original Dodge mill up in the Blackstone Valley had closed its doors forever, Black Thursday having delivered the final blow to a slowly dying beast. Father had few remaining relatives: an uncle, still in Providence, but now in his dotage, and two first cousins who moved to California years ago and retired to a quiet obscurity on the Pacific ocean when the Dodge family was still quite wealthy. We had not been in contact with them for many, many years. Father's vision of restoring the family, its wealth and position and optimism, had become his alone—and Oliver Fielding appeared to embody all of my father's last hopes for a life which had all but disappeared.

CHAPTER ELEVEN

When I arrived, a valet parked my car and I entered the restaurant through lead-glass-paned double doors pulled open simultaneously by two young, uniformed boys who stood at either side of the foyer. The interior of Henri's was dark, paneled in mahogany, with sconces on the walls between each table and small shaded lamps on the tables themselves, casting a warm, flattering glow over the starched white linens and gleaming silverware. Each table along the wall was tucked into a curved alcove, the walls undulating in and out around the room. A red leather upholstered banquette hugged the wall in each alcove, allowing diners to sit as close to each other as they wished, and affording a mostly unrestricted view of the parquet dance floor situated at the center of the room.

It was beautifully designed, I thought. Everyone's view was panoramic, unobstructed, but each table was secluded. Strategically placed palms provided additional privacy from the diners immediately to one's right or left. A band was playing on a slowly rotating, raised dais in the center of the enormous dance floor, and while it was early, and the restaurant not nearly as crowded as it would later become, there were already several couples out on the floor.

I did not see Oliver but felt shored up by the approving look the maître d' gave me as he looked me up and down in less-than-subtle appraisal.

"Madame, may I seat you with your party?" he asked smoothly. He was handsome, in an attenuated sort of way. His shiny patent-leather hair needed only the addition of a thin, waxed moustache and he would merit a Hollywood casting director's call.

"Thank you, but I'll wait here for my escort. If you don't mind."

I had found it somewhat disconcerting while I was driving to peer at the road through the black netting on my hat, but I found it very much to my liking at Henri's. I felt masked, hidden from view in a way that was quite freeing. Comparing myself to the other women in the room, I began to feel more confident. The sultry glow of the dim lights, the throbbing music, and the thin veil over my eyes made me feel a little mysterious—not excited so much as exciting. I wasn't used to it.

"Very good, madame," he said, with a hint of a bow.

I stood to the side as a couple entered the room from the street and spoke with the maître d' about a table. They blocked my view of the door for a moment, and I did not see Oliver come in until he suddenly stepped out from behind them and addressed me.

"Anne." The warmth in his voice, despite the simplicity of the greeting, actually gave me goose flesh.

"Oliver, hello," I said, feeling awkward. I extended my gloved hand, and he took it, turning and tucking it inside his crooked elbow.

"Shall we go to our table?" he asked, and at my nod the maître d' immediately sprang into action and led us to a recessed table in a corner of the room.

"Will this do, Mr. Fielding?"

"Yes, thank you, Robbie."

"Robbie?" I asked, after the man had departed. "Not Roberto, or Jean-Christophe, or Armand?"

"Hmm, I see what you mean. I'll speak to him about a name change later. Might improve business," Oliver said.

"Not that business needs improving," I said, looking around as the place filled up. There were easily a dozen couples on the floor now, and the swirl of silk, the gleam of satin, and the bare arms and backs of women were set off by the uniformity of the men's black tuxedos and white dinner jackets. The kaleidoscopic patterns they made wove in and out with the music.

Oliver didn't answer as we settled into our seats. I examined our tiny, intimate space, tucked into the wall, and approved the simplicity of the décor. The richness of the room was due to the quality and textures of the materials rather than anything flashy or bright: deeply upholstered leather, fine linen, heavy silver, muted colors, fabric lamp shades. It was exceedingly well done.

We took our seats on the banquette and, with minimal adjustments, left about a foot and a half between us. I relaxed a little.

Oliver sat so that he was turned slightly toward me, his arm draped casually across the low back of the banquette. He offered me a cigarette from a silver case, and I took one, though I hadn't had one since college. He lit mine, then his own, and I smoked for a moment, content to say nothing, watching the dancers.

When I looked at him I found he was looking at me.

"This is a very different look for you," he said, trying to read my expression behind the black-net veil and the smoke drifting up from my cigarette.

"It's not my usual style," I said, suddenly self-conscious.

"You look lovely," he assured me. "Very fashionable."

I grinned. "That's not something I hear very often."

He chuckled in response. "Will you drink champagne with me?"

"What are we celebrating?" I asked.

"Celebrating? So you're a stickler for form. Isn't champagne its own reason?" He was clearly amused.

"But then it would just be wine, wouldn't it? The fun of drinking champagne is in the context, not the taste—we celebrate our victories with it. That's why champagne tastes like winning."

"You're a rather intellectual young woman, aren't you?" he

asked, and I noticed for the first time that he had a deep dimple on the left side of his mouth, just at the edge of his clipped, dark mustache.

"I read—it's my shameful little secret. Don't worry, you wouldn't be the first to find it unattractive."

He snorted a little, just a tiny exhalation through his nose that sent a stream of smoke down toward the table, a gesture that suggested exactly the outlook I'd hoped for. "What kind of a fool would I be to prefer my women brainless?"

"What kind of a fool would I be not to object to the suggestion that I am one of your women?" I countered, simultaneously offended by and attracted to his unusual, forceful style. He was being pushy, and I found I wanted to push back.

He threw back his head and laughed, and suddenly I was in the mood for champagne.

"Well played," he said. "But let me be clear on this: I do not find intelligence unattractive in a woman. Quite the opposite, in fact. Women who bore me are unattractive, and intelligence is anything but boring."

"You're a rather intellectual man, aren't you?" I asked, mocking us both. I felt both pleased and annoyed. He was flattering me, of course, but I liked it, even while I felt the condescension at its heart.

"I don't care what other people think, if that's what you mean—that's *my* dirty little secret."

"How lovely for you to be able to ignore everyone's expectations," I said. "If you were a woman you would certainly tell a different story."

"If I were a woman and I believed that, I would only be confirming everyone's expectations," he retorted.

Oh, this is quite nice, I thought. *Maybe too nice. Be careful, Anne.*

I didn't see him signal anyone, but suddenly there were two waiters standing in front of our table—one in a tuxedo with a bottle of champagne, which he presented ceremoniously to Oliver, the other hovering just behind and to the right of the first with a starched white linen napkin folded over his forearm, two champagne flutes held upside down, and a silver bucket filled with crushed ice for the table.

Oliver read the label, nodded, and handed the bottle back. The wine steward decanted the bottle—with a lovely, resounding pop and a bit of frothing—and poured a small amount in one of the glasses, handing it to me. The champagne was icy cold and so effervescent that I wondered if I could contain my first small sip in my mouth as it bubbled and expanded against my tongue. I nodded to Oliver, and within seconds, it seemed, we each had a glass, the bottle was on ice before us, and the men were gone. I almost clapped, it was all so well rehearsed.

Oliver picked up his glass, raised it, and gazed directly into my eyes. "To new friends," he said.

"To new friends," I agreed, touching his glass with mine and drinking.

"If we must celebrate something," Oliver said, "and I think you may be right about that, you should choose. What shall we drink to?"

"Oh, there are a number of things I could name," I evaded.

"Such as?"

"Such as, my sister Maria Cristina. She's only recently come into my life, and she is a wonderful, happy addition."

"An excellent choice—and one that says as much about you as your sister," he said but did not raise his glass. "What else?"

"There's my boat, which I hope to have on the water in a few weeks. And there's the mill," I added. "This may be indelicate of me, but you must know that Father and I are both hoping that the family business will be resurrected, and that a lot of good people in Milford can begin to put their lives back together."

"Why limit ourselves to just one?" He raised his glass again and spoke, his eyes never leaving mine. "To Maria Cristina, and to family coming home. To the completion of your first boat, and to her maiden voyage. And to putting Milford back on its feet."

I couldn't speak. He touched his glass gently to mine and drank. I felt the lump in my throat, and my eyes burned, but when that brief moment passed I felt lighter, more hopeful than I had in a long time. Something about him—his confidence, his keen intelligence, his easy acceptance of who I was and what I wanted—made me feel that anything was possible.

I drank, more deeply this time, to give myself a moment before I had to speak, but Oliver deftly changed the subject and regaled me with stories about learning to sail at Newport when he first came to Rhode Island from the Midwest ten years earlier. He had tried to pretend he knew much more than he did, tried to blend in with the New England aristocrats who'd been born with silver spoons in their mouths and the helm of a yacht in their hands, and he had failed.

His father had been in automobiles—not in a big way, he said, but it was enough to get him to Yale, enough to get him to New England, to the ocean, and to the wealthy industrialists and bankers whose saltwater pastimes had been so alien to him. It was the funny, self-deprecating story of a self-made man, punctuated by physical comedy, and I liked him better for telling it.

He asked if I cared to dance then, and I did. We moved to the floor, and he put his arms around me for the first time. I had danced with boys before, of course, and with Will most often, but this was different. Oliver was older, in his mid-thirties, I thought, and his experience was apparent in everything he did. His arm was behind me, his hand firmly on the small of my back as he guided me around the floor with the merest pressure from his fingertips. The band was playing softly and a young woman in a strapless, sequined blue dress crooned "Smoke Gets in Your Eyes." Her smooth, throaty voice washed over us as we moved in perfect rhythm on the now-crowded floor.

Oliver was exactly my height when I wore heels, and this, too, was in marked contrast to Will, who towered over me when we danced. I had always enjoyed dancing with Will, even as teenagers when we were awkward and self-conscious, in part because his size had made me feel small and feminine by comparison. When Oliver pulled me close I had expected to feel clumsy and mannish, but I felt nothing of the sort. I felt every inch of my height in his embrace, and I felt no less feminine, no less desirable because I did not have to look up to meet his eyes. It was, quite simply, a revelation.

As we turned about the floor, our feet stepping in and out without falter, I became increasingly aware of the warmth of Oliver's hand on my back, his face next to mine, not quite touching. The netting on my hat brushed his cheek once—that's how close we were. I could feel his breath, and knew he felt mine.

And then the song was over and we returned to our table. Oliver ordered for us, after asking my permission, and we dined exquisitely on oysters Rockefeller, lobster tails with rich drawn butter, asparagus hollandaise, and pink grapefruit sections on watercress with creamy Roquefort cheese. We talked lightly throughout the meal, touching briefly on books—he said he didn't read much popular fiction and felt only disdain for all those American writers who'd run off to Paris, writing in self-important, critical tones about their country. He saw the danger of contagion in their disillusionment and too much ego in the endless self-analysis of their characters.

He liked biographies, though, and to my surprise he loved movie musicals, loved the big, splashy production numbers in *Gold Diggers of Broadway* and *Girl Crazy*. He liked any form of entertainment, he confided, where the underdog wins against all odds. I agreed, and told him that was why I was a Red Sox fan. Letting Babe Ruth go to the Yankees had merely insured we would always be the underdog, I explained. Boston was the team to root for, and we should all cheer to see New York defeated by anybody. He said he hadn't meant to suggest that winning made you the bad guy, but in terms of baseball he could see my point.

We finished the bottle of champagne and were lingering over coffee and some kind of lemony tart when he asked me about Will. He had been telling me that he hoped to sail leisurely up the coast to Maine with friends the following summer, since he hadn't had a proper vacation in nearly five years. He was no longer a hopeless sailor, he said. He now owned his own yacht and was hooked. Then he asked if I would be married by next summer, and if not, if I might like to go sailing.

"What?" I asked, completely taken aback.

"Married. You and your fiancé—Bill, I think your father said. Bill Dekker. When are you two getting married?"

"It's Will," I said. "And we're not." I felt as unsophisticated as I've ever felt in my life, despite the glamour-girl hat and veil. "I'm not engaged."

"No?" he pressed.

"No. Definitely not," I said firmly.

"Good. Now let's talk about that boat of yours," he said, changing the subject so quickly that I had difficulty catching up.

"What do you want to know?" I asked.

"I'm interested in it," he said, shrugging. "Is it for sale?"

"No," I said quickly. She was mine and I had no interest in parting with her.

Oliver smiled. "That's what I thought. But I liked what I saw of it, and your rationale for the design. You said you'd designed her for someone who wasn't an experienced sailor. How do you think someone who's never been on the water at all would fare in her?"

"Well," I hesitated, not sure where he was going. "I suppose it would depend in part on the person, his general good sense and judgment. It would depend on the weather, and where the boat was taken. But I'd say a complete novice would do just fine in her, provided he was given some clear instructions for operating the motor and didn't do anything stupid, like take her on rough seas or out of inland waters. She's not made for either."

Oliver was nodding, listening intently, watching my face as I spoke.

"Okay," he said at length. "How would you feel about becoming a professional?"

"I beg your pardon?"

"How would you feel about taking a boat order from me?"

"Oh! I don't know. I suppose I— Really?" I interrupted myself, unable to contain my excitement and play the seasoned business-woman. "You want me to build you a boat?"

"I've been out to Mr. Johnson's since I saw you last. I had other business in Milford and decided to take another, closer look at your boat. I talked to him about your experience, your craftsmanship. He says you're a first-rate carpenter, and that your design is a good one for my purposes. I believe he knows what he's talking about, and I'm willing to bank on it."

"Well, I'm kind of slow," I hedged, thinking fast—would I get a down payment, a construction draw to buy my materials, or would I have to scramble with the household money and get it back in the end? "How many boats are we talking about?" I asked, suddenly alarmed.

"Take it easy, kid," he said, laughing as he watched me, my mental calculations no doubt written plainly on my face. "I'm talking about one boat. One boat, identical to the one you're building now, finished by June next year for the summer season. I want it for my largest cottage, which, frankly, is hardly a cottage. The same family has rented it each summer for the past three years, and they've got two sons who would love a boat like yours. I like to keep my tenants happy, and I don't want to lose this particular family. He's a district court judge in Providence, and has been helpful to me on more than one occasion.

"So," he said. "What do you say?" He leaned in, eyeing me intently, and his tone became soft and persuasive. "Maybe in a few years you'll have your own yard, with a dozen master carpenters on the payroll, and you'll design and build only your own models."

I clasped my hands together over my chest, my smile wide, and laughed out loud. "Oh, what a fabulous dream—but I could never do it," I finished, the joy draining out of the moment for me.

"Why in the world not?" he asked, a little impatiently.

"You don't understand. You're talking about me. About me working—in a man's job, no less. A ship's carpenter for hire. Have you met my father?"

He laughed at that. "Yes, I have. I see what you mean. But the

Samuel Dodge I met is immensely proud of you, and he clearly adores you. The only questions you have to ask yourself are what do you really want, and how badly do you want it. Nothing else should matter."

"But he's my father," I said, with no hesitation. "And he wouldn't want me . . . I mean I work down at Ezra's now but it's private . . . and temporary. I couldn't."

"Well, that's your choice, I suppose," he said, shrugging as if he had lost interest.

"I don't know . . ." I said, wanting him to somehow make it happen or show me how I could.

"Look," he said. "Don't decide now. Think it over. Get used to the idea first. Then we can really think about how to make it work. You have to take these things one step at a time—otherwise you'll be too overwhelmed to move forward. Deal?" He put his hand out, the businessman's honor code.

I hesitated for just an instant, then put my hand in his, and we shook. I felt a little guilty, and even looked around, as if I had agreed to something that I hadn't really thought through yet, something that would disrupt the fragile balance of my family.

"Okay, we'll talk about it later," I agreed, gently pulling my hand from his. "Let's talk about you."

"All right, but I warn you: I'm not a particularly fascinating topic."

"I'll be the judge of that," I said sternly.

"What do you want to know?" he asked, lighting a cigarette.

"For starters, I want to know if your reputation for union busting is deserved."

He coughed on the inhale, and I waited while he shook out his match. "You don't fool around, do you?" he asked.

"Well, I've reason to be interested in the issue. I'd like to know where you stand."

"Where any ethical man would," he said easily, recovering his poise. "I stand for jobs—reasonable pay for an honest day's work. I stand for profit, without which jobs are not even remotely possible."

"That's not exactly a stand. Who would disagree with you?" I asked, impatient to discover who he really was.

"Fair enough," he said. "I meant what I said, but what you really want to know is whether I accept the premise that so many do, that those who work for me have a say in how I run my business."

"Well, without them you wouldn't have a business to run," I said.

"That's true, and the gamble we all take is whether I can find someone willing to do things my way. If I can, then I've won, and any employee who was betting I'd have to give in to his demands in order to keep my business running has lost."

"And the unions upset the balance?" I asked, fascinated by him despite myself.

"And the unions upset the balance," he agreed, squinting as the smoke from his cigarette drifted upward.

"Some would argue that the unions restore the balance," I countered, oddly eager to cross this man. "You can't really argue that you and the individual worker are on equal footing."

Oliver frowned as he stubbed his cigarette out in the ash tray. "Look, Anne, I'm not ignorant of the hard knocks workingmen have taken these past few years. But I am not willing to cripple my ability to make money—which does, in fact, produce jobs—by giving away what I have. In the long run, while it may feel and sound noble, no one is served, not even the most humble worker, by simply spending money—money must be put to work. It may not be pleasant or popular, but I have a responsibility to think about the long term, even when people are starving."

I hesitated, drawn to his explanation. He was a capitalist like my father, and the familiar-sounding views about money and class urged me to forget what I'd felt at the union rally. But something from that day still remained, and I seized it. "It's lonely at the top? You poor thing."

"Touché," he said, laughing, and I think he really meant it. "But don't dismiss my point, Anne. If I gave my wealth away instead of using it to make more—more for me, and for everyone who works for and with me—in a very short time the tiny fraction of poverty I had been able to eliminate would reappear, and I would be powerless to do anything about it. I'd be standing in the breadline with everybody else."

"Okay," I said, "very persuasive. But are those the only alternatives: profit, where everybody wins, or poverty, where everybody loses? I don't know that the choice is that stark, or the outcomes so sure. I also think there's a difference between jobs and wealth. Your employees don't build the kind of security you do simply because they have jobs, and yet you alone determine what and how much of your business you will risk.

"And," I chided, smiling to soften my lecture, "you've avoided my question about organized labor entirely."

"You're not making this easy for me," he said. "I'm not used to being on the witness stand."

He really was charming, I thought. "I'm not trying to make it hard for you—or easy, for that matter. I just want to know what you really think."

He paused and looked at me appraisingly before he spoke. "What I really think is that everything I have I earned. I think that you would be outraged if someone tried to strong-arm a workingman out of his meager pay in order to give it to someone who needed it more. What's the difference? I've earned more than a common laborer does, but does that make it any less reprehensible for someone to take it from me? I might even argue that it's *more* reprehensible, because only the worker and his family benefit when he gets paid. When I make money, I don't bury it in the backyard in a coffee can. I build my business. Each job I'm able to create, each family that eats on the salaries I pay—they're all dependent on my making money. I own a resort, commercial properties, two worsted mills, and an interest in a carpet factory—that's more than two hundred employees, most of them with families to feed. Will you be the one to choose the men I have to fire because the money I would have paid them has been given away to some other men, somewhere else?"

I couldn't answer him. His argument appeared unassailable, his position amoral at worst—and his conviction was overwhelming. I felt young, out of my depth. I tried to recapture the feeling I'd had standing at the Sullivan's truck listening to the labor organizer rally the townspeople yesterday, but the immediacy of the experience was gone, and Oliver was sitting right here.

"Well, of course, when you put it like that . . ." I said, the uncertainty apparent in my voice.

"How would you prefer I put it?" he asked, pressing me. I had begun this interrogation, undeterred from asking him hard, personal questions, and he had every right to insist that we play it out.

"I don't know," I said, angry with myself for my inability to make my case, but stubbornly refusing to concede. "I suppose you think you've won," I accused him.

"Don't think of it that way," he said, taking my hand and leaning in toward me. "Listen to me, Anne. This is important." He waited, refusing to let go of my hand, forcing me to meet his eyes. "I don't want you defeated, or embarrassed. If you agree with me, now that I've said my piece, it's not because I've won but because you're smart enough to change your opinion when you hear a better argument. You'll go to sleep tonight wiser than you were when you woke up this morning, and if you're lucky that'll be the case every day of your life. Surely that's not defeat. How can that be anything but a victory?"

I had heard this kind of thing in college, from my professors, but it had always seemed so abstract, mere mental exercise. Did Oliver think this way—talk this way—all the time? I felt sharp, challenged, and I imagined feeling this way every day. I was enamored, I knew, and it made me nervous—there must be a catch, something dangerous here.

It would be so easy, I thought, to grant him the position of mentor. But pride reared its ugly head and drove all thoughts of pleasing him from my mind.

I withdrew my hand, sat up straight, and said in the iciest voice

I could manage, "You misunderstand me. I am not conceding defeat. I am simply acknowledging that for now I cannot hope to persuade you. At best you have my withdrawal."

"My *God*, you're a stubborn woman!" he said, dropping my hand in annoyance. He turned from me then, staring moodily at the dance floor and lighting a cigarette. He did not offer me one.

"I tried to warn you," I said, gathering my gloves and bag from the seat beside me. I stood and muttered a stiff good-night, but he stopped me.

"Where are you going?" he asked, rising as well, his manners intact.

"Home," I said simply.

"Don't be silly," he said. "You're not a child—stop acting like one. I haven't had this much fun in months, and I doubt you have, either. Sit down. Please."

I looked at him, frowning. "Fun! This is fun?"

"Yes," he said. "Of course it is. Haven't you heard a word I've said to you tonight?" He rolled his eyes, exasperated. I couldn't help but laugh. I was indeed being childish. I sat back down and so did he.

"God, what's wrong with me?" I wondered out loud.

"There's nothing wrong with you. You're smart, you're stubborn, and you hate to lose." He smiled then, a twisted little smile, before draining the last of his champagne. "Sounds like somebody else I know and greatly admire. No wonder I like you so much."

I was relieved that we appeared to be on friendly terms again. But something had changed, and the evening was clearly over. We were both guarded now.

He asked if I wanted more champagne, or coffee, and when I said no, he suggested that I might want to get on the road since I had a thirty-minute drive back to Milford. I agreed, and he got up from the table, stepping back to let me precede him to the front door. When we reached the foyer Robbie was nowhere in sight. I handed my valet ticket to one of the uniformed boys who ran to bring my car around.

We were alone in the dark-paneled foyer then, and Oliver grabbed my hand and led me behind a palm tree.

"I'd like to see you again," he said softly. "Don't let a spirited discussion chase you away. In fact, I'm hoping it will draw you back for more. There must be hundreds of things we can argue about."

"Well, yes," I said, holding up my hand and pretending to count the possibilities off on my fingers. "There's the existence of God, President Roosevelt's tax plan, the Red Sox starting lineup—"

"Come here," he said, his hands on my upper arms. He pulled me in close to kiss me, and I saw gold flecks in his eyes. My body trembled, waiting for the first touch of his mouth on mine, and then we heard the street sounds coming through the open front door and the discreet cough of the valet.

I retreated from Oliver's embrace, touched my hat to confirm it was on straight.

"Ready?" Oliver asked.

I nodded, and he took my elbow and walked me to the curb where my car sat, engine purring, ready to go home. Oliver opened my door, and I turned in the circle of his arm and the door frame to face him.

"Thank you, Oliver," I said, meaning it. "I had a wonderful evening."

"The pleasure was most certainly mine," he said with a sincerity that pleased me. I held out my hand, but when he took it he turned it over and, with his other hand, gently spread my fingers. Then he raised my open hand to his mouth and kissed the tender skin of my palm, just in the center, very lightly. It was shockingly intimate, and desire washed over me.

"Good night, then," I said, my voice shaking, as I pulled my hand back.

He let go immediately, and I climbed into the driver's seat. He shut my door without a word, and I drove back to Milford down the darkened coastal roads, marveling at the beauty of the moonlight flickering over the waters of Narragansett Bay, the skin of my palm where he had pressed his mouth still burning.

CHAPTER TWELVE

August in Rhode Island is a volatile, untamed thing. Some days are blisteringly hot, hazy and breathless. Others are foggy, the constant drip and drizzle of moisture bone-chilling, the condensation so thick it is indistinguishable from rain. The light changes, becoming diffused, as if shining through a silk veil in an effort to soften the coming blow. The days shorten as the month progresses, and the winds that blow inland bite, a reminder of how bitter—and inescapable—winter is. Summer spends itself on squalls that spring up unexpectedly, pounding the coast with rain and ripping shingles off homes. Hurricanes gather themselves in warmer waters until September, when they lumber inexorably up the eastern seaboard, the onslaught of wind and tidal surge wiping out whole towns, crops and livestock and hope.

I have always loved August for its sheer unpredictability. Each deep inhalation of warm, late-summer air insists I pay attention, appreciate, store up warmth and food and memories for the bleak, brutal days ahead.

August that summer kept a slow, even pace so as not to call attention to itself, and we were happy to oblige. Its first days were deceptively calm, warm and dry, inviting us to relax. I went to Ezra's nearly every day, intent on finishing the boat. I was so close, eager to get her out on the water before it grew too cold. And, of course, after my dinner with Oliver, I had begun to think about what it would be like to keep doing this, not as some quirky hobby, an indulgence of my father's until I was safely married, but as a career, designing and building through the years, growing and changing along with the boats I built. I imagined myself an independent businesswoman, a skilled and respected craftsman.

My daydreams during those first days of August were all about boats, and about a life I had never seen a woman live. I allowed myself a glimpse—just a glimpse—of a life with purpose, making things that were beautiful and useful. The act of doing something that mattered stretching out endlessly in front of me. I began to believe that I had the strength to fight for that life.

August lulled me with its blue skies, scudding white clouds, gently lapping tides that marked the passing hours I could never get back. I dreamed of my boat when I was away from her, and when I was at Ezra's I rolled her in the cradles when the planking was complete, eager to get started on the deck and seats. Maria Cristina waited at home, or wandered Milford alone when Deirdre Sullivan was busy with chores. I was obsessed with finishing the boat now that she had begun to take on her finished shape beneath my hands. When I caught sight of Maria Cristina digging in the sand with a stick, or standing silhouetted against the sunset while I worked, I told myself that we would have a lifetime to spend together. I could not be bothered with her just now—or with guilt, either.

Ezra watched, saying little. He had steadfastly refused to talk about the Da Silva murder, about the missing chisel, and—though I'm ashamed to say it—I did not pursue it. It was a tragedy, but not mine, and I was content to let it slip from my consciousness.

Still hungry for facts about my parents, about Inêz and her family, I instead badgered Ezra about them while I worked, trying to pry information out of him. He was reluctant, and sometimes walked off without a word in answer to a pointed question. Other times he talked, even if only cryptically, and I pressed him hard when I could. It was all I had.

"Ezra," I asked on one such day, "how did my father and Inêz come to marry? It seems so unlikely to me—he talks as though he hated her."

Ezra, clearly annoyed by my lack of perception, answered tersely. "Well, a' course he didn't always feel that way."

"So he did love her once, and she loved him?"

"Guess so," he said.

"But you were there, right? You were her godfather. What happened?"

"I wasn't a part of that," he said. "She was young then, younger than you are now, an' she didn't want nobody tellin' her what to do, godfather or not." He shrugged, indicating that there was no story here, nothing of interest. "They met. People do. She was strong-willed, didn't care what her folks thought. They got married."

"But didn't it seem odd that he would marry a young Portuguese woman whose parents barely spoke English?" I asked. "You know him. Doesn't that seem unlikely?"

"I s'pose," he conceded. "But he was young, too. I expect he knew what he'd become, but for a time there, maybe he didn't want to. Maybe he wanted to be somebody else."

I thought about that as I nailed supports for the middle and forward seats on the side cleats. I was putting in the reinforcing pieces for each interior seat, but it was tricky, involving compound cuts at each end and top, fitting both the flare and the angle of the sides, all the while trying to imagine my father as a young man, desperate to break free of his own father's expectations, doing something passionate and outrageous. It was not an easy picture to conjure.

"So he married Inêz as a form of rebellion?"

Ezra shrugged, pulling on his pipe. "Who knows? I'm jus' sayin' that was a part of it. For both of 'em."

Of course, I thought, her parents would have objected as well.

They had spent their entire lives isolated among other immigrants. What must they have thought, or feared, when their young daughter announced her intention to marry this rich, conservative young Protestant whose family was so powerful that they employed most of the local Portuguese workers in their mill? What had they felt when their daughter left the Catholic Church to marry him? What had Inêz felt?

"What was my mother like as a young woman?" I asked.

Ezra paused before he answered. He had not started a new boat after Stevie Sullivan's. He sat in his chair down by the water instead, idly whittling while I worked. I knew his leg had been bothering him. Occasionally, without thinking, he reached down to gently massage his swollen, mangled knee, but I couldn't say anything. My concern would only annoy him.

"She was a handful," he said. "Ben spoiled her, an' she got too big for her britches. She hurt 'em sometimes, things she'd say to 'em. But all kids hurt their parents, an' then they grow up."

I felt a little uncomfortable, wondering about the ways I had hurt my own father when I was younger. The ways I still hurt him.

"So she saw my father as a way out of that, a way to have a more exciting, interesting life?"

"Who knows what she thought?" Ezra asked.

His refusal to draw any conclusions, make any firm statements, was maddening. I scowled in frustration, sweating and squinting in the sun. The cuts on either end of the forward seat board were done, but before I could fasten it to the supports and the reinforcing piece spanning the hull, I had to bevel the top edges with the plane and round the corners a bit with a chisel where the seat met the upright cleats.

"You never talked to her about Father, before they got married?"

"No," he said. "It weren't my place."

"Did you approve?"

"I don't know whether I did or didn't," he said. "It was a long time ago." He inched farther up toward the edge of his chair in an attempt to ease his leg, his pipe clenched between his teeth as the wood shavings dropped from his knife to a small fawn-colored pile between his feet.

We worked in silence then for a time until I thought of another question.

"Once they got married, do you think she was happy?"

It took Ezra so long to respond that I began to think he wouldn't answer at all. When he finally did it was with a surprising mixture of reluctance and compassion, as though he wanted to remain silent but could not, in good conscience.

"I expect she liked the freedom. She— No, Annie, for her bein' married *was* freedom," he insisted, seeing the look of disbelief on my face. "She was a modern girl, with old-world parents. You can't imagine it," he said, with a pointed look at my work pants and stained cotton shirt, the tools at my feet and in my hands. "Not you or Maria Cristina, now that she's livin' with you."

He was right. I had been struck by how isolated and protected Maria Cristina had been, how formal her manners were when she first arrived. Now, after only a month or so, I was happy to see her exploring her world, making friends, gaining a level of both independence and self-confidence that I thought was healthy, despite what our grandparents had obviously thought. I could only imagine how much more difficult Inêz's situation had been all those years ago. How she might have seen the big house, the money, playing the well-dressed hostess to important men as freedom—freedom from her parents, and from the Church, too, which appeared to work very hard to keep the old ways alive, in part by tying girls to motherhood, or God, or both.

Inêz must have dreamed of a different life, dreamed the way I dream, I thought, feeling a kinship with my mother that I'd never expected to feel. "It sounds romantic. They risked a lot to marry. So why didn't it work?" I was more confused than ever.

"They grew up," he said.

"What does that mean?" I asked.

"It means life catches up with ever'body. Inêz decided her folks wasn't so bad after all, like most kids do. She wanted 'em around, and they obliged. They came up to the big house a lot, especially after Ben stopped working so much. When Samuel's father died the mill became his responsibility. But lots o' mills was closin', or movin' down South. He needed help, certain kinds of friends, and he found 'em in Providence, in his father's old cronies, the bankers and politicians. Pretty soon he was walkin' an' talkin' jus' like 'em. Inêz's family—Estevão, especially—was at odds with them folks, naturally. She filled up the house with her Portuguese family, their friends and their immigrant politics. Ain't nothin' worse than them kinda arguments in your own house." Ezra paused for a moment to draw on his pipe before he continued. "That was the end of 'em. Only one thing ever made 'em happy again, but it didn't last long."

"What was that?" I asked.

"You," he said.

I was stunned. "Me?" I had forgotten that these two young people were my parents. That Inêz had been pregnant, that I had been a baby they held in their arms.

"They was happy about you," said Ezra. "But you made it worse, too."

You're too old to get your feelings hurt by this, I told myself. "I made it worse?" I asked, and my voice sounded small to me.

"You know what I mean," he said, his gruff voice meant to convey his apology. "They wanted you, but it weren't enough to make 'em happy with each another. Nothin' could've done that, stubborn as they both were."

"Did she talk to you about it?"

"Nah. We wasn't too close for a coupla years, but after you was born she started coming down here again, like when she was a girl."

This was a new thought, my mother at my age coming down here to Ezra's. Maybe standing right where I was standing now, I thought, inexplicably pleased.

"Was she interested in boats?" I asked.

"Ha!" he said, snorting at the very thought. He pulled on his pipe and blew a thick cloud of gray-white smoke. "Not her," he said. "But she brought you, and here you are still."

I smiled and kept working. "Did she talk to you about her marriage to Father?" I asked. "About what was wrong?"

"Not much. Though she liked to chatter. 'Bout nothin'. She jus' needed the company, I figured. She was unhappy, and lonely. Thought the marriage had been a mistake."

We sat then, for a while, me imagining Inêz and he remembering her loneliness, her despair. I waited, listening to the bubbling, sucking sound of his pipe as he drew on it.

"I told her they was jus' figurin' out what all kids do, eventually. That you turn out like your folks, no matter how hard you try not to. An' that the person you've up an' married ain't the picnic you thought he'd be. I told her worse things had happened."

"Did that help?" I asked, hoping to hear that their relationship had improved, despite knowing how the story ended.

"No," said Ezra. "She said it was more'n that. Turned out she was right."

I was suddenly defensive. "Was that her excuse for having an affair and leaving us?"

He didn't answer, just pulled harder on his pipe, and I moved around to the starboard side of the boat. I was relieved that the momentary empathy I'd felt for Inêz, the shocking sensation of feeling close to her, had been replaced by the familiar sense of her absence, the certainty of her betrayal. I couldn't see Ezra anymore with the boat positioned between us, and I needed the seclusion. After a moment, I calmed down enough to talk to him again.

"Did she tell you about him?" I asked from behind the boat. "Maria Cristina's father?"

The wind had sprung up, and it cut coldly through my sweat-damp shirt. Some low clouds had moved in, and the sunshine was now only intermittent. I felt a chill run through me, and I shivered, straightening up and looking over the hull to where Ezra sat, silent and still, his knife clutched so tightly in his fingers that his knuckles were white.

He didn't look up, just went back to whittling, his back straight and his mouth shut hard. "I don't know nothin' about that," he said after a moment.

I cleaned up and collected Maria Cristina, and we made our way back down the sandy fork and the old mill road toward town. It was getting late, and we were both hungry. We picked up the pace to race each other the last hundred yards or so, and when we got close we saw that Mrs. Hatcher had her front door open and was beckoning us in. We veered toward her door, figuring the food would be better than anything we might find at home. We did not need to confer on the decision.

Mrs. Hatcher ushered us inside as the breeze whipped the drapes at the window into a crazy, flailing mess. She shut the front door behind us, and the sudden stillness in the living room made the coastal winds outside seem far more than they really were. Still, I wondered if it would rain, and if it did how long it would last. Days of rain would definitely delay the completion of my boat.

"Well, girls, how are you?" asked Mrs. Hatcher as she bent to switch on a lamp, flooding the living room with light.

I opened my mouth to answer, but Maria Cristina was sniffing the air like a hunting dog on a scent. "Excuse me, your kitchen smells good," she said. "Lemon squares?"

Laughing, Mrs. Hatcher crooked her index finger and beckoned us into her warm, brightly lit kitchen. Katie and her infant daughter were seated at the kitchen table, where a baker's rack of lemon squares was cooling.

"Katie," I cried. "What a wonderful surprise! I didn't know you were coming," I added with a reproachful look at Mrs. Hatcher.

"Don't give me that face, missy. I didn't know until this morning that they were coming. You weren't home to hear the news, so I've been looking out the window waiting for you."

"How long can you stay?" I asked, delighted to see her. Katie was two years older than I, but we had been very close before her marriage to Mike Flynn, after which she'd moved up to Woonsocket, just this side of the Massachusetts line. When I was growing up, Mrs. Hatcher had kept me over at her house every day after school while my father worked, and Katie and I had become fast friends. I was far more the tomboy than Katie ever was, however, and she was several years my senior. Predictably, she changed from a girl to a woman long before I did, and she left me behind in more ways than one.

"Just a few days. Mike had to come to—" She broke off at a glance from her mother, then flushed, finishing her sentence in a rush and tumble of words. "Mike had some business here. I decided at the last minute to bring Lizzie and come too."

I glanced at her, but then the baby shrieked in protest because we weren't paying her any attention, startling us all into laughter, which she seemed to find very gratifying. I hugged Katie then, and Mrs. Hatcher introduced her to Maria Cristina—or Maria, as she called her—and we settled down at the table with coffee and milk and still-warm lemon squares.

"Tell me everything!" said Katie. "I'm stuck in my house with a baby, just an old married lady who never gets out anymore!"

"There's very little to tell," I protested. "You know how it is—you haven't been gone that long. We keep up the house, go to church. A picture in Providence once in a while. We go to Dekker's, and Jablonski's, and the Sullivan truck to see what they've brought in—oh, Stevie Sullivan fishes with his father now, that's new. We go down to Ezra Johnson's."

"Well, the fact that it's 'we' instead of 'I' is new," Katie said, looking warmly at Maria Cristina, whose face was beginning to look as though it had been powdered with sugar.

"True, true," I said, eyeing Maria Cristina with affection. "It's been wonderful. It feels sometimes like we've always been sisters."

Maria Cristina nodded in agreement as she concentrated on licking the lemony filling off of her fingers, one by one. "Always," she said.

"And how is Will?" asked Katie with a sly look.

"Excuse me, Will wants to marry her," Maria Cristina said.

"Maria Cristina!" I said.

Katie laughed, and Mrs. Hatcher jumped into the breach. "Oh, Anne, honestly. Will wanting to marry you is hardly news. That poor boy has been mooning over you since you were children. And you treat him dreadfully—which isn't news, either."

"I do not!" I glared at Maria Cristina for steering the conversation along these lines, but she was completely unaffected, having just started on her third lemon square.

Katie was laughing at me while she jiggled the baby up and down on her lap and tried to keep her from twisting and lunging for the coffee cup which sat just out of reach on the table.

"Annie Dodge, you know it's true. Every girl in town gave up on Will by the time he was fifteen years old because he's never had eyes for anybody but you. He's got the patience of a saint. Are you ever going to say yes?"

"That," I said haughtily, trying my best to sound injured and yet somehow above it all, "is none of your business. Perhaps I won't marry at all."

"What about Mr. Fielding?" Maria Cristina asked brightly. "Does he want to marry you also?"

I closed my eyes, hoping it would all go away, but when I opened them again Mrs. Hatcher and Katie were both staring at me. I had some news after all, it seemed.

So I told them—in the briefest possible way—about Oliver Fielding, stressing that he was a business associate of Father's and that the conversation on our one and only date had been primarily about the mill. Katie was frowning, and I felt a little annoyed. What did she care if I stepped out with Oliver, I thought, or anyone else? I shot Maria Cristina a wait-till-we-get-home look, but she was smiling and laughing at the baby, pointedly ignoring me.

"What about this boy who was killed?" Katie asked, changing the subject.

"There's very little to tell," I told her. "It appears to be a murder, and Sheriff Tucker is investigating."

"Does he have any suspects?" she asked.

"No, not that I know of. Farley asked Ezra some hard questions at first, but he doesn't seem interested in him anymore." This was true, but if Farley didn't find another suspect I worried that he eventually would come back to Ezra.

"Remember when we ran away that summer?" Katie asked, and we both laughed. She had always been like this—sensitive to those around her, steering people away from what divided them and toward what they shared instead.

"What happened?" asked Maria Cristina.

"Will and I were, what, fourteen?" Katie asked, looking at me, and then addressed Maria Cristina. "Will and I decided that we were too old to be told what to do, and that we were going to run away. We had no plan at all, but we were determined to go. We were going to show everybody."

"It was me who came up with the plan—Boston, remember?" I asked, laughing at the memory. "They had a circus and we were going to get jobs feeding the animals!"

Mrs. Hatcher was laughing now, too. "Will had an old rowboat they'd decided to use," she told Maria Cristina.

"That's right," agreed Katie. "We had packed some sandwiches and a blanket, in case it took us more than a day to get to wherever we were going. We were just about ready to shove off when Anne showed up. 'Where are you going?' she whined. 'I want to come, too!' We tried to give her the slip, but she wouldn't budge. Finally I yelled at her to go home, that she was too young to come with us."

Maria Cristina stared at Katie, eating up the story. "Then what happened?"

"Well, of course Anne refused to leave, said she'd run and tell our mothers if we didn't let her come! I was furious—"

"Yes, and as I recall you pinched me!"

"Well, you deserved it! Will felt sorry for her and said she could come," Katie told Maria Cristina. "And of course she took over the whole plan, decided we would go to Boston. So we set off across the bay late in the afternoon, probably heading east toward Portsmouth. Will rowed, I kept lookout for rocks and sandbars, and Anne cried."

"I did not!" I protested, but my laughter undercut my indignation somewhat. "To hear you tell it I spent my entire childhood crying!"

"Excuse me, what happened then?" prodded Maria Cristina.

"Well, it started to get dark, and the bay was getting rough," said Katie, her voice low. "We had no lights, no life preservers, no more food—we had eaten our sandwiches while we were still tied to the dock! Will got tired after rowing for an hour or two and had just let the oars rest in their locks for a moment when the wind really picked up and we started to pitch. We grabbed the gunwales to steady ourselves, and the oars slid out and into the water. It was so dark that within seconds we couldn't see them, though they must have been floating right next to us, at least for a while."

I recalled that night, and the terror we had felt as the night and cold waters of Narragansett Bay seemed to threaten us from every side. When the oars slid into the water I knew what it meant.

"What did you do?" asked Maria Cristina, clearly alarmed.

"Well, what could we do?" asked Katie, teasing out the drama. "It was pitch-dark by then. At first we told one another that we were a few hundred yards from Boston, and we'd probably make landfall soon even without the oars. When that didn't happen, and when we heard far off ahead of us the foghorn of what was clearly a huge ship, we knew we were in deep waters, in the dead of night, drifting who-knows-where on a rising sea. The boat was pitching fearfully, the waves were getting bigger and coming over the sides, and we were soon drenched and freezing. I don't mind telling you that at that point we were all terrified."

Maria Cristina's eyes were huge. Mrs. Hatcher had picked up her knitting from the basket she kept on the counter by the back door and was working steadily, a smile playing about her mouth.

"We were feeling pretty desperate," Katie continued. "The boat was pitching and rolling, and we were taking on water. We had no idea which direction Boston was in—or home either, for that matter, which by then we all would've preferred. We were alone, wet and cold and scared, and when we heard *that sound*, we knew we were going to die."

"What did you hear?" asked Maria Cristina breathlessly.

"Pounding surf. We were approaching land, and the tide was running in to a rocky shore. The waves looked as tall as you are now, their troughs as deep again, and they sucked us toward the rocks. We knew the boat would be smashed to pieces and we would all be sent to a watery grave."

Maria Cristina had grown a little pale, and I looked at Katie with a warning in my eyes. "Well, it probably wasn't that bad," I said.

"Oh, it *was* that bad," she said, her eyes never leaving Maria Cristina's. "We could just make out the whitecaps leaping and foaming around us, and as the surf pulled us in closer, to the mouth of the river, inching us in toward those deadly, jagged rocks, the mill suddenly loomed out of the night, the only immovable thing visible between the black sky and the dark, towering sea. We had drifted back toward home, but into the bay off the mill where many a boat had been destroyed in foul weather. The ship's horn we thought we'd heard had come from the Point Judith lighthouse—it hadn't burned down yet back then. We drew closer, hanging on to the sides for dear life. This was the end. We would be crushed against the rocks, our boat broken like a toy. We were filled with fear and regret. We hadn't even told our families good-bye, and now they would find our bodies washed up on shore in the morning. We had all begun to cry— especially Anne—and our voices rose above the noise of the storm in a last, desperate wail," she said, then paused for effect. ". . . And then we heard it."

"What? What did you hear?" said Maria Cristina, anxious to know the outcome.

"We heard Ezra Johnson's voice, deep as the ocean itself, not fifty feet from our bow.

"'What're you fool kids doin' out here?' he shouted.

"'Save us!' we cried. 'We don't want to die!'

"'Nobody's dyin',' he said. 'Keep your shirts on.'

"And something happened then, something we've never been able to explain. The sky seemed to lighten and we found it was only dusk. The sea calmed right away. We looked at the shoreline, at those deadly rocks that spilled down from the mill property into the cove, and, lo and behold, the tide ran softly in and out, back to where we sat in our little rowboat, drifting back toward home."

Ezra had indeed appeared like a vision, grumbling about what fools we were and wading out to hip-deep water and catching our bow with a gaffing hook and pulling us in as the breakers tried to knock him off his feet. He pulled us to shallower water and picked me up, though he made Will and Katie jump out and drag the boat up, ruining their shoes in the process, because they were old enough to have known better, he said.

Ezra had carried me to shore, cradling me, my head on the side of his lame leg, and each time he took a limping step with it my head dipped alarmingly down toward the water, and despite being only a few feet from shore by then I clutched at his shirt, terrified that I would drown.

Mrs. Hatcher and I were smiling, and Maria Cristina, though clearly more relaxed, looked a little disappointed that nobody had died. Outside I could hear the steady, pleasant sound of a light summer rain on the roof. The sky had lightened to a whitish-gray just in time for dusk. I felt as weightless as the rain there in the safe harbor of Mrs. Hatcher's kitchen, surrounded by Maria Cristina and Katie and little Lizzie, by so much girlhood past and still to come.

Maria Cristina asked if she could take the baby to play on the living room rug, and Katie agreed, going with her to put the child on a blanket. She came back moments later and settled back into her chair at the table, flanked by her mother and me.

"I would have guessed her to be older than thirteen," Katie said. "Such a lovely girl."

"I know," I agreed. "She's smart and fun and pretty."

Katie laughed. "Just like you. Is she stubborn, too?"

"Yes, I saw the family resemblance immediately," said Mrs. Hatcher.

We all chuckled at that, and then Katie said, "What else is happening around here? How's your father?"

"Father is fine," I said, though somewhat tentatively. "He still works too hard. He's been dividing his time between the mill and this murder investigation. He likes Farley Tucker, thinks he's a first-rate sheriff, but Father's name just carries more weight in the area. He's been meeting with the parish priests in Warwick, asking them to urge their people to cooperate. He really seems worried about the boy's family, and of course he's worried about the mill. He's trying to reopen, and though he hasn't made any promises, I think a lot of people are counting on him succeeding. He's been looking for investors. He doesn't have the capital to do it on his own, and the banks aren't willing to lend that much with only the old structure and our house as collateral. Not these days, anyway."

"Has he had any luck finding a partner?" Katie asked, a strange sound in her voice.

Mrs. Hatcher focused on her knitting and said nothing.

"Well, Oliver Fielding is interested, but I don't think they've come to any agreement yet," I said. "What about Mike? Your mother told me last spring that he got a job in a small carpet factory in Cumberland—is it steady?"

"Yes," said Katie, without enthusiasm. "The pay is about half what he was making in the Woonsocket mill before it closed, and the hours are longer. Plus, we have to buy gas for the flivver so he can drive down to the factory and back every day. But it's better than nothing."

"Does he have a line on another job here? Oh, is that why you're all here? Katie, wouldn't it be wonderful if Mike found work in South County and you moved back home?" I asked, excited by the prospect of having her nearby again.

"Well, not exactly," she said. I heard that sound again, something in her voice that made me stop and look at her.

"What's going on?" I asked, looking from Katie to Mrs. Hatcher and back again. "What is it?"

They exchanged glances, and I could feel my heart beating. "You're scaring me—has something happened?" I asked.

Clearly uncomfortable, Katie opened her mouth to speak but stopped. Her neck and jawline flushed red. She could never hide her discomfort, not with that strawberry-blond hair and pale, freckled skin.

"We're here because of the mill," she said suddenly, and her mother attacked the tiny pink sweater she was knitting, her needles clicking nervously together. "Mike is here, and some other men, too, because of the mill. Because of Oliver Fielding."

"What?" I said, unable to articulate a clearer question.

"Mike's in the textile worker's union," she explained. "When a group of workers is in trouble, the others rally 'round. A show of support." She still looked embarrassed, and was having trouble meeting my eyes.

"Okay," I said slowly. "So Mike is here to support the textile workers. Do you mean he's here to support the reopening of the mill?"

She looked at me then with pity, and something else: impatience. She thought me naïve, sheltered, and she was right. Later I was capable of feeling gratitude that she didn't also see me as shallow and uncaring and stupid.

Her voice was gentle, the same voice she used with Lizzie. "Oliver Fielding is a union buster. He's not a nice man. Some people think he's a criminal. Mike and his friends are here to persuade your father not to make Fielding his partner. They're here to protest."

I didn't know what to say. A protest? Like a strike? But the mill wasn't even functioning yet! Oh, he was going to hate this—Father, who prided himself on being a part of the community, a friend to all his employees, a fair man. He would be wounded and angry. How could they make demands before the mill was even opened? And how could we open without Oliver?

"When?" I asked, but my voice cracked. I cleared my throat, licked my suddenly dry lips. "When is this supposed to happen?"

She paused, looking at me as though trying to see clear through to the bottom. I didn't look away, and she seemed satisfied.

"Sometime in the next few days," Katie said. "We came a few days early to visit Ma. Most of the men aren't here yet, but more are coming. Anne," she said, after glancing at her mother first, "I shouldn't be telling you this. Mike would be furious. But I don't want you to be blindsided, and who knows? Maybe you can help."

"Help? The men my father has worked so hard for and a bunch of strangers who don't even know him are accusing him of horrible things, and you want me to help?" I was incredulous.

"I thought maybe you could talk to your father."

I didn't know what to say. There was no answer that could possibly feel like the right one. We sat in silence, lost in our own thoughts. The kitchen clock ticked loudly, the clicking of Mrs. Hatcher's knitting needles keeping time.

"I have to go," I said, standing suddenly.

"Anne—" began Mrs. Hatcher.

"Annie, I'm sorry," said Katie. "You know how we feel about you and your father. It's not personal. "

"Of course it is," I said, astonished that she would say such a thing. "And it should be—you know my father, personally."

"I'm sorry you feel that way," she said, and I was struck by her steady gaze and dignity. "But we have a family to feed, and there are thousands of families just like us. We've been hungry—Mike and Lizzie and I. Actually hungry. Did you know that? Does your father know that?"

I couldn't hold her look and dropped my eyes to the floor. *Of course he knows,* I thought, and then I heard that traitorous little voice in my head.

Then why hasn't he ever said so?

"I didn't think so," she said, smiling an unhappy smile. "I'm sorry you're upset, sorry if I've hurt you. But as much as I love you, your hurt feelings are nothing compared to people going hungry."

I felt the hot tears behind my eyes and bolted out of the kitchen, through the back door and the gap in the hedge that Katie and I had used a thousand times as we ran back and forth between our two houses. I didn't look back, and nobody tried to stop me as I ran, hard and fast, away from the devastating truth that we were all grown-up now, whether we liked it or not.

CHAPTER THIRTEEN

I got up early the next morning in order to catch Father before he left the house. I had not decided what I would say about the workers' demonstration at the mill, about my concerns regarding Oliver's reputation, about anything. I only knew that I had to see my father, but whether it was to reassure him or myself I did not know.

I came downstairs and found him in the kitchen with his coffee and the morning paper. He looked up briefly and smiled before going back to the folded paper that he held out and away from him, his arm extended as far as it would go.

"Morning," I said.

"Good morning, dear. Sleep well?" he asked without looking up.

"I did. What are your plans for the day?"

He paused a moment, finishing the news story he was reading, then put the paper down. He looked at me while he took a sip of coffee, the steam curling up around his nose and eyes as he tipped the cup toward his face.

"Believe it or not, I'm going down to Ezra Johnson's this morning. Fielding's attorney needs documentation on the property line between the mill and Ezra's land, and I've got to ask him for it. Let's hope he's in a good mood," he finished.

Father, I noted, was certainly in a good mood.

"Mind if I come with you?" I asked, figuring it would be a chance to talk to him and I could stay and work on the boat after he left. Besides, it wasn't often that my father and Ezra Johnson willingly came face-to-face, and while it made me nervous, I certainly didn't want to miss it.

"Of course not," he said. "It's probably a good idea. I have the sneaking suspicion that the old man likes you better than he likes me. I'll probably get further with him if you're there."

I drank my coffee, stealing surreptitious looks at him while I wrote a note for Maria Cristina, who was still sleeping upstairs. Father seemed brightly energetic, enthusiastic—even happy, wise-cracking about Ezra not liking him. I thought we should talk about what Katie had told me, but I wasn't sure how to begin.

The right moment did not present itself until we were in the car driving toward Ezra's.

"Fielding is moving quickly," Father said. "He wants title and surveyed dimensions of the property confirmed. His bankers have already been out to see the mill. I think we'll have an agreement within the week."

That explained my father's mood, I thought. He believed that the mill would reopen, and soon. He seemed comfortable with the idea of Oliver as his partner, but he had said very little about the details of the impending investment.

"What will Mr. Fielding's role be, exactly?" I asked.

"He'll cover payroll for the first few months, and provide the capital necessary to clean out the plant, refurbish the salvageable machinery, and buy some new equipment that we'll need immediately. Even with the Depression, the industry has changed, and if we want to be competitive we'll have to update some of our methods before we begin. He will dedicate himself in the first few months to getting orders. He has a lot of contacts, and we're confident that we'll be running at full capacity within three months."

"That sounds terrific," I said. "What about management duties? What about everyday decisions? Will you retain control of the actual running of the mill?"

"Well, we haven't talked about that in much detail yet, although I expect to be on site most of the time, while he will do some traveling," he said.

For the first time, he sounded concerned, and I looked at him, waiting for more.

"He'll have a forty-five percent interest in the company, which means that I retain the controlling interest, but I'm not sure that that accurately reflects the way this will work. But without his help the mill will sit unused until it crumbles into the bay. Fielding is my last option. We will never reopen without him. I know it, and he knows it, which gives him quite a bit more power than the division of assets suggests."

"Are you concerned?" I asked. "Do you know him well enough to let him in, knowing that he'll have that much power?"

He hesitated before he answered. "Yes and no. I don't want to lie to myself, to pretend that he couldn't fight me over something we both felt strongly about—and win. But I have to take the chance. I've exhausted all of my resources, all of my contacts, every favor I might have called in. This is it, and I know what's at stake. I've thought of nothing else for months. I need him. Milford needs him. I've got to risk it."

This is the good man I know, I thought, and these are the problems he faces that Mike Flynn and his friends don't understand. My father cared, and he was struggling to bring the mill back and to do it in a way that would work for everyone, but it wasn't as simple as it might look from the outside.

"What's troubling you, Anne?" he asked, glancing at me as we took the left-hand fork off the mill road down to Ezra's. His voice was tender, concerned, and I swelled with gratitude.

"I'm not sure," I said. I did not understand my own hesitation, why I didn't just tell him. "A lot of things. The men. Oliver Fielding."

"What do you mean?" he asked.

"Father, you know about Mr. Fielding's reputation, don't you? About the way he treats his workers, about the union busting?"

"I've heard the rumors, Anne. I'm aware of Mr. Fielding's reputation. But everyone who owns a factory or a mill—everyone, including me—has that kind of reputation among the workingmen and the unions. It's in the job description of 'boss.' We all fall somewhere between bad and worse as far as the labor organizations go, and that's not just in textiles—it's in every industry. Fielding's reputation is worse than mine, but not so much as you might think." He put his hand over mine, lying on the seat between us. "It can't be helped, dear. Don't take it so hard. I could not possibly do the things that would make me an acceptable boss to the union. I'd be out of business in two weeks. They know that, but they have a job to do. The smartest men on both sides don't take it personally. I wouldn't worry about Oliver's reputation, or about mine."

He sounded so sure, and so reassuring, that I decided I could wait a little longer. I was happy to let him ease my mind as if I were still a little girl.

"What else is bothering you?" he asked.

"I'm worried about Ezra, about the murder investigation. I've heard almost nothing. What's going on? Is Ezra a suspect or not?" I asked, taking a chance that he would tell me despite his dislike of Ezra.

"I don't want to say too much," he said slowly. "Farley has taken me into his confidence to some degree, but I'm sure I don't know everything he does, or at least everything he suspects. As far as I know Ezra is a suspect, but at this point no motive has been established, and the evidence appears circumstantial. Unless something new comes to light, I'm not sure any charges will ever be brought against Ezra."

I felt an overwhelming sense of relief despite my conviction that Ezra couldn't have killed the Da Silva boy.

We pulled into the clearing and parked, and when we walked

up toward the house Ezra appeared on the porch, holding a mug of coffee. The steam rose up from it, an opaque white cloud in the damp morning air.

"Morning!" I called, hoping to start our little encounter off on a friendly note.

"Good morning, Ezra," said Father.

"What're you doin' here?" Ezra asked, looking directly at Father.

"I've got a few questions about property lines, and thought we might chat for a few minutes if you've got the time," Father said.

He sounded cool and business-like, though not very friendly—a good choice, I thought. They didn't like each other, and to have pretended otherwise would have made Ezra angry and suspicious.

"Not up here," said Ezra as we approached the steps up to the house. "In the workshop or down by the dock, either one."

I looked at Father and said quietly, "Do you have a preference?"

"No, it doesn't matter to me," he said. "Whatever the old fool wants."

"That's not helping," I hissed as Ezra came down the steps toward us. I was immediately alarmed by the slow, laborious way he was moving. He was clearly in a great deal of pain from his knee, and while a part of me knew that I shouldn't mention it, especially right now, I couldn't stop myself.   "Ezra, are you all right? Have you seen Dr. Statham about your knee?"

It took him a full two minutes to make it down the stairs, his knuckles white as he gripped the railing with each step. He didn't answer me until he was on the ground in front of us, breathing hard from his exertions.

"It's fine. Jus' the damp is all." He scowled at me, then shifted his attention to my father. "What's this about?"

"Why don't we walk down to the dock and sit so we can talk for a minute," Father suggested.

My concern for Ezra had not abated, though. "Why don't I grab a couple of chairs and you can both sit right here?" I suggested. I didn't want Ezra walking all over the uneven clearing. What if he fell?

"I'm not a cripple yet," said Ezra.

I looked at him for a moment, then ran to the workshop as he started to make his painful way down to the water's edge where his chair sat next to my boat. I threw open the doors and grabbed an old paddle off the wall, turned and ran back into the sunshine. He hadn't gotten very far, and my father was walking slowly beside him, keeping several feet between them. Neither said a word. I raced up to them and stopped in front of Ezra, forcing him to stop, too.

"Here," I said, thrusting the paddle out toward him. "Use this to help support your weight, at least, you stubborn old man." He looked at me for a moment, furious and scowling, his eyes peering out from beneath his thunderous brows. That face would have scared half the children in Milford home to their mothers. He held my look for a moment, then took the paddle from me without a word and continued on his way, the wide, flat blade of the oar planted firmly in the sandy soil with each step, the sturdy handle under his arm. I looked at Father, who shrugged a little, and we followed half a step behind.

Once Ezra was settled in his chair Father looked around and realized there was nowhere else to sit but the cedar stump I had rolled down to the water years ago so that I could sit with Ezra when we weren't working. My father took a look at that stump, then a look at his expensive suit and shiny black shoes. He sighed and took his seat, mere inches from the ground, his bent knees up around his chest and his pant legs riding up above his socks. He adjusted the slant of his fedora against the morning sun and looked up at Ezra, who was sitting much higher in his chair, wearing worn coveralls and a stained undershirt and eyeing my father through his customary squint.

"The place looks the same," said Father.

"It don't change," said Ezra. "Neither do I."

Father seemed to bristle at that, but he kept his temper. "You know about Oliver Fielding, about him coming into the mill with me?" he asked.

"Yep. Ever'body in town knows."

"Yes. Well, I need some paperwork on the property line, and I wondered if I might look at your deed and the original survey documents, if you've got them. Just to confirm the mill's papers. If there's no property-line dispute we can open the mill that much sooner."

"I got no quarrel over property lines," said Ezra. "Never did with your dad, neither. It's all clear and the deeds agree. I'll have to go up to the house for 'em, but you can take the papers and bring 'em back to me when you're through, if that'll do."

"That'll do fine, Ezra. That's perfect. Thank you," said Father, clearly surprised by this unexpected cooperation.

"Annie, go get my strongbox," Ezra said suddenly. It took me a moment to register what he'd said. In all the years I'd been coming down here I had only been in Ezra's house two or three times, and it had been several years since he'd invited me in.

"In the house?" I asked.

"Yep. The metal box, sits on the mantel close to the bed. It'll save me the stairs," he reluctantly admitted.

"Of course," I said, realizing what that admission cost him.

I raced back to the house and up the steps to the front door. I entered the cramped one-room house that was still faintly familiar, saw that nothing had been moved since the last time I'd been inside. The place was dark, the small windows allowing only a weak, watery light into the room. Ezra's old iron bed sat near the fireplace at one end of the room, and a table and chair over by the window faced the water. The plaster on the walls was badly in need of repair, but the old unfinished beams were still sturdy and had only grown more beautiful as the years passed. The wide-plank floors could use a scrubbing, I noted, and the windows— I looked at the salty, almost opaque glass panes and moved a little closer when I noticed my father had risen from his seat on the old stump and was pacing back and forth in front of Ezra's chair. Ezra appeared to be sitting quietly, watching and listening as my father talked in an agitated fashion. I couldn't hear what they were saying, but Father was clearly unhappy.

I hurried to the fireplace to retrieve the strongbox, wanting to get outside and smooth the waters between them. I couldn't imagine what they were arguing about, but I doubted if either of them needed an excuse.

I picked up the box and turned, intending to hurry back outside with it. But I found myself standing in the middle of the room instead, the box in my arms. Slowly, I lowered the box to the braided rug that lay on the floor in front of the fireplace and squatted down beside it. I sat like that, glancing up at the door, nervous but unwilling to stop myself from looking inside. It was as though my newfound curiosity, my sudden ability to ask questions about the past, had taken over my life. I knew I shouldn't open the box, but I did it anyway.

The simple metal catch lifted easily and the hinges at the back squeaked a little as I lifted the lid. The box was filled with papers, and a few scattered photographs lay on the top of the pile. I lifted them gingerly with the tip of my forefinger and thumb, looking for a more interesting find underneath. I was not disappointed. Just beneath the photos I found the last page of a letter written in lovely, flowing script. I sat back on my heels and began to read it.

You are my eyes and ears, now, the letter read. *I know nothing unless you tell me, so you must give me more, if you ever loved me. You don't write often and when you do you say too little. You cannot know the pain I feel. Give me more, Ezra. Tell me how she looks, the color of her hair and eyes in the sun. Tell me everything—even how much she hates me if that is all you have. Spare me nothing, as I have spared her nothing.*

It was signed, simply, *Inêz.*

I was suddenly a wild woman, frantically digging through the papers for the rest of the letter, other letters, for the date.

When did she write this? How old was I then? It had to be me she was talking about, Ezra the conduit between us. How much had been kept from me?

The papers were upside down, backwards, and my hands were shaking so badly I couldn't even see what I held. I jumped suddenly as Ezra yelled from his chair down by the dock.

"What're you doin', girl?"

"Coming!" I yelled back.

I stood up, put the page I'd read back in the box underneath the photographs, and walked outside. Father was standing down by the water's edge, looking out at the horizon. Ezra sat in his chair, scowling and smoking his pipe. They were not speaking.

I brought the box to Ezra and handed it to him. He looked at me sharply, sensing that something was wrong.

"The contents might be a little jumbled," I said, my voice still shaky. "I tripped and the box opened up. A few things fell out. I think I got everything. I'm sorry."

He looked at me long and hard then, and I thought, He knows I'm lying. He's wondering what I saw. Or read. His expression softened unexpectedly, and he spoke to me as gently as he ever had. "Don't worry, girl. Are you hurt?"

I could only shake my head.

"Then that's all right," he said. "Nothin' in here but a bunch of old things, papers and pictures of people long gone. None of it matters anymore. As long as you're okay."

"I'm okay," I said, sitting down on the stump.

He opened the box and looked quickly through the papers until he found an official-looking document with heavy blue backing. He looked through its several pages quickly, then closed the box, keeping the document with him.

"Here's the papers you'll want," he said to my father's back.

Father turned around and walked back toward us. He took the paper Ezra held out to him, lifted up the top sheet, and glanced through the document, nodding.

"This is it," he confirmed, then looked at Ezra. "Thank you. I really do appreciate it."

"No thanks needed," said Ezra curtly.

"Well, we both know you didn't have to give me this. You could've made me get the surveyors out here, drawn up new lines. Delayed everything. That's what I thought you'd do. I was sure of it."

Ezra looked at my father then, a hard, piercing stare that seemed to see far more than I did. "If you think makin' things hard for you is my aim—now or then—you don't know me."

"No more than you know me, I imagine," said my father, his voice stiff and just this side of courteous. His hand unconsciously moved up to touch his jaw, and then, realizing what he was doing, he jerked his hand away and scowled.

"I'm heading in to town," he said, indicating the papers in his hand. "I want to get these filed with the clerk."

"I'm going to stay," I said. "Work on the boat." I glanced at the hull as I said this, and Father's eyes followed mine. He had never seen her before.

"This is it?" he asked, actually taking a step nearer.

"Yes," I said, trying not to sound too eager. "She's almost finished. I'll have her in the water in a week."

He took a couple of steps around her, though he didn't touch anything. It was all I could do not to explain it all to him, tell him how I'd designed her, the months of labor I'd put into her, the love I felt for this simple wooden vessel, the pride.

"Do you like her?" I asked because I couldn't help myself.

"Looks like a boat," he said, trying to infuse the comment with warmth and approval and interest. All I heard was the trying, and my own pathetic longing.

He left then, after telling me he'd see me for dinner at home.

I don't care, I told myself. He doesn't have to like what I do. This is my boat. My life. I picked up a rock and flung it with all my might into the bay, then turned from the shore to my boat, more inclined than ever to rise to Oliver's challenge, to make a real break from Father's expectations. Oh, he would be so shocked, so horrified to have me living nearby, building boats, raising Maria Cristina outside of his influence. Everyone in town would see us, too. They'd all know. I relished the thought of his discomfort.

Ezra didn't talk to me for a while, and I was grateful. He picked up his whittling, a piece that was starting to look long and thin and graceful, though what its final shape and purpose would be I did not yet know. I hauled the rest of the teak down to the horses, and we whiled away the morning and a good portion of the afternoon with me finishing the deck and seating, and Ezra whittling what was beginning to look like a fish of some kind. At some point I realized I was hungry, and when I asked Ezra if he wanted something to eat he said yes and asked me to take the strongbox back up to the house, go into the kitchen, and fix us some lunch.

I carried the box up the steps and into the house, my hands itching to open it again, to find the letter and read it, to see if there were others. But Ezra trusted me, and I had let him down once. I felt guilty enough already, and the weight of it kept me from repeating the offense. I placed the box back on the mantel and went into the little kitchen ell to see what I could find for our lunch. He didn't have much, but it would do. I picked up a loaf of day-old bread, some blackberry jam, and a knife. The day was rather cool, with a fair sky and a stiff breeze off the water, and we sat down by the dock, Ezra in his chair and me on the old cedar stump, eating soda bread and jam.

"Thanks for giving the papers to Father," I said.

"I said it was nothin'."

"Not to him it wasn't," I pointed out.

Ezra only grunted in reply.

"Have you two always fought?" I asked.

"Well, we really only fought the one time." His lips twitched in amusement.

"You actually fought? You hit each other?" I asked, incredulous, trying to imagine my father engaging in a fistfight.

"Not exactly," he said, chuckling out loud. "I hit him, but he never touched me. He was flat on the ground, so it would've been quite a reach."

"Oh, my God," I said, trying to comprehend this scene.

"Well, like I said, it was just the once."

"Why would you ever do such a thing?" I asked.

He shrugged. "He made me mad."

I could only stare at him, appalled. Ezra continued to wield his knife, his hand sure of the vision he had in mind.

"Well," I said at last, "at least you behaved decently today, and I appreciate it."

"I hope he don't regret it," Ezra said.

"What, partnering with Oliver Fielding?"

"Yep. He may be bitin' off more'n he can chew, from what I hear."

"What do you hear," I asked, "and from whom? You hardly ever leave this place, and now that Stevie's not pestering you, nobody comes out here but me." I was amused by the idea that Ezra had his ear to the ground, knew what was happening in and around town, though I supposed he did see the local fishermen every now and then, and even Oliver had said he'd been out here.

"I talked with Father about the partnership on the way here this morning, and I think he knows what he's doing," I assured Ezra.

He didn't answer. He finished the last of his bread and wiped his hands on the legs of his coveralls. He bent to pick up whatever it was he was carving, stopped and shifted his weight before reaching into his pocket to retrieve his knife.

"Your knee seems pretty bad," I commented. "Have you seen the doctor?"

"No need," he said. "Dick Statham can't tell me nothin' I don't already know. I'm old, and this knee is gonna get worse every year. That's jus' the way it is."

I fastened the false stem and sawed it off at a downward angle, then moved to the stern and sawed the transom off flush with the gunwale. The cut piece fell to the ground with a solid, comforting thud.

"Ezra," I began somewhat tentatively, "when I went to get your strongbox, I . . . I opened it. I saw some pictures and a page from a letter."

He didn't answer. He knew there was more to come, and he waited patiently for it.

"I read just the one page. The last page of a letter to you from Inêz. From my mother. She was talking about me, I think."

I waited for him to say something, but the only sound coming from his chair was the sound of the knife slicing through wood, taking off just enough to reveal what lay hidden beneath. The discarded pieces floated down to the ground, curling just slightly as they descended, light as air. Only Ezra knew what it would look like when he stopped carving, and he had told me once that he was never quite sure until the piece was finished.

"Ezra, after Inêz left us, you talked to her." It was a statement, not a question. "She asked about me. And you told her things . . ." I paused, flailing in the dark. I needed him.

"We wrote," he said simply. "Not often, but we did."

"For how long?" I asked.

"Until she died," Ezra said.

I took this in, stunned. What was I to think? I had spent my life recovering from the seemingly indisputable fact that my mother didn't care about me, that she had walked away from me and never looked back.

I said nothing, at first. I clamped and fastened the gunwale scrub strips along her sides. The sunshine and the gentle sound of the waves rolling in against the sand and the dock settled upon me, anchoring me at my boat, Ezra by my side.

"I don't understand," I said. "She wanted to know about me? What I was doing, how I was doing?"

"Yep. She did. She was your mother. It was only natural she'd want to know how you was."

"There was nothing natural about her!" I cried. How could he say such a thing? "She abandoned me when I was *six years old*!"

"That's true, she did. And it was the hardest, most terrible thing she ever did. No one knew that better'n her."

I held tight to my rage, as if what lay beneath it was far worse. "There had to be some other way, no matter what her reasons were, if she really did care about me," I said. "It makes less sense to me that she did this if you're right and she cared than it does if she didn't give a damn about me at all!"

He had put the piece he was carving down across his knees, and he held the knife idly in his hand. He looked pensively out at the bay, and I wondered what he saw as he stared, unblinking, at the horizon.

"You can't never really know a person. Not truly. I could tell you some things, but you still wouldn't really understand what she did, no more'n I do, even now." He had not turned to look at me, but spoke as if he were talking directly to the water that lapped against the sand just beyond where we sat. "She left you—that's the hard truth of it—though she didn't want to. She would've rather done anything else, but she felt she had no choice. She was unhappy for the rest of her life because of it. She loved you, though, an' it seems to me that oughta be worth somethin'."

I couldn't hear this. I wouldn't. I felt the panic rise in my throat, pushed up by a growing emptiness so overwhelming I knew I could not look at it.

I marshaled reason to my side, instead, and fought the panic back down. "But she wasn't even that far away. No matter how bad it was that she left us, she only went to Barrington with Ben and Lucia. Why didn't she try to see me? Why couldn't I go to see her?"

"I asked her that very thing. For years I told her she could still see you, but she wouldn't do it. I thought she was wrong, but I didn't have to live with her fear."

"What about my grandparents? What about her brother, Estevão? They all left me. Why didn't they ever try to see me?"

"Ben and Lucia thought she was doin' right, though they loved you, too. Estevão was already gone by then."

"Gone?" I asked, startled. "You mean he died?"

"No, gone," said Ezra. "To Portugal."

"He went to Portugal?" I asked. "But I thought he wanted to build a better life here. Why did he leave?"

Ezra had picked up his whittling again, and I watched as a long fish tail came to life under his blade, the flip and curve of it suggesting power and grace and movement through dark water.

"He went back just before Inêz left Samuel. It broke his parents' hearts, but his dreams for a life here were never going to happen."

"What do you mean?" I asked.

"He wanted to go to the university. They all thought Samuel would help him get in, but he didn't. He disagreed with Estevão's politics, an' he didn't want it known they was family, especially not in Providence. Your father's friends were talkin' hard an' fast in his ear, and he had to choose. He didn't choose Estevão."

I sat quietly, for a time, my tools hanging idly in the loops of my belt. I tried to imagine my uncle's face, proud and fiery, but I could not. I had been too young when he left. My mother's face was blurry, the memories too old and scattered. When I thought of her now I increasingly saw Maria Cristina's face and expressions. Certainly the resemblance between them was strong, but they were blurring together for me, at least physically. But Maria Cristina was here, and she needed me at least as much as I needed her, while Inêz had abandoned me. According to Ezra, at least, she'd done so because she was afraid—of what, exactly, I wasn't sure. The only thing I knew beyond a doubt was how wrong she had been, and how unforgivable she remained.

Ezra cut and carved while I sat, and the sun began to sink below the trees. I looked at my boat, realized she would be ready soon, and I longed for the wind in my hair, the Rhode Island shore shrinking to nothing behind me. I was exhausted with trying to understand what my parents had done, and why, and even more so with having to pay for it.

I gathered up my tools and walked them back up to the workshop, finished for the day. I would roll the boat back over tomorrow and caulk the seams on her bottom. She was mere days from being put in the water, and none too soon—September was upon us. There was a distinct chill in the air, and I shivered. I hung my tools back up and walked back through the doorway to say good-night to Ezra before heading home. I stopped, though, my hand on the doorframe and my breath caught in my chest.

Maria Cristina had arrived, probably to bring me home for dinner. She stood in front of Ezra's chair, talking happily with him, her elfin face and petite form so like our mother's. She was animated, smiling, her hands moving about as she described some antic of Deirdre Sullivan's, while Ezra gazed adoringly at her, his face unguarded, a gentle, loving smile on his weathered face.

The setting sun bathed them in an unearthly golden light worthy of a Renaissance Pietà, and the suspicion came to me then, unexpected and unwanted, that Inêz's mysterious Portuguese lover had always been a lie, and that Ezra Johnson himself was Maria Cristina's father.

CHAPTER FOURTEEN

Sunday mornings had been the same for Father and me since I was a little girl, and they did not change with the arrival of my sister. Always an early riser, Father got up first and made us breakfast before church. He made the same thing each week: pancakes with maple syrup, and fresh berries, when they were in season. Eventually I had started drinking coffee with him, but Father still poured me a glass of milk every Sunday morning to drink with my pancakes.

Maria Cristina had willingly gone to Milford Congregational Church with us the first Sunday after she arrived, but it had not gone well. The entire congregation had seemed to turn as one to watch her as we walked to our pew. Their curious stares and the whispered retellings of our family scandal threw my father's head up higher and drew Maria Cristina in close to my side. When she asked me later that afternoon if she could go to a Catholic church instead, I could not say no. She offered to go to early Mass and still attend the later morning services with us, anxious as always not to be a bother. But it was a simple matter to ask Mrs. Sullivan if Maria Cristina could accompany them to Our Lady of the Sacred Heart each week. The Sullivans were happy to have her, and she often stayed overnight with Deirdre on Saturday in order to get up and have breakfast with the whole noisy Sullivan clan before Mass. It was easy to see that she loved it, and neither of us ever again mentioned her attending services with me.

At first I thought it might be difficult or awkward for us to go to different churches, but it wasn't. We were each happy with our choice, and pleased that the other was content with hers. I asked my sister once what she liked about being Catholic. It wasn't a matter of liking or not liking, she had said. It just *was*. Being Catholic was a part of her family, a part of her. She described the Mass to me, the prayers chanted in Latin, the priest's singsong voice. She told me of incense and the Holy Mother, of Christ on the cross and her own whispered prayers, her fingers moving over the rosary beads our *avó* had given her for a confirmation gift. She assured me that confession was neither strange nor frightening but a solemn accounting to God, a cleansing that rendered her featherlight and open to the joy of the Gospel, the homily, and Holy Communion. She was Catholic to her very soul, and Ezra told me later that she was very much like our grandmother Lucia in this.

On that particular Sunday morning in late August I woke to the smell of coffee wafting up the stairs from the kitchen. I laid there for a moment in bed, coming to terms with consciousness, blinking in the soft yellow light that filled my bedroom and sought out every crevice where shadows might lurk. The white muslin curtains blew in the cool morning air, and I was grateful for the heavy bedspread that I pulled up to my chin. It was deliciously warm underneath the covers, made more so in contrast with the breeze that blew across my face from the partially open window. I moved my bare feet and legs against the soft cotton sheets inside my cocoon, reluctant to leave its sheltering folds.

The clock on the table beside my bed was unrelenting, however, and I finally threw the covers off and swung my legs over the side of the bed. The fine wool rug, a remnant of wealthier days in the Dodge household, insulated the soles of my feet from any unpleasant contact with the cold hardwood floor. I quickly thrust my arms into the sleeves of the rather worn flannel robe I had hung on one of the four posts of the bed the night before and tied the belt around my waist. I leaned against the side of the bed, pulled a pair of thick wool socks onto my feet, and headed for the bathroom down the hall.

After brushing my teeth and pulling my hair back I walked past the unused bedrooms and sitting rooms, the built-in drawers and storage closets on the second-floor landing, and down the back stairs to the kitchen. I smiled, content in the Sunday morning ritual I shared with Father, and sat down at the table, where a pool of sunshine invited me to relax and stretch like a cat in its warmth.

"Good morning," said Father.

"Morning." I did love that kitchen on Sundays.

"Just you and me for pancakes?" he asked.

"Yes, Maria Cristina spent the night at the Sullivans'. She'll be back later today."

I watched him as he stirred batter in a large bowl, the round cast-iron skillet on the stove hot and ready. My milk was already poured, and I took a sip.

"Coffee's hot," he said, indicating with a move of his head the pot on the burner next to him. There was a small bowl of freshly washed blueberries on the table already.

I shuffled over to the stove and poured myself a cup of coffee. He always made it too strong. He said he preferred to get his two cups' worth of caffeine quickly rather than waste time drinking a second cup. I had to admit there was a certain logic to that, but I wasn't sure the trade-off was worth it. It was a vile brew, and I always poured only half a cup, leaving plenty of room for some of the milk from my glass.

I sat back down and sipped my coffee, observing him as he kept watch over the pancakes. Small bubbles began to form around the edges, and when he could just make out a hint of golden brown around the lacy perimeter of each cake he carefully scooped them up, one by one, and flipped them. They were, as always, perfect.

My father persuaded me to eat a fourth, and when I'd polished off the last bite I laid my fork down on my plate with heavy finality.

"That was delicious," I said. "But I shouldn't have eaten that last one."

"Nonsense." He had always insisted I eat, convinced that my appetite was an indicator of overall good health.

I had eaten many meals at the homes of my schoolgirl friends whose mothers had opted not to run away, but instead to stay at home and raise their daughters into proper ladies. Their breakfast and dinner tables had been a wholly new experience for me, presided over by slim, self-assured women who cautioned against any display of appetite. They taught their daughters that hunger is unseemly, self-denial supremely feminine, fullness and satisfaction somehow grotesque. At my own house, without the worldly wisdom of a mother to guide me in such matters, food was simply food: necessary, desired, enjoyed. Beyond that, my father and I never discussed it or gave it a second thought. It would not have occurred to either of us to do so.

We lingered over coffee, knowing we had about fifteen minutes before we had to dress for church. We were both enjoying the morning, the sense of tradition that always permeated our Sundays.

"I've been thinking about Maria Cristina," said Father without preamble. "We need to think about her future. You'll want the best for her, I know."

I couldn't argue with that, but I was wary. His beginning the conversation by telling me what I wanted was clearly designed to narrow my options.

"I don't really know what you mean," I said slowly. "She's not quite thirteen. I haven't thought about her future, other than that I want her to grow up safe and happy. I assumed I would be supportive, later, when she can make decisions for herself—not decide for her."

He heard the implied criticism. "I'm not suggesting she be railroaded into anything, Anne. But we can make sure she's well prepared for the right kind of life. The kind of life she'll want. We can help her."

"How?" I asked. I knew I sounded suspicious, but that's because I was.

"Well, I was thinking. She hasn't had the benefits you have had, the exposure to certain things. My mother had a hand in your early training, and Esther Hatcher has certainly had a positive influence on you. You've been educated at home as well as at school and the university, and it shows—to your advantage. You're fully prepared to take your rightful place in the world. Maria Cristina has not been so lucky in her upbringing, but we can attempt to remedy that now."

"Father, what are you trying to say?"

"I think we should consider a good boarding school for her. With the mill open again, we'll be able to afford it. I know you want the best for her, and I'm willing to spend the money for her sake."

I looked at him, but there was nothing to read on his face but the triumph of having delivered good news—news that would delight me, and for which he could take full credit.

"But I don't want her to be sent away," I protested. "I don't want her to go to some fancy school. Even I didn't have to do that—I would have hated it! She will, too. I want her to live here, to stay with me."

"Don't answer now," he said quickly. "Of course that's your initial response, but it's based on sentiment. I've made some inquiries, and there's an excellent school in upstate New York that I think you'd approve of, where she'd be surrounded by girls her own age, where she'd get an excellent education and training."

"Training for what?"

"Training that would counteract what she's gotten so far," he said impatiently. "She was completely insulated by her grandparents. She knows nothing of how to behave in decent company—you saw that when Reverend Brown was here. And if she stays in Milford she'll gravitate to the people who fish and farm. Or even toward the immigrants, up toward Warwick. Which would be fine, of course, if she weren't your half sister. You've got to think of your—"

He stopped abruptly, but it was too late.

"I've got to think of *my* future—that's what you were going to say, isn't it?" I asked. "Mine, not hers. Of course." The joy in our

Sunday morning together was gone. "And that's not the whole truth, either, is it, Father? You're not really thinking of me. You just thought that my own self-interest was the surest way to appeal to me. You're thinking of yourself."

I sat stewing for a moment. "It's Estevão all over again!" I blurted out without thinking.

He sat perfectly still for a moment, and I looked up at him cautiously. I had expected anger, but to my surprise he was actually thinking about what I'd said, considering its possibility.

"No, Anne. It's not the same at all," he said slowly. "I assume you've been listening to Ezra Johnson, but I did not force Estevão to leave—how could I? He was a grown man. He made his own choices."

"Even so, you don't think she's good enough, just like you didn't think he was good enough!" I argued.

"I'm sorry you see it that way," he said sadly. "Have I suggested deporting Maria Cristina, or finding some other family to take her in? No, I have not. What I have done is recognized that she faces a disadvantage, given her background, in terms of handling the opportunities that growing up in this house might afford her. I want to help her to reduce that disadvantage. If she is to take her place beside you in a way that will not cause either of you embarrassment or pain, I feel that we must do this."

He seemed sincere. I believed he meant it.

"Let's set this discussion aside for now," he said. "You're going to realize what it means to care for a child, to help her have the best possible life. It's not always easy. We'll talk about it again later."

I said nothing, dragging the tines of my fork through the thin film of syrup on my plate. Regardless of his rationale, I wasn't prepared to entertain the possibility of losing Maria Cristina, even if it was just to attend school. Not yet.

"Any news about the mill?" I asked, trying to fill the awkward space between us.

"I had a call from Fielding yesterday. We're meeting Wednesday afternoon—with our attorneys. I suspect that we'll be legal partners in the mill when we leave that meeting." His voice had an undercurrent of excitement, like the hum of electricity.

"That's wonderful," I said. "No second thoughts?"

"None," he said. "As I told you, this is the only way. Besides, Fielding's been successful at a time when many good businessmen have failed. I could do much worse."

"I hope you're right."

I wondered if he'd heard any rumors about the planned protest, and what it might mean for Katie and Mike if I told him about it. I was formulating a question in my mind, trying to figure out how to broach the subject without betraying my childhood friend, when he spoke, scattering my good intentions like ripples on the water. I could not seem to gather them up again.

"We'd better get going," he said. "We'll be late."

Thirty minutes later we were walking toward the Congregational church, the brim of my hat shading my eyes from the bright morning sun. The cool breeze I had awoken to just a short time ago had been sent packing. It was hot already, maybe the last truly warm day we would enjoy that year. We nodded and spoke to neighbors as they joined us in the current that carried us all down the sidewalk to the front doors of the church, thrown open to the town while the bells pealed the time and the start of the service.

Father and I went inside, moving with the crowd, and made our way down toward the front. We had sat in the second pew on the left my entire life, and we sat there now. Even if we arrived late, it would have been unthinkable for anyone else to be sitting in our customary place. Father immediately bowed his head in reflection or prayer—I had never known which. I wouldn't have dreamed of asking. We had only ever discussed religion from an intellectual standpoint, never our own personal beliefs. We respected each other's privacy. I looked around, soothed by the familiarity of the room. Sunlight shot through the stained glass windows, tinting the air we breathed, yellow, green, blue, purple. The plaster walls reflected the light, and massive oak beams soared twenty feet above our heads to the rafters, where half a dozen sparrows always seemed to be nesting.

I settled in, having long since grown comfortable with what it meant to sit before the altar for an hour each week. Surrounded by our neighbors, illuminated by the filtered morning light, I repeated the same words, heard the familiar lessons intoned by Reverend Brown, and sang the hymns I'd memorized long ago. I wasn't communing with God so much as I was communing with myself. I had never tried to explain this to anyone, and felt sure that if I had I would have been misunderstood. But I knew, somehow, that God did not need me to square things with Him so much as I needed to square things with myself, and with God looking on in this quiet, lovely place, I felt much more capable of doing so.

I believed. I always have. I know God is out there because His existence is simply beyond my ability to question. I cannot conceptualize this world without Him. But beyond that, I confess, I have always struggled with the contradictions I felt between a personal, sustaining faith in God and religious dogma or church politics. I believed in God, but I was skeptical of all the ways in which religion attempted to wrest that simple belief away from me and turn it into something wholly unrecognizable. For all I knew, my father felt the same.

As always, we sat right up front where we belonged, and the service made its meandering way toward the closing prayer. I felt calmed, refreshed, relaxed as we made our way back up the center aisle toward the doors, open once more on the bright lawn where the congregation lingered in good weather for fellowship.

I immediately spied Will and his parents, and Father and I joined them on the lawn. Elsa Dekker's print dress looked like a field—a very large field—of bright-red poppies. She wore a broad-brimmed hat and gloves, and her shoes looked like they pinched. Mr. Dekker and Will both wore gray suits, but where Will's clothes draped his slim, athletic body in a comfortable way, the buttons on Mr. Dekker's jacket were straining a bit across his midsection. I hid my smile as we approached.

"Good morning," Mr. Dekker called to us, then heartily shook Father's hand.

"Good morning, Wilhelm," my father said. "Elsa, how are you?"

I leaned down to kiss Elsa's soft, plump cheek, and the brims of our hats bumped a little, making it difficult to reach her. We both laughed, and she immediately took her hat off, pulling several strands of her fine hair out of the neat coil she'd arranged underneath. It made her look slightly unkempt, and she knew it. She pulled me to her and gave me a hearty kiss on the cheek. "A kiss from Annie after church on Sunday is more important than my old hat."

"I couldn't agree more," said Will, and I smiled at him.

Elsa linked her arm with her husband's and stood silent and supportive as he spoke with my father about the mill.

"So, Samuel, what's happening with Fielding? Any progress?"

"Yes, I think we're almost there. We've been negotiating the details—informally, you know, but we're meeting with our attorneys on Wednesday. If we can hammer out a final agreement, they'll draw up the papers."

Father looked every inch the industrialist that morning. The tired, drawn look he'd worn the previous few months seemed to have disappeared. He carried himself like the powerful, successful man he was, and I gazed at him with some wonder. This was the man I remembered from my childhood, and I felt happier than I had in a long time just to have him back.

Will took my arm in his and turned me away from our parents, and we took a step or two in our own direction, the three yards that separated us from them effectively creating some privacy. He looked at me intently, hungrily, and I found myself inexplicably receptive to that look this morning.

"What are you doing today, beautiful?" he asked.

"I'm going home to change, and then I'll go to Ezra's to work on the boat," I said.

Suddenly I clutched at the lapel of his jacket, leaning in toward him. "Will, I'm almost finished. I'm taking her out in a couple of days!" Will was one of the few people who really knew what this meant to me.

"That's wonderful, sweetheart!" he said. "Maybe I'll stop by Ezra's later, see how she looks." He saw my alarmed expression and hastened to add, "Don't worry, I won't interrupt your work. I just want to see it. You won't know I'm there."

I smiled, happy to include him. "That would be great," I said. "I've got the whole afternoon to work. Maria Cristina's at Deirdre Sullivan's, and probably won't be back until late afternoon. They go to Mrs. Sullivan's mother for Sunday supper after Mass."

"Sounds romantic, just you and me and Ezra . . ." he said, trailing off. "That's fine, Annie. I'll take what I can get!" he added quickly, laughing, when he saw my face.

Sheriff Tucker joined us then, offering a polite good-morning.

"How is the investigation coming along, sheriff?" Will asked.

Farley Tucker looked sad and preoccupied, I thought. "Well, I suppose it's coming along. I was out at the Da Silva house again this morning, before the service. Had a chance to talk to them kids, without their parents hovering. Learned a few things—finally," he finished.

"What do you mean?" I asked, alarmed, my mind racing as I tried to decipher his comment.

"Well, you think you know your neighbors—know your people—but there's always more to 'em, isn't there? More to everyday life than meets the eye. There's a messy, unhappy layer just below the surface—in any town, I'll wager."

"So"—I paused to swallow—"will you be arresting anyone?"

"Yep." The sadness was unmistakable now. "Some lives'll be ruined when it's all said and done."

Our attention was suddenly drawn to a group of men twenty feet or so from us. They stood in a small, tight knot, so close to each other that their dark Sunday clothes ran together into an indistinctly shaped shadow that shifted as they talked, their seemingly disembodied heads turned inward as they spoke in increasingly heated voices. I recognized several of the men who weren't wearing hats. They were locals—Earl Andrews, Mr. Hightower and his son Ben, Johnny some-body. They had all worked at the Dodge mill until it closed. One of the others looked familiar, and I frowned, trying to recall when and where I had seen him. At Mr. Sullivan's truck, I thought. He was pass-ing out signature cards for the union.

"No, *you* don't get it," Mr. Andrews was saying. "That's not how we do things in Milford."

The man from the labor rally spoke quietly to him, put a calming hand on the sleeve of his jacket, but Mr. Andrews shook him off, re-fusing to be mollified.

"Go peddle your wares somewhere else. We'll handle our own problems here."

Will had tensed beside me as we watched the group of men. The eyes of everyone on the front lawn of the church were drawn to them. I saw Mr. and Mrs. Hatcher, standing with Katie and Mike Flynn. Katie's eyes met mine, but after a moment she looked away.

Ben Hightower turned on Mr. Andrews. "We need them," he said, his youthful voice hot and loud in the morning air. "There's no-body here looking out for our interests."

"You're too young to know what you're talking about, Ben. Don't make a fool of yourself."

Ben's face burned with embarrassment, and Mr. Hightower at once put a restraining hand on his son's shoulder, then turned to Mr. Andrews.

"Earl," he said, quietly but sternly. "He's young, but he's not the only one who sees it that way. You're turning a blind eye to what it'll mean to have Fielding in here. We want some protection. For our families."

"He's right," said the man from the rally.

"You're not a part of this conversation," said Mr. Andrews savagely.

"He is if we say he is," said Ben Hightower menacingly, leaning in too close to Mr. Andrews, despite his father's restraining hand on his arm.

The sheriff made no move to interfere, but Will approached the group and spoke in a quiet voice. His back was toward me, and I couldn't make out his words. He spoke briefly, but I could see from the faces of the men I knew that he had reminded them that they stood on the lawn at church with their neighbors, that their children were watching and listening. The men looked around and then hung their heads sheepishly. The tension that had threatened to erupt into something physical seemed to leave their bodies. The expressions of the men I did not know, the agitators from out of town, remained inscrutable as Will talked. They merely watched and waited.

When he'd finished, Will waited for a moment while the men dispersed, walking back to their families, calling good-mornings and good-byes to friends, and beginning the slow walk toward home. The Sunday morning crowd thinned.

I looked up at Will as he came back to me. We walked together and I wondered why I always forgot how quiet and calming a person he was—or maybe it was that I always forgot how valuable that particular quality can be. I couldn't seem to hold him in my mind, somehow, and I thought it spoke poorly of me, not of him.

I turned from my scrutiny of his profile to see where we were walking and discovered too late that he had led me straight to Katie and Mike Flynn, still standing beside the Hatchers.

"Morning, Kate," said Will, kissing her on the cheek. "Mike," he said warmly, shaking his hand. "It's great to see you both. How long are you in town?"

"Couple of days," said Mike, his voice, I imagined, holding some menace.

"How are you, Anne?" asked Katie, and I knew what she was asking.

"I'm fine," I said, a little stiffly. Will heard it and looked at me, puzzled.

"I hope so," she said softly.

"I'm fine. And Father's fine."

Katie looked at me sadly, saying nothing. Mike, though, responded to the challenge.

"I'm glad you're both well," he said. "But your father's plans for the mill, while they might be beneficial to your family, are not in the interests of the men. Bringing Fielding in is a mistake, and I think you know it, Annie."

"I know nothing of the kind," I said. "My father will retain control, and you know him, Mike Flynn. The men have nothing to worry about. I don't know why you're sticking your nose in where it doesn't belong, anyway."

"Anne!" said Will. "What's wrong with you?"

I felt my face flame with embarrassment, but I couldn't keep my mouth shut.

"I'm sorry, Mike," I said. "But you know Father better than that. This thing you have planned seems so unfair." I heard the hesitation in my voice even as I said it. What, exactly *would* be fair? The workers left unorganized, without a voice? I didn't want that, didn't believe that was how things should be. I was on their side, at least in the abstract, but I didn't want them to blame my father, or to make things harder for him than they already were.

"Anne, you're thinking of it all wrong. The men want to talk to each other, and as a group to your father," said Will. "They have a right to think about their future, just like everybody else. Your father understands that."

"You know about the strike?" I asked.

"It's not a strike. It's a protest. A public demonstration," Mike corrected me. "Public association and speech. It's all there in the First Amendment—maybe you've heard of it?"

"It's nothing but a show of force against my father!" I said hotly.

"It is also that," agreed Mike. "But the law is on our side, and this show of force is in response to your father's show of force: bringing in Oliver Fielding."

"Well, it's wrong and it's cruel—I don't care what the law says," I said. "The men should know that they're worse off if the mill doesn't reopen at all. I don't know what's wrong with everybody!"

I seemed as incapable of framing an argument in favor of Father-as-mill-owner as I had been of articulating the workingman's position to Oliver Fielding. I felt ridiculous, and knew I was clutching at straws. If this hadn't been about my own father I would have been on their side. It was either betray myself, and pretend to those who knew me well that it wasn't what I was doing at all, or betray my father, which I couldn't do. I lost either way, and I resented everybody for it.

"When will it be?" Will asked Mike.

"Not sure yet," he said with a glance at me.

"Afraid I'll run and tell my father, spoil your surprise attack?" I asked nastily.

"Yes," he said quietly.

"Fine," I said. "I'll save you the trouble." And I turned and walked away, back to Father and the Dekkers.

We walked home together, and Father seemed oddly unper-turbed by the brief scene we'd witnessed at church. I supposed he saw it as a good sign that not all the men were in favor of the union com-ing in, and with so many obvious strangers in town, I had begun to convince myself that Father already knew about the demonstration, and about the union presence in town. I reminded myself that my father was completely aware of the ways the workingmen saw him. This wasn't new for him, and he knew how to handle it. At home I took the stairs two at a time up to my bedroom, happy to stop wor-rying about what I could not control. I couldn't wait to get to Ezra's.

I hurried down the mill road, eager to be working. I was so close now, ready to caulk her, make her watertight. As I approached Ezra's I recalled my suspicion that he might be Maria Cristina's father and resolved to just ask him outright. It would no doubt prove em-barrassing to us both, but I was determined to know, and I believed with all my heart that Ezra would not lie to me—not about this, at any rate. On other matters, I wasn't so sure. I wondered if I should warn him about what Sheriff Tucker had said after church, or if he'd view my warning as evidence that I believed he could have murdered Matt Da Silva.

When I left the cover of the trees for the brightly lit clearing of Ezra's yard, I saw him immediately down by the dock, standing with his hands on his hips. He was examining my boat.

"Morning!" I called as I approached. "How's she look to you?"

"She'll do fine."

I was pleased. In Ezra's book this was high praise.

"I'll do the caulking today, and the anti-fouling paint," I said.

He nodded his agreement. "You can make a first run day after tomorrow if the weather holds and you get her painted."

That was my plan, but to hear him say it made my body contract, tighten in anticipation.

"You think so?" I asked unnecessarily.

"Yep. You'll have to stay close in," he warned. "She's still not finished. You've got lights and a radio to wire, life preservers and such to stow. You'll want her safe and legal."

"Oh, I know. But maybe a quick run in the bay on Tuesday," I said, needing him to agree.

"Tuesday'll work."

He settled into his chair with his knife and the fish he was carving, though I could see now that she was actually a mermaid. "What's this?" I asked.

"Nothin'." He shrugged. "Thought Maria Cristina might like it."

I nodded, more determined than ever to ask him. But not just yet.

I marched up to the workshop, picked up my caulking cotton, a roller and mallet, a can of anti-fouling paint and a large brush, and carried everything down to the boat.

I worked quickly and in the way I like best: alone. Ezra was there, but after he helped me roll my boat over in her cradles so she was upside down again, he sat down and devoted himself to his whittling, and said nothing.

The caulking cotton I had brought down from the workshop was a woven hemp cord coated in tar. I used the mallet to drive the cord into the seams between her bottom planks. When I put her in water for the first time, the wood would swell, making the joints watertight.

I paused after a time, stood up to stretch my back, and looked over at Ezra. The late-afternoon light cast a golden hue over the cove, and everything looked warm and lovely, as if lit by a cheerful fire burning on the hearth. Somehow the warmth of the light only emphasized Ezra's isolation, the years of his lonely life spent in the decrepit old house with little sense of hearth or home about it.

"Ezra, how come you never married?" I asked.

"What kind of a fool question is that?" he asked, annoyed.

"I want to know. Why didn't you ever have a family of your own?"

"Ever'body ain't that lucky," he said, offering nothing more but saying a lot.

"Did you want children?" I asked, wondering if I did myself. Everybody assumed, of course, but I wasn't sure. It didn't seem to be a question anybody asked.

"What man doesn't, at some point?"

"Didn't you ever love anybody?" I asked. "Really love her, want to marry her?"

"If I did, it ain't nobody's business but mine," he said curtly.

I kept working, driving the caulking cotton into her seams until every crevice had been filled with the tightly woven cord. Ezra said nothing else, at first, but after a time he spoke again, as though he couldn't leave it alone now either.

"Now don't turn me into no tragedy."

I glanced down at the mallet in my hand, looking for courage. "So you did. Love somebody, I mean. You always loved her, but she was already married."

He sat and whittled in silence. The mermaid's body was beginning to take form, her narrow waist curving in from the round, scaled tail and rising up into the chunky, as-yet-uncut block of wood that hid her breasts, shoulders, and head. "If I did, it was a long time ago. An' if she was married, there weren't nothin' I could or would do about it."

"Didn't she love you back?" I asked, hurting for him despite the fact that it was my own father who had been betrayed by this love.

He shrugged. "Maybe. In her way."

The sun was encroaching on the tree line as I finished my work, and I knew we would soon have to call it a day. I opened the can of dark anti-fouling paint and began to apply it in a thick, even coat across her bottom. It would be dark in an hour or so—the days were getting shorter fast. I looked at the cloudless sky, tipped my head back and tasted the dry air, and knew I would paint her tomorrow. *My boat,* I thought. I was a boatbuilder, just like Benigno. Just like Ezra. The thought put us on equal footing.

"Do you still miss her?" I asked, even though I knew it hurt him.

He hung his head then, offering me no pretense. I glimpsed for the first and only time in all the years I knew him something of his grief, his loneliness, his regret. He sat in that old chair, his forearms hanging loose from the elbows that rested on his knees, the mermaid dangling from one hand, his knife in the other. I tried to picture him younger, still virile. In love with Inêz, who came to him for relief from her unhappy marriage. She must have turned to him more fully once, at least for a time. Before she left us all.

I felt a pang of sympathy for him, for making him relive it, but I needed him to say it.

"Do you miss her?" I asked again.

"Ever'day. Ever' blessed day of my life."

Me too, I thought.

CHAPTER FIFTEEN

Monday morning broke against my bedroom window with a vengeance. I stood on the bare floor in front of the glass panes facing Kingston Cove, the soles of my feet pressed into the wide planks of pine. The wind was high, gusting across the marsh and laying the tall grasses flat around the salt ponds. The sky was cloudless, the wind having swept everything before it. Even the birds were grounded.

It was a lousy day to paint my boat.

I sighed, reluctant to make the only choice I had, knowing I would make it anyway. I'd have to move the boat inside and finish painting her in Ezra's workshop. This kind of wind would lay so much sand into her paint that the finish would be ruined, but I couldn't bear to postpone taking her out tomorrow any more than I could bear doing a shoddy job on her paint. But I would have to ask for help moving her—she was too heavy now, fully assembled, for me to even think about doing it alone—and that was a bitter realization.

I presented a grim face to Father and Maria Cristina at the breakfast table, poured myself coffee, buttered toast, and sat down, completely absorbed in my own thoughts.

"Excuse me, will you work on the boat today?" Maria Cristina's mouth was full of toast and jam, her words a gooey mess.

"Yes," I said, as short with her as Ezra often was with me.

"I want to come." I found it increasingly annoying how often she made pronouncements that should have been questions, instead. She was not very good at asking permission, despite all the "excuse me's" that came out of her mouth.

"I'm busy today," I said, irritated to have to think about anyone else.

"I will not bother you. I promise," she wheedled. "Deirdre must do chores for Mrs. Sullivan. There is nothing to do."

Father sat reading the paper, saying nothing. In moments like this he made it clear that he was not interested in parenting Maria Cristina. I knew that if Deirdre Sullivan, any of her siblings, or any of the other kids in town had been sitting here, whining that they were bored, my father would have spoken up and told them sternly that there were plenty of chores to do and he would be happy to give them some in order to stave off boredom. Then he would have noted that there is no excuse for boredom, ever. That boredom is a sign of weak character, an undisciplined mind.

But he remained behind his newspaper, polite and disinterested, as if Maria Cristina were the child of a stranger he had encountered by chance for a moment and would never see again.

"You can come down, but wait until afternoon." I was imagining the weight and dimensions of my boat, anticipating the sweating and the grunting, my strained back and shaking arms as I moved it inside—all of that, and more, with Maria Cristina bouncing around me, asking questions, distracting me.

"Okay," she agreed without enthusiasm. "Can we eat pork chops tonight?"

"Sure," I said absently.

I finished the last bite of toast, gulped my coffee, and glanced at Maria Cristina as I stood to leave and saw a quick spasm of pain cross her features. She sat quietly, turned inward as if listening to some sad but lovely music.

"Are you all right?" I asked.

She looked up at me, a little worried, I thought, and smiled. Reassuring *me*. "Yes, I'm all right. My stomach hurts a little."

I was immediately relieved. A stomachache. "The bicarbonate is in the hall cabinet by the bathroom," I said. "That should help."

Father put his paper down. "Anne, why don't you broil some scallops tonight? Something light." I looked at him, then at Maria Cristina, both of them waiting for my answer. Waiting for me to make a choice between pork and fish—and more. Always more.

I turned without a word and left the house, left the two of them sitting there without me in between, and walked quickly to Ezra's.

As I walked I silently cursed the Sullivans for letting Stevie fish with his dad—he would've been my first choice to help move the boat. I would've paid him a dollar. Somehow it didn't touch me or taint my sole ownership of her if he helped and I paid him for it. Ezra's knee was so bad I knew he couldn't do it, and I wouldn't ask Father. I could've gone to Ben Hightower or his father, but I felt uncomfortable now among the workingmen. I went over in my head a list of everyone I knew, and then went over it again, conspicuously skipping over Will. I had known all along that he was the only one I could ask, but I tried very hard not to ever be in his debt.

The wind almost blew me off my feet when I left the trees and came out into the clearing. The gusts shook the trees, skirted around the buildings, and the waves were whipped up into whitecaps. The sun shone in a brilliant blue sky, unimpressed.

Ezra was nowhere to be seen.

I would have gone straight to the workshop or down to my boat, but I was worried about Ezra. He had seemed alarmingly frail lately, and I was uneasy. I climbed the steps to his house and knocked.

"Ezra?" I called over the wind. "You in there?"

I didn't hear anything, so I knocked louder. "Ezra?" I yelled.

I heard a noise inside, the sound of a chair leg scraping against the floor and the uneven clumping of Ezra's footsteps. He wrenched the door open and glared at me.

"What do you want?"

"Nothing," I said. "I just wanted to make sure . . . I wanted to ask if I could dig through the shop. I want to rig something to move the boat inside."

He scowled, and though I wilted under his look a part of me resented him for turning his anger on me. I knew he just hated being old, and I didn't blame him for being angry that it was happening anyway. God knows there's more power and independence in anger than acceptance, which is why He asks for acceptance and why we prefer anger. My concern for Ezra only reminded him of his own mortality.

"You paw through my things every day without askin'—why bother me this time? Leave me alone, girl! I'm busy."

I almost backed up a step, I was so surprised. I was used to his moods and his gruff way of speaking, but underneath I could almost always sense his love for me. This time I felt abandoned, alone. I turned away and walked back down the steps. After a moment's pause I heard his door close. I made my way against the wind to the workshop, letting the sharp, quick gusts push me around.

When I was inside the shop and had pushed the door closed I relaxed for a moment in the calm, still space. Ezra must be worried, I thought, maybe about more than his lame knee. Was it possible that the sheriff's resigned admission that someone would be arrested soon referred to Ezra? I did not believe—had never believed—that Ezra had killed Matt Da Silva, but what if I was wrong? I shook my head to dispel the traitorous thought. I couldn't do anything at this point but what Ezra asked of me: to leave him alone and finish my work.

The sound of the wind was muted to a faint, intermittent whine, like children crying. While the windowpanes rattled, I toured the room, looking for anything that would help me move the boat. It took me less than half an hour to realize that there was no pulley-and-winch system I could rig up that would allow me to bring her inside without help. I would have to go to Will's office and ask him to come out to Ezra's. Now that my mind was made up, there was no point in putting it off, I figured. I had my hand on the door latch when I heard the sound of a car motor over the wind.

I took two steps forward to look out the window and saw a sleek, powerful coupe pull into Ezra's yard. A man got out—a man who had the sense to take his hat off before climbing out of the car in this wind. A man I could not picture chasing his fedora across the clearing and into the surf.

It was Oliver Fielding.

I moved quickly to the wall, leaving only half my face exposed to the window glass so I could see outside without being easily seen. Oliver glanced at the workshop where I stood watching him, then leaned purposefully into the wind and walked up to the house.

It took a minute, but eventually Ezra came to the door. They spoke briefly; then Oliver retraced his steps and headed right for me.

I opened the door before he had a chance to knock and greeted him with a smile that told him I was happy to see him—which I was, despite my reservations about him.

"What brings you out here this morning?" I asked as he stepped inside and I shut the door behind him. I turned and stood with my back to the door, a sentinel set guard to prevent his escape.

"To see you, of course. To talk about the boat you're going to build for me."

"I haven't agreed to that—only to think about it," I said quickly, sliding out from between him and the door.

He smiled, and it infuriated me. I saw indulgence in that smile, and certainty, as though he knew me better than I knew myself.

"Don't push me, Oliver. I won't be pushed." I wanted to sound tough, but we both knew it was false bravado.

"I'm not pushing you. I'm encouraging you. You should learn the difference."

"Maybe I don't want you for a teacher."

"What do you want me for?" he asked softly.

I blushed and said nothing.

"Take it easy, kid. I'm also in town to see your father," he admitted casually, breaking the tension. He walked away from the door and toward the table, where Ezra's designs were scattered. "Samuel and I have an important meeting tomorrow, and I thought I'd come a little early. See you. Spend a day in Milford. See what's what."

I looked at him and saw a dangerous man. He could easily persuade me that I was the focus of his attention—and intentions—and a moment later walk away from me without a second thought. And I couldn't forget that I was tied to the mill—my father's heir. Of course he was here about the mill. The papers were being drawn up, the partnership between him and my father made legal and binding. Oliver Fielding would forever after be a part of the Dodge mill, and he was here to accomplish that—and to start throwing his weight around, I thought. Starting with me.

The men were right to be worried.

"Things are pretty quiet around here," I said, shrugging as if there was nothing to tell. "It's a small town. Not much happens."

"I know small towns. There's usually a lot more going on beneath the surface than you might suspect."

"You think so? I've never found that to be true here." I refused to get angry—it was what he wanted, what he expected.

"Really? Even with the recent murder?"

When I didn't answer, he casually remarked, "A little bird told me the old man's a suspect."

I would not be goaded. I simply returned his look and waited, standing on one side of the workbench, Oliver on the other. He took a cigarette out and tapped it on his monogrammed case, put it in his mouth, and lit it. I considered telling him that there were varnishes, oils, and gasoline stored in here. But Ezra was pretty good about keeping things tightly sealed, and I couldn't smell any flammables in the air, so I said nothing.

"How do the men feel about the mill reopening?" he asked when it became clear I had nothing to say about Ezra.

Was he digging for information about the demonstration, I wondered, or testing me to see if I would tell him anything? He had to know what the union was planning, I thought, a man like him. He was gauging my loyalty.

"You'd have to ask them. I really couldn't say."

He smiled then, a more genuine look of pleasure and ease than he'd worn since he arrived. "How's the boat coming?" he asked.

"I hope to finish her up today," I said, a grin I couldn't prevent stretching my mouth wide. "I'm taking her out tomorrow." Then my mood sobered and my voice followed suit. "If I can get her in here, that is. It's too windy to paint her outside today."

"Can I help?" he asked. "I've got some free time, and I can take directions." He was disarmingly boyish now, the sparring tone gone from his voice, the sense of danger I'd felt hovering about him vanished.

"Well . . ." I said, tempted by the prospect of getting the job done quickly without having to go back in to town to get Will. "If you're sure you have the time." I looked at him appraisingly. "You don't look like you do a lot of manual labor, though."

He laughed. "True, I don't do a lot of heavy lifting for my pay-check, but I think I'm up to the challenge."

"Okay then," I said. "I wish I didn't need it, but thanks. I'd appreciate the help."

"What do we do, boss?"

"We set up carpenter's horses—cradles—in here, and then we bring her in."

It took us almost no time to get the shop ready for her. Then we opened the double doors, securing them against the outside walls of the building. The wind whipped my hair across my face, and I paused a moment to pull it back again and tie it tightly behind my head.

"Your hair has a mind of its own," Oliver observed loudly over the wind and the door banging against the wall of the workshop. He turned and wedged the rock we were using as a doorstop up a little tighter to immobilize it.

"I know. I've half a mind to cut it all off into one of those new short and wavy styles."

"No, don't," he said quickly, and I looked at him in surprise. "I like it." He took a step closer. He grabbed a long piece of my hair and started to wind it slowly around his finger, and as it tightened, the space between us diminished. He drew me toward him until his face was inches from mine, only the wind racing through the narrow gap between us. "I like it loose, down your back and around your shoulders, like the first day I saw you. Don't cut it." He stood back, and my hair unraveled from around his finger. The wind blew me back a step.

"Stop fooling around," I said. "Let's get this done."

He nodded, without smiling. Will would have teased me right now, I thought suddenly. Gently but purposefully, lightening my mood. He hated it when I was serious. He wouldn't have rested until he had me laughing and smiling. He meant it when he said my happiness was more important to him than anything. I was lucky to have someone who cared for me that much, I reminded myself.

Oliver and I walked against the wind, down to the dock where my boat sat.

I paused for a moment, appraising the situation.

"I'll take the bow," I said. "She's up high enough that lifting her should be pretty easy. Use your legs. Center the stern over your head and grip the gunwales on each side, up by your shoulders," I said, demonstrating. My elbows were bent, my hands up level with my ears as though holding something over my head.

Oliver listened and nodded.

"We'll bring her in bow first, her stern closer to the door. When we set her down, don't let go until she's stabilized."

"Okay," he said. "Will we leave her upside down again?"

"No, we'll flip her back right-side up, but not until she's in the cradles. We'll roll her once she's stable."

"Okay," he said. "I can do that."

"Are you ready?"

The real danger didn't lie in her weight but in her width—she was wide and would be awkward to carry because our hands on each side would be so far from our bodies and our center of gravity. If one of us started to tip and the weight of the boat shifted from the center, we wouldn't be able to catch her and she'd fall. I didn't want to spend a week or two on repairs.

We positioned ourselves at bow and stern, the horses between us. We crouched down a bit, our hands up by our shoulders on the gunwales.

"Ready?" I called. Oliver was behind me, so I could only assume he was doing what I was doing.

"Ready!" he called.

"On three. One—two—three!"

I exhaled as I stood up straight, my legs shaking a little as my body took half the weight of the boat. We paused a moment, each of us adjusting, centering the boat, steadying ourselves.

"You okay back there?" I asked.

"Fine. Just say when."

"Okay, let's start toward the shop," I called, my face turned a little so my voice would carry behind me. "Slow and steady. The wind's going to catch her full across like a sail, so be prepared. And it's uphill all the way, though the incline isn't steep. If you need to stop, say so."

We walked then, taking it one slow step at a time. The wind pushed us hard, gusting against the hull like a battering ram, but we held her steady. I was breathing hard—she was heavy, and the ground was uneven. As I approached the open doors, my legs beginning to shake in earnest, I called back to Oliver.

"You doing okay?"

"Doing fine. We're almost there."

We were inside then, the wind gone so suddenly that we staggered in the sudden stillness. We walked the bow back to the far sawhorse, and I stopped just past it.

"Are you in place?" I asked.

"I think so—wait, hold on a minute." I felt the boat shift a little as he used his foot to angle the stern sawhorse in a bit closer. "Okay. I'm ready," he said.

We moved a few steps to the side, lining up with the horses.

"On three we're going to bend, lowering her until she's resting on the horses," I said.

"Okay."

"One—two—three." I bent my knees, leaning a little forward. My legs were shaking badly, and I thought for a moment I would drop her. Then I felt her touch the support, and the weight was simply gone. I ducked under her, my hand still on her side, and came up to look back at Oliver.

He was standing, his hand resting proprietarily on her side, grinning at me. "We did it!" He was triumphant.

"We did. Thanks for helping."

"My pleasure," he said, smiling.

We rolled her then, which was comparatively easy, until she was right-side up, ready for paint. Oliver sat down, his back to the wall, and took out his cigarettes, lighting one for each of us and handing me mine. I smoked beside my boat, smiling to think that I looked like Ezra.

"What's her name?" he asked.

"Oh, right, a name. I don't know."

"She's got to have a name. This isn't just any old boat," he said.

"True. I don't know why I haven't thought of one. No one else has asked." I turned to look at him, relaxed and comfortable. He seemed comfortable wherever he was. I drew on my cigarette, felt the hot smoke spinning down into my lungs.

"What do you think I should call her?"

"I don't know—but make it mean something to you." He paused, smoked for a minute, lost in thought.

"How about *Anne's Folly?*" I said. "That has a nice, natural ring to it." I was thinking of my father. I hoped, too late, that my voice didn't sound bitter.

"No," he said, suddenly serious. "You don't really think that. Don't take what hurts you and keep it."

I smiled. For a dangerous man, Oliver Fielding sounded like a nice guy.

"You're right. Maybe *Annie's Dream* or, even simpler, *Hope* or *Joy*."

"Any of those would do," he approved, but I didn't want a name that would just do.

"I'll think about it," I said. "I don't have to name her immediately. There's plenty of time."

We sat, smoking and looking at the boat.

"Oliver, what's going to happen when the men and the union organizers demonstrate?"

I was impressed that I hadn't startled him, or at least that he didn't show it. He didn't even turn toward me. There was no denial, no defensive posturing. He sat quietly for a moment, smoking, considering.

"I honestly don't know," he said. His bare forearm lay across his thigh, only inches from mine. His shirtsleeves were rolled up, and I stared at his tanned skin, the thick, fine brown hairs that grew down a little past his wrist until they thinned and then stopped altogether on the back of his hand. His nails were clean and neatly trimmed.

"It depends on what they want to happen. What their objective is."

"None of it depends on what you do?"

"This is their action, not mine. It's my responsibility, and your father's, to react. We have a vested interest in what happens at the mill—it's private property—and our role is to react and to try to contain, if necessary, anything potentially destructive to that interest." He looked at his watch. "You need me for anything else before I go?" he asked.

"No," I said. "But I'm not finished with you yet."

"I should hope not," he said, grinning.

"I have a bad feeling about this thing, Oliver," I said, pretending I hadn't heard him, pretending I didn't want to play, too. "Can you just let them have their protest, let them make speeches and cheer, and then let them go home? It doesn't have to be a confrontation, does it?"

"Annie," he said gently, "you're young and passionate—" He stopped when he saw my face. "Stop being angry for two seconds!

You *are* young, and you *are* passionate. Those things are plainly true, and they're wonderful besides. Stop being so goddamn combative! All I'm saying is that there are things about this you can't possibly understand. I couldn't have, either, at your age."

"Well, then, make me understand," I said. "I've heard stories about you, Oliver. About your workers, about how you respond to the unions. Make me understand how you can have a man beaten to death with a baseball bat because he wants to negotiate with you for a raise and a shorter workweek!"

"Where did you hear that?" he asked, no longer smiling.

"It's just gossip, but—"

"What it is, is slander," he said coldly. "I've never had a man beaten for anything. I don't break the law—I use it because it's on my side. I will never let the unions into my business. Ever. You're going to have to get used to the idea."

"Says who?" I asked, outraged. The Dodge mill had become the Fielding mill in his eyes, and the papers hadn't even been signed yet!

I stood up and moved away from the wall, facing him. "Don't forget for a second that my father holds fifty-five percent of the mill. And that one day I will. I'm not afraid to fight you on this, Oliver. I'm not afraid of you."

He stood up, brushed the sawdust from his trousers, tucked his shirt back in at his slim waist where it had ballooned out a bit from carrying the boat.

"I know," he said, completely serious as he looked at me. "It's one of the things I like most about you. But if you fight me, you will lose."

He walked straight out the door then without another word or a look back. I stood rooted to the spot, even after his car disappeared and the sound of his motor was lost in the wind.

I stood there, stunned, exactly as he'd left me. What happened? I wondered. I felt bereft, somehow, as if my last chance had just walked out the door. It was those words resounding in my head that brought me to my senses: *last chance*. My father saw Oliver as his last chance, as our last chance. It was clear to me now that I had begun to see him this way, too, not just because of the mill but because he would make it possible for me to gain some independence for Maria Cristina and myself by buying a boat. But that's not true, I reminded myself. It's the boats I could build that would make us independent of Father, free of everyone. Not Oliver. All Oliver has done is show me that I can sell what I make. He didn't need to be the buyer.

My determination restored, I turned back to the boat. Now that she was indoors I could finish her. I would take her out tomorrow, after all—if the wind didn't whip up too much chop in the bay.

I spent the next hour puttying all the nail and screw heads with seam compound. Then I applied a fast-drying paint, flat primer, and two coats of gloss, with a good sanding in between. Inside I used a good deck paint. She was white all over, with several coats of Red Hand copper at the waterline. She dried good and hard inside the workshop, though the process took about six hours. I couldn't detect any tackiness when I finally touched her. The sun had set long ago.

As I hammered the lid back down on the paint, I considered my boat, thought about what Oliver had said. She did need a name.

My head ached a little from the fumes, and I longed for the fresh air I would breathe as soon as I opened the doors, but it had been worth it to keep them closed, keep the sand out. Her finish was smooth and flawless.

I imagined Maria Cristina and myself in summers to come, exploring the bay in her, laughing and singing, gulls screeching overhead, the wind in our hair. I looked at the flat, wide stern, brilliant white now, where I would eventually stencil letters. I forgot my worries and uncertainties for that one, brief moment, and thought about her name.

Something happy, I thought. For once in my life, something hopeful. Things were different now that I had Maria Cristina. We would be inseparable: Maria Cristina and her sister, Ana.

I will put our names together forever, I thought.

My boat would be the *Mariana*.

CHAPTER SIXTEEN

The worst storms are born of things I love: salt water and sunshine. The earth spins, and in warmer waters the coupling of moist air and heat gives birth to monstrous progeny, swirling winds and rain that pulverize everything in their paths. The wind is always strongest near the center of the storm, where the rising heat from the doldrums creates low barometric pressure and the earth's rotation pulls the winds along.

I woke on Tuesday morning unaware, as we all were, that down the eastern seaboard, along Virginia and the Carolinas, the central hub of an enormous storm was approaching, sweeping northward over the sea at forty-five miles an hour and picking up speed. The quiet grayness we woke to held its secrets close.

I finished the breakfast dishes quickly, eager to get to Ezra's. The wind had died down overnight, and a thick fog had rolled in, but as soon as it cleared I knew I'd be out on the water in the *Mariana*. The vision was shattered, however, by the insistent ring of the telephone. It was my father, who needed me to bring him some papers he'd left on the bureau in his bedroom.

I felt somewhat agitated, but admitted reluctantly that this small delay was really no delay at all since I had to wait for the fog to burn off anyway. Maria Cristina and I set out with Father's papers, hurrying downtown to the courthouse.

When we arrived, we found Father waiting for us, hovering near the front doors, pacing.

"Did you get them all?" he asked, quickly leafing through the stack of pages I'd picked up in his room. "Good, good," he said, clearly relieved. He looked at me then and smiled. "Thank you, dear."

"Of course," I said. "What's going on?"

"Nothing new. I'm just in a meeting all day with my attorneys, getting ready for tomorrow. The meeting with Fielding." He glanced at Maria Cristina, who looked back at him calmly until he looked away and back to me.

"What do you have planned today?" he asked.

"My boat's finished," I said. "I'm taking her out."

There was no point in trying to sound blasé. I was thrilled, and it showed.

"I'm not going far and I won't be out long. It's just a test run. I'm going out to Ezra's right after I finish up here."

"All right," he said, turning away and taking a step toward the doors. "But be careful, Anne. I saw Sheriff Tucker this morning. He's getting a warrant. I don't know any of the details, but I don't want you to be upset by any . . . unpleasantness at Ezra's today."

"Oh, no!" I cried softly. "I thought there wasn't enough evidence?"

"Farley must've found something. All I know is that he'll be making an arrest sometime later today. And I don't want you involved."

"There's nothing I can do, anyway," I said forlornly. "But I would have protected him, if I could." My tone was defiant, but he merely looked at me with pity and I dropped my eyes. "Thank you for telling me, Father."

He started back inside, then stopped and turned back. "Do me a favor before you go, will you, dear? Run to the post office for me.

I've got a letter from the statehouse you'll have to sign for, and I won't have a chance to get out of the office today."

"Okay."

He turned to go, and Maria Cristina and I walked down the wide steps of the courthouse to the sidewalk.

"Your father does not like me," she announced.

My silence became a confirmation. I could detect no hint of hurt feelings or resentment in her voice as she said what sounded like a simple statement of fact. Which is, of course, exactly what it was.

"Maria Cristina, I don't know what to say," I began.

She shrugged. "When I came, I thought you would not like me, also."

We were walking to the corner where we would cross Main to the post office, a small brick building flying an American flag and, just beneath it, the state flag of Rhode Island. The metal clips on the rope's pulley clanked loudly against the pole—we could hear it across the street. It was a lonely, futile sound.

"Maria Cristina," I said, stopping and turning to face her. "I do like you. I love you. You're my sister, and nothing can ever change that now."

"I know," she said. "But I am sorry he does not like me—sorry because it makes you sad, I can see. I try to be quiet and polite and helpful, but it does nothing."

Maria Cristina was indeed doing all those things—she was a model child, for the most part, if a model child is rarely seen or heard, ever-conscious of adults' moods, careful not to attract attention or create a ripple, eager to please at every turn. She had done her very best to become invisible, to erase her presence like footprints in the sand. A light breeze could fill in the indentations, and no one would ever know she'd been there.

"I know. You've done all those things, and you're right, it hasn't helped. But it's going to change. I promise you." *Even if I have to leave that house,* I thought, startling myself.

Why couldn't I rent a small house in town—maybe even buy

one someday? The thought was exhilarating, like running fast. I could not understand how this had not occurred to me before. But suddenly, there it was. We could move out of my father's house. I could build boats for money, support us even if Father cut me off. I would be free, and Maria Cristina could laugh and sing and run through the house if she wanted to. Make deep, permanent footprints. We would never—either of us—have to be careful again.

I couldn't tell her yet. What if I failed? What if it took three or four years before I could make it happen? I would wait until I had money in my hand, maybe even a house I could walk her up to, waltz her in the front door and declare that we were home—and which room would she like as her own? I felt lightheaded at the idea of so much freedom. Maybe the day was just making me crazy, the boat giving me a courage and a vision that wouldn't stand up to my every-day responsibilities, my more sober, cautious self. But for that moment I believed it could happen.

I squeezed her hand. "It's going to get better," I said again. "Come on, let's get that letter."

We entered the Milford post office and proceeded to the counter where Mrs. Caulfield, a cousin of Mrs. Hatcher's, worked. She sold stamps, weighed packages and meted out postage, sent telegrams. She had been widowed in the Great War and had never remarried. When I was a teenager I had romanticized her loss, trying very hard to see her as tragic, but there was nothing about her that suggested stoicism or deep, well-hidden pain. Some people, I was eventually forced to conclude, got over things.

"Hi, Mrs. Caulfield," I said as we approached the counter. "How are you today?"

"I'm well, Annie. And you and your sister?" she asked, with a nod and a smile for Maria Cristina.

"Fine, thanks," I said. "I need to sign for a letter for my father from Providence."

"All rightee," she said, and disappeared through a door into another room. She came back almost immediately, carrying a letter and a box wrapped in brown paper.

"There's also a package for you," she said, indicating the small rectangular package. "Do you want to take it with you, save Joe from carrying it on his route tomorrow?"

"Sure," I said.

She handed me the letter and an official form, indicating where I was to sign. She tore off the receipt and handed it to me, stamped the remaining piece of paper, and filed it away in a drawer.

"There you are," she said. "Unless there's something else you need today?"

There wasn't. I put the letter in my back pocket and turned the box so I could read the address: "To Miss Anne Dodge." The return address was in Providence, I noted, but I didn't recognize it. Maybe Father had ordered something for me—my birthday was coming up, I remembered. That was probably it. The box was light and small, maybe ten or twelve inches long, eight inches deep. I shook it gently, but it made no sound.

"What is it?" asked Maria Cristina, her curiosity piqued.

"I don't know," I said. "Probably something my father ordered for my birthday."

"A present!" she said. "Let's go home and open it."

"It's probably socks," I said. "Or maybe cucumber seeds for next year's garden."

She laughed as we walked outside. The fog was beginning to burn off. I could see patches of deep-blue sky, and I wanted to be at Ezra's. I knew Maria Cristina would want to come and, while I wanted to take the boat out alone, I wanted her to share my excitement and the triumph of the day.

"You want to come to Ezra's with me?" I asked.

"Yes!"

"Good. Let's drop these at the house and go."

We walked briskly back the way we'd come, crossing the street at the courthouse and heading back down Main toward our house.

There was light traffic, people going about their business as happened most weekday mornings, but as we walked I began to notice a difference, like a scent in the air that I could just make out. At first I simply noted that I had passed a group of three men I did not recognize—not an unheard-of event in Milford, but not especially common, either. As they passed Maria Cristina and me on the sidewalk, I caught a glimpse of their wiry tension. I stopped, turned, and followed them with my eyes. At the end of the block they crossed the street and joined another man who stood on the corner before they all continued down Main, a tight knot of swinging arms and darting eyes.

We kept walking, but I was bothered. It was too much of a coincidence not to assume that they were agitators, brought in by the union to stir up trouble—which probably meant that the demonstration would be soon, maybe even today, I thought nervously. Father was planning to spend the day with his attorneys behind closed doors and might not get wind of any of it. He had told me not to worry, of course, that he had everything under control. I hoped he was right.

Just before we got to the Hatchers' place I looked up as a car engine grew increasingly louder, and we both waved at Mr. Sullivan, who was driving past. I had just enough time to make out Stevie in the passenger seat, looking unusually pale, and two men sitting in the truck bed whose faces I couldn't see beneath their hats. It wasn't until we reached our front door that it occurred to me that the Sullivans weren't out on the water, and they never missed a day.

Once we were home I put the letter and my package on the dining room table, and Maria Cristina and I quickly went upstairs to change our clothes. I grabbed an old wool fisherman's sweater to put on over my shirt in case it was cold on the water. I was grinning like a fool by the time I had run back down the stairs where Maria Cristina waited for me.

"Will you open your present before we leave?" she asked, eager as always for a surprise, even if it wasn't hers.

"Let's go to Ezra's," I countered. "I'll open it later. You can help me."

We left, despite Maria Cristina casting a longing, somewhat melodramatic glance at the package and heaving an absurdly loud sigh on the way out.

I set a record, I think, on the mill road, with Maria Cristina complaining that I was making her run to keep up. She was so moody! I asked her, without much compassion, what in the world was wrong with her.

"Nothing," she said. "My stomach still hurts."

"Well, if it's that bad perhaps you should've stayed at home," I said, knowing I was being unkind.

She didn't answer but trudged resentfully by my side.

By the time we came out of the trees and into Ezra's clearing it was only ten o'clock. The fog had lifted, and though there was an insistent, chilly breeze, the sky was clear except for a few gray and white clouds that occasionally obscured the sun.

I strode toward the workshop, going over in my mind the checklist I would have to complete to get the boat in the water. I had reluctantly asked Will to come down at lunchtime to help me move her down to the dock—the decision was somehow easier because I had avoided needing his help the day Oliver had showed up. In the meantime I needed to make sure she was seaworthy and get one of Ezra's two-cycle motors ready. I'd have to carry it down to the dock and fill the tank. I'd take care of the lights and safety equipment over the next few days.

I lifted the latch on the workshop doors and threw them open wide and discovered that my boat was gone. I looked again. I was stunned and stood there blinking like an idiot.

"Look!" cried Maria Cristina.

She had had the sense to look outside as soon as she realized the boat was gone. I turned, following her index finger that pointed toward the dock. My boat sat bobbing gently in the water, tied to one of the pilings.

She was beautiful! She sat gleaming in the sun, her bow curving gently upward to a point. She was elegant despite her girth, I thought. She looked like a woman, substantial and confident.

I was completely in love with her.

I heard Ezra's front door open and grinned. He'd been waiting for us, probably watching out the window.

"How did you do this?" I called as we walked toward his house.

"Will was down here with the Sullivan boy first thing this mornin'," he said, and some of the excitement I felt myself was reflected in his voice. "Said he knew it would just about kill you to have to stand around an' wait, so he came before he went to his office. Woke me up at sunrise."

Ezra tried to pretend he was annoyed, but I knew better.

We had reached the steps now and stood looking up at Ezra, who leaned over the railing toward us.

"So they moved her," I said unnecessarily.

"Yep. It wasn't nothin'."

"I'll get her ready then, if you don't mind," I said.

"She's ready now," he said, and I knew from his tone of suppressed pleasure that he had made his own contribution. "There's a brand-new two-cycle, eight-horse kicker on her, and her tank's full. She's ready for her first run."

"No!" I breathed, hardly believing it. "Really? I can't believe you did this—I can't believe she's finished!"

I was ecstatic, barely keeping myself rooted to the ground when what I wanted was to fly down the gently sloping yard to the water where she waited.

"Well, hold on now, she's just ready for a little test drive. She ain't done till she's completely outfitted. You buy what you need, get it stowed before you go out again." He was stern again, the crusty old man endlessly teaching.

"I know, I will, I promise," I said in a rush, interrupting myself to laugh, my joy uncontainable. "Can I go now?"

"Me too!" said Maria Cristina. "I want to go too!"

I caught Ezra's eye and in a flash he knew what I needed.

"Not this time, Maria Cristina," he said smoothly. "The skipper's got to take her out the first time, make sure she's seaworthy. It's part of her job."

"He's right, Maria Cristina. But you know you'll always ride with me after that," I quickly added. "You know the plan: we'll be Robinson Crusoe and Friday, escaping *to* our island instead of away from it! Today, though, I have to go alone. It won't take too long. I promise."

"I always have to wait. I don't want to wait anymore," she said, sounding angry for the first time since I'd met her.

"Maria Cristina, if you could just—" I began.

"No, Ana! You said when you finished this boat we would do everything together. You are finished. If you go, I want to go."

Why does she have to make her stand *now*? I thought, exasperated. Can't she just do what I ask, grumble a little, make me suffer through her pouting? She had begun to feel safe enough to challenge me, confident that I would not leave her. I might have focused on that, I know, celebrated our growing love for, and confidence in, each other. But all I could see was my boat, beckoning me toward the water and freedom. All I could feel was an overwhelming desire for Maria Cristina to simply go away.

"I want to come with you," she said again, her chin thrust forward.

"Not today," I said, and our eyes met and locked. Oh, we were sisters, all right.

"Why can't I go?" she asked, her voice louder, her arms crossed over her chest.

"Ezra has already explained that," I said, losing patience.

"You cannot say what I may or may not do," she said. "You are not my mother."

No, I thought, I'm not. I looked at Ezra for help, thinking, *If you are her father, now would be a good time to act like it.*

He looked back at me, raised one eyebrow, and said nothing.

"You can't go," I said with finality, and turned and started walking toward the dock.

"Excuse me, I do not want your stupid boat!" she shouted.

I could hear the anger and the tears in her voice, but I did not turn around.

Ezra and Will had made her fast to the last piling of the dock, and I quickly slipped her line and boarded her. My hand lingered on the smooth gunwale. My heart was beating fast, and a bracing wind blew inland off the water. I was glad of the sweater I'd worn. I turned, the sun high overhead, and went to her stern to start her up. Bracing my left hand on the transom for balance, I closed the choke and pulled her cord with my right. She flooded on me, sputtering and quitting altogether. I cleared the excess fuel, then opened the throttle partway and pulled the rope until she was clear.

I turned the fuel valve and tried her again, certain that the majority of our four-letter words were born of trying to start a boat engine. She coughed and sputtered and came to life, running strong and even.

The propeller churned up pale sea-green foam, and I slipped her rope and shoved off from the dock, raising my arm in a casual farewell that didn't fool anybody. Ezra and Maria Cristina stood on the shore up by the workshop, watching me as I moved away from the dock.

I put a few yards between me and the breakers before I opened her up. The bow came up, the propeller dug deep, and a little rooster tail sprayed up behind me. I couldn't keep from yelling from sheer happiness. My hair flew out behind me like a long, dark cape, and I pretended I might not come back at all.

I followed the shoreline away from Ezra's, toward the mill, about a hundred yards out. The water was choppy, but I was pleased with how she took the whitecaps without bucking. I watched as a huge cloud of barn swallows rose up from the marsh, flowing and twisting with inexplicable, perfectly executed changes in course. A few birds led, dipping and turning, and hundreds of others followed without dissent. It was a wonder.

The sun sparkled on the tip of each small wave whipped up by the wind. The light was refracted back at me from each one of them until the entire world sparkled, so brilliant I could hardly stand to look at it. The steady drone of my motor drowned out the gulls as they screamed overhead, the sky subtly changing from blue to purple off my starboard side, the horizon a deep bruise.

Twenty minutes later I reluctantly turned her around, the tiller in my hand, the rudder responsive. The waves were too big for comfort. I could've easily stayed until it was too dark to make my way home again, but I told myself to be patient. I would have endless days of this—just this, and nothing else.

When I got back I stepped out onto the dock and tied her fast to the dock cleat. Ezra had taught me to make a boat fast to a good, heavy mooring, if possible, but in any case to always leave her as though you expected a hard blow. It looked like we might get one. I stood up and looked down at her. She was perfect.

I didn't see anyone outside the house, so I walked up. Ezra came out onto the porch when I approached.

"How'd she treat you?" he asked.

"Like a captain," I said, grinning. "It was amazing. Not a single problem."

"Gettin' rough out there. The wind's picked up."

"A bit. Think we're in for some weather?"

He paused, and I waited while he looked at the hazy purple skyline, the white-capped waves in the cove. He seemed to be sniffing the air. I smiled, convinced that he did it for effect when he probably had heard a weather report just a few minutes earlier on the radio he kept on the mantel in his house.

"We might be."

"Well, I'm glad I took her out then," I said. "Is Maria Cristina inside? I assume she's still mad at me."

"She's not here. Ran off right after you left." He cleared his throat. "She was cryin'."

I frowned. This was all new to me, and I wasn't finding it particularly pleasant. She was going to have to learn to compromise and not throw a temper tantrum every time she didn't get her way. I would need to be tough, I decided. "She'll be fine. I'll let her pout by herself for a while."

Ezra looked skeptical but said nothing, unable or unwilling to help.

I looked back toward the boat, pitching a little but clearly secured.

"I'm going to do a little clean-up in the workshop," I told him. "I've left a lot of things lying around lately."

"I noticed," he said pointedly.

"Ezra," I began with some hesitation, "the sheriff's ready to make an arrest."

"I know," he said gently, surprising me. "You can rest easy now. It's all over."

"But . . ." I began.

"It ain't me that's goin' to jail."

"Then who?" I demanded.

"Ever'body'll know soon enough," he said, sounding as defeated as I'd ever heard him.

He went in the house then and shut the door. I stood a moment until I had convinced myself that all that mattered was that Ezra was innocent.

I headed for the workshop, whistling.

I had only been at it for a few minutes and was squatted down in front of the workbench, trying in vain to see to the back of one of the shelves underneath, when I felt a gust of wind as the door opened. Thinking it was Ezra, I called over my shoulder to him.

"Sounds like the wind is really picking up!"

"It is," said Oliver.

I came slowly to my feet, turning and rising like a waterspout.

"What are you doing here?" I asked.

"I came to wish you luck, to send you off on your maiden voyage—or have you already gone?"

"I've already gone."

"Ah, well, I couldn't get away earlier. Pity. How was it?"

"Great," I said, my mouth stretching wide in a smile I couldn't help. "Amazing. Wonderful."

Oliver laughed with a deep, genuine happiness that caught at my breath.

"She handles well, and she's incredibly stable. I've got to add a few finishing touches, but she's perfect."

"If you do say so yourself," he teased.

"Well, if I don't, who will?" I said, my spirits high. "Do you want a builder who has confidence in her work, or don't you?"

He took a quick, involuntary step toward me. "You're going to do it?"

"I'm going to do it," I said simply.

"Anne, that's wonderful news. This will be good for both of us."

"I'm looking forward to it," I said. "I need to make some changes in my life, and this will be the first step. So I thank you for the opportunity, and I accept your offer."

I felt a little self-conscious, but I needed to formally agree. And when I did, when I said it out loud, it was a step toward an independence I'd always wanted. I felt strong and in command of my own life. I wasn't pleasing anybody but me, and what pleased me felt right. I knew I would have to deal with my father, with the issue of the mill, but at that moment I did not care.

I closed the distance between us, my hand held out to shake his, to put the traditional seal on our partnership. He met me halfway, put his hand in mine. We stood like that for a moment, hands clasped, saying nothing, our eyes locked. I felt my heart hammering in my chest, and I swayed just slightly, my sea legs still under me. I could smell the salt in my hair and clothes, a briny perfume more heady to me than the most expensive dram from New York. Without thinking I pulled his hand, still clasped in mine, in toward me, and he let his body follow until his face was only inches from mine, our arms pressed in between us. I leaned in and kissed him.

He was so still I thought he might be holding his breath, waiting to see where my desire would lead us. I let go of his hand then, pulled my arm free, and pulled his head in toward me, both my hands in his hair. I was ravenous, tasting the faint air of tobacco smoke that clung to him and enveloped us both. I felt hollowed out and I crushed him to me, pulling him in, wanting nothing more than to fill that space.

And then care and caution were gone, his hands on either side of my face, his tongue in my mouth, demanding more. I fumbled at his trousers, wishing them off him, afraid to stop and think. He held me to him with one arm, allowing no space between us, and backed me up against the workbench. I felt the edge of it pushing hard against my lower back.

He crushed my breast with one hand and unbuttoned my dungarees with the other. Suddenly he pulled his mouth from mine and we looked at each other—I, startled; he, offering me a last chance to change my mind.

I put my hand behind his head and pulled his mouth back down to mine.

We half fell to the floor, and his weight pinned me down. He was hurting me, just a little, and I thought I would say something, ask him to let me breathe, but I bit his lip instead. He swept my trousers down with one quick movement and I lifted my hips to help. I felt the cold, dirty floor against my skin, wood chips pressed into my flesh. And then he was in me and I was straining toward him, the motion of the deck still with me, the heat of the sun and water everywhere, but it was we who moved, we who embodied the warm, wet world.

When it was over we lay bruised and filthy and breathing hard. After a moment, Oliver raised himself on one elbow and looked at me carefully, unsure of what to expect. I was a little embarrassed but forced myself to look him straight in the eye and smile. This would be my new life: certain, unapologetic.

"It's been quite a day," I said lightly.

He laughed, clearly relieved. I wondered with some amusement what he had expected. Tears? Recriminations?

"Yes, it certainly has. I wish I had champagne. I think we have a legitimate celebration on our hands."

We grinned at each other.

"I should get going . . ." I said.

"Here's your hat, what's your hurry?" he teased. "You'd better be careful, or I might start to feel cheap."

I was startled. Was he serious? "Oh, no," I said quickly. "I wanted to— I'm sure you could tell, but I thought you did, too, and I know that happened rather fast, but it's been an incredible day, as I said, and I—"

"Anne." He looked at me, amused. "I'm joking. You were beautiful, and I am so happy that you 'wanted to.' I certainly did—as I'm sure you could tell. Don't feel awkward or sorry. I'm glad I was here to help you celebrate. I think it was excellent timing on my part," he finished wickedly.

I shoved him, he laughed, and we both got dressed. I had sawdust in lots of unexpected places, and he looked like— Well, he looked like he'd been rolling around on the floor with somebody. I laughed, reaching over to smooth his hair down where it was sticking straight up.

"We might want to go get cleaned up before we run into any respectable people," I said.

He left then, without kissing me. There was no hint in his manner that things had changed, that we were a couple. No suggestion that the suspicion and antagonism between us had been resolved.

It was exactly what I wanted.

I locked up the workshop and began walking home, the wind tearing at my clothes, looking for seams and a way in. The waves had picked up speed and height in the cove, the faint purple horizon having materialized as dark storm clouds moving inland. Rain had begun light and fine, like mist, and I wondered if this would be a quick summer shower, blowing itself out in an hour or two. But the barometer had been falling steadily all day, I would later learn, and by nightfall it would plummet and the storm would make landfall.

I hardly noticed the rain then, though, light as it was, but it soaked me through as I trudged through the drifting sand. When I reached the mill road and turned toward town, the hollowness that had been my constant companion was gone. I felt full, satisfied, as I ambled back toward Milford, the trees bending and blowing around me as the storm crept carefully toward the south shore.

That feeling—and that naïveté—carried me all the way home.

CHAPTER SEVENTEEN

I let myself in the front door and stood for a moment in the hall. The house was dark, quiet, and tense. I listened for a moment, wondering if Father or Maria Cristina was home, but I heard nothing. I walked quickly then to the telephone table in the hall and switched on the lamp there. It cast a discrete pool of light on the chair and table, a smaller circle of light on the ceiling above that served mainly to illustrate the deepening gloom.

I took off my shoes and tossed them over by the wall where a puddle began immediately to form around them. I moved to the foot of the stairs and called loudly.

"Anybody home?" I paused for several beats for a response, even the sound of a footstep, a creaking floorboard. There was nothing. I went upstairs and quickly changed into dry clothes.

Back in the kitchen I turned on the wall light switch and saw that nothing had been prepared for dinner—not that I had expected it, but there was always hope. I opened the door of the icebox and saw little that inspired me. Finally I took out bacon and eggs, figuring that I could fry the bacon now, then begin cooking the eggs when Father and Maria Cristina arrived so the food would be fresh and hot within minutes.

I lit the stove and put a heavy, cast-iron pan over the flame. I covered the bottom of the pan with strips of thick bacon, the white, fatty edges covered in black pepper, and waited. I thought about Oliver, and about our afternoon. I felt myself blushing. I accused myself of loose morals and tried to sound convincing, but it was no use. I certainly understood how I was supposed to behave, but I wasn't sorry.

I felt myself growing hot in the face, thinking about Oliver. His mouth had found every part of me, and when I'd put my hand down to stop him he'd shoved it away. He'd been like a starving man, and I was sustenance. I covered my face, grinning as I remembered the heat of his mouth—I reached over to turn down the flame under the pan, as if the stove had anything to do with it, and laughed. It was the laugh of a pagan. My life didn't have to be shaped by other people's beliefs. I was free, and for the first time I thought maybe I deserved it. When I'd returned with my boat to Ezra's, that's who I was, and the joy of simply existing in such a world was more than my own body could contain. I saw Oliver, and I wanted him. It was that simple.

I would not apologize for it, even to myself.

The bacon began to hiss softly, popping occasionally as the fat liquefied in the pan. I recalled seeing the Sullivans this morning in their truck, and the strangers moving together purposefully down Main Street, and felt an uneasy urge to walk down to the mill to make sure everything was okay. I resolved to do that after dinner. I tried to convince myself that the men would decide to hold the protest during the day—and when the weather was better, I thought, listening to the howling wind pick up outside. I turned the meat with a long fork, one piece at a time, crisp sides facing up, and when they were done I lifted them out and placed them on newsprint to blot the grease, covering them with another sheet to keep them warm. Suddenly I heard the bang of the front door closing.

"Anne?" my father called.

"In the kitchen!"

He strode in the door, a scowl on his face. Water streamed from his hat brim and the collar and shoulders of his coat.

"What an awful night!" he said, peeling his coat off and hanging it over the back of one of the chairs, then hanging his hat on the back. "Have you been home long?" he asked, eyeing the makeshift dinner I was preparing.

"No, not long," I said. "I had no idea when you or Maria Cristina would be home, and I wanted to be able to make something quick—like eggs—once you got here."

He said nothing but crossed to the sink behind me and filled a glass with water from the faucet. He stood there, his back to the room, while he drank it slowly, deliberately, without taking a breath. When the glass was empty he set it down on the counter and turned back toward me. I busied myself at the stove, placing the last of the bacon strips on the paper, covering them, turning off the gas and extinguishing the flame. There was no point in cooking the eggs until Maria Cristina got back.

"I'm going out again, so don't bother cooking for me," he said.

"Tonight?" I asked, surprised. He often worked late, but once he came home he almost never went back out.

"Yes. I've got to go down to the mill."

It *is* tonight, I thought. "Are the men demonstrating tonight?"

He looked at me sharply but didn't ask what I knew, or how long I'd known it.

"Yes. I'm not sure what they intend, or if I'll make things worse by going, but I have no choice."

I could see that he was upset, agitated, worried. What does he think might happen? I wondered. "Father, it might not be that bad. Don't worry so much."

"You don't understand," he said, and the last word was a moan. The sound scared me more than anything he could have said. He always presented a calm and in-control face to the world, even in times of crisis. I hated that he felt he had to do so even in his own home, with me, but it had always been like that.

"Tell me," I said. A willingness to listen was all I could offer him.

"I've got to go. It's my property. People don't always think rationally in a group. I've got to see that everyone stays calm, nothing gets damaged. I can do that. They know me."

He paused, began to pace in front of the kitchen sink, his reflection materializing in the darkened window every time he passed. He ran his fingers through his thick white hair, making it stand on end. I felt my stomach clench. I'd never seen him like this before. Unsure, indecisive.

"I'm sure it will be fine," I said soothingly, but it was a weak attempt at comfort, and we both knew it. "Like you said, they know you."

"It's not that simple—I wish it were!" he said, stopping up short in his pacing, facing me, angry and frustrated. "If it were just about the men—even the unions! But I'm completely trapped. Caught in the middle."

"What do you mean?" I asked, and when he didn't answer I was afraid. "Father, tell me what's going on! I can't help you if you don't tell me."

"Fielding knows about the demonstration," he said. "He's known for several days. He'll— I'm afraid he's going to send some men in. Nothing's been proven, of course, but there's talk about the kind of thugs that seem to appear where he's involved. Outsiders, people nobody knows, who disappear when it's all over." He paused, looked at me so I'd hear this, get it at last. "Somebody could get hurt."

I looked at him, my mouth open. "But why would he do that?" I asked. "If he's going to be your partner, if he's going to be a part of the mill and the town, why would he do that?"

"Because that's what he does. He hits hard and fast. There are some who believe that in the long run it's better for business, even better for the men. A little violence early on, no problems later." He sounded bitter, and weary to death.

"But that's just unacceptable," I said, unwilling to reconcile this picture of Oliver with the man I had come to know intimately. I could still smell him on me, and I suddenly knew what it felt like to be unfaithful.

Father laughed, without a trace of humor. "Of course it's unacceptable!" he shouted, pacing again. "It's outrageous! In my town, my mill—my people! But we haven't signed anything yet, Anne. I could destroy the whole deal by working against him on this, and then where will we be? Where will the men be? My only hope is that I'll be able to keep everybody calm: the men—who are fighting among themselves, even—the union organizers, the outsiders who always show up for things like this because they *hope* things will get out of control. And the thugs Fielding sends."

"Take Sheriff Tucker with you," I said.

"He's had to drive to Narragansett—in this weather—to secure a capital crime warrant. It's the closest place with a sitting federal judge. As if this day weren't bad enough already."

He stopped and sat down heavily in one of the chairs at the kitchen table. He leaned his elbows on the glossy maple surface and put his head in his hands.

"I can't believe this," he said, his voice muffled by the bars of his fingers behind which he'd hidden himself. I reached out to touch his shoulder when Maria Cristina walked in through the door.

"Where have you been?" I asked, startled. I moved back from Father, protecting both of us, out of habit, from scrutiny and speculation.

She shrugged, sullen.

Clearly she was still angry about my refusal to let her come with me in the boat today, but I had little patience and even less sympathy. I was far more concerned about my father and about what might be happening at the mill. Besides, she looked warm and dry—she had obviously been somewhere in the house all afternoon, refusing to answer me when I called.

"Well, it's not very considerate of you to be out so late without a word to anyone," I said sternly. "I had no idea when I should make dinner, and it's dark out—I was beginning to worry."

My father was sitting up straight now, all traces of anguish and indecision erased from his expression. He watched her, his face carefully blank as she sat down at the table.

"I believe you owe Anne and me an apology," he said quietly.

She didn't look up. I stood only a few feet away, cracking eggs into a white milk-glass bowl. Maria Cristina crossed her arms over her chest and said nothing.

"I'm talking to you, young lady," my father said, his voice a command that I could not imagine disobeying.

"I know," she said quietly, not looking up. "Excuse me, but I am not talking to you."

I gasped, and the egg I held dropped down into the bowl. "Maria Cristina!"

She ignored me, staring down at the table.

"Maria Cristina," I said again, firmly.

"What?" she asked, looking up at me.

"You can't talk to my father that way. You shouldn't talk to anyone that way. You know that."

Her face was stony, cold, resentful. "I do not care," she said. "No one cares about me—I am in the way. Why should I care about anyone?"

"That will be quite enough," said Father. He spoke quietly, but I could tell he was furious. "I am shocked by your ingratitude."

He turned to me and through the outrage I saw satisfaction. "Do you see?" he asked, as if Maria Cristina wasn't there. "She needs civilizing. She's going away to school in September. Even you can see that now."

"What school?" asked Maria Cristina. She looked at me, scared, the suspicion that I had betrayed her just beginning to dawn. "You will send me away?"

"Maria Cristina," I began, but she turned and fled. I heard her

feet pounding on the stairs and the slam of a door. Father said nothing, and the seconds were ticked off by the sound of the water dripping off his slicker onto the floor. I stood looking down at the bowl
of eggs in front of me, the perfect yolks, the broken shell of the one
I'd dropped.

"You were right the other day, Anne—to a point. I have seen
this before with her uncle. They just don't understand that if they're
going to live like us, they've got to make some changes. Some sacrifices. It'll be best this way, you'll see," said Father with confidence.

"No, it won't," I said. "I'm not going to send her away, and
that's the end of it."

Something in my tone must have alerted him to the fact that
things had changed. I did not argue—I wasn't even interested in discussing it. I would make the decision about Maria Cristina, not him.
I knew this, without a trace of doubt. Besides, we had other things to
worry about.

He looked at me for a moment. "I don't really have time to eat,"
he said again, picking up two strips of bacon. "We'll talk about this
later. I'm going upstairs to change. Then I'll drive down to the mill."
And he left the room.

I leaned against the counter and closed my eyes.

What is happening? I thought. Father was upstairs, worried sick;
the men were gathering at the mill; Maria Cristina was locked in her
room, all our time together and the trust we'd built crumbling. I knew
I should go to her, and yet I hesitated. It was all too much, but her hurt
feelings were the least of it. I wandered into the dining room and saw
the package I'd picked up earlier. I stood there, picking at the tape.
Then I pulled out a chair, sat down, and opened it.

The brown paper came off easily, revealing a plain white box. I
lifted off the lid, and inside I found an envelope with my full, legal
name typed on the outside and another box—a carved, wooden box—
nestled within tightly balled-up tissue paper so it wouldn't move in
transit. It couldn't be a birthday present from Father.

I picked up the envelope and lifted the flap, pulling out a one-page letter, and two bank checks floated out, falling to the floor. I bent down and picked them up, then with trembling fingers opened the letter flat, smoothed it on the table, and began to read, the checks still in my hand. The letter was typed on familiar stationery—the lawyer in Providence who had notified me about Maria Cristina a few months ago.

Dear Miss Dodge, it began. *I hope this letter finds you well, and that your sister, Maria Cristina Caldeira, is adjusting to her new life in Milford. I am writing to tell you that your grandfather's will has been probated, and that you and Miss Caldeira are his sole heirs. He requested that his house and all other assets be sold, save for this box and the items it contains. All are enclosed. Please find with this letter two checks, made out to you and Miss Caldeira, respectively, for five thousand three hundred twenty five dollars each.*

Five thousand dollars! I looked at the checks, unable to believe it, but it was true. Maria Cristina and I had ten thousand dollars between us. From Benigno and Lucia. I read on:

This money represents everything your grandparents owned at the time of their deaths except for the items in the box that your grandfather explicitly requested should be delivered to the two of you. I apologize for the delay, but the sale of Mr. Caldeira's property took some time. His estate is now settled, but if you have any questions, please feel free to contact me at any time.

I was stunned. I couldn't wait to tell Maria Cristina that she didn't have to go away to school, especially now! We could get that little house—we *would* get it, there was nothing to stop us. I closed my eyes for a moment, tears stinging the backs of my eyelids. My grandfather had not forgotten me. Perhaps he had even loved me.

I picked up the box then and looked at its intricate design. It was small, offering limited space for figures, but the artist had carved a dozen into its lid and sides. I looked closely, recognizing the theme—it was like the door on our house, I thought, confused. How was that possible? But look, there's a similar whale, a geyser of sea spray shooting up from the blowhole. And there, a lone fisherman fighting the swells, an ominous thundercloud bearing down on him. I ran my fingers over the rough surface, the figures my grandfather had carved giving birth, in some comforting way, to the door Ezra had made for me.

Slowly, carefully, I lifted the lid.

Inside lay two heavy lockets on fine chains: one for me, one for Maria Cristina. They were identical and ornate, glinting yellow-gold in the soft light from the kitchen. I picked one up, found the clasp with my fingers, and pushed. The top sprang open, revealing two faded photographs, one on each side. Father, young and proud on the left, a smile hovering on his lips, reaching all the way to his eyes. I looked to the right, to the other photo. Inêz. That pointed chin, the wide-set eyes. She looked so much like Maria Cristina, it took my breath away.

They were achingly young, and I realized that this was how they had looked when they loved each other. My parents. And my grandfather had wanted me to see them like this. I had once had a family, he was telling me. No matter how things had turned out, these people had been mine, and I had been theirs. There had been love.

I snapped the locket shut, closed my eyes, and squeezed the thing hard in my hand, hurting myself.

I put the locket back in the box, slowly coiling the chain like a rope on a boat deck, then picked up Maria Cristina's locket. Her parents were here, too, I thought, weighing the thing in my hand. I pressed the spring-loaded catch and the lid flew up, revealing, just like mine, two faded photographs. Inêz, of course—the same photo.

And my father.

I quickly snatched at the other locket and opened it, now holding both in my hands, the four photos staring up at me. Inêz and Samuel. My parents.

Inêz and Samuel. Maria Cristina's parents.

Impossible. I looked around, frantic for another explanation. Samuel was not Maria Cristina's father—Inêz had left years before she was born! To my knowledge they had never seen each other again. It didn't make sense.

I stood up, paced behind the chairs lined up at the formal dining room table like good soldiers. I had suspected that the mysterious lover was a lie, had thought that maybe Ezra . . . but my father? It's not possible, I thought. There's got to be some other explanation for my grandfather sending these. He was old. He simply made a mistake when he put the photos in.

I heard someone coming back down the stairs, and I quickly put the lockets back in the box and covered it with the paper. My hands were shaking as Father came in from the kitchen.

"What are you doing?" he asked, seeing the opened package.

"Nothing. Just opening some mail." I thought my voice was shaking, but he didn't seem to notice.

"I've got to go," he said, pulling his dripping oilskin back on. "I don't know when I'll be back." He hadn't noticed the checks, lying right beside the open letter.

Say something, I thought. *Tell him about the lockets. Ask him to explain.* But I couldn't. Too many years of saying nothing, of asking nothing, pretending even to myself that I didn't want to know things that affected me so deeply. Now all those years, the silence and pretending, loomed between us, a gulf far too wide for me to cross.

"What's wrong?" he asked, as I stood there, dumbly.

"Nothing," I said. "I'm just worried about tonight." *I'll talk to him tomorrow*, I told myself. *Let us all just get through this night.*

"Me, too. Wish me luck," he added over his shoulder as he walked out of the room.

"I wish us all luck," I answered softly, but he was already gone.

I quickly climbed the stairs. I had no plan, no intention at all, simply a need to be in the same room with her. I knocked on her door but got only silence in return.

"Maria Cristina?" I said, knocking again.

When she didn't answer I slowly opened the door. She sat on the edge of the bed, looking out the window into the dark as the storm spat rain against the glass. She did not turn around as I came into the room

"Maria Cristina, why don't you come downstairs and have something to eat? I'll make us some eggs."

"I am not hungry," she said, her face still turned toward the night. Her voice broke my heart. She was resigned to being sent away, I could tell. To losing me.

"You have to eat," I said briskly, as though I were Mrs. Hatcher. "And we do need to talk about school—about you going to school in Milford. The same school Deirdre Sullivan attends. The school I attended. Classes start next week, you know."

She still hadn't turned around, but there was a stillness about her that suggested she was listening.

"My father does want you to go to a boarding school, but I don't."

She turned her head then and looked at me. "Excuse me, but he is your father. He will decide." She had reverted back to the kind of polite phrasing she'd used when she first arrived.

"Maria Cristina, what's wrong?" I asked gently.

She blushed, looking down at the quilt she was picking at with her fingers.

"You know you can tell me, whatever it is," I said.

"My stomach," she said, so quietly I barely heard her.

"You still have a stomachache?" I asked. "Maybe we should go see Dr. Statham tomorrow."

"No, it is not that," she said, and I frowned. I had no idea what to make of this.

"Maria Cristina, just tell me," I said impatiently.

"I . . . Please ask Katie and Mrs. Hatcher," she said. "They know."

"They know what?"

"They know about the blood," she said, hiding her face in her hands.

"The blood—" I repeated, confused.

And then I understood.

"Maria Cristina, have you begun to menstruate? To bleed . . . down there?" I asked, incredulous. I had been years older when I had begun.

"Yes," she said from behind her hands.

"Oh, honey, there is nothing to be embarrassed about!" I said, putting my arms around her and hugging her. "This means you're growing up."

"But it's horrible!" she said, taking her hands away.

I laughed. "Yes, I suppose it is in some ways. And you are very young to begin this, but it is perfectly natural."

We sat and looked at each other for a moment.

"Why did you tell me to ask Katie?" I asked.

"When I came back from Ezra's today I found blood on my clothes. I was scared, and you were not here, so I went to Mrs. Hatcher. She told me what it was, and Katie showed me what to do. Then we ate cake."

Katie and Esther Hatcher had provided the love and guidance my own mother should have given me, and here they were again, stepping in to help my sister. Only this time it was I who had abandoned a young girl, not Inêz. My guilt knew no bounds, but I pushed it down. I swore to myself that I would make it up to her. Now that the *Mariana* was finished I would be with her through everything, big and small.

"Let's go downstairs," I said.

She got up reluctantly, and we went down to the kitchen. I scrambled eggs for us, and we ate at the kitchen table in silence. I could tell she was worried about being sent away, but I knew that she would be staying with me in Milford, so my thoughts strayed to what seemed the far more pressing problem—what was happening at the mill.

I said nothing about the protest or my father's fears. I said nothing to her about the lockets or the money. I didn't have the time or the patience for all the questions she would have. She was so young, I told myself, and she wouldn't understand so much of what was going on tonight. It was better to keep some things from her. Easier.

Oh, how completely and utterly I was my mother's daughter, despite all my efforts.

As soon as she was finished I picked up our plates and washed them quickly. Maria Cristina sat at the table, saying nothing. She had fallen silent again, brooding and sullen. She was worried about being sent away despite all my reassurances. I felt she should trust me, and she didn't. Now that we had money, everything would be fine, but I didn't have time now to explain it all to her. I had to get to the mill.

I dried the plates and put them away in silence. "I need to go out for a little while," I said, turning to her.

"Where are you going?" she asked, but I had no intention of telling her. There was reason enough to believe that things might turn ugly at the demonstration, and it seemed as though a storm was indeed moving in. She had no business going anywhere near the mill, but if she knew what was going on she would insist.

"I've just got to go out, that's all. I won't be gone long," I said. I knew it seemed mysterious, but I didn't have time to think of a plausible story.

"I want to go with you," she said, quiet and stubborn as always.

"You can't." It seemed these imperatives were all I could muster. I moved into the hall to get my yellow oilskin and hat.

"I know where you are going," she said, the thick sound of tears still in her voice. "You are going to the mill with everyone else."

"What do you know about the mill?" I was surprised, though perhaps I shouldn't have been.

"I know that the Hatchers are going, and the Sullivans." She seemed to draw herself up against me. "Your father is going to do a bad thing. Everyone says so."

"You don't know what you're talking about," I snapped.

"I want to go." Her voice quivered. "Please."

I opened my mouth to tell her she could come with me, or maybe to tell her she had no right to speak of my father like that, not after everything he'd done for her. I honestly didn't know which. But a sudden gust of wind threw one of the shutters up against the side of the house with a bang like a gunshot, making us both jump.

"You can't," I said simply. "It's too dangerous."

"I want—"

"Maria Cristina, I don't care what you want! I have more important things to worry about. Just do what I tell you!" I thundered, pulling on my coat and smashing my hat down on my head. I was feeling frantic. I needed to be at the mill, now.

We faced each other in the dim hall, the lamp on the telephone table casting a feeble light that didn't reach us. I took one last look at her forlorn face and left without another word.

CHAPTER EIGHTEEN

Though we did not know yet how bad the storm was, we learned afterward that the Blue Hill Meteorological Observatory outside of Boston clocked its winds at ninety miles an hour. They might have been a bit slower up into the Narragansett Bay and inland of Kingston Cove, but when the wind hit me full in the chest as I walked outside our front door, I had to struggle to close it behind me. Rain was blowing horizontally, and the trees were bent low. Father had taken the car, so I made my way against the wind and ran down Main until I reached the old mill road. Once there, the trees offered some protection and I hurried toward the mill.

As I approached the closest building I could see, even through the dark and rain, a large crowd illuminated by dozens and dozens of lanterns. Most of them were ships' lanterns, fueled with oil, and they swung from handles which made the entire group appear as if they were moving. The men and women of Milford had gathered in a tight, restless knot up against the exterior wall of the main building, its smooth brick soaring up more than three stories high and offering some protection from the wind and rain blowing in hard from the cove. Many people wore the same yellow fisherman's oilskins my father was wearing when he left the house, and as I approached I despaired of finding him in the crowd. As I entered the property a reception committee of five or six sturdy men was waiting. They promptly approached me, shone a light in my face, then relaxed after deciding I posed no threat.

Until I said I was looking for my father, Samuel Dodge.

"You can't pass through," said the man who appeared to be in charge.

"What do you mean I can't pass through? This is private property, sir. My father owns the land you are standing on, and I'll walk on it if I damn well please."

I tried to walk past him, but several bodies closed ranks and blocked my way.

"Miss, we don't want any trouble," said another man, his face, like almost everyone's here, completely obscured by the darkness and his hat pulled low against the pounding rain.

"Really?" I said, hoping my voice fairly dripped with scorn and sarcasm. "Is that why you're here, trespassing, inciting these good people to trespass?"

"You can stay, miss, but you can't cross into the yard," he shouted so I could hear him over the storm. He refused to be baited.

I backed up a couple of feet, fuming, and took a closer look at what was happening. The townspeople stood awkwardly against the building, self-consciously shifting from one foot to the other, unsure of exactly what they were supposed to be doing. The wind whipped their coats and the lanterns swung from their hands, as if we all stood on a ship's deck together. Between the townspeople and me, standing perhaps twenty feet from me, were the union organizers, formed into a line that created a perimeter around the yard—keeping hostiles out, I thought, and keeping the workingmen of Milford in.

To the left of the workers crowded up against the mill wall was a small station under an oilcloth tarp where two women were pouring coffee, handing out cups. I searched the crowd for my father, though

I didn't expect to find him inside the union's perimeter. There were a few people outside of it, like I was, but they appeared to be alone, or standing in small groups of two or three, unorganized, unsure, watching. I didn't see Father's car, either, though several vehicles were parked just to the right of the road where it spilled out into the mill yard.

I was startled by a loud voice coming from the crowd. A man stood out in front, shouting through a bullhorn, the workingmen of Milford huddled in close behind him. Those of us on the outside of the union's human chain gathered closer together, listening.

"Friends, we are here with our brothers from the rubber, steel, and shipbuilding trades to offer a show of strength and support to the textile workers of Milford. To state our demands for fair working conditions on the eve of the reopening of the mill here. To insist, with the law on our side, that the union-busting practices of intimidation and violence be rejected by the owners, and that they instead treat the workers with respect and fairness."

The crowd erupted with cheers and clapping, whistles and shouts, but it sounded weak, battered down by the storm.

"To demonstrate that we mean business, we stand together— even when we sit!" With that he turned and made a motion to the crowd—he held his arms up, both hands high, and then brought them down by his side in a single, dramatic motion, like an orchestra conductor. As one, every man and woman who stood huddled together against the walls of the mill—well over a hundred people, I calculated—sat down on the ground.

I heard it then. It began as a kind of low twitter—as if a group of small birds was inexplicably singing while a storm raged—but the sound picked up strength and I saw that the townspeople were *laughing*, sitting on the wet ground and laughing in release, nervousness, and anticipation. They were gathered together with friends and neighbors, had probably been chatting together all night, and when they moved as one to sit down in the puddles in front of the mill, it simply struck them as funny.

I have thought a lot over the years about what happened that night at the mill. I have wondered how my neighbors and friends, laughing as the storm bore down upon us, could accept from strangers that my father—a man they'd known all their lives—was their enemy. I have felt at times that I would never be able to speak to a single one of them again, could not even live among them anymore, but after all, this gathering of friends and neighbors, the stirring words of the agitators, perhaps even the fury of the storm itself charged the air with purpose and power, a feeling they must have welcomed after the long, bitter years of helplessness. It was not my father who was ever their enemy. They knew this. They were simply caught up in something bigger than themselves, bigger than our little town. I have to believe that, even now.

Their lives in the hands of someone else, or some force beyond their control—*that* was the enemy. And who can blame them, in the end, for choosing to take their lives back? If some of them were duped, or looked the other way as menacing strangers appeared in their midst with clear intentions, that is not the full story, or even the most important one. They did what I believe most of us would do had we been them, living through those years, feeling the gnaw of hunger, watching our loved ones suffer, and trying to remember what dignity felt like.

"We are here tonight to demonstrate that we will act as a collective—not to challenge ownership, but to challenge privilege. The privilege of power over workers that results from the fact that most of us here live from hand to mouth, through no fault of our own."

The crowd sitting on the ground clapped and cheered, but I saw them more than heard them. Without the bullhorn, I doubt I would have heard a single word the speaker shouted. The wind was roaring around the sides of the mill buildings, and I could hear the thundering of the waves as they struck the rocks in the bay just beyond the seawall at the back of the property.

"My friends, we must ask ourselves: Is the ownership of production and property the only right that should be recognized in the American democracy?!"

"NO!" shouted a hundred voices in unison.

"Go home, you filthy communists!" shouted a man standing a few feet away from me, one of the growing number of people standing outside the union's perimeter.

I had been so focused on what was happening inside, up by the mill, that I had not noticed the dozens of people who had gathered near me, most of them wearing oilskins or slick black coats, faces hidden by hat brims pulled low, pacing outside the human chain on the side of big business.

The side where I stood.

I did not recognize the voice, and I could not see the face of the speaker near me. "Go home and leave us alone!" he shouted, cupping his mouth with his hands so his voice would carry to the sitting crowd, who appeared to hear him and booed in response.

I turned, looking behind me, and saw that those of us on this side were easily thirty strong. I recognized Ezra standing with Mr. Sullivan and his sons Stevie and young Fin who stood very close to his da. He's too young to be out here, I thought. He should be home, safe and warm with his mother. I swept the crowd for my father, saw Mr. Dekker. I didn't understand the lines of division and wondered if there had been a mistake. Did the Sullivans want to be inside with the mill workers and union members or not? What about Ezra? How did he feel about this?

Perhaps, like me, they were unsure, wanting only to watch, to stand in the shadows and not be counted. Perhaps we all simply stood in the place where we had stopped, thinking to watch others' drama unfold.

Facing back toward the road I saw a truck drive up and stop in the dark, away from the crowds. I watched as half a dozen men got out of the back—strangers to Milford, I was sure of it. They were big to a man, and they wore dark coats and hats. As they approached, slowly and cautiously, hanging back away from the lanterns, I saw that each one carried a billy club in his hand, down by his side.

Oliver, I thought. A wave of fear left me nauseated.

Several of the men came near, and I saw stubble on their cheeks, cold eyes that quickly assessed the area, including me. They looked like barflies, poolroom toughs, but they were alert as G-men. They spread out, stationing themselves two-by-two, and I saw that while one man in each pair kept vigil, constantly surveying the people around them, the other began to shout at the union speaker standing with the bullhorn in his hand.

"Commies!" shouted one man.

"This is un-American!" yelled another. "Go home or we'll send you!"

I hurried over to Mr. Dekker. "Have you seen my father?" I asked breathlessly.

Mr. Dekker jumped when I spoke. He had been watching one of the thugs, his eye on the billy club the man was now holding in plain view, slapping it lightly, menacingly, into the palm of his other hand.

"Annie, you shouldn't be here!" he said. "No, I haven't seen him. I believe he's gone to Judge Abbott to get an injunction, an order for everyone to vacate the mill property."

Judge Abbott was an old friend of my father's, and I knew he would come through for us. The crowd—on both sides—was agitated and had begun shouting at one another. Some of the townspeople had risen and walked toward the union perimeter, jeering at the toughs who now stood only a few feet away. The organizers who separated the two groups were trying to persuade the workers to go back and sit, that this was the purpose of their demonstration, but more and more people were rising, and no one appeared to be listening.

I saw movement from the corner of my eye and turned as a man ran from the jumble of parked cars toward the union line. It was my father!

"Wait!" I heard him shout as he approached. "The judge has ordered that everyone leave, immediately!"

Hope welled up in my chest, and I thought, It's going to be all right. They'll talk tomorrow, in the light of day. But my hope was crushed when two union men stepped in front of Father, blocking his way, their faces stony as they stared straight ahead.

"Move aside, sir!" I heard him demand as I crept closer. "I have a legal writ from Judge Abbott!" He held aloft a piece of paper, gleaming white in the darkness, but the rain immediately began to batter and wilt it.

The crowd, on its feet now and pressed up against the backs of the union leaders, wasn't listening.

"You've got to vacate the premises!" shouted Father. "You have no choice—it's the law!"

They laughed in his face. Nearby I saw Mr. Hatcher and Patrick Tully among the dozens of people I'd known all my life. Their faces were lit from below by the lanterns they held in their hands, and the wavering light moving over their shadowed features made them look like the monsters of childhood.

Several of the tough-looking men with billy clubs had moved together into a tight group, their weapons on display. My father turned and saw them, and his face blanched as he hurried toward them. Where is Sheriff Tucker? I thought.

"No, no! We don't need you here, we don't want you. We'll work this out on our own!" Father shouted, trying in vain to staunch the hemorrhaging of his life's work.

"Get back!" snarled the thug closest to him, shoving him out of the way. Father staggered, his foot slipping in the mud. He didn't fall, but in the moment before he caught himself the order to vacate flew out of his hand and landed in the mud. Mr. Sullivan sprang forward.

"Hey, now, there's no call for that!" shouted Mr. Sullivan, but two men with clubs stepped in front of him, one of them mashing the paper into wet pulp.

"Back up, mister!" said one of the thugs, putting his face right in Mr. Sullivan's.

"This is Samuel Dodge—the owner of the mill! Don't you even know whose side you're supposed to be on?!" Mr. Sullivan responded, furious.

"We know exactly whose side we're on," sneered the man, poking him in the chest with the end of the club, the braided handle in his meaty fist.

He jabbed at Mr. Sullivan, slowly stepping forward, forcing the other man to back up from the sharp little blows. Father moved off, looking for a break in the union line so he could get inside, reason with his people.

"Get your filthy hands off my dad!" shouted Stevie, but another thug grabbed his arms, holding him back.

"Stevie, be quiet!" yelled his father, the fear apparent in his voice. "Let him go," he pleaded, looking at the man who held his son while backing away from the man jabbing him in the chest. "Let him take his little brother home," he asked.

I looked over and saw Fin Sullivan standing behind me and looking on in horror.

"You're all lousy commies!" snarled the man who held Mr. Sullivan at bay. "There's not a real American among you!"

"Well, now," said an amused voice. "Americans can disagree, can't they? Ain't that the whole point?"

I spun around and saw a man limping into the light of Fin's lantern.

"Ezra!" I said, and he flashed a look at me that told me to shut my mouth and not call attention to my presence.

"You boys know these folks ain't what you're here for," Ezra said casually. "Case you haven't noticed, they're standin' on the same side as you."

"What about you, old man? What side are you on?"

"Well, I don't know that's any of your business," he said.

"Another commie," said one thug to the other, disgust—and excitement, too—in his voice.

"You a commie?" said the man holding Stevie, releasing him suddenly and taking a step toward Ezra. "Or are you an American?"

"Of course he's an American!" said Mr. Sullivan quickly. "We all are."

"Maybe he should prove it," said the thug.

"Say the pledge of allegiance, old man," interjected a third man, and the others laughed.

"Get down on your knees and say the pledge," said the man still holding Mr. Sullivan at the point of his club, though he'd stopped pushing him and was focused on Ezra.

"He can't!" shouted Stevie, his voice shrill with fear.

I knew immediately what he meant—with his crippled leg, Ezra could no more drop to his knees than he could fly—but the men chose to understand that Ezra couldn't say the pledge because he didn't know it, or wouldn't recite it.

Either way, it was all they needed.

"Get down on your knees, now!" snarled the man who'd bullied Mr. Sullivan, moving toward Ezra with his club. "Do it!" he screamed, spittle flying, his face contorted into something less than human.

The other two stepped forward, pushing in close, menacing, three billy clubs poised.

This is what they'd come for, I thought. It didn't matter much who was on the receiving end of it.

One of them reached out with his club, put it against Ezra's shoulder, and shoved, hard. Ezra stumbled back, and they advanced.

"On your knees!" shouted the man, the wind howling around us, rain slashing across my vision, but I could still see well enough to know that people were gathering around us, the union line in shambles, our friends and neighbors inching forward to see what was going on.

"Leave him alone!" shouted Stevie, a note of hysteria in his voice that seemed to set everything in motion at once.

As Stevie yelled, I heard in his voice a note of desperation that should have warned me. Mr. Sullivan made a quick move to quiet him. One of the thugs put a hand on Ezra's shoulder and tried to force him to his knees, and I saw the look of pain on his face as his good knee bent and his lame leg took the pressure. Stevie saw it, too, and before his father could reach him to stop it, Stevie lunged at the man who was forcing Ezra to the ground.

The man turned, raised his arm, and brought the billy club crashing down on Stevie's head, knocking him to the ground in a crumpled heap.

I screamed, and heard an echoing cry of anguish, like that of a wounded animal, come up from the very soul of Mr. Sullivan.

We stood stunned for I'm sure the briefest of seconds, though it felt like an eternity. Lightening flashed, and I saw arms raised, the milling bodies of our friends and foes indistinguishable from one another. I heard a sharp crack of thunder that might have been a gunshot. Stevie was still and silent on the ground, while those of us nearby stood staring down at him. I was vaguely aware of men fighting around me. One of the thugs still had his hand on Ezra's shoulder, though he seemed to have forgotten it was there.

He was looking at Stevie Sullivan instead, lying in the mud with blood on his face.

Mr. Sullivan dropped to the ground and gathered his son in his arms.

"Stevie! Stevie, can you hear me?" he pleaded.

Stevie didn't respond, and I saw his arm fall limply into a puddle.

"Oh, dear Lord," I heard a woman say, and I looked up, not realizing until that moment that I was on my knees beside Mr. Sullivan. People I knew stood close, pressing in all around, and among them were the union organizers, the out-of-town supporters, and the merely curious. The sounds of fighting had diminished or moved away. The thugs seemed few now, and somehow shrunken in size in the light of the countless lanterns that threw the scene into stark reality. They caught one another's glances and slowly backed away, turned and headed for their trucks.

Then my father pushed his way into the tight circle around Stevie, staggering when he saw the boy lying in the mud, held tightly in his father's arms.

"Everybody go home!" he bellowed. He turned to Mr. Sullivan. "Rory, I'm going to drive my car up here and we're going to put Stevie in the backseat. We'll take him straight to Dr. Statham's."

Mr. Sullivan nodded, too stunned to think or move. He clutched Stevie to his chest, unable to let him go.

People started to back away, holding on to one another. They were murmuring, crying, some still breathing hard from the melee, others holding cloths to split, bloody lips and noses. Ashamed and afraid, they walked toward town, or to their cars. I heard someone ask if Mr. Hightower was the one who'd been shot. Ezra stood on the other side of Stevie. I looked at him, but he seemed unaware of me, staring down at the Sullivans. I followed his gaze, saw the thick, dark blood on the top of Stevie's head, just above his right temple, and though his hair hid it pretty well, I saw what Ezra had seen: that Stevie's skull had been crushed by the billy club, his life spilling out into the rainwater that ran in little streams across the uneven ground, down the sloping yard and into the cove.

The headlights of my father's car swept across us, and I got up and moved aside. Father and Mr. Sullivan lifted Stevie's limp body into the backseat. Mr. Sullivan sat in the back, cradling his son's head, the blood soaking through his clothes, while my father, in the driver's seat, focused all his attention on salvaging what he could of our lives.

CHAPTER NINETEEN

I watched the taillights disappear into the trees until there was nothing left but the wind and the rain and the darkness. Someone touched my shoulder, and I turned to find Ezra standing next to me.

That simple human contact, the warmth of his hand through my clothes, started me trembling.

"He'll die, won't he?" I asked.

"Doc'll do his best," said Ezra, a warning in his voice as he looked pointedly over my shoulder.

I turned and saw little Fin Sullivan standing behind me. His face was completely expressionless, but in his hands he clutched Stevie's hat so tightly that his knuckles were white. I wanted desperately not to have said it. He had been the one to find Matt Da Silva, to stare down at that broken, lifeless body, and now his own brother had been struck down as well. How violent his world had become!

"Your ma's prob'ly wonderin' where you are," Ezra said to him. "Let's start walkin' toward your place."

It was probably two miles from the mill to the Sullivans' place. They lived on the other side of town, in the area where Milford proper began to turn into farmland. We walked in silence, all of us abreast, Ezra limping and Fin holding that hat as if handing it back to Stevie was the only thing left to live for.

We were all pretty well soaked through, and the rain did not let up. Hats and coats by this point offered little protection as the unpredictable wind blew the water at us from every direction. We were sodden and shivering, and at one point my jaw began to ache with the effort of clenching my body to stop its trembling. We moved slowly through the night, the walking wounded. After about ten minutes I felt something brush my hand.

It was Fin, staring straight ahead and saying nothing, as he groped in the dark for my hand. He was too big to ask to be held, wanting to be a man but not quite there yet.

I said nothing but wound my fingers through his and held his hand until we climbed the steps to his front porch.

The moment the porch timbers creaked under our feet, the front door flew open and Mrs. Sullivan ran out to meet us.

"Rory!" she called before she'd seen who it was. The sight of us brought her up short with a gasp, and she paled visibly in the yellow light pouring out from inside the house.

She took us in at a glance: the absence of her husband and Stevie, Fin holding my hand, the blood on my coat sleeve that I hadn't realized was there until I saw her eyes riveted to it.

Why hasn't it washed away? I thought, turning quickly to hide it.

Pale though she was, Mrs. Sullivan didn't hesitate. Hands on her hips she turned to her son.

"Well, it's a little late for you, young man, and in this storm! Come in by the fire and warm up. I'll heat up some milk."

Fin's shoulders lowered, releasing the tension he'd carried in his body for too long. He walked past his ma and into the house, and though I saw her try not to, she could not resist touching his hair as he passed her. Her mouth trembled, but she quickly regained her control.

Once her son was inside she turned to us. "What's happened?"

I hesitated, and Ezra stepped in. "There's been an accident. Rory took Stevie to Doc Statham."

She nodded, her lips pursed. Kept nodding, with no indication that she would ever stop.

"Mrs. Sullivan . . ." I began, but she put up her hand to stop me.

"How bad?" she asked Ezra.

His hesitation was so brief it almost wasn't there, but she heard it. Felt it stretching out in front of us all, telling her everything she didn't want to know. "Bad."

She closed her eyes, and her hand came unbidden to her mouth, holding in her fear and prayers and grief. I wanted to touch her, but I was afraid that she might shatter, or that I might.

"Ma!" shouted a small voice from inside. "Can we stay up if Fin gets to?"

She opened her eyes, her hand still clamped tight over her mouth. I wondered what she saw as she stared out into the night. Then slowly, deliberately, with the greatest effort of will I have ever seen, she took her hand away and brought it slowly down to her side. She took a deep breath, and she called back over her shoulder in a voice that was strong and even. "You can all stay up for another fifteen minutes, but not a minute more."

"Thank you," she said quietly, turning to us.

"Bridget, we're stayin' till Rory gets back."

"No," she said. "We'll be fine. Thank you."

And she turned and walked back in the house without another word. The door closed softly behind her, and we were left on the porch, the storm howling around us, the sound of a child's laughter drifting through the window.

"Let's go," said Ezra.

I wondered if Ezra had been hurt when those men had tried to force him to his knees. Regardless, this long walk couldn't be good for him. I made myself slow down, and we plodded along.

"Somebody'll have to tell the Da Silva girl . . ." Ezra mumbled next to me, though I barely heard him over the storm.

"What do you mean?" I asked, thickheaded to the end.

"Susana Da Silva. Matt's sister. Somebody'll have to tell her about Stevie. They was gonna get married."

"They were?" I asked, shocked. They were practically children!

"That was their plan," he said, wincing in pain as he walked. "They didn't tell nobody. Their folks wouldn't've let 'em so they was gonna wait till she was old enough to do it on her own. But her brother found out, tried to put a stop to it."

"You mean it was Stevie . . ."

Ezra nodded. "Matt had it out with his sister, heard it from her own lips, an' he lit out after Stevie. Caught up with him at my place, in the workshop, fussin' over the damn lights I was gonna wire up for his boat." He paused, and when he continued his voice was harsh, angry. "I'd told him to leave me alone while I was workin' on that damn boat, so he snuck out at night to the shop to look at her."

I stopped in the road, staring at him. "How long have you known?"

"Stevie come poundin' on my door that night, blood on his hands, shakin' and cryin'. I couldn't make it out at first, but I calmed him down enough to get the story. Matt had come at him, and Stevie grabbed what was near—that chisel—and just swung it, once, and it was over. He panicked and took the body out to the marsh, dropped the chisel in the tall grass. He wasn't gonna tell nobody. But he couldn't go through with it alone and came to me. I told him to wait, an' then I went down there and found the Da Silva boy. He was past helpin' and I couldn't see no reason to wreck two boys' lives when one was tragedy enough. So I sent Stevie home, and I said nothin'. Didn't touch the body—didn't seem right to bury it—but I did clean up my shop a bit. Seemed a small enough thing."

I couldn't seem to focus. Young lovers from two different worlds, those worlds bent on keeping them apart—somebody was always devoured in that kind of story. It's such a common story, I thought bitterly, and then I remembered. Maria Cristina. The lockets.

"Ezra," I said. "I got a package today. Benigno left Maria Cristina and me some money. And a carved box that looks like the door you made."

"It is. When I made your door, I was thinkin' of yer grandfather. He would've been proud of yer boat makin', too. I thought that th' door—with his kind a' carvin' on it—would be like him givin' you a present, too."

I tucked his words away, out of sight of this hideous night. Later I might feel some joy in them. "Ezra, there was a locket for each of us—with pictures of our parents."

I felt, rather than heard, the sharp intake of his breath beside me.

"Ezra, I need you to tell me. No more lies. Who is Maria Cristina's father?"

He kept walking for a moment, stepping forward with his good foot, then slowly swinging his bad leg out and forward.

"You need to understand why people lied," he said.

"Ezra, I swear to God, I don't care anymore. I don't think I'll ever give a damn about anything again. I'd just like to know, for once, what the truth is."

"Understanding why people do what they do is part of the truth," he said.

We stopped then, in the middle of the dirt road, though it would be more accurate to say that we stopped in the middle of a small, muddy stream. The rain had been pounding South County for five or six hours straight, and the ground had long ago reached its saturation point. There was standing water everywhere, and still the rain beat down upon us, the wind blowing it into our faces, making us squint, the water dripping off our hats and noses and chins as though the known world was melting.

"Your mother was an unhappy woman."

"I know that. You've told me."

"Samuel became a different man after you was born. He loved you, but it twisted him up somehow, made him hate Inêz. It was bad."

"What do you mean?" I asked.

"He may have loved her when they married, but after you was born he— Well, he seemed to think that Ben and Lucia, and especially Inêz, wasn't good for you."

"That's ridiculous," I said, my voice coming from far away. "She was my mother."

He said nothing, and I felt nothing, I realized. I was standing there as if I were someone else, watching this old man tell a young woman about her life.

"So what happened?" I asked.

"She started comin' down to my place, sometimes with you, sometimes not. Samuel had hired a woman to take care of you. Told your mother to go visit her family, stay as long as she wanted. One time she came back and he'd moved her things to another room. Out of his an' away from yours—that's the time I hit him. Only time I ever interfered, but when she come home and seen she was losin' you, she was just crushed. I couldn't help it. I went up to the house and I smashed his face."

"He was separating her from me," I said matter-of-factly. I could feel a stirring somewhere deep inside as the cruelty of what my father had done to his wife—my mother—dawned on me. The sensation of turning my lifelong rage against Inêz toward Father instead left me somewhat disoriented, as though my senses might be tricking me and I couldn't trust what I thought to be real.

"Yep. An' she knew it. First she was angry. Then she was scared. Weren't long after that she left for good."

"But that doesn't make sense," I said, starting to feel a little irritated. "Why would she leave me if losing me was what she was afraid of?"

Ezra paused, and I sensed the struggle between this moment with me and promises long kept to the dead. The sound of the wind seemed to die down, the trees bent low, listening as we stood on the open road.

"She left to keep from losing another child. She was pregnant."

My heart was suddenly hammering in my chest, and I unclenched my hands because my nails had cut into my palms.

There had been another child, before Maria Cristina? My head hurt, and I couldn't seem to grasp this new information. The storm raged over me, through me.

And then I understood. There had only been one child.

"Maria Cristina," I said, so softly I didn't think he'd heard me.

"Maria Cristina," he said.

I began walking, slowly, and he kept time with my ponderous steps.

"But—" I said, then stopped. I couldn't grasp it. "But she's only thirteen—"

"Anne, Maria Cristina is sixteen years old."

It came rushing in at me then, a succession of images of Maria Cristina since she had arrived in June, her unexpected physical development, her flirtatious looks at Will, her teenage moods, her surprising maturity. Her menstrual period.

Of course, I thought, and the sound in my head was the click of tumblers falling into place, the unlocked door swinging wide.

"Ezra—" I began.

"I've seen her birth certificate, Annie. Inêz showed it to me before she burned it. She made me promise to keep her secret, but it's on file at the courthouse in Barrington."

His face was filled with compassion, and I looked away.

"Inêz had already lost you, an' it was killing her. But a new baby—to have it happen all over again—she couldn't do it. She made a choice. She did it to keep Maria Cristina from Samuel, even though it meant leaving you forever."

"I feel so stupid," I said.

"You couldn't've known," he said gently. "Maria Cristina doesn't even know. They kept her at home, hidden for years. They postponed school as long as they could, till they felt safe enough. She started a couple years late, but she's a tiny little thing. Nobody ever asked."

"Samuel Dodge is Maria Cristina's father," I said slowly, trying it out. "We are truly sisters."

"Yep."

We walked on, in town now and drawing near to my house on Main. The numbness was wearing off, and I felt a little sick. I turned to Ezra just before we reached my front gate.

"Am I supposed to be happy? Or am I supposed to feel sorry for Inêz? Because I'm not, and I don't. She was my mother—she should have protected me—but instead she chose everyone else over me!"

"That is one way to look at it," he said grimly.

"It's the only way to look at it! She was willing to write me off, and so were my grandparents—"

"And it nearly killed them all," he said quietly.

"Don't defend them, Ezra," I snapped. "It makes it all too obvious that you're merely defending yourself."

I was crying now, openly, but the whole world seemed to be crying—we would all be underwater soon. I hardly noticed. I certainly didn't care.

"You've lied to me my whole life," I accused him quietly, sobbing. "I thought you loved me. No matter what, I thought you loved me. But you're just like the rest of them, leaving me in the dark—it's where I've lived my entire life."

"Annie," he said, sounding completely helpless.

"Don't 'Annie' me!" I screamed. "Your only thought has been to protect Inêz. She's the only one you've ever cared about!"

"No, Annie, it was Lucia! It was your grandmother—" He moved as if to grab my arm, but I twisted away and ran up the steps and into my father's house, refusing to hear what he wanted to tell me.

I stood in the hall, dripping and disoriented from the sudden absence of wind and rain. The lamp on the telephone table cast its soft light on the little chair next to it, and a faint sheen across the oil portrait of our colonial Dodge. After a moment I slowly, methodically began to unhook my oilskin. Then I peeled it off and hung it and my hat on the hall tree to dry.

I had no sense of purpose, no idea of what I should do next.

Maria Cristina was my father's daughter, and neither of them knew it. They hated each other, Maria Cristina because my father was unkind and unwelcoming, my father because—well, because he thought she was the child of Inêz and her lover. A lover who had always been a lie. I supposed she had made it up, written the lie in the note she'd left Father in order to keep him from going after her. But what an ugly lie. I had believed it my whole life, felt the humiliation and the degradation as though it were visible on my skin for everyone to see. I had lived my life believing my mother was a whore who had failed her husband and child. And fearing that I might be just like her.

Everything I'd thought true was now false—it was both better and worse than I'd believed, but somehow, more important than what was true was the blow of having been the last to know. I wandered into the dining room, toward the light that spilled out of the doorway.

My father sat at the table, his hair still damp, the letter and the lockets spread open before him.

"I see that you've come into an inheritance," he said, his voice distant and impersonal.

"Yes," I said, feeling no compunction to explain.

"Congratulations."

"I had thought to get a small house with it for Maria Cristina and me," I said, my tone matching his.

"Why would you do that?" he asked.

I shrugged. "I'm a grown woman," I said simply.

There was no need to argue with him about boatbuilding or boarding schools anymore. Neither of those things were his decision to make.

"Yes, I suppose you are," he said softly. He sounded beaten, and I suddenly remembered the mill. And Stevie.

"How is Stevie Sullivan?" I asked quickly.

"Dead."

I had known it, but I felt the pain nonetheless. I closed my eyes.

"And the men who did it?" I asked after a moment.

"Long gone. The state police are investigating, but they won't find them." He paused for a moment, then chuckled once, softly and with great bitterness. "I suppose justice has prevailed, though. I met Farley in town, after I left the Sullivans at Dr. Statham's. He'd just come back with a warrant for Stevie Sullivan. For murder. Over a girl, apparently."

We said nothing else for some minutes, and eventually I pulled out a chair and sat next to him. "Was anyone else killed?" I asked.

"Just one other. Mr. Hightower was shot in the chest, and there are several townspeople with broken bones from those billy clubs. Dr. Statham will be busy for days."

"What will happen with the mill?" I asked.

"Lost," he said. "Gone. Everything my family worked for. Gone." He paused, then took a great breath. "But I'd burn it to the ground myself before I'd let Fielding in now."

He said it with the last bit of strength he possessed, and I let the sound of it wash over me: integrity. My father had integrity, and it gave me the strength I needed to trust him.

"Father," I said. "I've found something out that you should know."

He looked at me, with effort. "What is it?"

"Inêz didn't leave us for another man," I began, thinking to work slowly up to the fact that Maria Cristina was his child.

"Who told you—Ezra?" he asked, bitterly.

I stared at him, at the sound of anger in his voice. At the lack of surprise. "You knew?" I said slowly.

I saw his eyes shift then. "Well, I suspected . . ." he began, but faltered and didn't finish his sentence.

I had no path to follow, it seemed, not even a faint track to guide my feet. My whole life was a lie, a fairy tale of mean, ugly proportions. Any betrayal was possible now, and so the final piece of the puzzle, the first lie really, occurred to me. "Inêz never wrote that she'd left us for another man, did she?" I knew it was true even as I said it.

"She didn't have to!" he said hotly. "I knew what she was capable of."

"Did she leave a note at all?" I asked.

He tried to stare me down with his stern countenance, but it was useless now and he knew it. He seemed to shrink before my eyes as his shoulders dropped and his head bent. He looked tired and old.

"Yes," he said. "All it said was not to look for her. And that she loved you," he added.

"My mother was not a whore." I said it out loud, for myself and for her.

My father did not even look up.

"She left, Father, because she was pregnant. With your child—a child she didn't want you to take away from her. Maria Cristina is your daughter."

The look on his face told me that he had never considered this, not ever. He was shocked, searching my face for any telltale sign of deceit. He found none.

"She's . . . Inêz was pregnant? Are you sure?"

"Yes. I'm sure."

"But . . ."

"Maria Cristina's older than we thought—older than she knows. She's yours. Ezra has seen her birth certificate."

He was stunned, trying to take it in. This was his one chance, I thought. He had thrown Inêz away, thrown her family away, and isolated me from so much that could have filled my life with love and a sense of belonging. But he could rise to this. I desperately needed to believe it because this was my last chance as fully as it was his.

"Father, you can make it right. We'll tell her now, tonight. We'll do it together. Maria Cristina is your daughter, yours and Inêz's. Just like me. We can be a family. You could love her—you could try. I know you can do it, Father. Please."

His face changed in the light, reflecting the battle that waged within him as he considered what I'd said, tried to imagine himself loving her, introducing her, being a part of her future. His daughter.

His Portuguese daughter.

That's what she was, and would always be. I saw the light of his integrity flicker and go out. All that remained was fear and pride, and his inability to see that he could be wrong, even when he'd been wrong about so much.

"I can't," he said simply.

"But Father, she's yours."

"No," he said, shaking his head. He stood up and began to pace behind me. "She's not. It's too late."

"What do you mean?" I asked, turning in my chair to face him. "How can it be too late?"

"She lived with them too long. She's too old, she's already— Besides, it doesn't matter anymore. She's gone."

"What are you talking about," I asked, standing up, my chair scraping backward on the floor. "Where is she?"

"I don't know," he said, and hesitated. "She left. I don't think she's coming back."

"Father, did you turn Maria Cristina out of this house?" I asked slowly.

"We quarreled," he said, like a little boy, resentful and put-upon. "I told her we were sick of her tantrums, told her Stevie Sullivan had been killed—that she was the least of our concerns."

I felt sick, not because he'd said this to her, but because *I* had only a little while before him.

"What did she say?" I asked, afraid to hear the answer.

"She said 'excuse me' a dozen times, crossed herself over the Sullivan boy—your grandmother used to do that endlessly. And then— then she had the temerity to tell me to my face that she would not go to boarding school."

He looked at me then, expecting after everything I now knew that I would join him in condemning her for her bad manners. When he saw nothing of the kind in my expression, he hesitated.

"I'm sure she's a fine person, in her own way, but she's not like us," he said quickly. "She doesn't really belong here—surely even you can see that. And it's not as though we haven't done the Christian thing. Haven't I provided a home for her? I don't think I can be blamed if she's not happy here, living the kind of life we live."

I said nothing as I stared at him. I didn't know him at all.

"Anne, don't look at me like that!" he pleaded, and for the first time in my life I realized that he had needed me all along, needed me to see him as he saw himself, despite all the evidence to the contrary. And I had been a dutiful daughter, until now.

"Look at you like what?" I asked. "Like I don't know who you are? Or like the sight of you makes me sick?" The horror of all he had done—in the name of love and family—was beginning to sink in.

"This is my house, my family, and it's my responsibility to take care of it!" he argued.

"But Inêz was your family. You made that choice and she trusted you! Did you tell Maria Cristina how you treated her mother, drove her from her home, belittled her until she felt like nothing? Is that how you take care of your family?"

"You don't understand!" he cried.

"Oh, I understand, Father, better right now than I ever have. Matt Da Silva was taking care of his family, too, when he decided that Stevie Sullivan wasn't good enough!"

"Yes!" He seized on it, twisted the ugliness to suit his purpose as he had done my entire life. "Why shouldn't they feel the same way, preferring to stick with their own kind?" he railed.

"But Father, you married Inêz. You loved her and made her your wife. She had your child and you threw her away . . ." I whispered.

"I am not responsible for that," he said, desperate for exoneration. "She should have changed when you were born—that was her responsibility to you! Her father was a fisherman and a boatbuilder who couldn't even speak English. I gave her the Dodge name, I gave her this house, and do you know how she thanked me? Not by bettering herself, becoming a mother you could be proud of, someone who could help me. Oh, no! She threw it in my face, after everything I'd given her. She brought her family here and their filthy immigrant friends, filling this house with their music and their food and their crucifixes. And she would have turned you into one of them—you, the Dodge heir. It was humiliating!"

"You took my mother from me," I cried. "How is it possible that you don't understand that?"

"Anne, I was thinking of your future."

"My whole life, everything you've done—it was all because you were afraid that I'd be like her," I said, shaking my head in disbelief.

"Yes, it's true!" he shouted. "They didn't know their place, any of them. Your grandfather thought he was as good as me, and Estevão—my *God*! What an upstart! He had some crazy idea about college, about law school and politics. They would have destroyed us, everything my family stood for. I had no choice! Inêz made it clear that she wouldn't cut them out of her life, so I had to cut her out of yours."

"This has all been because of your family pride? Because of your fear of what people might say?" I couldn't believe I hadn't seen it on my own. "You don't hate my building boats just because it's not feminine. You hate that I love something my grandfather loved. That I'm good at it! You and Grandmother Dodge tried to break me of any bad habits I might have picked up from them—like the color of my skin! Did you know that she hated me, Father? She told me I was dirty! You were both terrified that my Caldeira blood would ruin your good name, and the truth is that I'm the one who's ashamed— ashamed of you, ashamed that my name is Dodge!"

"Anne, you don't understand," he began, holding out a hand in entreaty. He was pale and shaking and irrevocably diminished.

"You threw them all out like they were nothing, like they were garbage! You took my mother from me, made me despise her." I was crying now, my eyes burning hotly. "All those years, when she was still alive—I could have known her, and she could have loved me," I sobbed.

He drew himself up in a final, pathetic effort to play the good man misunderstood. "I have lain awake every night of your life planning how to make you happy and safe. For more than twenty years I have worked tirelessly for you. Your life, your success, your position have been my only concerns. I did what any father would do!"

"No, Father, you're wrong. As hard as it is for you to hear, you're wrong. You've been selfish and cruel—things you've always stood against—and it was all so unnecessary." The weight of my sadness, of all I had lost, seemed too much to bear.

He said nothing, just stood and looked at me, still proud. Disdainful. Through the doorway I could see the portrait of our colonial ancestor hanging in the hall. I turned away from them both and walked out into the blackest night I have ever known.

CHAPTER TWENTY

I raced next door to see if perhaps Maria Cristina had gone to Mrs. Hatcher for comfort, but when Mr. Hatcher came to the kitchen door I knew immediately that she had not. He opened the door just wide enough to let me in, and for the first time the kitchen was neither clean nor well lit. Puddles and muddy footprints marred the normally spotless linoleum. Oilskins, hats, and raincoats had been carelessly tossed onto the table and over the backs of chairs, and they lay there still, dripping onto Mrs. Hatcher's floor. I heard the faint murmur of voices coming from the living room and the clink of a spoon against a china cup.

"What can I do for you?" asked Mr. Hatcher, whispering as if someone had died.

"I'm looking for my sister," I said.

"She's not here. Just the family," he assured me.

"Okay," I said, turning away.

"Annie, wait," he said, his voice halting. I paused, unable to help him ease his awkwardness. I stood with my hand on the doorknob, but I did not turn toward him.

"We never . . . You know, of course, that nobody wanted this to happen. Katie and Mike and the others. They feel terrible about the Sullivan boy . . . about Hightower . . . They were doing what they thought was right. It wasn't the union people, you must know that, though of course those murderers were here because the union was."

I stood for a moment longer, letting the words wash over me. "I know," I said softly. "I know who it was. But we all participated in some way, and just because the two who died were killed by outsiders doesn't make the rest of us blameless. We all were there, people were shouting at their friends, *hitting* their neighbors! Everybody thought they were doing what was right, and that makes it all so much worse. Look what happened, Mr. Hatcher. Even with the best of intentions—Father, Oliver Fielding, the townspeople. Me. Everyone trying to fend off the outsiders, even though our only hope was in the people we claim don't belong here—investors, unions, immigrants."

He didn't answer me, and after a moment I walked back out into the wind and rain.

I ran the few blocks to the Dekkers' house, so used to being pummeled by the elements by now it had begun to feel like my natural state. I felt like I was floating.

I knocked hard on the Dekkers' front door. I saw no evidence that the power was on, not on the whole street, but I assumed they were home and hoped Maria Cristina was with them. They might be in the kitchen, I thought, at the back of the house, sitting around the table with candles or an oil lamp casting a dim glow over them all.

I knocked again, harder and with more urgency. It hurt my knuckles but I barely registered it. The door opened suddenly, and Will stood in front of me.

"Annie! What are you doing out in this?" he asked, opening the door wide and pulling me inside with a hand on my arm.

"I'm looking for Maria Cristina," I said, a little breathless. "I came back from the mill and she's gone."

"Okay, come in and sit down. You were at the mill tonight?"

"Yes, of course! Were you?"

"I was. I didn't see you."

"I stayed back, toward the road, away from the lights and the union line," I explained.

"Did you see . . . ?" he asked, hesitating to evoke Stevie Sullivan's broken skull, his limp, dead body.

"Yes," I said simply. My voice shook, and I had to pause a moment. "I was standing right next to him."

"Come here," he said, his voice low and comforting. He held out his arms to me and I felt myself falling into him, but with effort I stopped myself.

"Will," I said. "Maria Cristina's missing. I've got to find her."

"I know, I heard you. I'm sure she's fine. I'm worried about you. You're shaking, you're pale, you're upset—"

"Of course I am—everyone is! It's been a horrible nightmare. Those men were going to hurt Ezra, and Stevie stepped in and— It makes sense that I'd be upset, is all I'm saying," I said impatiently, shaking off his hand on my arm. "What's important right now is finding Maria Cristina."

"I know, don't worry. I'll help you," he said, leading me gently to the couch. "But let's take a moment and think before we run off half-cocked. Where have you looked?"

"Just at the Hatchers'."

"Where do you think she might have gone?" he asked, sitting down only after I did.

"I would have thought the Sullivans', but I don't think . . . not tonight . . ."

"Was Maria Cristina at the mill tonight?"

"No, but my father told her what happened. They . . . they fought, I think. And I told her to grow up. Will, she thinks we're going to send her away, and there's more. Ezra told me—"

He took both my hands in his then and forced me to look him in the eyes.

"Anne, it's going to be all right. You've got to settle down."

"No, Will, I don't," I cried, tearing my hands from his and clenching them together in my lap.

"I'm just trying to help, Anne," he said gently. "It kills me to see you like this, honey."

"Well, it's not killing me—why should it kill you?" I snapped.

I got up and began to pace the living room. I had started to tell him about Maria Cristina, that she was Samuel's daughter, but now I didn't want to.

"Okay, so she wouldn't have gone to see Deirdre Sullivan tonight." He thought a moment, then spoke quickly. "What about Ezra?"

"Maybe . . . I don't even know if Ezra's at home. He might've gone back to the Sullivans'. But she might . . . Let's go," I said, pulling my hat back on and heading immediately toward the front door.

"Let me at least get you some dry clothes to wear," Will began, and I turned, incredulous. Had he heard anything I'd said?

"Will, stop it!" I shouted, and I heard the edge of hysteria in my voice. "We're going back out into the storm—I'll be wet again in a matter of seconds! What the hell difference does it make anyway?!"

"Okay, okay," he conceded, his hands up, palms toward me as though he were humoring a deranged patient, showing me he had nothing in his hands that could harm me. "You can't blame me for trying to take care of you!"

And just that quickly, the contradiction of loving him and yet not wanting to marry him was gone, my confused feelings of guilt and panic, desire and irritation made clear at last.

"Yes, I can," I said slowly, my back to the door. Outside the storm raged, but I stood and faced Will and his love for me in the quiet, enveloping warmth of his parents' house. "I can blame you," I said again. "And I do."

He looked taken aback, and a little offended. "Well, I'm sorry, but I love you, and that's what people do when they love each other, Anne. They take care of each other."

"No, Will, that's not what you do," I said. I finally saw it, and I wanted him to see it, too. "You hover over me. You watch my face, gauge my mood, listen to every inflection of my voice. You look for things to shield me from. I can never be angry or sad or mean or bored or dissatisfied or, or anything!"

He was looking at me, hearing me but not comprehending. "Well, I want you to be happy," he said, pushing his hair off his forehead as he turned the idea over in his mind, the crazy idea that his wasn't the best way, the only way, to love someone. The idea that I didn't want what he wanted me to.

"I know you do, Will, and I want you to be happy, too. But you want me to *only* ever be happy, so you treat me like a child, try to protect me from everything!"

"Yes, goddamn it, I do! And I'm not going to apologize for it!" he yelled, getting up to pace the room. "Goddamn it," he muttered, and then suddenly he punched the wall. "God*damn* it!"

He turned and faced me, breathing hard. I was stunned. I had never seen him angry like this. "I have loved you my entire life, Anne. And I have stood and watched while you put everyone and everything before me!"

I couldn't speak, and he began pacing again, waving his arms while he gave voice to his grievances.

"I give you everything I have, and you give me whatever you have left over from your father, your boat, your sister, that crazy old man, and, for all I know, Oliver Fielding!"

I jumped at the mention of Oliver and a flush of guilt crept up my neck, staining my face.

"In all these years the only thing I have ever asked of you is that you let me love you, and you never have. Never!"

We stood facing each other, several feet and miles apart, while he struggled to control his anger.

"Will, I'm sorry," I said, tears running down my face. "It's just no use. I don't want to be wrapped in cotton so nothing ever touches me. I can't be kept from my own *life*!"

"I wanted to build a life together—a life you wanted, too. I'd have made the kind of marriage you wanted!"

"I know, Will, I know!" I cried. "It's not that I think you don't want to. I just don't think you can. I don't think either of us can."

A moment passed as we looked at each other, then down to the floor, and back to each other again.

I had always known, I realized, but I'd been too cowardly, and too cruel, to make the futility of our relationship clear to myself, let alone to Will.

"I have to go," I said.

I saw the tears in his eyes before he turned his face away and stepped aside to let me walk out the door without him, alone in the night to search for my sister.

I half walked, half ran to Ezra's. The rain had abated somewhat, but the wind was stronger than ever, the air much, much colder. The effort of pushing my body through space, and through the drifting sand and standing water on the old mill road and the track to Ezra's, exhausted me before I even got there. When I came out into the clearing I stood for a moment, looking at the cove in shock. I knew it would be rough, but I had not expected this.

The waves were enormous, without uniformity. At their crest they reached well over four feet, coming in from every direction and crashing into each other, sending spray and foam shooting up into the air, pounding the dock and washing over it. The noise was deafening—much louder than at the mill, where the buildings had muffled the sound and the river had created a space between us and the ocean. Ezra's old chair was upside down halfway up the yard toward the house, and the trash barrel bobbed in the surf, alternately washing up to the beach on a fast-moving breaker and tumbling into the sand, only to be sucked back out into the crashing waves. Tree limbs littered the yard like fallen soldiers on a battlefield.

I searched the darkness for my boat, but I couldn't see the end of the dock. It was black as pitch, and the waves and rain obscured everything beyond a dozen feet or so past the shore. I looked up at Ezra's and saw a faint light in the window. I ran as fast as I could toward the steps up to his porch and banged both hands against the door.

"Ezra! Ezra!" I shouted over and over again, pounding on his door, water running down my face and into my mouth, a salty mixture of rain and sea spray.

He wrenched the door open, took one look at me, and moved aside so I could come in.

"What's happened?" he asked.

"Maria Cristina's gone," I said, and then I told him about everything—Maria Cristina's disappearance, Samuel's refusal to acknowledge her, my fight with Will. When the last word was out I stood there, sobbing and spent.

Ezra looked at me and nodded three or four times, lips pursed together as he thought it all through.

"Finding Maria Cristina's the thing. The rest can wait. You think she'd come out here?"

"I do, Ezra. It's the only place that makes sense. She loves you, and she feels happy and safe out here. After the fight with my father tonight, and the fight I had with her out here earlier today—"

I stopped, stunned, and our eyes slid toward each other as we thought the same thing.

The fight I'd had with her had been about taking out my boat.

I ran across the yard, trying to keep my feet in the face of the wind pushing relentlessly back against me from the shore. I couldn't see much of anything, but I passed Ezra's chair and then the wooden cradles, empty now with both our boats finished and winter coming on. I reached the first steps of the dock and climbed them quickly. The sodden wood was slippery, and the crashing waves hit my legs and threw freezing spray into my face as I held onto the rail and made my way down the dock. The planks shook from the pounding waves—I could hear their painful creaking even over the shrieking wind. My head ached with the effort to peer through the darkness, but I couldn't see anything. At the end of the dock I understood why that was.

My boat was gone.

"No, no, no, no," I heard myself repeating in denial and desperation. The wind nearly ripped me off the dock as I scanned the disorienting waves in every direction, but I saw nothing except blackness and the end of the world.

I turned back and made my way to Ezra, who stood, waiting for me, with his foot resting on the first step of the dock.

"Okay," he said, before I could speak. "She's taken your boat out. Let's find out if she's equipped."

"Wh–what do you mean?" I asked, shivering uncontrollably.

"Go on up to the shop and see if anything's missing," he shouted over the wind. "She heard us talkin' about safety gear. Maybe she took somethin' with her."

I tore through the grass. I wouldn't let myself think of anything but the task at hand.

I threw open the doors and felt the wall to the left of the door where Ezra kept an oil lantern on a nail, but it wasn't there. I made my way to the workbench, and when I got to the big vise grips mounted on the far-right corner, I felt down below it and found the other lantern and matches, lit it with shaking hands, and went to the shelf where he kept his safety gear. Three life preservers, a disconnected radio, and two flares—all present and accounted for. I turned to go, saw the old sofa, and noted the missing blanket that usually covered its stained fabric.

I ran back to Ezra, forgetting to close and fasten the shop doors, but he said nothing as they banged against the building. "She didn't take anything. It's all there," I said breathlessly. "Except for a blanket and the lantern that hangs on the inside wall."

"That's bad," he said, and I nodded.

I waited while he looked out to sea. He'd know better than anybody what we could do to fix this. Finally, he turned to me.

"It's bad, but your boat's sound. She won't capsize easily, and if Maria Cristina stays low and bails, she might make it."

Oh, God, I thought. *She might make it*—which was just another way of saying she might not make it. I poked at the idea, like a hole in my tooth I couldn't keep my tongue away from. Maria Cristina might not make it.

"We've got to go out and look for her," I said, snapping out of it. "We've got to go get her."

"Annie, we can't," he said, so gently, and with such love right there in his voice, that he might as well have pronounced her dead on the spot.

"You're wrong!" I shook my head and backed away from him as though his thinking were contagious. "You've got a boat out behind the workshop—"

"Annie, girl, that's a rowboat, and it needs patching. You'd last all of ten minutes in her."

"Ezra, we can't just leave her out there! How can I just leave her?!"

I was crying in earnest now, the night's events adding up to a terrible, inevitable sum. I was exhausted, my teeth were chattering, I couldn't stop shaking. The wind and the rain, so loud now for so long, had beaten me into submission. I sobbed, knowing I should be fighting instead.

"I know, Annie," he said. "But where would we look? We'd be sailing blind! We can't do nothin' but wait."

"Well, I won't," I railed, desperate. "I'll go get Mr. Sullivan—he'll take me out to look for her!"

"He won't," said Ezra, his voice sharp. "He's too smart. And you will not ask him to risk anything else tonight, before he's even buried his son!"

I collapsed then, sinking to the ground because my legs simply refused to hold me up any longer. I sat there in the mud, crying weakly like a child. Ezra helped me up, and together we limped our way up to the house.

"I'll radio the Coast Guard," he said. "We'll start with that."

I heard him, but he seemed to be speaking some other language I didn't quite understand. He grabbed my arm and walked me back up to the house with him.

"Lie down, girl, before you fall down," he said once we were inside.

I turned to the big iron bed that sat near the dark fireplace and laid down on top of the old threadbare quilt, my sweater and dungarees wet and cold and pinning me down with their weight.

I heard Ezra put in a Mayday to the Coast Guard. Then he turned the dials on the radio that sat on his mantel, searching for weather reports. At one point he brought me a glass of whiskey and made me drink it. I would not sleep. Maria Cristina was out there, and she needed me. But though I struggled against it, in the end, I simply was not strong enough. I closed my eyes.

Just for a moment, I thought. I'm so tired.

I woke to confusion, not knowing where I was for a moment. A few dying embers burned in the fireplace, and sunlight streamed in the window.

Ezra's. I was at Ezra's, I realized, as it all came flooding back.

I got up, stiff and sore, my clothes still damp. But once I'd found my balance, I walked swiftly across the floor.

I flung open the heavy oak door and stepped out into the wrecked world. Trees were down all over the yard, especially off to the south edge of the property, where the woods came right up to the stone wall. A huge tree limb, easily twelve feet long, lay across Ezra's porch, his splintered railing poking out from underneath. Seaweed was everywhere, and the stench of dead fish left on the sand after the waves and tide had receded hit me hard in the face.

I stepped out onto the porch and looked down toward the water to the bay, out past the dock, where I thought I saw a wisp of dark smoke. A dark shadow lay in the water, something floating low. A boat. Burned down to the waterline, just her spine left, charred and waterlogged.

For a moment I didn't know. Some small bit of hope in the clear morning air still survived within me. But it lasted only seconds, and then I knew it was the *Mariana*, gutted and empty, floating in Kingston Cove.

I slowly began to walk down the steps, and just as my foot touched the grass I heard a splash in shallow water and turned toward the dock to my left. From the other side of it I saw someone moving, and I began to run. Maria Cristina!

And then he came into view, rising up out of the water like the sea god I'd thought him when I was a child, and I froze. He was walking up from the other side of the dock, where he'd swum out to get her.

He limped heavily, holding Maria Cristina in his arms.

She's hurt, I thought, maybe badly—but I didn't move. She probably needs a doctor, I thought. And still I didn't move as Ezra walked slowly, painfully, up onto dry land. He stopped a moment when he saw me before resuming his slow march. I saw the seaweed in her hair, and one of her shoes gone. Her foot looked a little blue, I thought. She's going to want some warm socks.

"Annie," Ezra said, but his voice sounded funny, thick and slow.

I raised my shaking hand to stop him.

"Don't," I said softly.

So he stood there, just far enough away that I didn't have to see her face, ravaged by the freezing Atlantic waters, her wide-open eyes and gaping mouth—the look of terror she surely wore as she went down for the last time and inhaled the ocean into her lungs. They stood in the morning sun, gilded by the light. He held her lovingly, close to his body, her limp arm hanging down by his side.

I turned away and began to walk home. I entered the old sandy track, shaded by the deep forest on either side, and shivered from the chill in the air.

September, I thought. Summer is over at last.

$\mathscr{E}$PILOGUE

Darkness spreads across the sky like a plague until everything is black. Thrown once more against the starboard gunwale, the girl finally admits to herself that she shouldn't have taken the boat out, but she'd been so angry. And anyway, she has confidence in her vessel. Her sister made it, and her sister knows everything about boats. Still, the Mariana *is taking a pounding. The girl hopes the wooden frame can stand it long enough for the storm to move away or blow itself out to nothing.*

The engine failed some time ago, though she doesn't know why. She can't see the shore at Ezra's anymore, but she doesn't think she is that far out. She considers swimming for it, but her chin comes up and out and she frowns, remembering her sister's harsh words and Samuel's threats. It's all so very unfair, and now she will likely be sent away just as she's beginning to feel at home. She'll show them, she thinks. She'll stay out overnight, and when she returns they'll all treat her better.

She reaches down by her feet and picks up the oil lantern she's taken from Ezra's workshop, and the matches. She carefully pulls the wick out, holding it close so she can see it, her tongue pushed up against the gap in her front teeth. She takes the matches out of her sock, where she's put them to keep them dry, and sets the lantern down on the seat next to her. Carefully shielding the match with one hand and bending low to create a cave with her body, she strikes the match. The wind immediately blows it out before she can even move toward the lantern. She must get out of the wind, she thinks.

Grimacing, although she is already soaked through, the girl sits carefully down in the bottom of the boat, in the two inches of icy water that have accumulated along the keel from rain and sea spray and waves coming up over the bow. The wind is weaker here, where the sides of the hull come up to her shoulders. She puts the lantern on the deck beside her and hunches over, bending low over her matches. She strikes one and quickly cups her hand around the tiny, struggling flame, willing it to keep burning. She moves slowly toward the lantern and touches the flame to the wick, soaked in oil and ready. The wick catches immediately, despite the rain, but before she has time to lower the glass side of the lantern, the boat pitches and throws her down, knocking the lantern over.

Burning oil spreads across the deck and licks hungrily at her feet. She backs up on her hands and feet like a crab, away from the fire. The blanket she took from the workshop becomes a torch, and she snatches at it to throw it overboard. The burning fabric unfurls like a bedsheet in the wind, and pieces break off and drop onto the boat, one flying into the cubbyhole, which is dry and welcoming. She uses her hands now, frantically splashing water toward the fire, but there are several fires now, and she can't get enough water in her hands at one time.

The boat's upper structure is soon a furnace. Maria Cristina begins to scream for help, but her voice is dampened, flung down at her feet by the wind and water. It does not carry, and she knows instinctively that even if someone were near they would not hear her. She knows she is trapped, and that if she stays on this boat she will die horribly.

She stumbles and falls over the seats as she moves back toward the stern, half-crazed, anything to escape the hungry flames. She prays that the rain will douse the fire, but despite the omnipresence of water, it rages on. There is no light save the lurid flames leaping at her, the wind carrying sparks to singe her hair and clothes. Below her is the dark turbulence of the sea.

Desperation comes, and courage. She jumps, and the black water opens its arms to receive her. Shocked by the unexpected cold, she comes up to the surface, kicking hard and losing a shoe in the process, and the sea breaks over her, choking her, clutching at her as it tries to drag her under. She fights to keep her head above the waves—just long enough for us to come for her.

She watches the boat, a few yards away now, eaten by the raging fire until it has consumed each plank I laid, every seam and rail, every last bit of my heart. The rain beats down, sea spray flies, and she swallows the freezing, salty water, her face upturned as she rises on the crest of a wave, her terrified eyes reflecting the flickering firelight as she sinks down in the trough, the boat obscured by the walls of water that surround her.

Soon she cannot tell how long she has been in the water, but the boat is now far away, the light from the fire fading until she is alone in the dark, exhausted, still fighting the vast emptiness above and below because she cannot give up. They might still come.

Ana, she thinks. Ezra. Will. Someone.

She cannot feel her legs or her hands now as the frigid water makes her its own. She is too tired to cry or even think, her body instinctively moving to keep her head above water, struggling toward oxygen. She is reduced to an animal, simply fighting for one more breath. Then she hears it—the sea pounding the rocks in Kingston Cove—and she remembers those other children, afraid for their lives as the rocks drew near and the night pressed them close, those children who cried, regretting their foolish choices and the death that awaited them, only to be snatched from the cruel water by the long hand of Ezra, patrolling his cove and strong enough to do anything.

Her legs begin to fail her, the muscles too exhausted to do more than twitch, her hands capable of only a last flutter or two before they hang, limp, in the water by her sides. The next wave takes her under, but she struggles up once more, opens her mouth for air and finds only water as, coughing and choking, she slides back down.

They could still come, *a voice says quietly in her head, a voice that sounds like her* mamãe, *and she thinks,* They can't see me if I'm underwater. *Her feet come back to life, kicking, sending her up above the waves. She hears the breakers, closer now, and strains her eyes toward that sound, and there, far away to her right and looming in the moonlight as the sky begins to clear, is the faint outline of the mill rising high above the waves. She is glad, because while she cannot see it yet, she knows that Ezra's place is closer still, the dock and the beach and the workshop and the old man, all drawing her toward them.*

I'm almost home, Maria Cristina thinks, relaxing at last, letting the waves carry her in toward shore, where I wait.

This is how I think of Maria Cristina, in her last moments, alone and afraid, believing we would come for her. I imagine her dying.

I wonder if she sensed the resentment I often felt, the petty jealousies I harbored. I was selfish and bad-tempered, secretive and bossy and manipulative. And still, she loved me. If I ever deserved this gift, for even a moment, perhaps it was because I tried to do better. I failed more often than I succeeded, of course, but maybe success is not our only instrument for measuring ourselves or one another.

And so we come to the end, with only a little more to tell. I have written this in order to see, at last, what happened that summer. That I might close this book forever, and you might understand why I gave you up—why I gave my only child to strangers, in the hope that in them you would find a family.

I had a daughter. I say it out loud sometimes, in the darkest hour of the night. The words echo in my room, the walls whispering them back to me, lulling me to sleep in that old iron bed.

I had a daughter.

But I lost everything, including you. My sister and Will. Samuel, too. He writes to me still, but I have not responded. Soon, perhaps, but not yet. I saw him once after that night, at the cemetery, just before he moved to Providence for good. He stood before Maria Cristina's newly turned grave, and when he saw me by the gate he reached out his hand to me.

"Anne!" he called, his voice breaking.

But I said nothing, made no move toward him. We looked at each other across that span of gravestones, the starkness of his pain telling me that he at last saw all the world connected—and the part he had played in destroying it.

"Memento mori, Father," I whispered before I turned and walked back out the way I'd come, through the gates and into the retreating afternoon sun. *Remember, you are only mortal.* I intended it as condemnation, but I begin to realize that it is in our human frailty that we may find—and grant—second chances. To Father. Everyone in Milford. Maybe even myself.

It wasn't long after we buried Maria Cristina that I found I was pregnant. I could hear Oliver's voice in my ear, laughing, amused.

What do you want, kid? He would have asked. *How bad do you want it?*

But wanting had never gotten me anything but disappointment, both tragic and mundane, and you deserved so much more. The one thing I did right was to recognize what I could not do, at least not then.

I left Milford and took a room in a boardinghouse in Barrington, not far from where Benigno and Lucia had lived, where they had raised Estevão and Inêz. I had the money they left me—left us both— and I lived quietly. The months seemed to float by, broken up only by the letters Ezra sent. He was the only one who knew where I was, though I never told him about you. You were my secret, and I held you close while I could.

When you were born—only a year ago, though it seems so much longer—the midwife put you in my arms, bloodied from your first

battle. I loved you, but I did not have the strength to watch you struggle and suffer. To watch you live your life. I did not know then if I
would be able to live my own.

My landlady made some discreet inquiries, and within days a
woman came to my room, a Portuguese woman with a husband and
two small children of her own, and I spoke to her with a quiet intensity, a ferocity I have never known, before or since. For a brief moment I was your mother, you were my child.

"We are Portuguese, too," I told her. "She must have a Portuguese family. A sister and brother. A home with laughter and music
and a crucifix on the wall. She should play outside, go to Mass, eat the
sweets she will love. Build things if she wants to."

This is for you, Samuel, I thought. *Your Portuguese, Catholic
granddaughter.*

She took you away then, to introduce you to your life, but not
before she asked me if you had a name.

"Mariana Inêz," I told her.

She nodded slowly and repeated the name. And then you were
gone.

I went back to Milford a few weeks later. Will was polite, keeping his distance for both our sakes. In time, perhaps we will find our
friendship and affection have survived. Samuel had closed up the
house and gone to Providence, so I went to Ezra. He let me stay in the
workshop without pity or too much conversation. He had pulled the
wreckage of my boat out of the shallows and put it up on the cradles
down by the bay, waiting for me to come home—hoping, I suppose,
to entice me back to work—but the carcass of that boat repelled me.
He said there was always something worth salvaging, but it was
months before I could listen to him say it, longer before I could believe
it.

But eventually I picked up a plane and some sandpaper, and Ezra
said nothing. It took a long time, but I put my hands on the grain of
teak and cedar and white oak again, drew sawdust into my lungs, and
found that I was still alive.

Ezra died last month. I nursed him through his pneumonia and thought he was improving, but one morning he simply didn't wake up. He left me the property, and I'm building a boat—just a small one. I miss him. I miss working with him, the sun shining off the water and into our eyes, the smell of varnish and pipe tobacco.

I cannot stop thinking of you. You will celebrate your birthday in a few days. I had thought to leave you be, to let your new family create a pretty story for you. Something simple and clean about who you are and where you came from. I had thought to leave everything be, to deny myself everything—as penance, I thought at first. But I find I cannot, after all. I have had enough of lies, enough of loss. One day, when you are old enough, I will show these pages to you. You will know who you are, who I am—perhaps even Oliver, if I am strong enough. And I think I may be.

It is in the writing I have found my answer. I choose the truth for you, though I cannot know if I am right. What I do know is this: all that is possible for us is the willingness to be human. To beware certainty and to remind ourselves every day that we are fallible, lest we lose the ability to change our minds, our paths, our lives. And then we must simply do the best we can. We cannot lie down, not while we still live. Your story is not pretty, but it is yours, and I will not take it from you. We will build what we can from our stories, trusting that God, at least, will understand.

ACKNOWLEDGMENTS

I'm fortunate to have a life in which family, friends, and colleagues regularly ask, with genuine interest, "What are you working on?" To live among people whose default assumption is that everyone is doing something interesting, creative, and relevant helps make it true.

Thanks to everyone at The Overlook Press, especially Peter Mayer, who took a chance on a new author; and Stephanie Gorton and Kate Gales, whose expertise, accessibility, and enthusiasm for the work are what every writer hopes for. And to Scott Mendel, literary agent extraordinaire: your guidance, patience, and humor are unparalleled, but your belief in this book is the one, indispensable thing that brought *Daughter of Providence* to life. Thank you.

I had no qualms about asking anyone and everyone to read drafts and offer their thoughts and expertise; luckily, every single one of you said, "Sure!" Thanks to Sonia Mitchell and Suzette Maciel for their help with the Portuguese dialogue in the book, and to Bill Drew, Bill Lyons Sr., and Jim Drew for their knowledge of all things structural and mechanical, including the love/hate relationship that boat owners have with their outboard motors.

The following individuals read early drafts and offered astute feedback that helped me revise and make this a better story: Janet Bean, TJ Boisseau, Joyce Byrd, Sid Dobrin, Bill Drew, Bill Lyons Sr., Carolyn Sorisio, and Lance Svehla; thanks to you all for your time and support. Alan Ambrisco and Jenny Moore—two of my favorite people and writers—went above and beyond, reading multiple drafts, talking through plot lines and character development, giving generously, time and time again, of their knowledge and artistry. I owe them both special thanks, Jenny for her gentle and thorough take on every last page, her eye for consistency and structural integrity, the best reader I know. And Alan, always the poet, for his love of language, his indefatigable enthusiasm, and his earnest hope that he'll score a bit part in the film. I know you have your SAG card at the ready. And to Ray and Amanda Lyons, who gave us a month at their beach house so I could write, every day, the sound of seagulls and Red Sox games my only distractions. 9 Arbeth is where this book was born.

In the most fundamental way possible I owe an enormous debt to my parents, Bill Drew and Joyce Byrd. They taught me that a creative life is not only possible, it is necessary, and not reserved for the leisured class. Without benefit of higher education or any money to speak of, my father took a childhood love of cinematic heroes and their feats of daring-do and turned it into airplanes he designed and built, climbed into and flew, sometimes upside down, and always with panache. He showed me the artistry in how-things-work. And my mother, who as a girl earned money for new school clothes by working in the tobacco fields, raised four children while she painted and read, played the piano, quilted and glazed, never once apologizing for the time she took to create and appreciate beauty. My childhood smelled like oil paints and fixative, sawdust and turpentine. My parents imagined things, and built them; they craved beauty, and made that a part of all our lives. I thank them for valuing their own imaginations enough that I can value mine.

To Philip and Brian Anderson: you are the delight of my life, and two of the brightest, funniest, kindest, and most interesting people I know. No parent could be more fortunate in the love and support of their children than I.

Finally, my most profound thanks go to my husband, Bill Lyons. To say that he was supportive throughout the making of this book would be damning with faint praise. He read and listened and brainstormed, cooked and cleaned while I wrote, offered sage advice or a sympathetic ear as warranted, and in every way made my authorship his priority. Thanks, honey. I am, as always, humbled by how well you love.